I0671711

A CORPSE for COZUMEL
ADIE STURM MYSTERY

ANASTASIA AMOR

BRODT PUBLISHING

BRODT PUBLISHING
AnastasiaAmor.com
Copyright © 2006 by Anna Brodt
All rights reserved.
ISBN: 978-0-9918062-6-3
Cover art by Anna Brodt
Author photo by Kristen Wells

ACKNOWLEDGEMENTS

Big hugs to my friends for their encouragement at the beginning of this journey. Many thanks to my karate instructors and fellow students for their support in the creation of the fight scenarios. Big hugs to Bruce for his edits.

by **ANASTASIA AMOR**

ADIE STURM MYSTERIES

Corpse for Cozumel
Days of the Dead
The Curse of the Carnaval
Dead Delicious

PARANORMAL FANTASY SERIES

Havana Heat

EROTIC ROMANCE

Exploring Irresistible

Praise for ANASTASIA AMOR

A CORPSE FOR COZUMEL: ADIE STURM MYSTERY

"…hot sexy men... thrilling suspense… keep looking over your shoulder. You won't guess who the killer is until it's too late."
—*Night Owl Romance Reviews*

"5 Stars! Detailed local color and flavor combine with intense mystery and intrigue as well as steamy romance ... Excellent descriptions, well-developed characters, and great action keep you right in the story, turning page after page to see what happens next. Sexual tension is high …Adie Sturm is a wonderful character to help you enjoy another world from the comfort of your own home or beach chair. **Gripping story, hot characters, realistic dialogue and fantastic action!**" —*Readers' Favorite*

"…suspense starts in the first few pages…strong, sexy characters and intense sexual tension keep you wanting more…great read that's hard to put down."—*Two Lips Reviews*

"…good suspense...expanse of detail of the locations and the plot, creating a vivid world for all..." —*Enchanting Reviews*

1

Rancid sweat and stale cigarette smoke. Darkness. I wasn't alone.

A few minutes ago, a rosy-hued sky reflected on shimmering Caribbean waters. Now the hotel drapes were shut. I stared into the blackness. A flash of steel. Wrapping my wet towel around my hand, I whipped it at my target and heard the satisfying clatter of a knife, followed by a guttural curse. I screamed, kicked him and ran, but he didn't want to let me off easy. He came at me from behind, his arm tightening around my throat. I was losing consciousness, but at the last minute I thrust my hand out behind me over my shoulder, making contact with something wet and slippery. Jerking back in pain, he withdrew but was pumped and wouldn't be stopped. He was enormous and wanted me dead.

This was not my idea of a fun vacation. Instead of a romantic evening out, I was fighting a losing battle for my life.

***

A couple days back...

I was home resting on the couch, eyes closed, day-dreaming.
A white powdery beach, a frothy strawberry daiquiri and a cool guy beside me—buff and tanned with incredibly sexy eyes.
Magic hands soothe my skin, massaging in slippery suntan oil, sending pleasurable tingles down my body until I'm aching for more.
Escape. That's what I needed. My Christmas reality was too much for anyone to handle, what with my overbearing brother, his tactless wife, not to mention snotty little Tasha. When the phone rang, I let it. I felt comfortably relaxed, my cat curled on my lap. I had another sip of red wine, a soft-in-the mouth shiraz, and ignored the noise. Let the answering machine deal with it.
My fantasy man slowly brushes my hair aside, his fingers

lightly stroking my neck before he kisses my throat, capturing my skin with his lips. His tongue trails to my shoulder and flicks over to the rise of my breast—silken and hot, feathering downwards to the flimsy fabric of my bikini. I thread my fingers through thick clean hair, smelling of soap and balmy ocean breeze. My hands glide over his broad shoulders to his muscular arms. He's firm and powerful, yet he's all natural, untamed and wild. The intense passion in his eyes fills me with longing. He wants me as much as I want him.

The phone trilled sharply. Closing my eyes, I drifted away again.

He lowers my strap to caress my breast, tracing the contours of my nipple with his tongue. Like a bird flying too close to the sun his lips sear my skin with their heat. Lightly his hand slides along my thigh and hesitates before teasing me with his lingering touch. My hips move in response—every nerve ending sparks, igniting into flames.

"Adie, pick up—hear me? Where's that slut? Bitch owes me an f'n grand." His voice grated in my ears. "Tell her to pay up or she'll be dog meat by the time I get through with her. *Adie!* Where is she?" He growled, " Friggin' bitches—" The tape cut him off.

Loser! If Boris was here, I would have smacked him good. Better yet, a whack to the groin would have given him something to think about.

When the phone rang again, I was sure it was Boris. He can't just let off like a normal person, maybe because he wasn't one. As leave the message after the tone, came on, I heard a beep and Marg's quiet voice.

Pushing my furry friend aside, I rushed over to the phone. "Hello, Marg. Sorry, didn't hear what you were saying."

"Adie," Marg murmured, "it's Libby—" she coughed and muttered haltingly, "she's skippin' school, smokin' and there's a boy."

Libby the thirteen-year old computer geek?

"And my mom's senility is worse." Marg's voice wavered as if she was losing her grip on the phone.

"Marg?" I waited, but she didn't say anything more. Could she be ill? "Marg? Are you there?"

"She's practically given away our cottage, and my new

2

supervisor—" Marg yawned, before she went on, "—is a nurse. My boss says Uma doesn't have to sign in like us. She comes and goes whenever she wants."

"Sleeping with her, is he?"

"For sure, someone is," she murmured faintly. "That woman owns a Mercedes and a house with a pool."

Her voice was so odd, I thought. Was she on something? No-oo. Marg was definitely not a pot-head. She wouldn't even recognize the smell. With the phone between my head and shoulder, I made my way over to the counter and switched on the kettle. When the phone slipped, I lost some of the drift before I placed it up to my ear again.

"...swore at me, and called me a *ho*," Marg whispered. Was it formerly sweet teenage Libby or the nurse-slut-supervisor she was talking about? Marg continued distractedly, "Boris came by to pick her up when I wasn't here, took all her things, the furniture, and left me a nasty letter from his lawyer."

Whoa! This blew me away. Boris hadn't taken an interest in Libby in years and now he wanted her to live with him? A teenager with hormone problems? I knew he was a nutcase but this was downright bizarre. "Why?"

"Three thousand-a-month support payment. Two thousand I now have to scrounge up somehow."

"Marg, Boris phoned. You need to be careful. He's looking for you."

"Never mind that noodle-brain. I have a plan, Adie. There's this deal I'm handling for my patient. He's paying me ten thousand dollars to pick up a check but I have to..." I heard the doorbell ring. She mumbled, "We're making the final arrangements. Ah, got to go, Adie."

"I'm coming over," I said quickly, but there was silence from Marg's end. Her phone clanged as if the receiver had been dropped abruptly. I could hear distant voices, a man and a woman's. Boris. It had to be him. I needed to get there fast!

Shrugging on a coat, I grabbed my purse on the way out. Large snowflakes whirled about in the cold breeze as I got into my car. Turning on my windshield wipers, I backed out of my driveway and drove through the snow-covered streets of Kitchener, ABS brakes flipping on and off, my car hitting ice patches. At

3

Ottawa Street South, I veered left and headed out of town to Marg's.

The evening sky was dark with angry gray clouds. The wind whipped snow on my windshield, the visibility getting worse as I drove further out of the city, forcing me to switch on the fog lights. Snowflakes danced wickedly in the yellow beams of my lights. My eyes grew heavy from the hypnotic rhythm of a million white specks lightly tapping on my windshield. I clutched the steering wheel tightly, watching the car ahead of me lose traction, swerving unsteadily as it turned onto an intersecting farm road.

Boris losing control, feeling resentful that Marg left him, could only mean that she could be in danger. *And she was strangely out of it. What was wrong with her?*

The upcoming street lights and a white sign that read Mannheim warned me to let off on the speed and slow down before entering Schulman Road, the major street in the subdivision. Single-dwelling brick houses stood close together, on both sides of the road. I headed down a narrow street bordered by tall pines, past houses lit up with strings of colored lights. Arriving at Marg's modest townhouse, I eased into her driveway and parked behind her rusty gray Corolla. Hers was one of many houses in beige brick with russet trim—one monotonous row, each house resembling the last, varying only by the type of glowing Santa and reindeer decorations on the snow-covered properties. The street was crowded with cars parked on the road, a modern version of *Jingle Bells* blasting loudly from a nearby house. A party well underway. Shutting the door of my VW sparked off a frenzy of barking from the neighbor's backyard—pit bulls behind a wire fence.

In my high-heeled boots, I kept contact with the sidewalk, sliding rather than walking to Marg's door. I pressed the ringer. Oddly, Marg's bad tempered Doberman, Demo, was quiet. I listened. Ringing it again, I looked around as I waited to hear some activity from within. The neighbors on either side weren't home, or at least their driveways were empty. Should I leave? She'd been there twenty minutes ago with a man, but now she didn't hear the bell or couldn't come to the door.

I tried the handle. The knob turned. Marg would be the last one to leave a door unlocked and chance a break-in. But she'd had quite a shock—her daughter taken by the crazy ex, a mother whose elevator didn't reach the top floor, and a slut boss who'd slept her way to the executive suite. I stood there, hesitant to go in.

But what if she was in trouble? I pushed the door open, holding my purse as a shield in case Demo bounded out. On tiptoes I worked my way over the tiles listening for the clicking of dog toenails but heard nothing.

"Marg?" I called out climbing the stairs. My only reply was the hum of the fridge and the dripping tap in the nearby bathroom. Things didn't seem right. When the hairs on the back of my neck stood up I retreated outdoors to my VW. I knew better than to ignore my instincts.

With my purse planted on the passenger seat, I unzipped my karate bag and pulled out a dragon-embellished broomstick two feet long. A Filipino weapon—an escrima. It packed a wallop. Demo had large teeth and an ugly disposition, and then, of course, there was Boris.

Inside there was no sign of Marg. From next door the growling grew irritatingly loud. I glanced over to the tiny living room. Near the kitchen, a floral peach couch and wing chair was grouped with a square pine table. A hammer along with a framed print of a horse lay on the table.

A door opened onto a miniscule deck with steps down to the back of the property. Frenzied frantic barking brought me to the west window. Where a low fence separated Marg's place from the pit bulls, a leafless oak allowed me to see into the neighbor's yard. There was a different sort of Christmas bash going on out there. A porch light illuminated shadowy figures of black beasts grappling and snarling over a lumpy blanket, partially buried in powdery snow.

Imagine coming home after a stressful day to that noise? I thanked my lucky stars my neighbor, a retired dentist, had indoor cats. And I never saw the weirdo plumber guy with the ferret.

Rounding the corner, I looked around for anything to give me a clue as to where she was. The kitchen was immaculate. This was no surprise. A stove was a mystery to Marg. She's a salad-type woman. Not much mess that way, either, unless she spills the mayonnaise.

A note lay on the kitchen table.

Marg, I took Tia to Darlene's. Demo is at the kennel. Have a great trip! Jeannette.

My eyes lit on a small pad on her kitchen counter next to the phone. I studied it and seeing some indentations in the pad, tore the top sheet off, folded it, and stuck it in my jean pocket. Picking up my escrima again, I prepared to search the rest of the house.

"Marg!" I yelled at the top of my voice, in case she was asleep. I wasn't about to scare her in the state she was in. Worried, I crept slowly up the carpeted stairs to her bedroom.

At her closed door, I listened, my ear to the wood. It was disquietingly still in the condo. Strangely, the pit bulls had stopped barking. My shoulders tightened. Perspiration dampened my armpits.

"Pull yourself together," my Logical Voice ordered. "Nothing's wrong. It's your imagination. She's probably doing some last minute shopping."

My Emotional Voice broke in. "Yup, for the trip she never mentioned. Some gff!"

I shut down my overactive brain and knocked. Not hearing any sounds from inside, I turned the knob slowly, shoving the door open with my foot. The hinges creaked. I froze.

The single bed was rumpled, the floral duvet draped off the bed, a ruffled pillow lay on the hardwood, and the closet door was ajar. A wooly gray sweater had been haphazardly thrown on a rocking chair near the window. This wasn't like Marg. She was obsessively neat—OCD if ever anyone was.

Thinking that Boris could be somewhere in the house, I clutched my escrima tighter and crept to the next bedroom. Libby's door was wide open—void of all teenage life. The furniture was gone. A Beyonce poster ripped on the bottom end, hung forlornly on the wall. One dingy white sports sock was buried in the corner with dust balls and cat fur. Scrapes and gouges on shiny yellow laminate. Someone had dragged heavy furniture across the floor with a don't-give-a-damn attitude.

The screech of sirens. One and then a second, further away. They were getting louder by the time I raced down the stairs to the front entrance window. An ambulance, lights flashing, was pulling up behind a parked pickup truck at the pit bull residence. Another demanding siren wailed loudly—a white police car with rotating red lights approached from the far end of the street. Suburbanites gaped out their windows. Partygoers plodded through the snow up the street, some jacketless, to see what the commotion was all about.

"Get the hell out of here!" my Logical Voice screamed. "Something big is happening. You don't want any part of this."

Hurriedly, I zipped up my jacket, clicked the door shut behind me, and paused momentarily to watch the crowd gathering. A gust of winter wind swept grainy snow pellets into my eyes. Brushing the icy grit off my face, I focused on a guy in a brown wool coat, standing apart from the chattering neighbors, huddled behind the ambulance. He eyed me curiously as I joined the throng in their sweaters, ski jackets and sneakers. In my black leather jacket and high-heeled boots, I stood out like a sore thumb. I needed to go before someone noticed and pointed a finger at me.

An unmarked white Ford, lights flashing, manoeuvred its way up to the pit bull house and parked. Two men in winter coats got out—one trim and dark, the other bear-like and tall. They seemed to know what they were doing, heading straight to the front door. Halfway up the sidewalk, the man in brown intercepted them, pulled out his notebook, and struck up a conversation with the big guy. Brushing past them, the slim man strode into the house without bothering to ring the doorbell.

The ham-faced blonde beside me started babbling, hands gesturing wildly to a bald beanpole. "I tell you, it's Karl! He should've taken it easy after bein' sick like that!"

"No way, Dagmar!" Baldy glared in my direction. "It's a robbery. There've been enough cars comin' and goin' around here. People waitin' to rip us off. Karl's dogs—" His attention riveted on the police officer coming out of the house.

I had a sick feeling about this. Time to hit the road. I was about to when I saw the man in the brown coat sidling up to the pit bull house, scribbling away in his notebook. He stared into the neighbor's window until a cop came over and told him to leave. He traipsed over to Marg's property and leaning against the siding, went back to the note taking.

Reporter was written all over him. Edging through a couple of women, I crept close enough to peer over his shoulder. Out of the corner of his eye, he noticed me. Abruptly he shut his notepad and swung around.

Slick, maybe too slick. He reminded me of the smarmy TV show investigator with the dark gelled hair and mustache. He smirked, his eyes crinkling at the corners in a practiced manner. "Hey, honey! You were next door. See what happened?"

I swiveled about and started towards my car without replying.

Slick grabbed my arm. His eyes shot over to my VW parked behind Marg's Corolla. "Got time for a coffee? I'm buyin'."

"No, thanks." Shaking his hand off, I headed to the driveway.

"Lemme introduce myself," he said smoothly, at my heels. "Bernie Scharf, *Kitchener Today*." How about it—can we talk?" He rubbed his frost-nipped hands together, bouncing up and down on the balls of his feet, his attention wandering to the cops. "I hafta finish up but let's say thirty minutes?"

A uniformed officer shouted out to the crowd. "Let's go, folks! It's all over—go home!"

Thick snow landed on my hair and a chilly wind froze the exposed skin on my cheek. What was going on and where was Marg? Slick must know something. "Okay, Gunther's. You know it?"

"On Victoria Street. " He grinned gleefully, despite the snow flicking into his eyes.

I strode over to my car, swung the door open and climbed in. Checking my rear-view mirror, I backed out the driveway, barely missing Baldy with the attitude.

***

Home—at last. The shepherd's pie had hit the spot but Slick was a little much to stomach. It was trivia night at Gunther's and at first, that was all I got from the big hot-shot reporter. I kicked off my boots and turned on the lights. I felt depressed. Maybe it was winter blues but more likely Marg and the mess she was in.

In the pub, I'd watched Slick gobble down mouthful after mouthful of delectable chocolate—an eruption of chocolate curls in cream, studded with nuts over a chocolate base. Sharing wasn't Slick's thing. Can't say I wanted anything from his spoon, either. There was no denying a sacrifice was involved for a bikini trim body. Consuming something that tantalizing in front of a pleasure-addicted chocoholic is a recipe for disaster—the image burned into my brain.

Thirty minutes later, I had a melt-down. I needed Mayan Magic—now! To me nothing was better, except maybe some afternoon delight. I sighed. A warm tropical beach with a sensuous man with needs as powerful as my own, whose touch drove me insane with desire. Chocolate would give me that feeling.

Knowing the powerful pull of my addiction, I had the foresight to order a chocolate eruption to go. Five seconds in the microwave and it was perfection. An orgasmic feast. My tongue caressed it, savoring the smooth texture, letting it dissolve slowly in my mouth. Pure bliss. I closed my eyes a moment and made myself a promise. I would find that man in Cozumel.

I mulled over my meeting with Slick. In Gunther's, he finally gave me the goods. One dead white male. Tim Reich. On my computer I Googled Reich. The University of Waterloo professor appeared, with a description of various research papers published.

I had this visual—snarling dogs gnawing on a lumpy coat, lying in the snow. Slick was convinced Marg knew the guy. He wanted me to spill the beans. Little did he know that I didn't have any beans to spill, or let's say my beans were limited to that little piece of paper I'd picked up at Marg's.

From my jacket pocket I took out it out and laid it flat on my kitchen table. The information was guess work until I lightly scribbled over with a pencil. The words popped out.

Dr. Reich, UW-ex 2134-paranoid personality? Contact: Alvarez: Royal Investments, Cozumel flights: 1-900-555-9359, North Jet. Caravan Tours.

Was Marg in Cozumel? I thought back to the note I'd found on the table. Darlene was my cat sitter. On my cell, I scrolled through my contacts and pressed her number. No answer.

Before I got into bed, I tried Marg's land line. It rang and rang. I let it, feeling the emptiness of the house, deserted by Marg and Libby. And a dead man next door—Reich. A chill ran down my body.

Where was Marg? Boris couldn't have done something to her, could he? I remembered his fun party personality. True, he could be nasty, but a killer? Marg had to be all right. She was in

Cozumel, listening to the rush of the surf, a warm salty breeze softly tousling her hair.

In bed, I pulled the covers up closer, covering my shivering shoulders, trying to focus on reading. When the words finally blurred, I dropped my book and fell into a restless sleep—ghostly images of pit bulls darting out at me.

2

Deadly Pit Bull Attack.

My eyes shot ahead.

Professor T. Reich was found dead in the backyard of Karl and Marion Stedmenn's townhouse in Mannheim yesterday. The Stedmenns had never met Reich and were surprised to find the dead man on their property.

Marg knew him—according to the note.

The police are treating the death as suspicious.

Glancing back at the article, I noticed something was off. I sat down and studied it. I shook my head in disbelief. Suspicious, eh? Slick hadn't been upfront. Why hadn't the little newshound told me?

I turned to Section C9 of the newspaper and checked the death notices. Sure enough there was a Professor T. Reich. No family. But there was an ex—Uma Farber-Reich. The obituary mentioned Reich as a biology professor at the University of Waterloo. The memorial service was today at five. If it was murder they would keep the body for an autopsy. The police would be looking for suspects.

The hospital. I needed to get into Marg's office. In difficult situations—dress for success. I put on a gray flannel suit over a white camisole, topping it off with a leather coat, and at the last minute snatched up my attaché case and strode out to my car. Props help.

After cleaning off a thin dusting of snow, I started the engine and backed out of my driveway. Swinging into the traffic, I had green lights all the way, getting there in less than fifteen minutes. I tried parking on the lower floors but ended up on the empty garage roof. With a bitter breeze biting my face, I headed to the stairs. Put off by the dingy stairwell, I took the steps two at a time to the main level and walked to the doors.

The psychiatric wing was in the old part of the hospital. I had to turn left at the yellow arrow, follow the green arrow down an empty corridor, and when I had just about given up hope, found a room with a reception desk at the end of a long hallway.

Two females sat at a curved desk. A girl with china-blue eyes looked up. Over-processed blonde hair hung limply to her shoulders. She inquired robotically, "Is there something I can help you with?"

"Marg Beige?" I studied her split ends.

Before the blonde could reply, the plump redhead butted in with a snooty British accent. "She's not here." She pursed her lips and peered down her long hooked nose at me as if I were alien bug life.

"What? But we have an appointment!"

"She's off." The blonde shrugged. "A flu, I think."

Miss Congeniality pursed her thin lips. "She always has her little excuses, Brittany." Pulling on her faux-fur coat, she gave me a disdainful look and stalked out the door.

"Lunch?"

"Oh, yes, she goes exactly at twelve. Me, I have to go at one when her highness gets back," Brittany whispered confidentially, "I'm so hungry..." Gold stars scattered on fuchsia nails flicked up as she brushed back a feather peacock earring.

"Must be rough working with her."

Brittany examined her manicure.

"Hey, girl, nice nails."

The receptionist grinned. "Done them myself." She waved them in front of my face. "Awesome, aren't they?"

"Sure are!" Nails don't turn my crank but she needed sugaring up. "You know, if you feel like taking a break, I don't mind covering for you." I didn't think she would actually need to eat. Nobody gets that thin from food.

"Na-hh, couldn't do that."

I leaned in. "You can trust me, I'm a teacher," I improvised.

Her lips flapped like a fish out of water. "Get out!"

Whipping out a pair of wire glasses from my purse, I set them low on my nose.

Brittany's eyes widened. "Well, maybe a short smoke break." She snatched up her purse. "Thanks! I won't be long."

"No problem."

"You're a lifesaver!" Brittany called back, throwing her coat over her shoulders before she rushed out. When the anti-smoking by-law came into effect, smokers either quit or put up with the elements, which in winter is no picnic. Addiction has its price.

After she disappeared down the hallway, I made my move. I saw two offices. The nameplate on the left was labeled Margaret Beige. I turned the knob and found it locked. Quickly, I raced back to the secretary's desk and checked her top drawer. The usual. What about the other drawer? Bingo! Taking the ring with the attached keys, I tried them, got the third one to fit, zoomed back and tossed the keys in the drawer.

Marg's desk was piled high with papers. A framed picture of Marg in happier times with Libby, minus Boris, was perched on the desk near her pad. I glanced over her calendar and saw yesterday's date circled but no notation made.

The filing cabinet was in the corner. I scanned the labels on the front. At *M-Z* I tugged but found it locked.

In my experience keys are usually in an obvious place. In the middle drawer of her desk, I found two keys on a ring. On the second try, the drawer opened. The file was thick with scribbled notes. With time running out, I shoved the papers into my attaché case, closed the cabinet and clicked the door shut behind me.

The adjacent office nameplate read *Uma Farber-Reich*. Could she be the slut nurse supervisor? And wait a minute…she was the ex. Even more reason to snoop. I knocked, waited a moment and tried the handle. It opened.

Curiosity has always been my downfall. I peeped over my shoulder and seeing no one, stepped into a Martha Stewartish office, decorated exclusively in greens and ivory. A few English garden prints hung precisely at the right height. The desk was cleared, with the exception of a framed photo and a brass pen set. No work for this woman. The photo showed a slim raven-haired female on water skis, attractive in a boyish sort of way.

As I turned to go, a hand grabbed my arm, claws digging deep into my skin. "Just *who* are *you* and what are you doing in *my* office?"

I looked up at a pale face, splotched red with anger. I shook off the talons. "Sorry, I was looking for Marg's office."

Uma Farber-Reich pointed one of her long red acrylics at Marg's door. "That is her office! The one with her name on it."

My eyes flicked to the pen set on her desk. "Needed a pen to write her a note." I patted my tote bag.

She curled her fire engine red lips and thrust out her hand. "Give it here."

"No worries. I'll send her an e-mail," I said, over my shoulder as I strode into the outer office and nearly collided into Brittany. The blonde gritted her teeth. She reminded me of a friend's gerbil I'd kept. When my cat Minnie knocked the cage down, the door sprung open and the gerbil fell out. Frozen on the spot, it was about to become a cat treat. Luckily, I snatched it up before Minnie had a taste. Wrapped in a towel, the little guy revived.

Brittany had that gerbil look."Took a washroom break, Uma. I told her," she gestured vaguely in my direction, "Marg wasn't in."

Uma glared.

Trembling in patent leather stilettos, Brit was ready to be wrapped in a warm towel. Making a hasty exit, I heard the two of them getting into it, voices raised, one in anger, the other an octave higher, frightened out of her gourd.

At the double-door entrance, I noticed a Starbucks to my left. My rumbling stomach told me this was as good a place as any for a little sustenance.

I brought a tea and chocolate brownie over to a small table near the door and started to read Marg's notes. Cookie crumbs and coffee stains marred the lined paper. Neat-freak Marg had to be stressed to get this messy.

Royal Investments, Reich's suspicions involving Uma, and his associates were the focus of his paranoia. On the verge of a breakdown, Reich couldn't function effectively in his job. Marg had referred him to a psychiatrist but he had refused to go. He wanted Marg to pick up his cashier's check from Santiago Alvarez in Cozumel.

A detailed drawing of a Boeing 747 had been sketched in the margin. Marg wasn't much of an artist but planes and engines turned her on. I, on the other hand, liked pilots. I nibbled on the last bit of my brownie contemplating that long steamy night in San Juan. I had been younger and stupider then. Still, there was something about a handsome man in a white pilot's uniform sitting in a cockpit controlling a super size jet.

On an unoccupied table I saw a copy of the *Kitchener Today* which reminded me about the memorial. If I hurried, I could take in my karate class first.

***

The Japanese name for a training school is *dojo*. The brunette at the desk greeted me cheerfully. "Hey, Adie! You'd better hurry. *Sensei* is raring to go."

I raced down the hall to the change room, slipped into my karate wear and grabbed my weapons. Being late meant pushups. When my teacher, entered, we kneeled.

Kicks, strikes and jumping jacks. Ten, twenty, thirty, and still more. *Sensei's* counting grew frantically loud, until he screamed at the top of his lungs like a drill sergeant. I was beginning to wonder if I would make it through class when *Sensei* stopped us and gave us a lecture. "If an attacker tries to kill you, how many seconds do you have to move out of the way? Your life depends on strength, endurance and muscle memory."

Afterwards, I trudged out to my car, shoulders aching from the pushups and legs sore from kicking the heavy punching bag. I was such a masochist. Who would be attacking me anyway?

***

The thick magenta carpet in Martin's Funeral Home muffled my footsteps. A solemn looking man with a pinched pale face in a black suit directed me to the second door.

The room was full. At the far corner I saw a tall trim brunette. I should have guessed Claws would be here. Dressed to the nines in a fitted designer suit, her thin figure took on some curves. The suit must have cost a small fortune. I wanted to take a closer look, but I wasn't crazy about getting near that woman. The indentations she'd made earlier would easily last a week. I should have brought my cat clippers and offered a free manicure.

Next to me, a dark-haired man, a youngish Al Pacino checked out the crowd. He was familiar. Where had I seen him before? His glance stopped on Uma. She looked like she'd been crying, but carefully, so as to not smudge her eye makeup.

"You were friends?" Pacino asked.

"With Reich?" I coughed nervously. "No, not really."

"So you're part of the Cancer Society group?" He was close enough for me to smell his aftershave. Spicy.

"Mm-m, excuse me." I stepped beside a bald man speaking to a dowdy lady with comfortable practical shoes—definitely university crowd. I blanked them out as I focused on Claws.

Uma was surrounded by men. A stocky fellow with a protruding belly sporting a tweed jacket, stood beside her. On her right, a tall, wiry gray-haired man patted her hand. A blond fellow in an expensive suit—maybe Valentino or Armani, for sure, designer Italian, offered her a drink. She smiled until she caught sight of me. If looks could kill...Uma jerked her chin in my direction and made some sort of remark. Her fan club looked over to see who had displeased the queen. I stepped back to hide in the crowd.

"The fat dude's Dr. Dreitup, an oncologist," a voice answered my silent question.

I whipped about. "Bernie?"

"So whatcha doin' here, Adie?"

"Why are you here?" I said, checking out the doctor guffawing loudly over the buzz of the crowd.

"Hello! Duh, I'm a reporter."

"And Drietup? What's his connection?"

"Reich donated generously to the new oncology wing. Guy was big on charities." He brought his lips up to my ear and whispered, "Reich was one of *the* Reichs."

"What?"

"Shoes, Adie," he added, as if he were speaking to an imbecilic child.

"Oh-hh." Reich Shoes were comfortable shoes sold all over Canada, something like Rockford. I flicked my eyes back to the group. "Who's the blond guy?"

"President of the Rotary Club, Alec Bauman. Criminal lawyer."

Really? That would explain the duds but seriously, a plastic surgeon, maybe, or a Hollywood hairdresser would be more like it. No male vibes here or my gay detector was on the blink.

"Reich was the past president. Quit suddenly. Health problems. Bauman's on the board at the hospital, as well."

"Oh?" My eyes flicked over his flawless symmetrical face once more before lighting on the solicitous distinguished man in a pinstriped suit. "And the tall guy?"

"Hamilton F. Morgenson, hospital director."

As I watched, the man stalked over to the side table and poured himself some water. He glanced over at us, his teeth drawn back in a sneer, passed off as a smile.

"Say, Bern, did you find out why the police think Reich's death was suspicious?"

"I keep askin' my contacts, but no luck so far. I was hopin' I would see somethin' here."

"You mean someone. The murderer could be here, couldn't he?"

"Yeah." Slick stroked his nose with his forefinger. "If I come up with the murderer, I could win an award, notta mention a Toronto Sun job, but, you, Adie, what do you get outta this?" He snuggled close. "You must think your friend's involved." He nudged me with his elbow. "Beige and Reich. Bet they were hookin' up. I'm right, aren't I?" He poked me in the ribs. "Come on, spit it out, Adie."

Annoyed, I spun around and headed to the door.

Slick came right after me. "Adie, wait! Gimme a break, here."

"Good-bye," I hissed through clenched teeth.

But Slick was like a terrier with a bone. He grabbed my jacket sleeve and held on. "Notsa fast, honey. Fess up. Tell Uncle Bern."

I tried to get away but his grip tightened. He pulled me so close I could feel his breath on my neck. I twisted ninety degrees and with the knife-edge of my hand struck his forearm. He let go, backing into the table, jiggling a pitcher of water and glasses.

The funeral director, swooped over, glaring at Slick, his face beet-red. While he gave Bern a piece of his mind, I escaped into the hall, on my way accidentally bumping into an old lady drinking coffee. I muttered an apology. Over my shoulder, I checked for Slick. He was giving chase.

I pulled out of the lot and headed onto King Street as he jumped into his red Toyota. A few blocks further, I saw a bar on the right. A neon yellow sax player holding a brilliant purple instrument flashed above the *Blues Brothers* sign. I checked my rear-view mirror, and seeing no hint of Slick's Toyota drove in and parked on the other side of a Chevy van.

A heavy black man tinkered away on the piano as I came in and took a seat at the bar. He was good, St. Louis Blues oozed out of the piano, slow and easy. Ordering a vodka and tonic with a twist of lime, I looked around.

At the far end of the bar, a red-head with blue snake tattoos huddled with a beefy biker. The bartender, a clean-cut university kid, wiped the counter before placing a coaster. The place was on the seedy side but it was early—rough types came in after nine.

The singer's gravelly voice rocked *The Thrill is Gone* and I remembered. The round slice of lime became his wide grin. With him I'd reached that precious moment when passion peaks. Pleasure I hadn't had with anyone. I'd thought he was the "one".

I poked the lime straight in the center and watched the pale green slivers detach and float into the vodka and tonic. Betrayal and lies. My rings and necklaces stolen—for his *other* fiancée. What did it matter how good a lover he'd been? I squished the lime repeatedly, mashing it into tiny pieces. Love makes us all losers.

I sensed someone taking the seat beside me, the scent of his aftershave, familiar and pleasant. Spice. I tried not to stare at Pacino from the funeral home. He shuffled uncomfortably, looked around and ordered a Sleeman ale.

His fingers tapped nervously on the counter.

"Trying to quit smoking?"

Pacino glanced in my direction, sipping his beer. "How'd you know that?"

"I can tell. Saw an acupuncturist. Hey, you should try water as a substitute." I met his eyes. Expressive and brown. "You're not a reporter are you?"

"No, a cop, actually, a detective."

I was right. He had gone into the pit bull house.

He held his hand out, "Ilya Kharkov, nice to meet you."

"Adie Sturm." I shook his hand. "You're on the Reich case?"

"Yeah." He stared. "You were at the service. Said you didn't know Reich."

"I didn't—not exactly."

"Then why go to the funeral home?" He shifted his body closer.

"A friend needed some moral support."

Ilya peered at me suspiciously. "Yeah? Which friend?"

I twirled a strand of my hair, thinking fast. "Bernie Scharf. Know him?"

"Reporter," he muttered derisively.

"So, is it a murder?"

Ilya gulped his beer before he replied, "Well, I wouldn't normally discuss this but at this very moment the chief is speaking to *Channel 12*. They want anyone with any information to contact me or the department. Got anything for me?"

"No-oo." I sipped my drink. "If the dogs didn't do it, how'd it happen?"

"We're still waiting for the autopsy."

"You must have an idea?"

"He was mauled badly, Adie. Someone was trying to cover up the real cause of death."

"He was thrown to the dogs?"

"Um." Ilya glanced at me curiously.

I sipped my drink, thinking. I had to ask, "From where?"

"Next door. Residence of Margaret Beige."

Whoa! This was worse than I'd thought.

The detective studied my face. "You know her, don't you?"

"She's a friend, but she wasn't there."

"And you know this because?"

"I stopped by her house." I motioned to the bartender. "Could I get an order of chicken fingers, please?"

Ilya joined in, "Make that two. I'm buying." He drained his beer and set it down on the counter. "We're looking for her for questioning. Do you know where she might be?"

My eyes shot evasively over at the bartender wiping the counter.

He pressed on my arm forcing me to face him. "Where *is* she, Adie?"

Marg was screwed if I said anything. "Can't help you there."

Kharkov looked skeptical. "Can't or won't?" He slid his card towards me. "This is serious stuff, Adie. A man's been murdered. A good citizen helps the police."

This cop would have made a good Jewish mother. I take that back, my grandma was a carefree creative type, with a laissez-faire attitude. "I would certainly call," I smiled, "if I could tell you anything."

I watched the bartender place two baskets of chicken in front of us.

Ilya glanced at me skeptically, before he dug a carrot stick into the dip.

Distractedly, I picked up a piece of chicken, bit into it, and promptly burned my tongue.

"So you know Scharf. He your boyfriend?" His dark eyes dug into mine.

Slick? He'd be the last man on this planet I'd want. No, make that the second last. I deliberated, thinking back to my doomed relationship with Jay. The tonic was bitter on my tongue.

"From the look on your face, I'd say no," Ilya surmised. "I need another beer. Would you like another drink?"

"No thanks. Got to drive." I focused on the food. Not bad, I thought, biting carefully this time, into a crisp finger.

Ilya signaled the college kid, who brought over another beer and the bill.

Wiping his hands, the detective pushed his basket away, and guzzled down half his beer. In a quick gesture, he brought out his wallet and threw some bills on the bar.

"Thanks for the fingers," I said.

Ilya smiled, "No problem. You're a cheap date," he winked adding, "and cute." He took a last swig of beer before he stood up. "See you around, eh?" he said significantly. "Call me." He grinned. "Put my number in your contacts."

As he put on his leather jacket, I gave him a quick once-over. Nice buns and flat abs. This cop must work out, definitely not a jelly-donuts type.

When I got home that night I kept thinking about Uma. Nurses weren't paid much. Government workers were barely getting cost of living increases. But she could come from money. Money marries money, doesn't it? Reich had been seriously loaded. If Reich had been involved in some deal and let Marg in on it, he might have involved Uma. And then there was the suit...*I want that suit.*

Just out of curiosity I got on the computer and Googled her address. She was listed on Old Grande Road. The houses there were referred to as homes by real estate agents. No fresh off-the-boat immigrants in that neck of the woods, unless they bribed the realtors.

Tomorrow I had a few hours before I left for Cozumel. I could drive by and check out Claws's lair. Maybe I'd see something. And on the way, I'd pick up some waterproof mascara and some heavy-duty sunscreen for my trip. I rubbed my tired eyes. I'd nearly forgotten my cat nanny. This time she picked up.

"Hi, Darlene, it's Adie. Everything's ready. Minnie's looking forward to seeing you. So anyway, sweetie, I was just wondering, is Marg staying at the Grand Cozumel?"

"Adie, I'm not sure I should say anything."

"Come on, Darlene," I begged, "I lost her address and we wanted to connect."

"Well, I guess its okay," Darlene considered. "She's at the Hotel Maria."

"Thanks so much, Darlene. Marg's going through a tough time, right now."

"Hope you both have fun down there then. Bye, bye, Adie."

I slipped into bed with a book. When the phone rang, I didn't pick up. "Go away," I muttered. The machine ignored me and said its bit. I waited. A man's husky voice came on.

"It's Ilya Kharkov—I'll try another time, okay?"

I was jealous. Pineridge Acres—an exclusive subdivision. Large homes spaced far apart, each with a different builder. Claw's house was on the edge of town past the ski club. I slowed down to glance at the numbers, and guessing hers was next, I parked.

The zipper on my black leather jacket done up, I walked uphill. At the top, I saw a gray brick, Colonial-style house with a triple garage and an enormous frontage. A silver Mercedes was parked in the driveway. No sign of activity. On a leafless maple tree, a lone robin that had forgotten to migrate, chirped happily, unaware of what winter could hold. So now what? I hiked back to my car, got in, and sat thinking.

Turning the engine on, I eased down the road to the next house where a silver Lexus was parked in the driveway. Silver was an acceptable color for the well-to-do. A stooped gray-haired woman in a ski jacket was examining a damaged tree with a broken branch next to the road.

I parked and got out. "Hello!" I called out.

The old lady looked up and frowned. "I'm not buying anything."

"I'm not selling anything. I just wondered if you've seen Uma."

"Oh, her. Not if I can help it. You a friend?"

"No, I need a file from her."

"Well, I can't help you there." She turned away and looked at the tree again.

"Did she just get the Mercedes?"

"I guess the Lexus wasn't good enough." Her mouth pursed downwards. "She probably asked one of her 'friends' to buy her something better."

"Men like her."

"Too much, I'd say." She pinched her lips into a narrow line, hissing through her teeth, "Cat in heat, that one. Last summer when she moved in, there was such a racket I couldn't sleep worth a dang."

"Her boyfriend likes parties." I scratched my head. "What's

his name again?"

She sniffed contemptuously. "Don't know, don't care. I've got things to do, young woman. Do you mind?" Ignoring me, she shuffled back into her house, shutting the immense oak door behind her with a dull thud.

Interesting. Uma sleeping around. Which wealthy sucker could it be?

Back in my car I drove to the junction and turned left in the direction of the pharmacy just over the bridge. It wasn't rush hour, yet the traffic was almost at a standstill, bumper to bumper. Near the Grand River I caught a glimpse of cobalt blue water, frigidly uninviting with its scattered ice patches.

As my Bug crawled slowly over the bridge I could finally see why. "Expect the unexpected" is something we're told in karate, but I can't say I was expecting anything like this.

Usually the area is quiet in the winter, with only the occasional person walking their dog. The riverbank below was swarming with cops. The road that led to the Grand River was cordoned off with yellow crime tape. On the other side of the bridge, I turned into the pharmacy parking lot. After I locked the Bug, I hoofed it back. A group of people stood looking down over the railing at the commotion below.

Police. A team of uniformed cops and forensic people in white jumpsuits were examining the muddy embankment and the pathway along the river. Paramedics shoved a yellow body bag into the back of an ambulance. I glanced about and saw a familiar man in a brown coat standing with the crowd. "Hey, Bernie!" I shouted.

Slick broke off from his conversation with a bearded chunky man and looked over. He smiled when he saw me. "Hi, honey. How're you doin'?"

Just as I reached him, his cell began a rendition of the Austin Powers theme. Taking it out of his belt case, he muttered a few monosyllables before shoving it back in.

"What happened?"

"Drowning. You might've met her. Uma Farber-Reich."

My jaw dropped. "Uma?"

Slick nodded, and got out his notepad. "I'll catch ya later, eh? We've gotta talk." Jotting notations on his pad, Bernie didn't notice me leaving—he had a story to write.

In a daze, I made my way back to the Pharma Mart. I wandered around the store, picking up makeup and sunscreen, my thoughts jumbled. First Reich and now Uma? Why?

After paying the cashier, I got into my car and decided I'd have to brave the traffic going over the bridge. It was still stop-and-go. I glanced down as I drove across—broken ice floes covered the surface of the river. Even for someone like Claws, this was a horrible way to die.

When I got home, I searched my purse for Bernie's card. I phoned his cell, left him a message and then pressed in a new contact number. "Detective Kharkov, please." I felt a little tense. Phoning the police is stressful, even more so when the detective is attractive.

I heard a click. "Detective Kharkov."

"Hi, it's Adie."

"Hey. What's up?"

"I was driving on old King Street and noticed it was closed off at the Grand River. A friend told me the dead person was Uma Farber-Reich."

"You sure get around, Adie. You're not with the press, are you?"

"I'm a tour consultant."

"I wouldn't mind a consultation," he said softly.

My mind flashed back to his soulful brown eyes. "Is that what you wanted last night?"

"It would've been a nice start. So, what's your interest in this, Adie? Anything you'd like to tell me about Beige?"

His "good cop" interrogation method probably worked, but I was more into deal making. "If I do, will you tell me what the cause of death was?"

"I might be persuaded," he said, his voice husky. "I could come by after work…"

"I'm leaving for Cozumel in a couple of hours."

"Lucky you. Where're you staying?"

"Hotel Don Juan. My e-mail is kiaicat@hotmail."

"Got it. Now, what about your friend? Where is she?"

"She's in Cozumel as we speak."

"Okay, I'm biting. Where?"

"I just found this out and I don't think she'd like it if I told you."

"It'll be far worse for her if I have to take her in at the airport."

I sighed. "Okay, you win. Hotel Maria. Now tell me, how did Uma die?"

"No autopsy results yet."

"And your guess is?"

"We won't know for at least three days, make that four, with it being a weekend."

"It's connected, isn't it?"

"I don't believe in coincidence."

***

North Jet Flight 124 from Pearson International Toronto was right on schedule. It was a charter flight with cuisine choices ranging from sandwiches to sandwiches. The flight attendants, comedian wannabees, cracked jokes in between explaining flight evacuation procedures.

By the time we descended for landing it was late afternoon. The sun was low in the horizon. Below, sparkling blue waters surrounded the green island of Cozumel. The name means "Place of the Swallows". It's only twenty-eight miles long and eleven mile. wide. A diver's Mecca. They come for the fish and the second largest coral reef on the planet—Palancar.

A blast of warm humid air hit my face as I stepped down the metal stairs onto the pavement and made my way towards the airport terminal. It was like taking a walk in a sauna. Inside, passengers scattered to get into immigration lineups. After my luggage was inspected, I headed straight to the Hertz desk, and rented a Jeep.

Topes, impressive little speed bumps on the ocean front road and limited streetlights, as well as people scurrying out in front of the cars made the driving difficult. *Calles*, streets going to and from the waterfront, and *aviendas*, streets running parallel to the waterfront, ran alternately one way, or so it seemed, except when they didn't.

Located close to the ferry crossing, the Hotel Don Juan, a

yellow stucco building with a red tile roof, was a typical three-star hotel. A dive shop was off to the right of the parking lot.

Automated double glass doors opened. A doorman helped me bring my luggage into a comfortable lobby, furnished with white wicker furniture and green floral pillows. At an identical set of doors across the lobby facing the sea, a group of divers, gear in hand, headed out to the wharf for a night dive.

With people coming and going, the air conditioning at the reception area was cool, but not cold. At the front desk I registered with a clerk with a distinctly Mayan appearance, a prominent hooked nose and a slanting high forehead.

The other front deskman, with "Manni Lopez" on his nametag, smiled widely when I glanced in his direction. A dark haired brown-eyed sort-of hobbit. A doppelganger for Frodo in *Lord of the Rings*. "Let me help you, Señorita." He picked up my suitcase and led me up the stairs to my room on the top floor. After showing me the usual highlights, he said, "I'm the assistant manager, filling in for the bellhop. If you need a guide, I'm at your disposal. A good guide is difficult to find."

"Sure," but *no thanks*, Manni. I'm no babe in the woods. "Do you know of any karate schools in San Miguel?"

"An English karate school opened on 40 Avenida Norte, Calle 10—Maple Leaf Martial Arts Academy. He opened the door. "We could negotiate a fee. I do this on my days off, and so," he swept his hands out significantly, "I do some business, make some money."

"I'll let you know."

I clicked the door shut behind him and walked over to the twin beds, covered by red and blue patterned duvets. On a table between them, a clay statue of Ixchel, the Mayan fertility goddess, sat next to the lamp.

Kicking off my shoes, I examined the room. No use having two beds. Before rearranging them I needed a little insurance. From my suitcase, I took a can of Raid, reached under the beds and sprayed in a wide arch. Satisfied, I stepped back, but not fast enough. A large black cockroach danced over my naked toe. I gasped. Backing off, I bumped into the dresser behind me. My butt smarted but I kept my focus, finger glued to the spray button, pushed to high heaven. But the roach was strong and wouldn't be stopped. With all the force I could muster, I smashed the can down. Once, and then again—annihilating the beast.

That bit of cleanup satisfactorily completed, I changed into a clingy black dress, slipped on silver high heeled sandals and headed down to the restaurant. Above the palapa of the open-air restaurant, the multi-hued sky reflected on sparkly lavender patches of ocean. Past that, there was a sandy beach with a few jagged rocks and a jetty. A lush jungle of hibiscus, heavy with bloom, bordered the pool and restaurant. From the puddles at the restaurant entrance, I surmised it must have recently rained.

The maitre'd greeted me with a smile. "*Buenas noches, Señorita.*"

"*Buenas noches.* A table, please."

"Is anyone joining you?"

"No. "

"This way, Señorita," he said, leading me to a table overlooking the ocean. A few younger people sat at the bar chatting and only two other tables were occupied. The waiter came over with some chips and salsa, handed me a menu, and asked what I'd like to drink.

My first night in Mexico deserved something special. "*Daiquiri de fresas.*"

"Yes, of course, Señorita."

When he returned with a strawberry daiquiri, he took my order. I leaned back against my chair, holding my frozen drink watching tiny waves lap against the shore. The warm ocean breeze blew a strand of hair into my face. I brushed it away and took another sip. It was sweet, yet there was a curious trace of bitter lemon in the finish.

The bar lights glistened on the water but the beach itself was shadowy. It felt good sitting out here after the flight and the hassles accompanying traveling. If I wasn't so hungry, I'd take off my shoes and dip my toes in the water to feel the nip of the salt on my skin.

I caught some movement on the beach. Something was out there. Whoa! Be still my beating heart! From out of the night, a tall dark figure appeared, his athletic body clothed in black, his hair catching the lights, gleaming silver. The man suddenly turned. Startled, I dropped my stir stick. His slow smile was one I could never forget.

The sea god's eyes glinted dark blue. "Adie, I can't believe it."

On a breath I whispered his name, "Wolf Du Lac."

He pulled out a chair and sat down. "Long time, Adie," he said softly, his gaze intense.

My eyes fixed on his windblown hair falling into his cool blues. "Years, Wolf," I said, thinking, who's fault was that? "Are you staying here?"

"No. I came by to see if there was any decent snorkeling."

"And is there?" His face was an interesting combination of features that spelled rugged, rather than handsome—his jaw strong and his nose imperfect but in combination, everything together, seethed sexuality.

"Could be. The reef's twenty meters off shore. How about you?" His gaze was so direct, I felt my cheeks flush. "You staying here?" Wolf casually motioned for the waiter.

"Um-mm." His lips were oh-so-sensuous.

"Dos Equis, *por favor*." The waiter nodded and headed to the bar.

"Is it okay that I join you? You're not expecting anyone?"

I met his eyes and saw something I'd forgotten. Was that a spark of lust for me or was that just the substance of this man that appeared to every woman. My throat felt suddenly dry. I sipped my daiquiri to collect my thoughts. "No." Was there a woman in the picture?

The waiter brought over Wolf's beer and my chicken fajitas.

"Are you on vacation?"

Wolf sipped his beer contemplatively. "I'm looking into buying property, but no luck so far."

The T-shirt hugged tightly to his shoulders and well-developed chest. He could just sit there. He wouldn't have to say a word. Eye candy, to be eaten slowly—every succulent morsel savored. This vacation was looking better by the minute, good food, delicious drinks, and a smoking hot man. A girl couldn't get luckier than that, could she? I filled a tortilla and rolled it up with anticipation, especially after the North Jet cardboard sandwich experience. "Problems?" I thought I'd better speak or he'd get bored and leave.

He got that serious look men get when they talk about business. "Mexican law. Foreigners aren't allowed to own land fifty kilometers from the waterfront, at least not outright. Everywhere on Cozumel is too close to the water." He examined the honey sparkle of his beer. " Now if I picked a site in the middle of Mexico…"

"Yup, everyone wants to rent a condo on a bare hill with some goats." I bit into my tortilla.

"Exactly." He grinned, flashing white teeth. "But there's always the benefit of authentic banditos."

"What's Mexico without holdups? Just what the average tourist wants to keep from dying of boredom on the beach."

Wolf eyed my black dress, cut low over my breasts. "There are other ways." Smiling suggestively, he took my hand. "Did you just get here?"

I was blown away—his hand was so warm and strong. An electric charge shot through me. Tingles of arousal. I shifted in my chair uneasily, glancing away.

"Adie?" His eyes were a dark crystal blue, like a freshwater stream.

I tried to concentrate on his question but the tingle between my thighs was becoming more pronounced. I glanced at my arms. "I suppose you can tell by the death pallor?"

"Your skin is not white, Adie. I'd call it—" eyes flicking to my cleavage, "golden."

Wolf was different somehow—a player? "You've obviously been here for a while."

He nodded. "A few days. Are you here with someone?"

"No. I'm a tour group leader. This trip is research but also a vacation."

"Good job?"

"Usually." My eyes were drawn to his full lips, wondering what they'd feel like to kiss. Thoughtfully, I traced a finger around my own lips.

Wolf's eyes followed my finger.

"And you, Wolf—are you alone?"

"For now. If I buy land, it'll be with my brother. He may decide to join me."

My fajita finished, I took a last sip of my daiquiri. I didn't want to go, but I had to. It was getting late and Marg liked to hit the sack early. I asked the waiter passing the table for my bill.

I couldn't get over it. Cozumel was full of surprises. Imagine meeting up with Wolf after all these years? I'd forgotten how magnetic he was. "I've got to go."

Wolf stood up and laid a few dollars on the table. His deep blue eyes met mine. "Why don't we get together?"

Oh, yes! Could he hear the thud of my heartbeat? "Call me. Room 209." I signed for my bill and got up to leave. I was so cool. Not like that girl I'd been years ago, the insecure one that had cried when he had found another girl.

Wolf pushed out my chair and took my hand. "Want to go out to Delores tonight?" He stroked my fingers, rubbing the fleshy part of my hand. "You like dancing."

How'd he know that? He had promised to take me dancing, but never had. I was suddenly nervous. The very thought of having his arms around me set a hot surge in motion, blitzing down to my thighs. Could he feel the dampness from my palm? "I'm afraid I can't tonight, Wolf. There's something I need to do." No that was too vague—I didn't want to lose him. I explained, "Before I left home, something happened. My friend's in trouble. I have to get over to the Hotel Maria to see her tonight."

"Sounds serious."

"It is." His fingers rubbing my palm communicated pleasurable messages to my body. "You wouldn't believe this."

"I'm staying at the Maria. I'll go with you. You can tell me all about it."

That was something I had always liked about him—how he had listened like a friend. And yet he was so totally male. Scorching lava flowed inside me—my needs and emotions churning as we made our way outside. On the uneven sidewalk, wearing high heels, it became a precarious walk. With every step I took, I became increasingly aware of my dangerously exciting companion.

***

Marg's room was on the corridor to the right. I knocked. Marg opened the door abruptly. She looked wiped. Her dark brown hair was standing on end, her face was clean of all makeup, and her glasses were slightly askew. We hugged and I stepped back to study her. I could see she hadn't been sleeping well by the shadows under her eyes. Was the puffiness from the drugs?

"What are *you* doing here, Adie? How did you know where to find me?"

"Cozumel research. And in answer to your other question— that's a long story." I sat down on a rattan chair.

Marg nodded slowly. "Knowing you, this will be good." She plopped herself down on the edge of the bed to face me.

"I think *your* story will be more interesting. You had me scared, Marg."

"Why?"

"We have a lot to talk about. I'll call room service and order us drinks," I picked up the phone, asking for a daiquiri, as Marg whispered, "Same."

Minutes later we were sipping delicious red concoctions on the balcony. Marg downed her drink quickly as I told her about the murders.

"I can't believe this, Adie." Marg's hand shook as she set her glass down. "Tim was a sweetheart. I really liked him." She paused, her voice catching, as a tear escaped.

Digging around in my purse I came up with a clean tissue and handed it to her. Marg blew her nose, cried a few tears, wiped her eyes and stared into space.

"You were close?"

My friend sat silently.

"Marg?" Maybe a drink wasn't such a good idea. The drugs could be hitting her hard. Alcohol might have made it worse. "Marg?" I said, louder this time.

She looked up startled. "We had dinner together a few times— candlelit dinners at nice restaurants." In a faraway voice Marg spoke softly, as if remembering. "Who knows what could have happened between us if…" Another tear appeared at the corner of her eye, which she pushed away with her fist. "This is so awful. It should never have happened to him. I can't say the same for Uma. Couldn't stand that witch."

I glanced at my arm, the scratch marks still visible. I would have called Uma by her proper name starting with a *B*.

31

"What did that detective say about me?" Marg asked distractedly.

"Not much, but I distinctly got the impression that he urgently wants to speak with you. I wouldn't be surprised if he phones you here."

Marg straightened. "Here?" She sounded annoyed. "How does he know where I am?"

"Sorry, Marg. I had no choice."

"What do you mean, no choice? You always have a choice. You like this cop, don't you? That's why you told him." She stabbed the air with her forefinger. "Listen to me, Adie. Avoid these men!" she warned. "Cops are mean alcoholics not to mention workaholics."

I was beginning to wonder about her mood swings. Drugs? "Well, you're the expert," I said, to pacify her. She should know. Boris was a workaholic, besides being a despicable human being with a drinking problem. "So why did you come here anyway, Marg?"

"Tim paid me to pick up his cashier's check at a company called Royal Investments. Ethically, I know I shouldn't have gone for it, but Adie, I'm desperate. Tim gave me ten thousand dollars plus a package deal at this hotel. It was a godsend. Believe me that money will come in handy with those outrageous support payments. And now that I'm here, I'm going to have a good time." Marg smirked. "Maybe even let loose a bit."

"Why didn't Reich get it himself or just send for it?"

"Poor sweetheart suffered from severe paranoia and a fear of flying. This person I need to see—he didn't trust him either." Her lip trembled. "Tim was so charming and intelligent."

I patted her hand and asked, "What are you going to do now?"

"Tomorrow I see Santiago Alvarez."

"And he is?"

"The owner of Royal Investments and a lawyer, as far as I know. Tim said he had contacted Alvarez about getting the check and it's been okayed."

"But he's dead."

"Well, I have to go ahead and do what I was paid to do. Besides, Tim gave me this fabulous break. I owe him."

She brightened. "I'll give the check to his lawyer."

"His estate gets it."

"Yup. He must have some relative who needs the money."

"Where's Alvarez's office?"

Marg reached for a card on her dresser table. "40 Avenida Norte, Calle 8."

"Hm-mm. It's close to the karate place I wanted to go to. You want a ride?"

Marg yawned. "Okay, but, let's do lunch first."

"I'm one block from you, at the Hotel Don Juan. Meet me in the lobby. I have a snorkeling date at ten, so I should be showered and ready by twelve."

"A date?" Marg's eyes widened. "I'm impressed. You just got here, didn't you?"

"Yes." I grinned. "But, I know him from back home."

"Maybe he's got a friend?"

Had Marg winked or blinked? Did she really mean it? But then again, once you've driven a standard, you never forget. It takes a while to rev Marg's motor but watch out when she hits that highway!

4

Strong, slightly calloused hands rhythmically massaged my back, the warm suntan oil spreading down to my bikini bottom. His fingertips lightly stroked my thighs, jump-starting my hormones into a wild ride. Physical labour in his dad's construction company and probably a weight room had helped that athletic body, but the magic hands were all his own.

When I started to fantasize about what else he could do for me, I knew I'd better sit up. "Why don't I put some on you now, Wolf?

"Sure, where were you thinking?" He grinned, stretching out on the towel.

"Cleanse your mind," I ordered, wondering if I shouldn't follow my own advice.

"And with that comes a flow of energy?"

"Um-mm." My energy was gearing up, scanning his flat six-pack. I dabbed suntan oil on my hands and smoothed it over his chest. His body was perfect, so strong and firm. Touching him took a lot of self-control. I heaved a sigh of relief when he turned over onto his stomach.

"Any suggestions as to what I should do with all that energy? I'd hate to waste it." Wolf eyed me lazily over his shoulder, sipping his beer.

I spread the oil over his broad shoulders and admiring his muscular back, I remarked, "There's a great big ocean out there waiting for you."

"I was thinking more on the lines of us."

"Good things come to those who wait."

Wolf reached behind him, placed his hand on my leg and squeezed lightly. "I can do that. I may not want to, but for you..." his voice trailed off, his attention on a dark patch of reef. "It was great out there, wasn't it?"

Colours flashed in my mind. "It was beautiful," I said, thinking back. But his skin distracted me—so velvety and smooth. His biceps were clearly defined. Hard and powerful but not like those muscle-bound workout junkies. It took an effort to refocus on our topic—snorkelling. So many fish in the sea… "Was that a Queen Angel or a Blue Angel?"

Wolf handed me an icy goblet of coconut delight. "Difference being?"

"One is minus a crown." I peeked over my piña colada at him.

"Could be a good thing. With a crown comes responsibility."

"I have more than enough of that."

"Your job?"

"Not this time. My research here should be interesting." My mind flicked from Mayan ruins to this very touchable man in front of me.

Wolf studied my face. "But you're concerned about Marg."

"It would be a relief if they'd find the murderer." I sighed. "I need to relax."

"I'll help you with that."

Yes, I thought, but was I ready to get into a whirlwind romance? "Do you think those nurse sharks come close to shore?"

"If they do, they sure would love to get a taste of you." He added softly, "You have incredible eyes, Adie."

He must be kidding! My face had red mask marks left from snorkelling. I set my drink down, eager to hear him continue, not that I really believed any of it.

"Luscious lips, too."

My lips were good. Everyone had always said so. I smiled at him encouragingly.

"I'd be lying if I said I liked your hair."

Ouch! What was the matter with him? Didn't he know that truth hurt? I stuck a finger into the sticky, salty mess on my head. "It's awful, isn't it?" I dug down deep into my beach bag for my denim cap and was about to stick it over my head when he snatched it away.

"Wait," Wolf said, taking the cap and pulling it over my hair, slanting it down over one eye. He leaned back and studied his work. "Sexy," he said, his voice husky and low.

I was caught somewhere between embarrassment and feverish excitement. Idly, I picked up my camera.

My Hormone Voice breathed, "Look at him! He's so hot. Move closer. He might kiss you. A kiss from him will recharge every battery you ever had and then some." Hormone was right. My lips parted and I moved my chin up.

"Stop, you fool!" Logical ragged in my brain. What's wrong with you? How many kicks in the teeth do you need before you wise up? Can't you see what he's doing? You'll only be one of many, another notch on his belt, a vacation fling. Once he has you..."

"Señorita? You want me to take a picture?" our waiter interrupted, seeing my camera.

Before I could think about it, Wolf handed the waiter my camera and drew me in close. His body was warm and strong and I liked his arm around me. *Click!* Wolf was captured on film, but was I letting myself be captured by him?

"Adie, I'd better go. I have a meeting at the El Presidente." Wolf pulled on a shirt and tossed his snorkelling equipment into a bag. "How about dinner and dancing at Delores tonight?"

He was like a category four hurricane. Comes in strong, stirs things up, creates havoc and then leaves in a wave of devastation. "Okay," I said a little uncertainly, wrapping my paraeo low around my hips.

"Seven?"

I nodded, watching him zip his bag. I touched his arm tentatively. "Wolf, I was wondering, could you find a cute guy for my friend, Marg?"

Wolf rubbed his chin reflectively. "I know this guy from California. Women seem to like him. What about Marg? Is she hot?"

Marg had certainly trimmed down, at least twenty pounds. "She looks fantastic. Call my room around five. I should be back by then and I'll ask Marg about joining us. If she changes her mind, you can always bring him anyway."

Wolf's eyes met mine. He ran his finger over my lips and whispered, "I don't like sharing."

***

Lunch at the Don Juan was a diner's dream. Delicious quesadillas. Marg and I weren't concerned about calories either. After all, we were on vacation and part of a good vacation is food.

I sat back, checking out Marg's svelte body in her navy sundress. Her workout had been running after Libby for years, until Libby started running after boys. But her real weight loss plan had been Boris and stress.

"Why does your hot-stuff detective think he needs to talk to me?"

"Hello? Who knows both the victims?"

"So-oo?" Marg drawled.

Was she being deliberately stupid? "You weren't exactly Uma's bestie, either."

"Nobody liked her except the head secretary."

"Snotty English woman?" I picked up another quesadilla.

Marg added some sour cream to her plate. "You met Jacqui?"

"A lot happened after you left, Marg," I pointed out to my spacey friend.

"You'd better start from the beginning, in that case."

I hesitated. Maybe Marg wouldn't like hearing this—me, breaking and entering her house. Well, not actually breaking, just entering. "I went over to your townhouse because I was worried about you meeting up with Boris. He was furious on the phone, swearing and threatening you."

"Boris called?"

"Yes, don't you remember? I told you. And he's done it before, leaving messages."

"I didn't realize…" Marg's fist clenched around her fork.

"Well I thought he was losing it, so I drove to your place. When I got there, you weren't home. I would have left but I found your door open—so I went in."

Marg frowned, her tone unnaturally calm. "I had to leave in a hurry—the limo service arrived. Tim was looking at my broken fence and I thought he'd lock the door when he left."

I examined Marg's face. I couldn't get over the change in her. I mean she's not an excitable person but this was totally weird. "Are you on anything? I mean tranquillizers or…"

"Anti-depressants—but only temporarily." She brushed the crumbs off her dress. "I'm gradually going off them." I wasn't sure if she was trying to convince herself or me.

She crossed her legs. "So when was Tim murdered and how?"

"Someone threw him to the dogs next door."

Marg dropped her quesadilla. "The pit bulls! That's why the detective thinks I murdered Tim?" Red blotched her cheeks. "That's utterly insane! I wouldn't murder him and I couldn't throw him over the fence."

"With help you could."

Marg's eyes widened.

"I don't mean to say I think you had help, or that you were even involved, but that's what Ilya might be thinking."

"Ilya? You're on first name terms already?"

"We kind of got to know each other over dinner."

"Dinner!" Marg's eyes widened. "Do you have a date with everyone you meet?"

"Not everyone—only the good-looking ones." I poured some more bottled water in my glass. "Seriously, it wasn't a date or a real dinner. We just accidentally met at a bar."

Marg exhaled in exasperation. "Adie, you are unbelievable!"

"Well, believe this Marg—you are a suspect. In fact, so far, the prime suspect."

Marg lowered her eyes, rubbing her temples. "But wasn't Uma drowned?"

"Ilya says they are waiting for the autopsy results but my guess is murder."

"I see." Marg paused. "Couldn't it have been an accident?"

I rolled my eyes. "Yeah, she was walking the dog and she slipped in the river."

"Well, that's possible isn't it?"

"Did she have a dog?"

Marg furrowed her brow. "She wasn't an animal lover."

Or a people person either, I thought, glancing at the scabs on my arm.

Marg pointed a finger at me. "You don't think I did anything, do you?"

I patted Marg's hand. "No, but what I think doesn't count. But I'll help you, if I can."

"Thanks. Looks like I'll be needing it," Marg said dryly.

I wiped my mouth with the paper napkin. "So what was Reich doing there?"

"Tim came over to bring me my travel package."

"And he was still there, when you left?"

"He was outside fixing my fence."

"So, between you leaving, and me arriving, someone murdered Reich."

Marg clenched her fist, scrunching her napkin. "This is so upsetting, but Adie, we can't find out anything here in Cozumel."

"Maybe we can. A reporter I met said he'll contact me here."

"He'll phone you?"

"E-mail. There are internet services everywhere. I was thinking of going to the one across the street."

"If you hear anything," Marg hesitated, "you will let me know, won't you, Adie?"

I nodded. I hoped Slick would come through for me.

After paying the bill, we hopped into the Jeep for an exciting Cozumel driving experience. Hefty Spanish women in skin-tight spandex outfits carrying groceries, skinny boys on bicycles zigzagging all over the road, and other inept tourist drivers, not to mention one-way streets, made it the route from hell. It was like an obstacle course in *Survivor*. The reward challenge was to reach your destination alive. It was a shocker, but we made it, our flag held high.

I found a parking space with a yellow line on the curb. Good lines, I guessed, thinking the red ones meant trouble. We were half a block away from the Royal Investment office. It was a classic Spanish-style white stucco building with a red tile roof, two doors down from the Maple Leaf Martial Arts Academy. Marg said she'd meet me after her appointment with Alvarez.

The *dojo* reception area had a curved counter and a few vinyl bar stools. A couple of big guys carrying gym bags passed me as I came in. The slim tanned man behind the counter eyed me inquisitively. He could have been Mexican but something about his face didn't add up—too angular.

"*Hola*," he said smiling.

"Hey. This is an English-speaking *dojo*, isn't it?"

"Sure is," he said, stretching out his hand. "Steve Vidjik, Torona."

Torontonians always say Torona just as Philadelphians say Philly. Other people wonder where the letters come from.

"Adie Sturm, Kitchener."

"Oh yeah," he said thoughtfully. "I went to a shiai at the

Vanier School of Martial Arts."

"No kidding! That's my *dojo*."

"*Kee-iii!*" Loud, enthusiastic screams rang out from the *dojo*. A *kiai* is a meeting of the spirits, an intense scream that is essential for self-defense. The louder the better. While I paid a fee for practicing, a few karate people left the training hall. An older, massive man strode out after them. Joe Brick was Steve's partner. I shook hands, exchanged pleasantries and headed to the change room.

A lone female was pulling up a mini dress. This brunette had abs to die for.

"Hi," I said, thinking I should cut out the chocolate. "Working out?"

"Um-mm. You a member?"

"Yeah. I'm Sandy Weiss. Steve's *my* boyfriend."

Was she trying to make a point? "Adie Sturm." I opened my bag and pulled out my uniform. "Where're you from?"

Sandy pushed her uniform into her gym bag and zipped it up. "Detroit. I met Steve at a *Shiai* and came down here to live with him."

I slipped my uniform on and tied the belt. "How do you like it here?"

"Hot, hot, hot, but who's complaining?" Sandy picked up her gym bag. "Nice to meet ya!" she called out over her shoulder. At the desk, she treated Steve to a passionate liplock for my benefit. Kind of like finders keepers or possession was nine tenths of the law. Steve was interesting but he didn't have that sheer animal magnetism that Wolf had. Sandy pulled away. Steve's eyes glazed over. Joe handed Steve a cold water bottle. I wasn't sure if it was for Steve to drink or to pour over himself.

The empty training hall was off to the right. I bowed before entering the large room covered with blue mats. I could hear Spanish rock from the cantina across the street. The smells of roast chicken from a rotisserie barbeque down below wafted up. A moist hot breeze flowed in from the open door. No fan or air conditioning here. Karate people believe in working out in the heat. They claim it releases the proper energy.

From the window, I could see to the front door of the Royal Investment building. No sign of Marg. She must have gotten in to see Alvarez. I would have at least half an hour to practice my *katas*. I felt at peace in the training room.

Remembering the importance of warm ups, I ran around the room and did stretches before I started practicing my nunchaku form. The idea of nunchakus is to grip the two handles together to strike the opponent with the butt ends or they can be pulled out so the chain in the middle loops around the opponent's neck and brings him in close for a strike.

I twirled them about in a sequence. I was impressively fast but sloppy, clipping my cheekbone and my hairline in one quick twist of the wrist. When I wiped my forehead, a dribble of blood appeared on the back of my hand, but I continued until my arms ached. I stopped to look out the window. Marg was coming out of the Royal Investments building into an empty street. I watched her ambling along, pausing at a flowering hibiscus tree. From the alley, a swarthy man in a red t-shirt and baggy rapper pants, stepped out and grabbed her by the arm. Marg pulled away but he hung on.

Nunchakus in hand, I ran out to the lobby. Steve and Joe stared as I rushed by yelling, "My friend's in trouble!" I flew down the stairs to the street. Rounding the corner, I saw them. "Leave her alone!"

With Marg hoisted over his shoulder, Apeman started down the alley. With all my strength, I ran up and jump-kicked out to the side of his knee. He grunted, dropping Marg abruptly in the dirt. His small eyes squinted meanly as he came at me. I screamed my loudest *kiai*, thrust out the nunchakus, and struck his ribs. He winced but his fist flew out. I spread my nunchakus wide and countered his punch. Like the street fighter he was, he brought his foot up and kicked. I blocked with my leg. The impact pushed me backwards. I fell hard, hitting the dirt in a not so perfect break-fall. Curled up into a tight ball, I covered my head with my hands.

Just as I thought game over, a terrific *kiai* resounded. Steve and Joe, formidable in their karate whites, warrior fierce at the alley entrance started towards us at a run. Apeman's face paled. He sprung away and hightailed it down the laneway. Steve and Joe sprinted up. Joe helped Marg to her feet. "You okay?"

Marg broke into a flood of tears. Joe patted her back awkwardly. "It's okay. He's gone," he said gruffly. Marg hung tightly to him.

Steve helped me up. "Anything broken, Adie?"

I shook my head, rubbing my leg. "No, but he sure whacked my shin."

Marg's dress was filthy, her neck was red and her elbows and knees were scraped raw. I came over and put my arm around Marg, giving her a quick hug.

She whispered, "I was so scared, Adie."

"Me too." Stained with dirt and who knows what from the alleyway garbage, my uniform was a mess.

Released of his responsibilities, Joe's eyes shot down the alley and back at Steve. "Let's get 'em." Together they rushed down the passageway. At the end of the lane they stopped. Standing there for a moment, they looked around, before jogging back to us.

Frustration was written all over their faces. Sweat rolled off Joe's brow. "Sorry girls. No sign of the dude."

"You did great, Adie," Steve praised, as we walked back to the street.

"Thanks, but if wasn't for you guys…"

Marg nodded in agreement.

"Too bad," Steve said, clenching his jaw. "It would have been fun."

Joe grinned. "Yea-ah."

I rolled my eyes. Male hormones. "You think?"

Steve winked. "Get your stuff. We'll wait here with your homegirl."

After I got my bag, I hurried to the Jeep. "Thanks, guys. Again, we really appreciate it." As they headed to the dojo, I started the engine. Marg sat head bowed, hair covering her face. "You okay?"

"No." Her voice trembling, she whispered, "he was so…"

I patted her arm. "It's hard to believe. Cozumel is a safe place."

"I can't believe this happened to me."

"It happens. I was attacked a few years ago."

"Attacked? Here?" Marg stared. "Adie, we're best friends and you never told me?"

"Not here. In Europe. That's why I decided to take karate, so if it ever happened again I'd have a fighting chance." I glanced at

Marg. "What do you think he was after?"

She shuddered. "I don't know. He didn't take my purse."

"Did he say anything?'

Marg shook her head. "No, he just muttered under his breath," she continued, reverting to her counselor mode, something she found safe. "Drunk, possibly low functioning as well." Marg folded her arms into her body. "I deal with assault on a regular basis, Adie, but this is real." She took a deep breath and looked at me. "But don't worry. I won't let this spoil anything. I *need* this vacation." She bent her head down. "You know, Adie, I hate my life." A tear squeezed out of her eye. She wiped it away with the back of her hand.

I patted her shoulder. "Let it go, Marg. Rest. Take a shower. Do you still want to go out tonight?"

She took a deep breath and nodded. "I've got to forget about this. I'm sure my mood will improve with dinner and a cute guy. Did you find one for me, by the way?"

Marg was bouncing back just fine. A divorce and a troubled teen toughens you. "Wolf knows a guy."

"Hope he meets with my requirements."

I returned her smile. "Well if he doesn't, at least you'll have a free meal and get out dancing."

"Anything can happen in a horse race."

Horses were Marg's thing. She went riding as a child and loved horses, hence most of her adages are horse-oriented. Me, I like animals too, but I prefer cats. I relate to how they do their own thing and their obsession with sleep.

Driving through the labyrinth of Cozumel's *avenidas* and *calles*, I found my way back to the Hotel Maria where I dropped Marg off. After I parked the Jeep behind the Don Juan, I crossed over the street and entered the Internet Café. It wasn't busy. I got a computer immediately and logged on. There were two messages. The first was from kharkoveclues@yahoo.

Hi, Adie. Having a good time? Love to have a business trip like yours. We're in the process of questioning all the usual suspects. Cause of death looks like a blow to the back of the head. Ilya

I scrolled down and clicked on berniescharf@hotmail.

Hey Adie. IMO Reich and Farber were involved in something

shady. What does Beige know? Wish I were there to rub that suntan lotion all over you. Bernie

Slick was a pervert but his opinion was right on. What kind of shady deal had led to murder?

The Chedraui Market was in the same plaza as the Internet Cafe. In stressful times, my urge to shop becomes all-consuming. Shoe shopping makes me feel good and believe it or not helps me problem solve. I visualized a pair of open-toed fiery-red sandals but searching the rack spotted a pair of pink wedges. I tried them on. They fit. On the bottom the price in pesos translated to ten dollars? My kind of deal. My mood improved. After all, I was in Mexico and had an evening to look forward to.

Manni waved to me as I passed the front desk. "If you need a guide tomorrow, I am free."

"Sure, Manni."

I headed up the stairs to my room and unlocked the door. I started stripping off as soon as I came in, dropping my clothes on the bed before I peered in the bathroom. I wasn't looking for perverts, only cockroaches. One thing I've learned is that roaches can be anywhere, when you least expect it. Just as I finished drying my hair, the phone rang.

"*Bueno?*" I said, practicing my Spanish.

"Hey, Adie. Don is coming tonight. How about your friend?"

"Marg's willing and able. But, Wolf, something happened today."

"Not a good something, I gather?"

"Tell you later."

"All right. See you at seven."

I punched in Marg's number. I would have to think carefully about a dress to wear. I had a hot man to look good for.

Marg answered on the first ring. "Hello?"

"We're on for tonight, Marg. You have a date."

"What should I wear?"

"Something that shows skin. It's dinner and dancing at Delores."

"Fancy?"

"Could be, but remember, no one dresses up much in Cozumel."

"Are you picking me up?"

"Wolf is driving—thank goodness. I don't think I want to drive at night unless I have to."

"That's what a man is for."

"That and other things."

Marg chuckled. "His name is Wolf, as in the big bad?"

"I wouldn't say he's bad," I said defensively, "of course, time will tell.

5

The insistent beat of a primal meringue pounded from the floor below. Even though the sun had set a couple of hours ago, a warm breeze caressed my skin. We sat around a table outside, on a balcony overlooking a small dance floor. Fragrance from the flowering trees wafted up from below. In the distance, sparkling silver glints flickered on the ocean, reflecting the lights from the beach bar.

Don was a friendly teddy bear type, causally attired in a short-sleeved orange shirt and tan shorts, curly brown hair framing his round face. He enthused, "You ladies sure look fine tonight."

He wasn't quite what I had expected, but then who could predict what a friend of Wolf's would be like. "Thanks, Don. After what happened today, a compliment is just what we both needed."

"Ah-hh, a woman with a story." Don winked at Wolf. "You didn't tell me she's a lady of mystery, besides being gorgeous."

Wolf's dark blue eyes seemed almost black in the evening light. "Twelve years ago she was an alluring girl, but now, she's fascinating as well as beautiful." Slouched in the rattan chair, his legs stretched out, Wolf looked sleek in his dark shirt and jeans, his blond hair windswept.

I don't mind attention, but this was embarrassing. *"Salud!"* I toasted. Marg and I clicked our strawberry daiquiris with the guys' beer as the waiter brought over our entrées.

Wolf added, *"A muchos amores."*

Not to be outdone, Don shouted enthusiastically, *"A muchos dolares!"*

They were good ideas—love and money. I could do with both, and maybe some luck thrown in. As we ate, I told them what happened.

"Your arm looks bad, Marg," Wolf commented, glancing at the scratches and bruises on her arm. "Did you get hurt, too, Adie?"

"A few scrapes and a bruise on my shin."

Wolf studied my lightly tanned legs in the high-heeled black sandals.

"You said you had a meeting," I said, touching Wolf's hand. "Did it go well?"

"We were asked to invest five hundred thousand into a project on the north end of the island."

Don leaned back in his chair. "Construction is about to start."

"Sounds interesting. What do you think? " I glanced at Wolf.

"I'm not so sure." He steepled his fingertips. "I'll have to find out more."

"I want to see the north end. I've read its all jungle and uninhabited. It would be cool to get away from the touristy part of Cozumel. I could check these condos for you too."

Marg set her glass on the table. "How would you get there?"

"There're dune buggies and ATVs for rent. Saw it on the internet before I came here."

"Why don't we go together tomorrow? You don't mind if I go too, do you?" She tossed her hair back, defiantly. "At least they can't find me there."

Wolf turned to Marg. "Wait a minute. This man that attacked you, Marg, are you saying this wasn't a mugging? It was deliberate?"

"Uh-huh." Marg nodded.

"Marg thinks Alvarez, the owner of Royal Investments, is behind the attack."

"Alvarez?" Wolf frowned. "We met with him—that condo project on the north end of the island."

I grabbed Marg's arm. "Isn't that a weird coincidence? Alvarez. He didn't give you that check, either. What was his excuse?"

Don leaned forward. "What's this about a check?"

"I was to collect a cashier's check for my patient." Marg pushed a strand of her shoulder length hair behind her ear. "Alvarez told Tim he'd have it ready, but when I went to his office, he said I was misinformed. Said it would be best if I went home and let him deal with the details of the investment himself. Told me it was complicated. Might take a while."

"Could be true," Don said, frowning. "Legal stuff takes time. Took me a month to round up lounge chairs for the beach bar because of all the red tape."

Wolf explained. "Don's the liaison man for a California

company. They want to buy up a string of hotels."

"Well, I don't believe it. Tim was right." Her eyes narrowed. "Alvarez's a liar and a swindler."

"What do you know about Alvarez?" Wolf asked Don.

"He's loaded, a multi-millionaire. Holdings everywhere." He shot an incredulous look at Marg. "You think Alvarez wants to get rid of you?"

Marg's cheeks flushed. "Your guess is as good as mine. This creep dragged me into the alley and roughed me up. Alvarez knew I had just left. I wouldn't be surprised if he sent someone after me. He probably thought if he scared me, I'd give up on getting the check and go home."

I don't know," Don said doubtfully. "He's an important man around here. His family is one of the elite Spanish families in Mexico. I doubt if he'd bother about a minor matter like this."

"Minor?" I argued. "We're talking about millions here. That's hardly a tiny amount. Besides, when you've got money, you can afford to hire help and get rid of people."

"To top that off," Marg said, "I got a call from a detective in Kitchener."

"Ilya Kharkov?" I asked.

Marg fiddled with her swizzle stick. "He said he's spoken to you. Told me to come to the police station when I get back." The plastic stick cracked in two. "I was counseling Tim Reich," she explained to the guys, "treating him for paranoia, but now, I'm not so sure my diagnosis was correct. Tim begged me to do this for him. Bought me a travel package for Cozumel and paid me to get his cashier's check. I feel obligated to see this thing through, even though he's been murdered."

Don stiffened. "Murdered?"

"The police think I had something to do with it." Marg grit her teeth. "I think, Alvarez is in the thick of it."

"There were two murders in Kitchener. Reich and his ex." I waved my fork for emphasis. "Both murders took place within two days, and the police think they're connected. And now there's a mugger, conveniently close to Alvarez's office."

"Ladies, ladies," Don held his hand up, "pure speculation here. I don't see how these murders could have anything to do with what happened here today. By the way, Marg, have you got in touch with the police about the mugger?"

"I reported it by phone," Marg said tightly, "but personally, I'm not so sure they're doing anything. They told me to fill in a report tomorrow."

Mañana. We all knew what that meant. Caribbean vacation spots are different from the US or Canada. Cozumel's pace was slow. Maybe they'd get to it by the time Marg was ready to leave Cozumel—maybe not.

Don stroked his moustache reflectively. "What do you think of the place otherwise?"

I gestured at the palms swaying gently in the breeze. "Love it. You have no idea how awful our winters are."

Don nodded in agreement. "San Francisco has way too much rain for me. You know," he paused reflectively, "I wonder if Royal's building project in the north end of the island is on the up and up. I might want to invest in it."

"Are there tours going there, Adie?" Marg asked, her eyes sparkling.

"A few times a week."

Wolf took up my hand. "I'd go with you but I have a meeting tomorrow."

"Don't worry, we'll be with a group."

Don summoned the waiter for another round. "Ladies, drink up! Look we're here for a good time, not a long time." He stood with his arms gyrating in large circular motions, moving his hips enthusiastically with the beat. "Let's dance!"

I laughed. You had to love the guy. He was such a party animal. Then again, it wasn't him that got into it with Apeman. The bruise on my shin would be black tomorrow.

They were playing a zesty salsa and Wolf was no amateur dancer. A bit of pressure from his fingers led me into a spin. Salsa's a sexy dance full of hip motion and promising innuendos. His masculine body swaying suggestively was a definite turn-on.

"Why don't you wait a couple of days, then I could go with you."

I stole a look over my shoulder. "We'll be okay, Wolf. Tour guides have to do this sort of thing." I swivel-stepped towards him. "Besides, I could check out that condo development for you."

The salsa booted up into a wild merengue—an equal

opportunity dance that lets the woman take up the lead, whenever she wants. A touch of insanity in a Latin tempo. My inhibitions flew away as I swung Wolf around, grabbed his waist, and pressed tightly to his body. I could tell he liked the attention by the way he returned the pressure.

Strobe lights flashed above us, and we twisted around, our backs together, our arms spread wide. He had no problem with my innovative style. Seductively, I slid against him. He maintained contact—curving his body to me. I was hot-wired. The warmth from his shirt radiated out to my skin. Around us, the club crowd was going crazy with the music, trying outrageous moves all the way to the floor, until the merengue crashed to a sudden finish.

The band shifted into a rumba—the dance of love. Wolf held me close. I shut my eyes taking in his scent of soap and ocean breeze.

"You sexy woman," he whispered in my ear, "you don't know what you're doing to me."

"Mm-mm," I murmured. I felt like a cat with a bowl of cream.

Wolf's husky voice cut into my thoughts. "Have you ever driven an ATV?"

"I'll learn."

"I'm sure," his said, softly into my ear, "you will." I felt his lips kiss my neck, letting myself drift into the music and the magic of the man.

***

It was after two when Wolf parked the car at the Hotel Maria. We left Marg and made our way to the Don Juan. Dark shadows on the uneven sidewalk made the walk a challenge. My heel caught on a crack and I leaned into Wolf to right myself. One wrong move and I'd end up falling flat on my face. That would not be cool. Smoking hot men don't go for klutzes. When I tripped again, Wolf said, "I could carry you."

Clumsy women appeal to big strong men? I thought about his powerful arms lifting me. The heat of his body. I'd like that. Would he actually do it or was he just teasing?

Outside the Don Juan, Wolf put his arms around me. It had been months since I'd been out with a man, and this wasn't just any man. Slowly kissing me, the tip of his tongue explored the inside of my mouth, sending a quiver down my body. His lips broke away way too soon.

"You'll call me when you get back?"

I nodded, not trusting myself to speak. His kiss was sweeter than honey. Silky smooth, creamy rich—like chocolate. I stood there for a minute, my eyes following him, a black clad figure disappearing into the misty warm night.

Manni was behind the front desk when I walked in. The rest of the room was deserted, except for a couple chatting quietly in the corner.

He looked up and smiled. "Can I help you, *señorita* Sturm?"

"ATV tours."

Manni opened a pamphlet and pushed it in front of me. "They go three times a week."

Reading the information, I frowned. "But not tomorrow."

"No problem, Señorita Sturm. I am off tomorrow and I could be your guide."

"What about the ATVs?"

Manni shrugged his shoulders. "It can be arranged. I know these guys—amigos, you know?"

"How much?"

A hundred dollars." Seeing my expression he said, "Okay, eighty. I got to pay them something too."

"My friend is coming. Make me a better deal. There's two of us."

Manni grimaced. "Seventy each and I bring lunch."

I shook his hand. "Deal."

He grinned. "You will have no regrets, Señorita Sturm."

She was too perky for her own good. Hair swaying, Marg flounced into the lobby where I sat slumped on the couch. It was six something—too early for any normal person to function.

I was ready with snorkeling equipment and other necessities. True to the karate motto "be prepared", I was in body, if not in mind.

"Hi Adie!"

I blinked languidly watching Marg plop herself down beside me. "Taking your car?" She asked in a cheery voice.

"Mm-mm." I yawned, thinking hyperactivity must be a side effect of her drugs.

"I'm so excited, Adie. I've never done anything like this before."

I, on the other hand, was having major problems waking up. I motioned to Manni to come over. "Meet Manni, our guide."

She smiled serenely and extended her hand. "Marg."

Manni took up Marg's hand and made the European kiss-the-wrist gesture leaving Marg entranced.

"So pleased to meet you, Señorita."

Manni was barely an inch or two taller than Marg so when their eyes met, their eyes locked. He was slim and trim—a Mexican Frodo. Although a bit shrunken, Manni was cute as a currant and definitely not dried up. He was ready to be the spark plug to start Marg's malfunctioning motor, if she'd let him.

I waved a hand for attention. "Say, do you two mind if we stop for coffee and something to eat?"

They both nodded automatically, no longer aware of my presence. I figured they didn't care where we went since they were obviously pumped without food or coffee. I drove over to Rudolpho's Bakery, a few blocks from the center of town and parked. They were busy. We sat down at a white patio table overlooking the street. People were scooting in, leaving quickly with small brown bags. Rudolpho's was Cozumel's version of Starbucks.

Manni and Marg struck up a conversation meant for two and I focused on the activity in front of me. Motorcycles and bikes seemed to be the most popular form of transportation as well as the old style VW Beetles, extinct everywhere else in the world. I nibbled on a chocolate-filled roll as a vintage black Beetle pulled up to the corner and parked. No one got out.

The chocolate was rich in the light puff pastry. I sighed, thinking I hadn't had chocolate for two days. Endorphins started bouncing up and down in my system—the pleasure principle released.

Chocolate makes me happy. I began to think of last night. Such a romantic evening. Wolf's kisses were so arousing and so was he, his shirt silky smooth to the touch, his body sizzling. The dancing had been so sensual. He had made me want him.

"Adie?" Marg said. "Are you okay? You look flushed."

I glanced at her. "Um-hm."

"Manni thinks we should go," Marg added, taking a last sip of her coffee.

I swiveled around. Manni had disappeared into the bakery. There was plenty of time to eat. I had a last bite, chewing slowly. At the edge of my plate, I noticed a chunk of chocolate. I pushed my index finger into the soft mound and brought it up to my lips.

"Adie?"

One last chocolate fix. I closed my eyes savoring the bittersweet taste. Just like my memories of Wolf. The French River at his parent's cottage. That hot sultry day on that isolated lake— our bodies wet, his eyes so blue. I swallowed the chocolate.

"Adie?" Marg tapped my arm. "Do you want to go now?"

I nodded.

Marg called out to Manni and we left together. When we got to the Jeep, Manni stopped and stooped down to peer at my tires. "Señorita, we have a problem."

"Call me Adie. What's wrong?"

"Your tires are low. Let's stop at the Pemax station. What about gas?"

I shrugged in reply, unlocking the Jeep for Manni and Marg to get in the back. I sat down. The needle on the gas tank was close to empty. At this rate we'd get there by late afternoon. Manni was right, but what was it with guys anyway? Were they all born with this annoying mechanical gene that activated near a vehicle?

The streets were filling up and the shops were all open as we headed out of town on the Avenida Benito Juarez. The sun was a bright yellow glow in the sky. To get the breeze circulating, we left the plastic windows unzipped. Manni pointed out places of interest to Marg, while I took note of restaurants I should try.

Two cars trailed behind—a yellow Jeep and a black Beetle. The open-topped Jeep was crowded, holding too many teens with some of the girls sitting on the boys' laps. At a shack that advertised cervesa, the Jeep turned off and parked. The Beetle continued on the cross-island highway heading east, just as we did. Roadside stands sold cheap colorful blankets. Flat fields along the way blended together in a brown blur.

I slowed down as I sighted another road meeting the main highway. Manni told us that the road went along the east coast, and would continue around the south point of the island eventually becoming the west coast highway. We were at the farthest accessible point. From here on, tours with dune buggies or ATVs were the only methods of transportation. A rundown shack stood alongside a dirt parking area surrounded by a few scruffy palms and spiky underbrush. A large garishly painted green sign announced the location of ATV tours. Several ATVs were parked in a row near the far side of the lot. I parked near the shack.

Across the street, the dusty black Beetle parked alongside the beach. A gaunt man got out. He stood smoking a cigarette, looking at the ocean.

Manni jumped out of the Jeep and made his way to the shack. Marg and I leaned against the vehicle, and waited.

Raucous laughter. A chunky square-faced man with black hair and a dark complexioned teen came out of the shack. The older man kept shaking his head as he approached us and I was beginning to think our plan was a dud.

"You see, Señorita, we do not let the ATVs out without no tour group."

Wasn't this guy one of Manni's amigos? What was that saying about honey attracting flies? I pulled out a fifty from my purse, and waved it around. "Are you a Mexican or a Mexican't?"

He hesitated a second before he snatched up the money, pushed it furtively into his pants' pocket, and handed me the keys to the ATVs.

"Enjoy your trip, Señorita."

I nodded. *"Gracias."*

The chunky guy walked over to the storage shed to fuss with one of the ATVs, leaving the gum-chewing teen to stare at us. Manni came out with disappointment written all over his face. When I casually opened my hand to reveal the necessary keys, his eyebrows arched in surprise.

"You have the magic touch, Adie."

I glanced at the tractor-like vehicles. "Know how to run these suckers?"

"No problem." After ten seconds of Manni's technical talk, I zoned out. When he saw my expression, he gritted his teeth. "Just keep it in second."

Expertly, Manni started his up. Behind him, holding on to his waist, Marg sat stiffly, a look of consternation on her face. A few tries later, I cranked mine up and drove straight into the nearest bush.

After I'd picked out the leaves and branches stuck in my helmet and hair, I steered the ATV to the right, backed it up and tried going forward. Marg smiled encouragingly. I repeated the process several times. Finally it worked. I was out.

I wiped the sweat off my brow with my forearm. An annoying mosquito buzzed around and landed on my cheek. I swiped at it, but it got away, only to come back in for a second attack. I brushed the air ineffectually, shifted into second gear and wondered if it could get any worse. It did.

The sun high overhead, was uncomfortably hot and the dust in the wake of Manni's ATV flew into my eyes. Narrow and fairly flat, the road became more manageable as we drove. Just as I began feeling pleased with myself, the dirt path changed into hills. Jagged coral boulders. Sharp thorny bushes bordered the path. I was sure it would only be a matter of time before I would get thrown off into the shrubs with my ATV going on without me. I gripped the handlebars tightly, my knuckles turning white with the pressure. I tried taking the hill directly, inching over the coral. The ATV was incredibly powerful, like a miniature army tank, crawling over the rocks.

The jungle plants surrounding the passageway blocked the

breeze. I could feel sweat trickle down my neck. The helmet felt unbearably hot. I shuddered. What would my hair look like if I ever got a chance to take it off? I had to rethink why I was doing this. Yes, I was a travel guide. But did I really need to know about the north end of the island? Other guides would have stuck to investigating sensational sandy beaches. And then there were the deluxe hotels, like the exclusive El Presidente. Wolf was probably relaxing on the shady veranda overlooking the ocean, having a leisurely brunch.

When Manni signaled me to pull over, I was glad I had chance to rest my numb fingers, clenched into claws. Swooping hawks would have nothing on me.

A caravan of dune buggies was heading up the road behind us. I was hoping their drivers were experienced, as even a slight nudge would send me straight into the shrubs. This was not the case.

Their idiot male leader came first taking up the width of the narrow road. There was a great big hump of rock in the center and the dune buggy had its wheels on either side struggling slowly along. He didn't care where he was going because his attention was completely riveted on the cute babe in the tight white spandex-top sitting next to him. Mouth open—drool escaping his lips.

Two more vehicles followed, red dust flying into our eyes as they passed. One of the girls in the back waved to us, laughing loudly.

Could be she thought we looked dirty sweaty and loser-like. Glancing at Marg and Manni with a layer of dirt smeared unevenly over their faces and then tasting the dust on my own lips, I had to agree. But the advantage of these ATVs was, we would survive, spines intact. They'd be lucky to walk as upright as their monkey ancestors after a few days.

A short distance later we stopped. I stepped down, muscles cramped and stiff. Manni told us to follow him. We took a path through the trees to a stone shrine with an archway large enough for a small person to stand in.

"Women have come here for hundreds of years to bring gifts to the goddess Ixchel and to wish for babies." Manni's voice was hushed over the whispering breeze.

Marg snatched up her camera. "Pose, Adie."

I stood under the arch and closed my eyes, communing with

the goddess. I felt her presence and I begged her to hold off on the baby, since I needed to decide on a man first. In my head I came up with a tall blond sea god, who had an amazing resemblance to Wolf. The wind ruffled my matted hair, rearranging the clump on my head into a less tangled state. Was Ixchel sending me a message?

Photos taken, Marg and I trudged over to the sandy white beach. The azure ocean sparkled brightly with the noon sun as the waves crashed into the shore. In the distance, I could see a small snorkeling boat.

Marg whispered to me, eying Manni at his ATV. "He's hot to trot."

I played dumb. "Who?"

"Manni, of course. Did you see the looks he gave me?"

"Now that you mention it, I was surprised he didn't want to stand in Ixchel's arbor and receive her blessings on your behalf."

Marg giggled. "He's cute."

"I gather Don didn't turn your crank?"

"He's a good dancer."

"That could be an indication of his other skills."

"A dark horse in the running, so far."

"Manni's yours, if you want him, Marg," I said, watching the little guy return with a small cooler laden with sandwiches and water bottles.

He apologized. "Sorry, no beer. I did not think you would like to drive and drink."

"You thought right," I commented dryly. "I'm a total screwup without any beer."

Manni nodded understandingly and passed me a sandwich. Marg spread out a blanket and we made ourselves comfortable. It was a beautiful sandy beach with the water an aquamarine blue. I finished the sandwich and had a sip of water.

The surf crashed loudly into the shore setting off a spray of white as it hit the coral that jutted out on the point. The steady rhythm of the waves made me sleepy. I lay down and closed my eyes.

A while later I felt someone shaking my shoulder. "Adie, we can go to the next beach and you ladies can try the snorkeling. The waters are more calm there." Manni gestured to Marg gathering broken coral from the shore. Her eyes shot up and she smiled.

Swimming would be heaven after another ride on that ATV. "Sounds good to me," I said to Manni, feeling the perspiration under my armpits. It was pleasant here with the moist breeze blowing in. I dreaded putting the helmet back on.

Packed up, we carried our bags over and fastened them on the ATVs before we climbed back on. I was sore from the jolting motion and my aching arms were reluctant to take up the driving again. I envied Marg. She had Manni. I glanced over. I couldn't believe it! She was fluttering her eyelashes and whispering into his ear. I was floored. Could be she was on to something, though. I frowned, thinking if I had taken Wolf up on his offer and waited, I would be holding on to his waist, my chest pressed close to his back, breathing in the ocean scent of his body.

Back on the dusty rocky road, I concentrated once again on steering. This time, the drive was shorter. At our stop, I couldn't believe how abandoned the beach was. The only sign of human presence was two kayaks tied to a mooring. The water shimmered silver as the waves rolled over the dark patch of reef in the bay. But large gray clouds were rapidly moving in from the north. We'd have to hurry. It wouldn't be long before it clouded over.

This had to be the place. Wolf had told me the condo site was at the snorkeling bay. I peered up. There was a sign at the top of the hill but I couldn't quite make out the lettering. I decided I'd climb up. At the summit, I knew I'd hit pay dirt. It read, *Royal Investment Condominiums*. But as I scanned the area, I could see no evidence of construction. I watched the turquoise waters wash onto a powdery white beach. The concept of building condos here was a realistic possibility. Alvarez could be a genius thinking of this. I could imagine a condo here, with access limited to the rich and famous. Yes, Brad Pitt would love this place.

My attention turned to the beach as Manni started shouting incoherently at me, his words lost in the rush of the ocean. He had dragged the kayaks into the water, strong little hobbit that he was. Both arms waving, he gestured for me to come down. Marg was sitting placidly in the tandem kayak, waiting for her slave to paddle her to the reef. I was to paddle the other one. I wouldn't have minded, but I was running on empty and I wasn't sure how much more abuse my shoulders could take.

It wasn't that bad—the kayak surprisingly quick. In a few minutes we were just south of the reef about two hundred meters off shore. Marg and I got on our gear and eased into the warm water, while Manni stayed with the kayaks holding the ropes.

Brightly striped fish surrounded me, their large yellow eyes staring expectantly. At first I was puzzled but then I clued in to what they wanted. They'd have to be disappointed. I didn't dare take the chance of feeding. A moray eel might decide that my arm might make a tastier lunch than some dried up breakfast leftovers.

The water was pleasantly refreshing. I began to feel sorry for Manni up in the kayak. It felt so good that I didn't regret the uncomfortable ride through the dust anymore, nor the swarms of mosquitoes, not to mention the scratches from those offensive bushes. Marg was a few meters ahead of me. She motioned for me to surface. I popped my head up.

Marg was ecstatic. "This is the most fantastic snorkeling I've ever done, Adie. You wouldn't believe the fish I saw. They're enormous!"

"Where?"

"Further over. Follow me." She stuck her mouthpiece in and dipped her head in the water.

Close to the reef, I saw what had her so excited—gigantic green parrotfish. They puckered their lips on the coral and bopped away, only to return again. Almost like kissing, I thought. But I wasn't the only one that didn't trust them or their kisses. In a mad rush, a school of white grunts shot by me.

I put my head up out of the water to see how far we were from the kayaks. Manni and the kayaks were heading in to shore. Marg swam up beside me to see what was going on. Small stones plopped into the water, striking the coral.

"Get out of there! Quick!" Manni shrieked at the top of his lungs. "Snorkel to shore!"

In the distance, just beyond the reef, I could see a small boat. A man was pointing a rifle in our direction. Gunshot pelted the water, just meters away. Frantically, we kicked our fins, propelling ourselves forward. I glanced behind me. The scuba boat was edging closer, but the reef was a deterrent. If they got too close they could damage the hull. Bullets rippled the water behind us. Rambo was badly in need of target practice. At last he clued in that we were out of range, and no matter how many times he swept the reefs with bullets, it was a lost cause.

Ahead of me, Marg hesitated. I motioned for her to go on and dunked my head down. The waves came in higher, and the current gained strength. I was terribly tired. I felt like I'd never make it back, but I kept on going. When Marg reached the shallow water, I was right behind her. Exhausted from the swim, our movements became erratic, as we attempted to tug off the fins and steady ourselves against the increasing pull of the current. Feet sinking in the sand, we made it in.

The sky, holding heavy black clouds, threatened us with a rumble, like the roar of a lion. Lightening flashed a jagged line in the sky. The wind picked up, the palms on the hill waved as if in warning.

In the distance, I sighted the snorkeling boat heading away from the reef, to the far side of the bay. They weren't done with us yet. "We've got to get to the ATVs! They're coming in."

Manni pulled Marg along to the ATV parked at the edge of the beach. I followed at a run. Ominous dark clouds hung low. Thunder boomed and crashed into the waves behind us. On the hill, lightening struck near the Royal Investment post, silhouetting the sign against a bright white flash.

A cloud of dust appeared on the access road, and two dune buggies drove in and parked. A Mexican guide with four chattering Japanese tourists, found a spot further down the beach, under the protection of some trees. They sat down with their cooler, looking apprehensively at the sky, wondering as we did, whether the storm would strike or pass us by.

I felt their eyes watching us as we hurried to the parked ATVs. Thunder crashed in the hills and sand blew in my face as I turned my key in the ignition. Raindrops fell lightly, sprinkling my arms and back. But by the looks of the black clouds pushing in from the water, I was sure this was just the beginning. Glancing back, I saw the guys from the boat had found their way to the beach, but without a vehicle they'd have to give up their chase.

The rain gushed as if someone had emptied a dam on top of us, soaking us through in seconds. The downpour was so dense it was difficult to see ahead more than a few feet. The hollows of the uneven rocky road filled up with deep puddles but the ATVs persevered and ploughed on like little miracle machines.

I swiveled around in my seat and scanned the road behind us. In the distance, I could see them bouncing along wildly in a dune buggy. Where'd that come from?

At the twist in the road we lost sight of them but pushed on. The rain washed sea salt into my eyes. I rubbed at them with one hand, steering with the other the rain beating down. I glanced over my shoulder. I saw them. One was holding a rifle.

Lightning backlit the shrubs ahead of us. The rocky road straightened out into a dirt path. We were getting closer to the end. I had to keep it together. Any mistake now could be my last.

The road formed a muddy river. Grimy water splashed up on my legs and shorts as I hit a deep rut, but the ATVs continued over mud, water, hills and rock—nothing would stop them. If anything went wrong it would be me, losing my focus and ending up in a bush, a perfect target.

A bullet hit a muddy puddle, splashing dirty water on my cheek. I turned back for an instant to see the shooter, leather hat pushed low on his forehead, standing up in the dune buggy, aiming his weapon. Rock splinters filled the air, stinging my face.

A round hit the metal of Manni's ATV, narrowly missing Marg's leg. Her face was white, slick with sweat and rain. Suddenly, I saw her expression change as she focused on something behind me.

I swiveled around. It was better than I had hoped, my silent prayers answered. They were stuck, their rear wheels deep in the mud. It was the break we needed.

I can't say it was smooth sailing from then on, but we finally made it to the last stretch of the road. As the rain eased off, the late afternoon sun emerged from the clouds. Manni gave me a thumbs up at the clearing. He jumped down, grabbed my keys and made off to the shack. Marg and I threw our snorkeling gear and the cooler into the back of the Jeep and waited with the engine running. Our whole trip seemed unreal, life going on as usual with another group of tourists, German this time, arriving to take the north road with their guide.

When Manni returned, I eased the Jeep into the highway. I picked up speed as we rounded the corner to the cross-island road. In the rear view mirror, I saw Manni putting his arm around Marg.

I dropped them off at the Hotel Maria and drove on to the Don Juan. I parked and sat there. I began to feel secure again, back at my temporary home, but I kept thinking—*who wanted us dead and why?*

Through the window of my hotel room I saw the crimson glow of the late afternoon sun. I took a deep breath and rubbed the knots in my neck before I phoned. Wolf picked up after the second ring.

"I'm back."

"I'll come over."

I hesitated. "Give me an hour. Something happened, Wolf."

"You, okay?"

"Tell you about it when you get here." I couldn't wait to shower off. Mud-stained shorts and bikini landed on the bathroom tiles. I was a mess. Dirt and salt crusted my skin. Sweat matted my hair. I planned to take my time—I needed it.

The warm water flowed soothingly over my aching muscles, renewing my energy. Mentally, I went over the events. They must have stolen the dune buggy from the Japanese tourists. And that guy in the black Beetle? He told them where to find us. With a towel wrapped around me, I opened the door. Something was not right.

Rancid sweat and stale cigarette smoke. Only a few minutes before I remembered seeing the blush of the sun streaked on a sheet of pale blue. The blinds were shut. I backed up into the bathroom, letting my eyes adjust to the dark. Then I saw it.

I eased my towel off, wrapping one end around my hand. As hard as I could, I flicked it. A glint of steel. The knife clattered as it hit the tiles.

"Fuck!" he growled. As he scrambled on the floor, I switched off the bathroom light. Then I came out strong—screaming a *kiai* before kicking at his head.

I scored but the game was far from over. In the dim light his eyes glimmered dangerously. A big hand circled my damp ankle and pulled me down. I landed in a front break fall, the impact all in my arms. He had me pinned—knees tight around my hips. An easy two hundred pounds against my one fifteen.

"Now I've gotcha, bitch—cleaned up and naked just for me."

He swung me around. Muscle memory kicked in. With the

heel of my hand, I struck up at his nose, making contact with bone and cartilage. He jerked back.

Twisting onto my stomach, I crawled out from under him. He came at me from behind, an arm tightening around my throat. I had to gain air space. With my hand over his, I pressed hard on the web of his hand to loosen his hold and twisted it away. The pressure was off. I could breathe.

"I'll fix you good." He fumbled with his zipper.

My rage brought on an adrenalin rush. Extending the fingers of my right hand, I jabbed them over my shoulder in the direction of his eyes. I scratched a smooth slippery surface.

With a gasp he wrenched one arm away, giving me an opening—an elbow into the chest. But he was brick solid. There was only one way out. As hard as I could, I bit. He pulled away and I was free.

With his groin wide open, I kicked. He fell back, knocking down the bedside table. From the floor I seized Ixchel and with her female power smashed his head. This was my break. I raced to the door. Like a drunken sailor, he staggered after me.

Footsteps pounded in the hall. A familiar voice shouted, "Adie!"

"Help!"

With a tremendous crash, the door jam splintered. Wolf stepped in the room. "Adie, are you okay?" Seeing the intruder, Wolf gripped his shirt. "What the hell are you doing here?"

The man flung off Wolf's hand. A chain whipped out. Wolf stood back. In the hall, people protested as the biker knocked them away, barging past.

"Security should be coming," Wolf turned to me. "You all right, Adie?" The light from the hallway backlit his form. "What happened. I heard the—" Wolf didn't finish. He stepped into the room, pushing the door shut behind him. I realized what he was seeing. Hastily, I picked up my towel, wrapping it around and tucking it in.

Wolf flicked on a light. "You alright?"

I nodded.

Blood dribbled down his cheek. "Who was he?"

I shook my head.

Noticing the knife lying on the floor, Wolf picked it up,

running his finger lightly over the blade, his expression intense. He frowned. "I'm sorry, babe. I should have gone after him." He pulled me close. "What happened?"

I had trouble speaking for a moment and when I did, my voice was shaky. "He was waiting for me. I saw his knife before I saw him. I whipped my towel on the knife and ran, but he caught my leg and took me down." Pausing, I gulped back my sobs. Wolf's arms tightened around me. "He started choking me. I scratched his eyes and I—"

Wolf turned to look at the broken table and the fragments of the Ixchel statue. "You used that?"

"Mm-mm."

Wolf tilted my chin up and I met his gaze. "His belt was undone—Adie, did he hurt you?"

"He wanted to rape me."

"You don't have to tell me..."

I felt the warmth and strength of him. I needed to talk. "He held me down. I was powerless. Thought it was over."

"You did good, Adie. That bastard eats steroids for breakfast."

I closed my eyes. "I'll have nightmares tonight."

"No, you won't." Wolf stroked my hair. "I'll be with you."

"I'm okay now." The heat of his body comforted me. "Really, he's gone. It's over."

Wolf clenched his jaw. "I should've taken him out."

"It doesn't matter, you're here now."

Seeing his intense expression, my reaction caught me off guard. Adrenaline caused my body to quiver or was it something else? I stepped away from him. "I'm getting dressed." Wolf watched as I opened my dresser drawer, dug up some clothes and carried them into the bathroom with me. As I closed the door I heard Wolf on the phone ordering room service.

The shower ran warm. The shower gel smoothed over every conceivable area of my body wiped away the memory of his hands. The warm water stopped the trembling in my body. I dressed, put on some makeup and willed myself an armor of confidence before I stepped into the room.

***

Sultry guitar rhythms. Through the open patio doors, *Santana* floated up from the bar below. The voices in the hallway had subsided. Wolf was sitting on my bed holding a beer. A half finished plate of corn tortilla chips and salsa sat on the coffee table."Drink," he said, handing me a goblet filled with a red mix.

The frosty daiquiri was ice cold on the roof of my mouth. As it reached my stomach, I felt it burn.

Wolf watched me before he spoke."Feeling any better?"

"A little." A numbing effect spread through my body.

He held out the chips. "Eat."

I dipped a chip into the red sauce.

Wolf's eyes scrutinized me. "The manager came by while you were in the shower wondering if you needed anything. He said you can call him. Maybe a doctor should check you out?"

"No, not right now. I'll see how I feel tomorrow. Did they catch him?"

"I don't know." Wolf put his arm around my shoulders and pulled me close. "The manager said they're looking. We'll know when the police get here."

"You'll stay, won't you?"

"Yeah," putting an arm around my shoulders, "I won't leave."

I needed to forget about the biker. I rubbed my forehead with my fingertips, making an effort to focus. "How was your day?" I laughed, thinking how stupid that sounded. "Must have been better than mine."

"That wouldn't be hard to beat."

"What about the meeting?"

"A waste of time." Wolf shot a glance at me. "You don't have to make conversation, Adie. I can be a good listener. It might help for you to talk about this."

His arm felt warm and comforting. "I know you are, Wolf. I appreciate it." I stared at the corner where the broken table pieces had been. They'd cleaned up the mess while I was in the shower and replaced the table. "I'm okay. It's tonight when I try to sleep…"

"Don't worry, Adie. I won't leave you."

I placed my hand over his. "You're a good friend."

His eyes met mine. "With potential for more?"

"Let's talk about your meeting."

Wolf grinned. "Okay, no pressure." He tipped back his beer.

"Don and I were thinking of investing in a beach bar with a friend of his. The owner agreed to have lunch with us."

"That's great."

"Not really."

"Why?"

"Don never showed."

"Oh?"

"The story is he ran into a damsel in distress—a beautiful woman with car trouble on the highway. He took her home and completely forgot about the whole thing."

"Didn't even phone?" I picked up another chip.

"Turned his cell off. The beach bar owner was so pissed he left. I've kissed that deal good-bye."

"There's nothing you can do about it anymore?"

"Maybe it wasn't meant to be."

"You believe in fate?"

"Yeah." Wolf stroked my cheek, gazing into my eyes as he placed his beer on the table.

I examined his face. The bruise on his cheek and the dried blood on his forehead, gave him a dangerously wicked appearance. I picked up a serviette and tentatively dabbed the scrape with the cloth. He watched me silently—eyes intense. The air was charged with electricity.

I dropped the cloth abruptly. His fingertips slid over my straps, pushing them slightly down while his hand slid over my shoulder. "Nice flower," he said softly, his eyes sweeping to the tiny aqua flower adorning the strap. "Same color as your eyes." Wolf pulled me close. I let out a sigh when I felt his lips caress my shoulder.

Worried that I'd upset my drink or worse yet, spill the icy stuff on his lap, I froze uncertainly. Seeing my dilemma, Wolf smiled, took the glass and set it on the table and then, sinking on the bed, brought me down with him. Our eyes met like in a dream. The kiss was hot. Fire flamed my body.

I pressed against him, wrapping my leg over his. Wolf's hand moved along my waist his fingertips stroking my skin under the fabric of my top. Sparks flew down the length of my body. My head fell back against the pillow. His lips brushed my throat. At the hollow of my neck his tongue licked lightly over my skin, triggering delicious pulsing between my thighs. I weaved my fingers through his silky hair, thrilling to touch his soft strands. His hand wandered to the base of my breast, encircling it momentarily before he worked his fingertips over the peak.

A loud rap on the door caught us off guard.

I shot a look at Wolf.

He frowned. "Police."

Getting up reluctantly I pulled on the knob.

"Adie, what the heck happened? This thing is broken." Marg stepped forward.

Manni peaked his head over her shoulder. "Hi, Adie."

I raised my hand to block them. "Listen guys, this isn't a good time."

Marg pushed past, followed by Manni. "We need to talk." She was dressed to the nines in a sequined tank top and black capris while Manni sported jeans and a floral shirt. I concluded they were on a date.

"Hey." Wolf waved, a beer in hand.

"Hi," Marg flushed, suddenly aware of how rude she was. "Adie, I'm sorry. I didn't realize—Wolf, my friend, Manni." She gestured to Wolf. "Manni, Wolf."

The men did a guy handshake.

"Beer?" Wolf handed one to Manni who nodded.

"Water for me, please." Perched on one of the wicker chairs, Marg asked, "Have you told Wolf?"

"No, not yet." I offered the chips to Marg and Manni who had taken the chair next to her.

"Adie, we've got to talk about this. This is important." She looked at Wolf. "On our trip a guy tried to kill us. Shot at us from a boat—"

"They were after you there and now here." Wolf took my hand. "Do think the biker was the shooter?"

Marg's eyes widened. "You mean that's why the door is broken?"

"He was waiting for me in my room." I glanced over to where the new table stood with an identical goddess. "I fought him off. Luckily, Wolf came."

"This is awful."

"Don't worry, Adie." Manni's eyes darted to the broken

statue. "The *policia* will catch him."

Wolf set his beer down. "Tell me about the trip."

By the time he heard most of the story, a knock sounded on the door. I trekked over and flung it open.

"*Buenas noches,* Señorita. Good evening." A slim man in a police uniform stood waiting. He surveyed the others sitting around the coffee table before he said, "I am Officer Hernandez of the Cozumel Policia. I have been questioning the owners of the hotel and they tell me that it was your room that was broken in to."

"That is correct, Officer."

Hernandez pulled a notebook and said, "The room is registered to Señorita Adie Sturm?"

"That's right. That's me." I motioned for him to come in. "These are my friends."

Hernandez frowned."They were here at the time?"

"No." I sat down. "I was alone."

"When I arrived the intruder was running out," Wolf added.

"And you are?" Hernandez asked.

"Wolf Du Lac."

"Can you describe this person, Señor?"

"I'd say three hundred pounds or more, with a reddish beard and a shaven head."

Hernandez looked at me. "Is this what you remember, Señorita Sturm?"

"He was large, Officer, but I didn't see him well. It was dark. The drapes were closed and the lights had been turned off."

Checking the door where it had been forced open, Hernandez took out a pad and scribbled down some information. "Were you robbed, Señorita?"

"No."

Holding his pen poised, Hernandez asked, "My pardon for speaking so directly but did he rape you?"

I hesitated. "He wanted to, but he was interrupted by Señor Du Lac."

"The man had a weapon?"

"Yes." I motioned over to the table where Wolf had left the knife. "That's it, over there."

Hernandez stepped over and picked up the knife. Pushing a button on the handle, the blade retracted. He dropped the switchblade into his pant pocket.

He turned to me. "How long will you be staying here, Señorita Sturm?"

"A week."

"We will pursue this matter further, have no fear, Señorita." Putting his pad and pen into his shirt pocket Hernandez added, "I have yet to interview some of the other guests who saw this man and our police force will be on the lookout for him."

"Thank you, Officer." I walked him to the door. "Could I contact you for an update?"

"Certainly, Señorita. Have a good evening." Abruptly, the police officer left, leaving me standing by the door and the others sitting in silence.

"Marg, did you see the men on the boat?" Wolf asked suddenly.

She shook her head. "Not really. At first we were in the water snorkeling when he started shooting, so I was more intent in getting away. Then when they followed us down the road, the rain was coming down hard. It was hard to see anything."

I nodded in agreement.

Wolf turned to Manni. "What do you remember about them?"

"One was big and the other—not so much."

"So this man tonight might be one of them?"

Manni shrugged.

Marg shook her head as Wolf offered a beer. "So we still know nothing."

I glanced at the broken door. "I want to know who's behind this and why."

"There is something you should all be aware of," Marg said slowly. "Boris has a problem—anger. He resents our separation." She slouched in the chair. "He's told me several times now he wishes I was dead. My lawyer thinks I should get a restraining order."

"Marg, you didn't mention this before." I was puzzled. "And I thought you said you were divorced."

"No, not yet." Marg looked at Manni. "We're in the process. Things are not going smoothly. Even though I helped him in his investment business with the bookkeeping work, he wants all of it for himself. And now he wants support payments as well."

Manni got up and stood behind Marg. He placed his hand on her shoulder and gently massaged her shoulder. Marg reached up and put her hand on top of his. "Boris has hidden away his financial assets. I know he must have millions by now." Marg paused significantly. "I believe he's quite capable of hiring a hit man to kill me. He hates me for leaving him and he doesn't want to split any of the money from his business."

"So you really believe Boris could pull this off?" I picked up my daiquiri and sat down beside Wolf.

Marg nodded.

"What makes you think he's capable of this?"

Marg looked away for a moment. "After he left the insurance firm, he was struggling. At one point he was watching the stock exchange. When he saw the value of one of the stocks drop he lost it—picked up a beer bottle and threw it at the TV screen."

"The man is a nutcase." I'd seen sides of Boris that were downright scary.

"There could be another scenario." Wolf gave my shoulder a squeeze. "Reich might have been involved in something illegal. Alvarez has a condo deal that's in the gray area."

"Maybe not. I saw it, Wolf. The condo project is a good bet. Alvarez could be honest."

"Alvarez is a shyster." Marg poked the air with a pointer finger. "We need to check his office records. The big question is how?"

Manni rubbed his nose thoughtfully. "I know. We can get Daniella to help."

"Who?" I said.

"She's my brother-in-law's second cousin."

"And she'll do what exactly?" Wolf picked up his beer and tipped it back.

Manni ignored us. He took out his cell and punched in a number. Hurriedly, he spoke in Spanish and then he turned. "No problem, she's coming right away."

I was getting frustrated. "So? How can she help us?"

"You'll see. She's very upset with him," Manni said. "She may want to get even."

Wolf's brow furrowed. "Why?"

"She'll be here soon." Manni shook his head. "I don't know

for sure if she will help but we are old friends."

Wolf's cell phone vibrated. He glanced down and then walked over to the window to take the call.

Manni started talking to Marg in quiet undertones. Not wanting to eavesdrop, I got up and went into the bathroom. I picked up a comb and methodically smoothed my hair, all the while thinking about the biker and how he would have killed me. A drawn pale face stared back at me in the mirror. I felt exhausted. I should pack it up and go home. I wanted to help Marg but whatever she was involved in, was becoming too serious. I was in over my head.

Someone tapped the bathroom door. "Adie?" Wolf said softly. "You all right?"

I swung open the bathroom door and left it ajar. "Come in."

Wolf's dark blue eyes searched my face. "You're upset."

I nodded. "I know I should help her, but Wolf…" I felt a tear wet my cheek.

Wolf held me to him. "It might be a good idea to talk to the doctor." He pulled out a card from his pocket and glanced at it. "A female."

Three sharp raps drew our attention. Wolf took my hand and we went back in.

Daniella was a walking piece of dynamite. Her skin tight black leather skirt was glued to her curved hips and her apple shaped breasts were almost falling out of her low cut silver halter, not to mention the fuck me high-heeled sandals which she clicked in on. She demanded attention as she paused dramatically leaning one arm up against the doorframe. Her long coal-black hair was pulled to one side in a silver clasp, to expose a bare shoulder. "*Hola,*" she said in a throaty voice.

Manni greeted her with a kiss and turned to us. "May I present Daniella?"

"I am Daniella Consuela Puntez de Fuego," she announced self-importantly.

Wolf pulled a chair over for her. "Wolf Du Lac." He extended his hand, which she shook. He gestured towards us, "My friends, Adie and Marg."

"*Buenas noches,*" she said, keeping her eyes on Wolf. Carefully, she crossed her legs. Her skirt hiked up to the top of her bare thighs.

"Did Manni fill you in?" I asked.

Daniella nodded.

Manni grinned widely. "Daniella and I are childhood friends. We go way back." He chuckled. "We were neighbors and played together." He sighed. "Give me a moment to explain to Daniella."

He started to speak rapidly in Spanish and as he went on Daniella nodded significantly. She asked a few questions some of them including Wolf's name. This continued for a few minutes while the rest of us waited impatiently. Every once and while the woman would lick her lips and twirl her sandal at Wolf, checking him out. This was followed by a quick *si*." She was a sly cat with a mouse in sight. I didn't trust her one iota.

Finally Manni said, "Daniella is Alvarez's personal assistant. She'll be leaving his employment this week and is already working for Paradise Properties."

Wolf asked, "Can you tell us anything about the condo development on the north end of the island?"

"No," Daniella said shortly. "Santiago has many dealings. He is secretive. I am not always privy to his business but I can tell you this, I am not so sure they are all ethical transactions."

"Is Alvarez hiding anything?" I asked.

"It is possible."

Wolf touched her hand. "Please tell us what you can."

She fluttered her lashes and leaned forward giving him an eyeful of cleavage.

"Daniella, my friends have been attacked several times now. I am concerned for their safety. I would appreciate any help you can give us."

Daniella frowned, shifting uncomfortably in her rattan chair. "Santiago has connections outside of this island as well as many right here, in San Miguel. He is very powerful."

"Mob?"

"Family."

"Your hesitation, is it because you are loyal to him? Are you friends?" Marg probed in her counselor mode. Seeing the color in Daniella's cheeks, she added, "Or is it more? You have feelings for Santiago Alvarez?"

Daniella uncrossed her shapely legs. "I have integrity,

Señorita. This is not about feelings! He's a liar! I would like to see him ruined," Daniella hissed. "He said he would marry me but his family said I was unsuitable."

I glanced over at Wolf. He had the same thought I did. Wolf glanced over his beer. "You will help us, then?"

Daniella's dark slanty eyes shot over to me and then to Manni and Marg. "Do all of you promise to keep silent about this?"

We nodded.

"No one must know I am involved, or my reputation will be worth *nada*!" She wiggled her chest, causing all eyes to focus on her protruding peaks. "I have made many important deals while Santiago sat back in his chair reading magazines. I was his executive assistant and have a great deal of experience with land development. My new realty job will depend on my reliability."

"I would appreciate your assistance," Wolf said softly.

Daniella ran the tip of her tongue over her lip. She purred in a throaty voice, "Alright, I will help you. I will unlock the door. But you must be careful, Wolf." Suggestively, she placed her hand on his forearm, running her fingers down to his wrist. When she crossed her legs, her sandal fell off her heel. "The mayor of San Miguel will do anything Santiago wants of him." She reverted her attention back to us. "His family is important in Mexico. We could all end up in jail."

Marg's jaw dropped.

Daniella leaned in closer to Wolf and snatched his hand in hers. "Santiago has bodyguards and security men."

Wolf stared intensely into Daniella's eyes. "I would like to access his files. Do you know his password?"

"He changes it regularly." She smirked. "But the fool hides it under his keyboard."

"This is insane! Maybe, we should go to the police," Marg suggested nervously.

Daniella looked at her as if she were a few pickles short of a jar.

Manni patted Marg on the shoulder. "No, my innocent one, Alvarez is a wealthy powerful man here in Cozumel. The Commander of the Cozumel Policia is the cousin of Alvarez." He shrugged. "Besides, police are bought off in Mexico with sufficient cash flow. So you see?"

Marg stared blankly. I sighed, thinking Marg needed a reality check. Sometimes she was like an alien dropped off on planet Earth.

"Tomorrow night. Will that work for you, Daniella?" Wolf asked.

She nodded. "There will be no one on the street at ten o'clock. Pick me up at my house." Giving him her business card Daniella quickly penned her address, phone number and cell on the back. This woman had more than revenge on her mind. *She was out to bag my man.*

Wolf nodded. "As for this evening, I suggest we call it a night as Adie and I have things to do." Everyone stared at me. "We need to move Adie. She's not safe here."

8

Sunlight warmed my face. I looked around wondering where I was. Nothing looked familiar about the spacious bedroom. I was lying in a king-sized bed covered with a green-patterned duvet. Mayan prints, hung on the white stucco walls, were artfully situated above the rattan furniture. It came back to me. Last night Wolf had moved my things into his suite at the Hotel Maria. It was late and we had ended up on the bed. I was just telling him what a lovely room it was when I noticed he had closed his eyes and was lying perfectly still. His breathing was slow and steady. He slept quietly, not even a hint of a snore. Dark eyelashes on his tanned cheeks, blond hair brushing his forehead. If he had been food, he would have been a chocolate truffle—creamy rich and sinfully sweet.

When I propped myself up on my elbows I spotted a note on the pillow.

Adie, order room service. Let's go snorkeling. I'll be back at 12:30. We need some down time. W

The clock radio showed 11:15. I took a quick shower and dressed in shorts and a top while I waited for my eggs to arrive. I wasn't sure I should be here with Wolf, but I knew I didn't want to be alone.

I opened the balcony doors and stood there a moment awed by the beauty of the place. The waves and the wind were low, indicating a day of sunshine. No El Norte. It blows in every little while, bringing rain. Usually, the weather on the east coast is drier and sunnier as the El Norte blows in from the west, but not always. There is no predictability in Cozumel, nor was there any in my life.

When I heard a knock, I checked the peephole. Room service. I asked the waiter to take the tray to the balcony. I brought out a hotel brochure from the living room table. Scanning the information while I ate, I noticed there was internet on the main floor near the lobby. If I wanted to get there and send off some e-mails, I had to hurry.

I was about to head over when I remembered Marg. At the end of the corridor, I found her room and knocked. Someone rustled around in the room. I knocked again. This time I heard an indignant, "Hold your horses!"

"It's me, Marg!"

The door swung open. Marg's face was flushed, her glasses sliding down her nose. "Adie."

"Can I come in?" I asked as she continued to stand there as energetic as a zombie. Too many anti-depressants? Shouldn't a social worker know better?

"Yup, sorry. I'm just in such a rush."

Her room was smaller than Wolf's suite. It would have been pleasant enough with the palm tree-cushioned couch and matching duvet but for the mess of clothing covering the furniture and tile floor.

"What are you doing? You're not going home are you?"

"Well I don't think that would be so unreasonable, after everything that happened, do you? I'm surprised you aren't leaving."

"You are in trouble with the police, Marg, remember? And you haven't got the cashier's check yet, have you?"

Marg plopped down on her bed, knocking down a pile of undies. She sighed. "No, you're right, Adie. I can't go home until we know who murdered Tim." Distractedly, she picked up a dress and placed it in the suitcase. "I don't want to talk to Alvarez but I'm not a quitter. I decided to move out."

"Where?"

"Manni's sister's house." She glanced away to the window, avoiding eye contact. "It's completely above board."

I grinned.

"Seriously."

"For now?"

Marg blushed.

"What about tonight? You want us to go ahead?"

"Yes, and Manni and I are coming too." Marg stuffed a dress into her suitcase and said, "We'll be your backup."

"You mean, lookout?"

"Um-hm. You and Wolf are doing this for me," she said gently, touching my arm, "and Adie, I'm grateful."

"Give me your address and phone number. We'll pick you up at a quarter to ten." On the night table, I found a pad and pen and handed it to her. Marg jotted down the information.

"Don't do anything I wouldn't do." I winked as I left.

Down at the computer room, I opened my e-mail. There were five messages—four from Fleischer Travel and one from Slick. After I replied to the work e-mails, I opened Slick's.

Hey, hottie. Have you gone to the topless beaches yet? Send me some pics. FYI the police think your buddy Beige has a motive. IMO they're wrong. Bernie

Slick and I were in agreement on one thing. No way was Marg a murderer.

***

I tied a purple and black paraeo around my hips, over my black string bikini. I was just about to stick my feet into a pair of sandals when I heard the door click. My heart stopped. An image of the massive biker flashed before my eyes. I breathed out in relief when I saw it was Wolf.

"You okay?"

I nodded.

His mouth curled slightly upward. "Hot."

"What?"

"You," he said, lifting my chin. My pulse raced. His lips were soft, his kiss demanding.

When he released me, it took an effort for me to speak. "You want to go snorkeling?" I squeaked.

"I'm in no hurry."

I wasn't either, but today I felt a need to think before I acted on impulse. Wolf didn't have to do more than twitch his little finger and I'd come running but that wasn't the way I wanted to play it. "Go get changed, Wolf," I shoved him away quickly. He was too great a temptation and I wasn't sure I was ready to plunge in deep water with him just yet, unless it was in fins and a mask.

He smiled that slow smile that implied he knew exactly what was in my mind. "Give me a minute." He walked into the bedroom and I could hear him rummaging around. It was odd sharing space with a man. I was so used to living alone, well almost, there were the cats, but they didn't talk much. Wolf wasn't big on speech either—he was definitely more doer than talker.

When he came back out he was wearing a bathing suit and a white unbuttoned shirt. Superb muscular legs and there was certainly nothing wrong with that chest. He looked good enough to eat, but to my disappointment, instead of grabbing me and shoving me into the bedroom for some raunchy sex, he grinned wickedly, snatched up the snorkeling bag, and opened the door.

At the end of the hall, a flight of stairs went down to the hotel's garden. Flowering lavender bougainvilleas edged the steps and continued to the lower arched doorway. Further to the right, there were tennis courts. A free-form pool with a waterfall was surrounded by a jungle of plants. From the landing, Wolf pointed to a large dark patch of coral reef in the ocean. "That's it, Adie."

It didn't look that far away but even if it was, the water was calm and salt makes swimming easy. On the left of the bay a dive boat was tied to a dock just past the hotel gardens. Close to the wharf, an open-air restaurant was situated next to the crescent shaped beach dotted with palapas, lounge chairs and palm trees. Reggae music drifted over from the band with a touch of Jamaica. Negative vibes lingering from last night gave way to a mellow energy.

At the beach, we set our bags and towels on one lounge chair and sat together on the next chair. Wolf draped his arm around my shoulders. I dug my foot in the sand, feeling the fine powdery grains between my toes. His foot stroked mine. I pushed sand on Wolf's feet and buried them. "Why is it you've never tried your own hotel for snorkeling?" I asked curiously.

"Wanted to save this to do with you."

"Yeah, right, Wolf," I commented dryly, "as if you knew I'd even be here in Cozumel."

"Psychic."

"What else can you predict?"

"The details aren't coming in yet," he turned to me, "but it would start with something like this." His arm encircled me and his lips touched mine. I got lost in that kiss, the touch of his tongue slowly igniting a fire. Pulling away, he smiled. "It would go on indefinitely," he went on, tracing my lips with his finger, "and my predictions are very accurate."

"You would think so."

Wolf's expression got serious. "About tonight. You don't have

79

to put yourself at risk again, Adie."

"What are you saying?" I asked, taken aback. "You don't want me to go?"

"I'm just thinking of all the stuff you've gone through lately. You could stay in the car with Marg. Manni could be the lookout. Daniella can open the door and go back to the car to stay with you. I could do it. You don't have to do any of this, Adie."

Okay, maybe I was nervous about breaking and entering. Who wouldn't be? Especially in Mexico where the rules were different—guilty until proven innocent.

I hadn't ever broken the law. Well, at least not deliberately so. No, that wasn't quite true. There was the time I slightly nudged someone's car when I backed out and there were the speeding tickets but I'd been a law-abiding citizen for most of my life.

"Admit it," my Logical Voice nagged. "You're scared. Why risk a Mexican jail?"

I squeezed his hand. "You're putting yourself at risk for someone you hardly know. I can Google-search, but information about company accounts won't be there." Business was like nuclear science to me besides the fact that this whole thing had to happen lickety-split. "But you know how to do this better than anyone with your computer experience."

Shaking his head, he said sadly, "Yeah—you're right. You three would be lost without me." Then seeing my expression, he grinned. "Made manager at Blackberry before I started my company."

"Mom told me. You didn't happen to bring a flash drive and a computer with you?"

"No, but we might not need any records. Besides, maybe Boris is behind the attacks."

"If he's not, we need to see names and numbers. Our time is limited, remember?"

"True. No use getting caught."

"Sending records as an attachment won't work."

"Right, he'd see that in the sent file." Wolf squeezed my hand. "Don't worry. We can do it the old-fashioned way."

"Right...a printer. Alvarez must have one."

"He will—relax." Gazing out at the gentle waves lapping the shore, Wolf indicated the sea with his chin. "Hey, time to get in there."

With that comment, some of my scary teen memories returned. Wolf had been a reckless boy charged by testosterone back then, doing anything on a dare. I'd learned how to live on the wild side.

Wolf's fingers on my shoulder, jolted me out of it. "Adie?" He opened his snorkeling bag and handed me my mask and fins.

Within minutes of entering the ocean's secret world, we were surrounded by a school of yellow grunts. Coral was everywhere. A mass of brown pillar coral stuck straight up like ugly furry penises in the midst of waving purple fan coral.

Wolf grabbed my hand. Romance under the sea. Who would've thought it. Felt good.

The current pushed us to a large hunk of knobby brain coral. Somehow it made me think of that slimeball with the shaved head. Who had sent him anyway? If Boris was behind it, I would personally cut off that little nerd's *cojones* and feed them to the fish. He had never liked me. I was a bad influence on Marg. But was he so angry he wanted me dead?

The warm water soothed my stress. When a pair of bright orange filefish dipped back and forth around us, I let go of Wolf's hand and zoomed my camera in to snap a picture. I swam around and took photos from different angles. Ready to go, I looked for Wolf. When I didn't see him I poked my head up on the surface, spotting a yellow snorkel fifteen meters ahead.

Wolf gestured for me to come closer. He pointed to a treelike branch of coral. I swam up. At first, all I noticed were some tiny yellow and blue wrasses scooting out through the boughs. Then I saw it. It was bigger than most I've seen—a silvery five foot barracuda. Not as scary as a shark but that jagged grin with a double row of pointy teeth threw me off. When two more barracuda joined the first one, my curiosity dissipated in record time. They say they don't attack you unless provoked, but there's always a first time.

With a gesture, I pointed to the beach. When Wolf followed a weight lifted off my shoulders. Barracuda attacks can happen anywhere—especially the two-legged kind.

After the warmth of the ocean, the cold-water shower on the shore was a shock to the system. I quickly rinsed off and headed for the ladies' room.

The lighting inside the washroom was dim. Sand dusted the tile floor. Once I'd washed the salt off my face, I applied eyeliner and lip-gloss. Back at the lounge chairs, I noticed two plastic glasses filled with a greenish liquid and ice on the table. "Margaritas?" I asked, seeing the salt on the rims.

Wolf nodded. He studied me approvingly and said, "You're all woman, Adie."

I wondered what had brought that on. I examined Wolf over the rim of my glass. He was a prize—tanned, blond and succulent, and apparently unclaimed.

"Are you going out with anybody back home, Adie?"

"No, not right now. You?"

"I didn't feel like getting into anything permanent after my divorce," Wolf said.

This was a shocker, why hadn't my mom told me? Our mothers were friends. But then, maybe she had. When she started her stories, I usually tuned her out when it came to the gossip. "How long have you been divorced for?"

"Almost two years."

Confused by this news, I tugged out a pair of binoculars from my bag and focused them on a cruise ship in the distance. I collected my thoughts. He'd caught me off guard with this one. I didn't want to ask but I forced myself. "Do you still have feelings for what's-her-name?"

"Samantha."

"What broke you up?"

"She's into power."

What kind of a nutcase would try to control Wolf? I swung the binoculars around to the shoreline, and closed in on the restaurant. I focused in on the three people seated near the railing overlooking the rocky cliff. A massive man, wearing a white linen hat with black sunglasses, long sleeved black shirt and baggy casual pants sat slightly behind a brunette. Across from her, a dark haired athletic man dressed totally in white held up a glass of wine. The woman fluffed up her hair, laughing at something the man said. "Take a look at that table, Wolf."

I handed him the binoculars. He readjusted the focus. "Daniella."

I had always wanted big hair like hers. Instead I journeyed through life always on the edge of hair disasters. This woman irritated me in a major way. "That's what I thought. Who do you think she's with?"

"A bodybuilder and the other one looks like..." Wolf passed me the binoculars, leaned back and met my eyes, "Alvarez."

"Really? Why's she so chummy with him, after all she said last night? You know how she hates the guy and she's got all this integrity, etcetera."

"She probably doesn't want to burn her bridges. He could be useful to her in her new job." Wolf smiled. "Speaking of lawyers—I've got a joke."

I pulled up my legs close to my body and sat back in the lounge chair, regarding him expectantly.

"This big-time lawyer was sitting beside a pretty blonde on a plane. He was bored and wanted her to play a game with him. This is the way it goes, he told her. I ask a question and if you don't know the answer you pay me five dollars, and then you ask me, and if I don't know I pay you five. The blonde said no, she didn't want to play. She wanted to read. The lawyer didn't give up but she still refused. Finally he said he'd pay her fifty if he can't answer, but she would just pay him five if she didn't know. Okay, she said, to get him off her back. The lawyer asked her what's the diameter of the earth? She paid him a fiver and asked him, "What goes up a hill with four legs and comes down with five?" The lawyer didn't know, so he called up all his friends and they didn't know either. He gave up and handed her fifty dollars. When she started reading again, he got really angry. Well, he said, "What's the answer?" She handed him a five dollar bill."

"Oh-h-h." I said, getting it. "Good one—unusual, a smart blonde."

Wolf smiled. "Not really. You're blonde, intelligent and attractive—a deadly combination."

"Deadly for whom?" I grinned.

"Deadly for that bastard last night. He must still be feeling the pain."

And how am I doing with you? I searched his face, but his sunglasses hid his eyes.

"One thing, though, Adie. You are way too noticeable."

"You want me to wear a bag over my head?"

Wolf pulled his sunglasses off and gazed directly into my eyes. "It wouldn't hide that sexy body."

"You're thinking a disguise?"

"A change."

I grinned. "Great minds think alike." Glancing at my watch, I noticed it was close to two-thirty. "Got to go, Wolf. Need to shower. Have a three o'clock appointment."

"Oh? Need any help?"

"Help?"

"Scrubbing those hard to reach places."

I ignored him. "Is it okay, though? It is your room."

Wolf handed me an access card. "No problem. I thought I'd go to the gym for a while. Let's meet in the room at six-thirty. We can go out for dinner."

Taking a last sip of my margarita, I nodded, setting it down on the table as I stood. "Sounds good. Where did you have in mind?"

"A restaurant near the naval base." He got up and pulled me close, bending down to stare into my eyes. "Blue like the ocean and just as mysterious."

His hand pushed my chin up. On tiptoes my lips were just inches from his. Soft lips pressed sensuously against mine. The kiss was bliss. Charged with supreme will power, I overcame the urge to ravish him. I stepped away.

Wolf's eyes glittered. "*Adios*, sexy."

9

Alejandro plucked at the matted mess, ranting, "This is impossible!" With a flourish he signaled his apprentice to join us and pointed to the sink at the back of the shop. "Teresa, take this unfortunate lady for a shampoo." His eyes rolled."We cannot work with this!"

Following Teresa's tightly contained ass to another busy area of clients and stylists, I sat down as she placed a towel around my neck and started the shampooing process. The job completed she lead the way back.

"What were you thinking, Señorita?"

"Highlights, blonde streaks mostly, maybe a few brown and red ones."

Alejandro stroked his chin searching for the key to hair spirituality. "Not impossible if we cut."

Did I hear that right?

He nodded for emphasis.

"No-oo!" Cut is a dangerous word—anything could happen when they cut.

Alejandro swept his hands up in exasperation. "I did not think you were a woman without courage. Señorita," he said patiently, "in order to achieve the halo of perfection needed to entrance the man you no doubt have in mind," he pulled my hair, for emphasis, "you must have a cut!"

I shook my head. "I hate short hair."

He shot me a look. "Not that much, perhaps two, maybe three inches."

"Three! You must be kidding." All those months of hair growth lost forever.

Alejandro crossed his arms over his chest.

"Can you keep the length?"

My hair guru sighed heavily.

"Okay, go for it." Hoping I made the right decision, I said a small prayer, knowing a fatal error could not be recouped for months. Teresa handed me a magazine with beautiful models sporting chic hairstyles, some of which I wouldn't be caught dead in.

After sitting there a good forty minutes, my hair sticking out wrapped in cellophane, Teresa came to shampoo and condition my hair. She raved, "You will see, Señorita, what fine work he does. He is so creative!" She sighed. "If I could only learn his skills."

Playing with my hair a minute or two before combing it out for the cut, Alejandro scrutinized every angle of my head before he started to randomly snip my hair. I crossed my fingers as my hair fell to the floor. I was then directed to lean forwards as he blew my hair dry.

"Excellent color," he commented positively.

When I was allowed to see for myself, I wasn't disappointed.

"Such genius!" Teresa squealed. Who would have thought anyone could do this with such hair."

Thanks a lot, Teresa. But she was right. It was extraordinary what he had accomplished. Dark blonde hair, streaked with platinum and vibrant brownish-reds in a layered jagged cut, fell over my shoulders. A flowing free-spirited sort of look.

"I like it. Thanks." I placed a tip on the counter and paid on my way out.

Since the hairdressing shop was part of the Hotel Maria, I was back in the room in a few minutes. I grabbed some clothes, along with lacy lingerie, and carried them into the bedroom. When I came back out, I heard water running in the bathroom. I started fantasizing. Wolf in the shower, getting soapy wet, the foam clinging to his well-formed chest. Stop it, I told myself. Any more of this and I'd drive myself insane. By the time the bathroom door opened, I had assumed a causal position on the couch reading a paperback that I had hastily picked up.

Clad only in a white towel, his wet skin gleaming, Wolf paused to appraise me. "You never disappoint me, Adie."

I couldn't take my eyes off him. "Oh?" I tried to sound calm and collected.

"Your hair, Adie." Wolf slowly stroked his bottom lip with his index finger. "It's wild—suits you."

My Hormone Voice started chattering in my brain. "Imagine that hot man without the towel."

I did. I tried breathing normally, but I was having difficulty, having held my breath ever since I saw him emerge from the bathroom.

"Hungry?" he asked.

"Yes." For you," Hormone said, excitedly.

Wolf smiled, paused and then walked into the bedroom.

Wasn't there air conditioning in this hotel? This room was like a PMS flash. Getting up, I opened the balcony doors and let myself out. Lights sparkled on the pool and on the palm trees below. Darkness had enveloped the hotel grounds and a cool breeze brushed my skin making me shiver involuntarily. I nearly jumped out of my skin when I felt warm strong arms encircle my waist.

Whispering in my ear, Wolf asked, "Cold?"

"Not anymore," I said, feeling his body heat against me. "Maybe, we should go."

"If you want."

"Want? Take him you fool—he wants you!"

But my Logical Voice interrupted, "Your brain needs food. You aren't thinking straight. Don't you remember anything? He was flighty back then and he's just as fickle now. Men don't change and you can't change him. Remember the karate motto— 'the mind is stronger than the body'."

I took Wolf's hand and steered him back into the room. "Wait, I'll get my shoes." High-heeled sandals for a little pizzazz. As I slinked towards him, his eyes zoomed in on my legs.

"Hot!" Wolf's clear blue eyes sparkled. A black silk shirt tucked into black linen pants, cinched with a woven leather belt around his narrow waist—he was a burning inferno. He couldn't have appeared sleeker. In contrast, his blond hair was mussed, as if some woman had just had her way with him. Get a grip, I told myself. Chemistry isn't everything. There are more important things.

"Like what?" Hormone broke in, "Isn't he what you want?"

I closed my eyes and massaged my neck with my left hand.

Stepping up to me, Wolf lightly massaged my shoulders. "Tight. Are you stressed about tonight?"

It took me a second to realize what he was talking about. The sexual energy between us was not what he was referring to. "You mean, checking out Alvarez's computer?"

Wolf smiled slightly. "You're tense about something else?"

"No, of course not. I'm too hungry to think straight."

"Let's go, then."

***

The Hotel Maria was a short walk away from the El Pescado, a seafood restaurant right at the waterfront. Wolf held the door open as we entered a dimly lit room. The maitre d' gave us a table near the ocean overlooking the beach. The guitar beat of nouveau flamenco filled the room. The rhythm both excited and relaxed. There was something mysterious and haunting about the Moorish chords, which stirred emotions deep inside me. I glanced at Wolf sitting across from me and wondered if it did the same for him.

We sat back in our rattan chairs with our drinks. So much had happened since I arrived here in Cozumel. Who would have thought I would have met up with Wolf and ended up sharing a suite?

"You look like the cat that swallowed the canary," Wolf commented.

I wasn't about to share my thoughts, so I shared my conjectures. "I was thinking about Boris."

"Marg's ex."

I nodded.

"Is there any reason to believe he could have hired hitmen?"

"It seems like a tall order, but Boris was making a lot of money with his investment work after he quit his job at Mutual Life."

"I can see you and Marg being targets for him, but why Reich and Uma?"

"Marg was tight with Reich," I speculated. "Could be Boris was jealous."

"They hooked up?"

"I don't know for sure, but they were getting close, according to her. That would have upset Boris. He liked to have complete control and he was the jealous type. I would get phone calls late at night ordering me to tell him where she was."

"Reich was Marg's patient, though, wasn't he?"

"The relationship looked professional enough from the notes

she kept."

"You saw her files! How did you manage that?"

"Well, before I left, I paid a visit to the hospital and I snuck into her office."

Wolf raised an eyebrow. "You got into her computer?"

"Hard to believe?" I said annoyed.

Wolf grinned. "I'm impressed."

"It was a paper file."

Wolf laughed, took a long swallow of beer and asked, "Did you copy it or just steal it?"

"Borrowed it. I'll give it back to Marg, but right now she could be in serious trouble with the police."

"And you're saving her."

"Correction, we're saving her. Anyway, it could be Boris is not guilty. In that case, it's Alvarez or Daniella we should be watching." The waiter placed my entrée on the table. "Are you still thinking of buying property here?" I eyed Wolf's plate of mahi-mahi, mixed veggies and potatoes.

"Yeah, I phoned my brother."

I picked at my fish and ignored the rice. Meals here always came with rice. It's possible to feel potato-deprived in Cozumel. After several days, visions of mashed potatoes and gravy start to enter my REM sleep. "How can you buy property when we're so close to the shore?" I stared at his potatoes jealously.

"Well," he paused, "we're in a restricted zone, but if a foreigner wants to buy something here, he gets a bilingual lawyer who contacts a bank that keeps the property in trust. Alvarez is a government appointed official that checks the property for liens and approves the purchase."

"He's a notary public? I thought he was a lawyer?"

"Notary publics are lawyers in Mexico."

"Oh." Grudgingly, I ate some rice. "Are you planning to do that or just invest with someone else?"

"Twenty years ago the law was changed for business people. If a person has a corporation, which I have with my brother Mike. We could own something directly if that property is for commercial use, even in a restricted zone." Wolf shot me a look. "Is something wrong?"

"No, not really."

Wolf's lips twitched.

"You're not planning to build something, are you?"

"I'm not inclined to after seeing all the problems other people had." He added, "Things aren't always what they seem here in Mexico."

"Things are never what they seem," I said, wondering about Wolf's feelings for me.

"They have a price."

"What?"

"My potatoes." Wolf took a serving spoon and pushed his potatoes onto my plate.

"Wow! Thanks, you don't know how much I missed them." I peered at him suspiciously. "What's the price?"

"Eat up," he said. "It'll be something you'll like. Now tell me about this guy, Boris. Did he strike you as a violent type?"

"He hated to lose anything."

"Competitive?"

"One weekend, we played tennis. At one point, my boyfriend and I were winning and I teased Boris about it. I was just kidding, but Boris went berserk. Played like a fiend 'til he and Marg won." I frowned, thinking, if he hadn't won he would have jumped the net and squashed me like a bug with his high-end Wilson racket.

When the waiter came over and asked if we wanted dessert, I shook my head but Wolf asked for the dessert menu.

"They'll just have ice cream," I said.

"That's not dessert?"

"Not in my book. Chocolate cake or nothing."

"Yeah, I'm into chocolate."

My kind of man! Rich sinful milk chocolate—Belgian, German or Swiss.

Wolf signaled the waiter for the check and took out his wallet. "We've got an hour to kill, let's go shopping."

A man who likes shopping? No, he's only trying to be nice. What do men shop for anyway? San Miguel wouldn't have hardware stores.

A huge fifty-foot Christmas tree with lights and decorations had been set up in the main square. Along the coastal street, Avenida Rafael Melgar, groups of tourists were out checking the goods. Salesmen would shout out about their great deals, except in the air-conditioned jewelry stores, where salespeople in smartly cut suits stood sedately waiting to assist tourists interested in diamonds and tanzanite.

Away from the harbor front street, down the cobbled pedestrian-only road, the prices became more reasonable. The small stalls and stores carried anything at tourist would want for a souvenir.

"Hammocks!" I said surprised, when Wolf started examining them.

"Gotta get one before I go back. You like silver?" He asked as we left the store, and strolling further past a gift store.

The shopkeeper perched on a wooden stool called out, "Come see, Señorita. Almost free!"

Jokers. I shook my head. "No gracias." I glanced at Wolf. "I didn't bring very much money with me."

We stopped in front of a stand displaying silver bracelets, necklaces and rings. The squat owner grinned a jagged smile. "My name is Ricardo." He pitched, "Let me show you some fine necklaces."

I glanced at the rings. "Cool is the rule when it comes to bargaining. I tried to look disinterested but the turquoise jewelry beckoned.

"And excellent rings."

I ran my fingers down a bracelet with turquoise heart-shaped stones inlaid in heavy silver. It was so pretty I had to ask, "How much?"

"Forty."

I laughed. "Surely you don't mean dollars, do you? I can pick up something just like this at home for far less."

"This is Mexican silver, lady."

He had a point there. The silver here was much brighter and heavier but it didn't matter if I didn't bring the cash. "Let's go, Wolf." I tugged on Wolf's arm.

"Wait, Señorita! What price would you be willing to pay?"

"I was thinking of an ankle bracelet. Do you have any?"

"I can extend any of these." He pointed to several silver bracelets with turquoise stones, cut in various shapes. "What's your best price?"

Mentally, I converted my pesos to dollars. I rubbed my

forehead and frowned—math not being my strong suit.

Ricardo thought I was stalling for a better price. "I can give it to you for thirty, Señorita, and I will make this bracelet fit you perfectly. Let me see your ankle." I allowed him to pull my foot onto his knee and place a bracelet around it. "You have a very slender ankle, Señorita." He ran his hand down my calf to my ankle. "It will only need a few more links. I could have it done in ten minutes."

"I'm afraid your price is too much for me."

"Señorita," he shook his head, "you drive a hard bargain. I will do it for twenty-five. Come on, you can surely pay that?"

I glanced over at another silver stall across the street, and Ricardo sighed. Wolf took out his wallet and smiled at me. "This one's on me."

I shook my head and opened my purse.

"Adie, I want to get it for you." Closing my purse with his left hand, he handed Ricardo the money.

"If you wait, it will take only a minute or two, Señorita."

"The one with the heart-shaped stones," I said, pointing to a bracelet. "Thanks, Wolf."

After adding some links to my selected bracelet, he asked if I wanted to wear it. I nodded and he pulled up my leg again and fastened the bracelet around my ankle.

As we walked away, Wolf commented, "I think Ricardo was enjoying himself too much when he was sizing that ankle bracelet."

At last, some reaction! Male territorialism coming into play. I lifted my foot to admire the turquoise encased in silver. "It's pretty. I've been looking everywhere for a nice one.

"It was amusing to see you bargain. Where did you learn that?"

"My Pop. I used to die of embarrassment when I was a kid and he took me to buy a coat at Vandoor's. He would walk away if he didn't get forty per cent off. But it worked. They would run after him and he'd get everything he wanted."

"Smart man, your father. You've learned well from him." His clear blue eyes gazed at me searchingly, as he took my hand, "Are you getting everything you want, Adie?

10

Like a diva on stage, Daniella sauntered out of her house. pausing dramatically on the step as if awaiting applause. With her glossy tresses hanging loose to her shoulders and a green halter dress clinging to her every curve, she swayed down the steps to Wolf, catching his hand in hers as she led him to the fence. Wolf opened the wrought iron gate and together they made their way to the Jeep.

She tossed her bangs back off her forehead. "Where shall I sit, Wolf? If we squeezed Aggie to the window, I could share that seat with her."

"Right, there's so much room," I said dryly, "and it's Adie, Daniella." Maybe she thought she could push me out the window—anything to get rid of me so she could have Wolf all to herself.

Daniella smirked, taking my remark as assent and opened the passenger door with every intention of jumping over me and inserting herself between us.

"There's room in the back," Wolf said quickly, sensing the tension in the air.

Daniella's ruby red lips twisted as I stepped out so she could get in. She knocked her purse against Marg as she seated herself next to Manni. The cloying scent of opium perfume filled the Jeep. Smiling wickedly, Daniella whispered something in Manni's ear and kissed him on the cheek. Marg folded her arms over her chest and glared, as Wolf eased the Jeep into the street. Daniella stared defiantly at Marg and rubbed her leg against Manni, before she settled herself back in the seat.

It doesn't take long to go anywhere in San Miguel. We were soon parked a block away from the Royal Investment building. A dog barked from inside a neighboring courtyard. It was getting late and the streets were quiet with only an occasional pedestrian passing by.

Daniella flipped her hair tossing a dark strand straight into Marg's face. Daniella ignored Marg's tearing eye and set about explaining the situation. "I will unlock the door and then I will come back. All of you wait here. Be on the alert for Santiago's security people."

I got out of the Jeep and pulled the seat up. "And we will know the security how?"

"You will know." Daniella paused, her face pale in the dim light. "One is large and ugly, and the other, thin and vicious. Watch it, they carry knives."

Daniella slid out the passenger side, shoving her round ass dangerously close to Marg's indignant face before she climbed out. Looking cautiously both ways, she crossed to the other side of the street and clicked along the uneven sidewalk in her four-inch stilettos at a pace to be envied by those of us without the extra high-heeled navigating gene. As I watched her unlock the large oak door at the entrance of Royal Investments, I sat nervously thinking about the conditions of a Mexican prison. This should not have been on my "to do" vacation list. Any sane travel consultant would be checking out the partying at Carlos & Charlie's to see if it was up to standard, instead of creeping around avoiding baddies and the police. I'd heard all kinds of stories about police corruption, but never in Cozumel. Honest cops might not be a good thing though, if I had to bribe my way out of prison.

When we saw Daniella manoeuvring her way back to the car, Manni and Marg got out and joined us on the sidewalk. Our plan was for them to stand out in front ready to warn us, while we made our search. Wearing my black outfit with Nike Airs, instead of the high-heeled sandals I had on earlier, I was prepared for anything— well almost anything, at least, I could try running away, if they came after us.

Wolf took my hand and led me to the door, which was slightly ajar. Making sure we closed it behind us, Wolf shone the flashlight down low onto the marble floor ahead. On either side of the hallway there was an office. Down the corridor we saw the exit. Daniella had briefed us to remember it in case things went wrong. My job was to listen for a signal from Manni if anyone approached the building. Hopefully, I would be able to hear him warn us in case the police arrived, or worse yet, some of Alvarez's security men.

Wolf turned off the flashlight. Dressed completely in black, and with the corridor shrouded in shadows, Wolf's lean form was hard to see. The darkness didn't scare me but the situation did. I reached out blindly for his arm but ended up touching his jeans. "Wolf," I whispered.

"Adie, this isn't a good time—but, hey, I could see how this could turn you on."

"Oo-oh, sorry." I withdrew my hand. What part of Wolf had I touched? It had been hard and firm—no, I couldn't have.

Drawing me closer, Wolf whispered in my ear. "Relax, Adie. It's not like I haven't been touched like that before." Slowly, he kissed me on the neck, his tongue feathering down. I shivered with pleasure as his lips pressed on my shoulder. "It was nice," he said, cupping my breast, his fingertips stroking the lacy material of my camisole. Warm lips moved on mine as his firm body pressed against me. I was overcome by an ache that escalated with every second. I ran my fingers down his narrow waist, feeling the warmth of his body through the silk shirt. I closed my eyes, taking in his ocean scent and brought my hand to his cheek. He caught my hand, his lips enclosed on my fingertips and slowly sucked them. I exhaled, aroused by the sensation.

Abruptly, Wolf stopped. "That should be good for a few potatoes."

"What?"

"Remember at dinner? I said you'd have to pay me back."

"Right." I thought back. He'd said the payment would be something I'd like.

"We'd better get at it."

Shocked, I gasped, "Here?"

"No, there." Wolf snatched my hand, switched on the flashlight and guided me along to the office at the back. Shining the light on the computer, he booted it up and checked under the keyboard for the password. "Hold the flashlight for me, Adie."

Breaking and entering is a good distraction from sex, but I had to wonder how he could just drop everything and get down to business. I shone the light on the heavy antique cherry desk, and watched Wolf take out the password from under the keyboard, and log in. Hastily, I turned on the laser printer next to the computer with my other hand.

His forehead furrowed in concentration, Wolf clicked on

different file folders, opening and closing files, still not locating anything nefarious in nature. "I'll try a search for Reich and what's his ex's name again?"

"Uma Farber-Reich."

Silently, Wolf scanned the files and our luck changed. As he began to locate documents about land development and bank transfers, he repeatedly pressed the print icon. When the laser printer chugged out sheet after sheet, I began to see light at the end of the tunnel.

With the flashlight propped up, I headed back down the hall to the front door. I was concerned how long we'd been there. In order to be successful, a break-in had to be completed in five minutes or less. It was time to check.

From the street, I heard raised voices. Through the venetian blinds, I could see Manni making back off gestures to a bruiser of a Mexican. That guy could be a security guard. I darted back to the office where Wolf was hunched over the computer. "Wolf, we've got to go, now!"

Wolf moved fast, shutting down the system. From the tray, he grabbed the hardcopies and tugged me to the door.

"Wait!" Breaking hold of his hand, I rushed back into the office and switched off the printer's blinking green light. Papers popped out. With these tucked into my top, I flew back to rejoin Wolf. Unfastening the back door, Wolf stepped into the night. He turned to pull me along, closing the door just as we heard the front door lock snap open.

The moon was our only light. Dark shadows on the concrete in the alley made it hard to see. Treading on an empty pop can, I twisted my foot and stumbled, scraping my hand on the stucco wall as I tried to regain my balance.

Wolf's hand shot out to steady me. "You okay?"

"Um-mm." My hand smarted.

A sulphuric stench turned my stomach. Twenty yards away from the building, Wolf switched the flashlight back on and we sped up, although with all the junk cluttering the alley our progress was only marginally faster. Without Wolf, I might have fallen face first into a pile of dog poop, but he managed to divert my stride before I messed up my favorite Nikes.

Nervously, I glanced back to the rear exit of the Royal

Investments building to see if one of the bodyguards had followed us. So far so good. With relief, I saw an opening on our right. We kept to the wall until we got to the sidewalk, dimly lit by the streetlight. The Jeep was parked half a block away. Manni rested his back against the car, holding Marg in front of him, his arms around her waist. Wolf motioned me to stop as he peered up the empty sidewalk. He whispered in my ear, "We're okay." He took my hand and we headed to the vehicle.

I opened the door for Manni and Marg. They climbed in, quietly waiting for me to shut the door. After inserting the key, Wolf said, "We've got something. I don't know if it's what you need, Marg, but we'll find out."

He started the motor and pulled out. It was close to eleven and the streets were empty, with the exception of a few men standing around smoking. No sign of Alvarez's security people.

"Thanks, Wolf. We had quite a scare when that man came but Manni convinced him we were lost and he finally left us alone." Marg leaned forward. "Adie, could we meet for breakfast and talk?"

I swiveled around. "The Rock'n Java at ten?"

Marg nodded. "We could go shopping."

"Shoes?"

"Ah-huh."

Wolf slowed down and made a right onto Calle 10.

"There it is," Daniella said tightly, pointing to her house with the porch light illuminating the nativity scene on her lawn.

After parking the car at the curb, Wolf stepped out and went around to open the door on the passenger side. I got out and pulled up the seat for Daniella.

"Goodnight Daniella, and thanks," Marg said politely, as Daniella kissed Manni good-bye. Wolf held his hand out. She latched onto him, her body molding to his, as they made their way to the front gate. Wolf stopped to exchange some words with Daniella but they spoke so quietly, I couldn't make out what they said. She pressed in to him explaining something in hushed tones. His blond hair glimmered in the dim streetlight, but the darkness hid his face.

I pushed the lever forward and sat back down, thinking how glad I was that there was no reason to see her again. She had officially made my "least favorite people list".

The car's interior light flicked on when Wolf opened his door, his expression distracted.

"Could you two check the printouts for me tonight?" Marg asked, once Wolf pulled out onto the street.

"Sure." Wolf turned his head slightly towards her. "You're still at Manni's sister's?"

"Yes, Manni thought I would be safer there since these criminals are looking for us. Do you think Adie is safe in your hotel suite?"

I could see Wolf's lips curl up at the corners. I nudged his arm and replied for him. "I don't think anyone knows where I am and I don't know if you noticed, but I changed my hair."

Manni threw his head back chortling. "I think it will attract more attention, Adie, but it looks awesome on you!"

I shrugged. "Oh, well. I tried."

Marg shook her head exasperated, "Wolf, you'd better take good care of her. She's predictable in her unpredictability."

***

We let Manni and Marg off at the Chedraui Plaza and drove on to the Hotel Maria. When we got in our suite, Wolf opened up the balcony doors to let in the cool night air. It was breezier now and the sky was draped with heavy cloud masses. The El Norte was blowing in. We were in for some rain tonight or tomorrow. I stood and looked out at the whitecaps illuminated by the beach bar lights as Wolf went to the bar fridge and got out two beer. Uncapping both bottles he handed me one and we sipped the beer, listening to the music from the bar—Enrique Iglesias crooning a sultry love song.

Sitting on the edge of the couch, I untied my laces and kicked off my Nikes. When I glanced up, Wolf was taking off his shirt.

"Just getting comfortable," Wolf explained, noting my expression. "Come." He steered me into the bedroom, and grabbed a couple of pens and magazines.

"We're reading *Star Spot* tonight?" I sat down beside him.

"No, we're going to take a look at what's down your cleavage."

I was speechless.

Wolf dropped his hardcopies on the bed with the magazines and grinned. "The last printouts you put in your top, remember?" He lay stomach down on one side of the bed and picked up a pen, looking at me expectantly.

I glanced down. My camisole was misshapen with the folded papers stuck in my bra. I scooped them out with one hand while still holding the beer in my other hand and flung the papers on the bed. I took another sip of the Corona and set it down, glad I hadn't spilled the beer in my embarrassment. Sorting the papers out, Wolf placed some on top of a magazine in front of him and positioned another pile on my magazine. I lay down beside him and picked up a pen.

Music from the bar downstairs floated up, a duet about a kiss. Entranced by the idea of a kiss lasting forever, the words on the hard copy blurred and the song made me think of Wolf's lips, the way they moved on mine. And then I remembered how his body felt against me, his hands stroking my skin. I stopped reading. Out of the corner of my eye, I noticed how his tan contrasted with his hair, bleached a streaky blond by the tropical sun, and yet his lashes remained dark. His elbows pressed down into the bed, he lay there reading, displaying clearly defined, muscular biceps. My eyes followed the line of his back until it met the belt of his jeans and then continued uphill over the enticing curve of his firm butt. I closed my eyes a second to force myself to keep my attention on what I knew was important, but I had difficulty centering on the print as the image of his body kept blurring my concentration.

Wolf's fingers touched my forearm lightly. "Here's a deposit from Reich for half a million." Wolf circled the amount and underlined "Reich".

What was the matter with me? I forced myself to focus. My eyes swept down the sheet and fixed on a transfer of seven hundred thousand from Uma Farber-Reich. "Look at this, Wolf," I said, underlining her name.

"Wolf?" Before I could look over, I felt his hand on my shoulder, pivoting me about. Flat on my back, I gazed up at his startling blue eyes, my research efforts forgotten. Mesmerized, I froze as he lowered his mouth, moving sensuously on mine until my lips parted eager for him to enter. And when he did, our tongues danced rhythmically, each in tune to the other's tempo. I felt my pen slide out of my fingers, roll off the bed, and click as it hit the tile floor.

His tongue teased. I was trapped in a net of smoldering heat. My fingers traced his sides, along to his narrow waist—reveling in the velvety warmth of his skin. When his hand pushed my top up, gliding smoothly over my belly. I stiffened self-consciously. A man like this had his pick of females—tall super-thin model types—something I was not.

"You feel so good," he said, softly breathing into my ear, "your belly is so nicely rounded," before he flicked the contours of my ear with his tongue.

Wolf liked fat? I sighed in relief, letting myself go—floating away into his warm caresses. At that moment, Enrique started to sing about his love addiction. I understood completely. Wolf's tongue flicked the hollow of my neck, setting me on fire. I ran my hand over his strong shoulders and traced my fingertips down his bicep. The heat radiated from his body to mine. I felt out of control, like a moth flying into a powerful light.

"I'm collecting for the rest of those potatoes, princess," he whispered, before his lips slowly trailed down my shoulder. He was right about the price—it was everything I wanted. I closed my eyes and drifted up on a cloud of yearning, sighing softly when his kisses descended to my breasts. My body was leaving logic and reason behind. It didn't matter what I should do anymore. His magnetism was powerful and I was a miniature element that could no longer resist. When his hand pulled down the lacy material edging my bra, I tried to stop him. "Wolf…"

"Ss-hh, just taking care of you." He pushed my bra strap down. Cupping my breast, he bent his head.

"Um-mm." Speech deserted me as the tip of his tongue tantalized my nipple. Tingles raced to my thighs.

"Let's take this off." Sliding the silky material up over my breasts he paused, his eyes glimmering with desire

I had no resistance left. I wanted him to make love to me. I raised my arms, reveling in the feel of his hands on my body as he pulled the delicate material off, tossing it on the bed.

His finger traced the outline of my parted lips. "I want you, princess," he whispered, his voice husky, "and I'll give you everything you need."

His mouth moved slowly on mine stirring the embers inside me into a flame. As his lips withdrew, he reached around me, unhooking my bra. I could feel it slipping off, yet he didn't rush, instead he kissed the soft skin slowly as if savouring the taste.

I slid my hands over his firm ass. The scent of ocean and soap assailed my nostrils. I felt his hand on my breast, massaging. His lips captured a nipple, sucking it before wandering over to the neglected breast to give it equal attention. My fingers wandered into his silky hair, threading through the strands, lost in the sensation. My hips squirmed with a will of their own.

Wolf undid my zipper and eased my slacks off. He licked the length of my inner thigh and along the edge of my lacy panties. My passion fired like a rocket. I was moist in anticipation.

A heavy knock on the door jerked me out of this delicious surreal state. My eyes met Wolf's.

"What the—?" Wolf sat up equally disconcerted by the noise. "Not Marg?"

A fist hammered the door every few seconds, getting louder with each impact.

Ignoring it was impossible when Daniella shouted, "*Hola,* Wolf! Open the door! It's important!" She giggled loudly before she solidly banged the door again.

"Sounds like she's wasted, Wolf."

Wolf whispered in my ear, "I'll answer it, Adie. She's making so much noise someone is bound to call in a complaint. That's the last thing we need—to draw attention to the fact that you're here with me. We need to keep your whereabouts hidden." He kissed me sensuously before he left the room closing the door behind him. I lay there a moment, my body in shock before I realized what this meant. Springing up off the bed, I pulled the door slightly open.

I could see Wolf kicking my shoes under the couch before he unfastened the door a crack, thinking he could stall her. He was wrong. Holding a bottle by the neck, Daniella wedged herself in the door and pushed through. She sashayed her way over to the couch where she sprawled back against the cushions, and crossed her legs, revealing a great deal of thigh.

"Get some glasses, Wolf." Her eyes studied Wolf's bare chest and shoulders. She wet her mouth with the tip of her tongue. "This bottle of merlot is at the perfect temperature and it's open." Her eyes lit on the table near the fridge where several clean glasses had been set. "Those will do."

Not seeing any response she got up, took the bottle over and poured out a substantial amount into each glass before making her way back. She patted a cushion beside her, indicating where Wolf should sit and stared at him significantly. Standing at the doorway, he met her gaze, an eyebrow raised.

"Oh, come now, Wolf. I won't bite. Join me. I have important developments to discuss with you. You will be pleased by my news."

Wolf took the chair across from her, stretching out his long jean-clad legs.

Daniella shoved the glass filled with red wine into his hand before she lifted the glass to her lips. "This wine has a rich bouquet. Exactly right for this occasion."

"This couldn't wait 'til tomorrow?"

I couldn't believe this. They were meeting tomorrow and he was coming on to me, tonight?

"There are two, I repeat," she held up two fingers to make her point, "two good reasons for me to be here tonight." Daniella thrust up her chest, displaying for his viewing pleasure two semi-covered mounds, emphasized with a dark black ribbon crisscrossing under each individual breast and continuing into straps holding up the dress. "We have something to celebrate," she purred, "and I'm definitely in a party mood after what happened." She sipped her wine, eyeing him from beneath sooty black lashes.

Appraisingly, Wolf tilted his head surveying her charms, seemingly amused. I wasn't. "Not tonight, Daniella." He grabbed the shirt he had thrown on a chair earlier and put it on.

"My news may be the break you are looking for." Daniella pouted. "Surely, you're not intending to go to bed?" she murmured, her eyes flitting towards the bedroom. She grinned slyly and suggested, "But if you are, perhaps you'd like some feminine company?" She stood and perched herself on the armrest of his chair. "I know you are attracted to me, Wolf and as far as I can see, there are no other women here to distract you."

Oo-oh! I fumed. This woman was worse than yesterday's garbage.

"I'll buy you a drink, Daniella, and you can tell me what's so important." He pulled her up off the couch and got her teetering off balance in her four-inch stilettos, or she faked it, because the next second she fell conveniently into his arms.

"Ah-hh, Wolf, a fine wine, like a fine woman shouldn't be wasted." She ran her fingers down the back of his head and pressed her lips on his. From where I was, I couldn't see his response. They separated and Daniella quickly grabbed her bottle before Wolf steered her towards the door. With one arm around her, he swung the door shut behind him.

I didn't know who to be mad at, her or him. Pacing the room, I picked up the beer and downed it in a few gulps. I let out a burp as it made its way down. Beer doesn't agree with me, but I had a right to drown my sorrows when I had to put up with a maneater like Daniella. Didn't she know I was seeing Wolf? Wait a minute, here. Realization struck—she knew and didn't care.

11

A tremendous throbbing in my temples extended to the back of my head. I remembered having had another beer and then falling into a restless sleep. The printouts on my side of the bed were scattered on the floor. When did Wolf come back, or *did* he come back? His side of the bed was slightly rumpled with an indentation on his pillow. The hard copies Wolf had been examining were placed in a neat pile next to the lamp on the right of the bed. The evidence was clear enough. He'd been here, but for how long? And where was he now?

What was that pounding noise? Was it my brain? Walking into the lounge area of the suite, I stopped. Giant raindrops pelted the glass of the balcony door. This was some wicked storm the El Norte had brought in.

I reached in the fridge for a water bottle. Slumping down on the couch I took a satisfying swig before I swung my feet onto the coffee table.

That's when I noticed the small cardboard box. Propped against it was an envelope. Curiosity overcame etiquette. I ripped open the box. Inside was a Blackberry. A nice sleek super-thin cell. I powered it on and saw a text.

Adie, didn't want to wake you last night.

Yeah, right—probably afraid to.

I'm going to the east side with Daniella to see some cottages.

He was with that barracuda?

Hope you like the phone. I'll call when I get into town. Have fun with Marg. Wolf

Marg! I pressed the power button on the cell. Nine-twenty. I raced to the bathroom for a quick shower and makeup. On my way out I grabbed my umbrella and headed down the stairs to the lobby. Ten minutes to spare.

The computer room was quiet. I paid and logged on. Going directly to my mail I saw two messages.

I opened *kharkovclues@yahoo.com.*

Hey Adie. Uma was drugged with roofies, hypothermia followed by a heart attack. Ilya

That was bizarre. Roofies were date rape drugs, not a typical murder weapon. I e-mailed— *Hey Ilya. Was Uma raped? Adie.*

The next e-mail was from *borisinvest@aol.com.*

What the heck? He was shouting.

WHERE IS SHE ADIE? TELL HER TO GET HER FAT ASS BACK HERE. TELL HER TO CALL ME IMMEDIATELY OR SHE'LL BE SORRY. BORIS

Psycho! How did he know my addy anyway? He must have snooped in Marg's computer when he went over to get Libby. The rain outside matched my miserable mood.

The uneven streets and sidewalks had filled up with a flood of water. People walked barefoot, afraid to damage their leather shoes. My sandals, on the other hand, with their three-inch plastic wedges were indestructible.

When I saw the dark windows of the Rock'n Java, I was afraid the place was closed. At the front entrance freshly baked cakes and pies were displayed at the cashier's counter. Rectangular tables scattered around a large room with a counter to the side. Marg sat drinking a coffee, staring through the window at a naval ship loading crates.

"Hey, Marg! Waiting long?"

"No, just got here, Adie. Can you believe this rain?"

"Seriously intense."

"I'll say. I'm sure I ruined my sandals. Good news is they gave me coffee on the house."

A tall dark complexioned man came over. "So sorry, ladies. We have gas, but we don't want to make anything with meat or milk just to be safe."

"Chocolate croissants?"

Marg nodded and the waiter smiled, glad we had decided to stay. "Coffee for you, too, Señorita?"

"Yes, thanks."

He poured some coffee from the carafe into my cup.

I added two sweeteners. "How are you getting along with Manni's sister?"

"Oh, she's fine, but are the kids ever noisy."

"Not much privacy there."

"True. At this rate, Manni and I will never be alone."

I smirked. "It's not too late, you could check into a hotel."

Shaking her head, Marg sighed. "No money for that."

"Can't you stay with him at his place?"

Marg's eyes widened. "We're not at that stage of our relationship, Adie. Not like you and Wolf."

"Me?" I took a bite out of the chocolate croissant the waiter had set down in front of me. "These are fantastic! Don't you just love chocolate?"

"Come on, Adie! Out with it." Marg leaned in and whispered, "Isn't he a good lover?"

What could I say? His touch set me on fire, but did I want to get involved?

"Something wrong in paradise?"

"Daniella."

"What do you mean? Is she making moves on Wolf?"

"The slut practically jumped him last night."

"What!" Marg exclaimed. "But we dropped her off at her house."

"And the cat came back, the very next day. In this case she made her appearance at midnight—totally wasted."

"She was drunk?"

"Right. Wolf had to lure her down to the bar."

Marg smirked. "I'll bet that wasn't hard."

I frowned. "I would hope *it* wasn't hard."

Marg smiled, shaking her head. "Oh, Adie."

"It was a problem getting her to leave. She wanted to join him in the bedroom."

"But they didn't, did they?"

"Who knows? She could have taken him back to her house."

"Do you think he did?"

I shrugged. " She's attractive in a trashy way. I don't know." I took another bite of the croissant. "Let's get some more croissants." I no longer cared if my belly looked fat. Comfort food was needed.

"You know, I was thinking of mentioning this to you. I saw Wolf at the hospital a few months ago meeting with the CEO."

"I detect some animosity?"

"That man makes mega bucks but I don't see the hospital

improving one iota."

"But why was he with Wolf?"

"Probably making a deal. Wolf put in a bid in for constructing the new wing."

"Well that's Kitchener for you. It's not that small but people keep popping up." I sipped my coffee. "Do you think Wolf recognized you?"

"I doubt it."

"Why?"

"I'm not his type."

"That type being?"

Marg laughed. "You, hopefully, not Daniella."

I frowned. "Speaking of losers—one of my e-mails was from your husband."

"Boris?"

"You don't have any others, do you?"

Marg rolled her eyes.

"But you're not divorced yet, right?"

Marg examined her fingernails. "No. Manni's upset about that. He's getting serious ."

"And you're not?"

"Adie, it's different for me. I have Libby, pets and responsibilities."

"And, I don't? Well, aside from not having a child?"

"Yes, okay. I admit you are not completely footloose and fancy-free. But your life took a different turn when you stayed single."

"Well, I don't just want a fling anymore, either. I'd like a serious relationship."

"You want to get married?"

"Maybe, I don't know."

Marg had finished her second croissant and signaled for the waiter to bring the check. "Are we shopping? It's still raining but not as bad."

Taking out my credit card, I paid the bill, adding a tip for the waiter. "It's on me today, Marg."

"Oh, thanks." She sipped her coffee. "If it's any consolation to you, I like him. I think he cares about you."

"You do?"

Marg nodded.

"What worries me is…"

"What?"

"You. Marg, we've got someone after us and you look the same as you did when you got here."

"What do you mean? I look the same as ever—perfectly fine."

I nodded. "Yes, you do, but seriously, Marg, it's not a good thing. We don't want the shooter to recognize you."

"What are you saying, Adie?"

Marg had her back up. I could tell with that eyelid tic. "Listen to me. It has to be done. I'm taking you to the hairdresser."

* **

After a couple of hours with Alejandro, Marg was ready. Auburn waves cascaded to Marg's shoulders, angling around her face showing off her cheekbones. With a fresh makeup application, her face glowed. Marg had been transformed from a blah married professional to a hot single babe.

"You look fantastic!" I gave her a hug as Teresa cleaned up.

"Thank you." Marg beamed like a pop star on stage.

"I'll pay for it, girlfriend. It'll be your early Christmas present from me."

Marg shook her head. "No, Adie, it's too much."

"I insist." I grabbed the bill. Amazing how the bright color livened up Marg's sallow complexion.

Teresa waved good-bye as we left. Heavy gray clouds covered the dull blue sky as we started out down Rosada Salas, the shoe store street. If I didn't find any red shoes there, I'd try the Chedraui Plaza across from the hotel. Marg wasn't too interested in fashionable shoes. She liked those practical specialty shoes that come in the extra wide width, like Rockford or Reich. I'm a fashionista, but the leather has to be soft where it touches my feet.

Marg tapped my arm. "What did you find out?"

"Well there's lots of money being transferred back and forth."

"How so?"

I picked up a red sandal. Nice, but it was way too flat. I'd feel like a midget beside Wolf. "Half a million last month to Alvarez from Reich and seven hundred thousand from Uma."

"And there would have been more throughout this year."

"How much, do you know?" I picked up a fuchsia sandal from the rack with a wide stretch material across the front and a two-inch heel. Comfy, but too clunky.

Marg pursed her lips as she probed a brown sandal. "Every month for a year, he's sent money down, until he decided Alvarez was into something illegal."

"How did he know this?"

"He didn't," Marg said. "He was suffering from paranoia but I can tell you one thing—Uma got him into this big-time."

"Oh? Did they still have a relationship?"

"Tim had stopped sleeping with her after…"

"After he met you? Were you having an affair?"

Marg picked up a black sandal and angled it in front of her.

"Marg?"

"Uma went from one wealthy man to the next. Sex appeal, Adie. The men were attracted to her. Who knows why."

"Did Reich own all the shoe factories?"

"His family business."

"He must have been filthy rich."

"True, and he was generous."

I placed the red sandal back on the rack. "You see anything you like?"

"This one." She pointed to the low black leather sandal.

Seeing her gesturing at the shoe, a petite brunette scurried over to ask if she would like to try them on. Marg nodded.

"I will bring a few." The girl said, running out to the back.

Marg perched herself on one of the vinyl chairs, tapping her fingers nervously on the metal arm rest.

"Was Uma's family well off?"

"I think so but she also had a divorce settlement from Tim." Marg tried on a pair black sandals that the lady handed her. She pranced around, pausing at the mirror.

"The suit she had on for Reich's funeral was to die for."

"Yes, indeed." Marg pursed her lips. "And I guess she got hers." Head bent down, hair covering her face, Marg scrutinized the black sandals.

"That's kind of spiteful isn't it?"

"Well, just because she got murdered doesn't promote her to

sainthood. She made Tim's life hell, always asking for things." She pulled off the sandal, adding, "And he gave her jewelry, even though they were divorced."

Remembering her sharp claws embedded in my skin, I revised my opinion. "Can't say I liked her."

"Just that idiot, Jaqui did." Seeing my puzzled expression, she went on, "the English secretary at the hospital. Didn't I tell you about her?"

"Er, no." I didn't want to get into how I still had her file.

Marg nodded to the saleslady. "I'll take these."

After the saleslady rang in the sandals and boxed them we continued our search further up Rosada Salas, but with no success.

By the time we got to the main plaza, the sun had filtered through the clouds and the rain on the sidewalks evaporated rapidly into a steamy haze. As we entered the outside pedestrian mall, more vendors appeared, selling anything from airbrush paintings to hemp chokers.

"Did you look at all the papers?" Marg asked, as we entered a pottery shop stocked with blue and red Mayan designs.

"Sorry, we didn't get too far last night, what with Daniella coming and all."

"She's something isn't she?"

"Something doesn't describe that barracuda."

Marg chuckled. "Well when you go home, you'll have him all to yourself, won't you?

I hadn't thought about that. "I guess it all depends on whether he finds what he wants. He might stay here." I winced, thinking what chance was there for me then, with Daniella here and eager to get her hooks into Wolf?

In the next store, seashells, octopi and flowers, tie-dyed on orange and aqua paraeos dressed the window mannequins. If one of my bikinis matched I could...

"And what is it he wants?" Marg broke into my thoughts. "Wolf?"

Marg giggled. "Have you got some one else?"

"Hardly had time for that, did I? Well, let's see—property to renovate or to invest in."

"What's Wolf's financial status?"

"From what he's said, he's doing all right. But his company

could be in debt for all I know." I took the orange one off the peg and wrapped it around me and slung it low on my hips before I knotted it.

"What do you think, Marg?"

"Do you have a bathing suit to match?"

"I've got an aqua bikini."

"I like the octopi."

"Me, too." I handed the saleslady the money.

Checking her watch, Marg said, "Adie, I've got to go. Manni's sister wants me to help her with some curtains."

"No problem. What time is it?"

"Nearly two. And Adie, could you take a look at those other papers? I keep thinking something in there might help me."

"Sure. But you realize there's a lot there."

"Really, oh..."

I hugged her. "Don't worry, I'll look."

Giving me a last brave smile, she trotted down Calle 2 towards 25 Avenida. I wasn't too worried now that she had a makeover. Besides, Manni's sister, Anita, lived only a few blocks away.

Here it was almost Christmas, I chided myself, and I hadn't looked for a gift for Wolf. I saw a shop with onyx chess sets in pale pinks and greens, but I didn't know if Wolf played chess. Another store had silver jewelry. I admired the shiny chains but maybe he wasn't a chain sort of guy. I was beginning to wonder if I really did know him.

With vendors hassling me every few seconds, I was ready to give up my search but when I saw Ricardo's stall I stopped.

"Hola, Señorita!" He smiled broadly. "You are back. Perhaps to get a ring?"

"I'd like to get a silver bracelet for my friend. You remember him?"

"*Si.*" He waved at the silver bracelets looped over a bar.

"These are all for a man—some have a very heavy silver." He picked up a thick chain. "This would look good."

"How do I know what length would be right?"

"His wrist would not be bigger than mine, would it?" Holding out his thick wrist, he fastened the bracelet and displayed the design. "Sixty dollars is a good price for this silver."

I pictured Wolf's tanned wrist. It would look great with his skin. I hoped he would wear it. Then again, maybe we had already broken up. Daniella would have had all day to hook up with him if she hadn't already. After last night with me, I couldn't believe he'd go for her, but I'd been wrong before. I ruffled my hair contemplatively. I could always give it to some future boyfriend. Turning to Ricardo, I said, "A good price for you is not a good price for me."

Ricardo stoically folded his arms. "Forty-five and we have a deal."

I opened my purse and took out thirty-five dollars, waving the bills in the air. He grabbed the money but I held on tightly.

Flicking the bills gingerly with one finger, he protested, "But this is thirty-five dollars!"

I nodded.

He sighed resignedly, placed the bracelet into a plastic bag, and gave it to me. "Amiga, come back, okay?"

I smiled and waved before I turned away to walk to the main plaza.

It was mid-afternoon and I was getting hungry. In the square, a gigantic Christmas tree was elaborately decorated with garlands, lights and ornaments. Waiters stood at the entrance of each café beckoning the passing tourists to choose their restaurant, offering them a menu to peruse. A friendly rotund waiter with a big smile handed me a menu from Lorita's.

"Adie," an attractive brunette called out from a corner table, "come join us!" From the patio Sandy and Joe waved me over.

"Hey," I returned, pulling up a chair. "No classes today?"

"Not 'til tonight." Joe took a deep swallow of his Corona beer. "Good stuff, this Mexican beer—" He suppressed a burp and slugged down some more.

Sandy explained. "We're having a late lunch. Steve went to workout at the fitness center."

"Did you order yet?"

"Just beer."

After last night, beer was the last thing I wanted. When the waiter came by, giving me a menu, I waved it away and ordered lemonade and soup. Joe and Sandy placed their orders while another server brought chips and salsa to our table.

When the waiter returned to the table with my drink, I caught

Joe's curious look.

"I drank too much beer last night."

He laughed. "I wouldn't have pictured you as a beer drinker."

"I'm not, that's the problem."

Sandy joined in. "I'd rather drink daiquiris myself, but when you live here you pinch your pennies and beer is cheaper."

"Must be great to live here, though." A glimmer of sunlight shone through the white web of clouds. "I think it's clearing up."

Sandy shrugged. "Don't count on it. The El Norte usually stays for three days."

"Too bad. I really wanted to do some more snorkeling."

"You could try the other side of the island. It's usually clear if this side has the El Norte."

"Where would you recommend, Sandy?"

"Chien Rio—if the water's blue."

Joe hiccupped and gulped his hot tortilla soup down too quickly. He took a compensatory swig to cool off his throat. A tire was building up around his middle and noticing his liking for beer, I could now understand why. "What do you mean blue? Isn't it always blue?"

Joe guffawed loudly. "That place gets yella water some days."

I ran my fingers through my hair. "You serious?"

They nodded.

"Yuck." Pollution crept in, even in this perfect piece of paradise.

The crowd in the park was getting noisy. "What's happening?"

"Band in the square today, I guess." Sandy turned to watch the gathering crowd. The tables at the café were filling up as more tourists arrived to listen to the music.

Two men sat down at table close to the entrance. I recognized the stocky fellow in shorts and Hawaiian shirt. It was Don from the other night. His friend pulled out a map from his attaché case and spread it out. I peered over to get a better view, but he was sitting away from me and I couldn't see his face. My companions fell silent as I stared at Don and his friend.

Sandy nudged me. "You know those two?"

"The guy with the Hawaiian shirt. His name's Don."

"The fashion police would arrest him. Oops, he's not your

boyfriend, is he?"

"No, I met him when I first came here. A lot has happened since then."

"You mean that mugger that attacked your friend? Steve told me about that."

"Ye-a-h…awesome," Joe said.

"Right." I rolled my eyes. "It all got worse the next day. We were on the north end of the island when a guy on a boat started shooting at us. Then, when I came back to my hotel room a creep attacked me with a knife."

"You okay?" Sandy asked, concerned.

"Um-m." I shuddered, thinking back.

Joe's eyes shot up from his beer. "What defense moves did you make?"

"Kicked him in the groin and poked his eyes, but that didn't do it. I had to bite him."

"Sweet!"

"Not for me. It was bad enough being shot at, I didn't need this creep trying to rape me."

"Omigod!" Sandy gasped. "He didn't?"

"No, luckily my friend came and he ran out."

"They know where you're stayin' now?" Joe asked in concern.

"No, I moved."

"Are you with a guy, Adie?" Joe persisted. "I don't want to be nosy or anything, but I would think…"

"You are *so* sexist, Joe. Isn't he, Adie?"

"I'm staying with a male friend, but personally, I don't think any living breathing man could have stopped this guy."

"Take a look at my ankle." I showed them the greenish-purple swelling on my ankle. "That's where he grabbed me."

Sandy glanced down. "Omigod!"

"See the scratches on the back of my arm?" I showed them the raw marks.

Joe patted my shoulder. "All signs to be proud of."

"I guess." I trailed off, thinking pride before the fall. In my case, it was only the fall. When the waiter came over, I paid him. "It was nice seeing you two again. Would you excuse me? I'd like to say hi to Don."

Sandy winked. "Take care, girlfriend."

Joe gazed at me sternly. "Pay attention to details. Be aware."

I nodded. He was a black belt—knew more than a brown belt in-training. Anyone could be gunning for me. I had to be alert.

For a second I surveyed the crowd. Tourists and locals were waiting for the band to start. In the park kids played tag, squealing and running in between adults. It was getting noisy.

"Adie!" Don called out from his table. When I walked over he jumped up and wrapped his arms around me in a big teddy bear hug—comforting and warm.

Sitting back from the table, his legs outstretched, Don's companion flicked his hazel eyes up. Black wavy hair, a lean face, full lips—drop dead sexy! Inclining his head towards me, he stood and waited for an introduction.

"Adie, let me introduce you to Diego."

"Santiago Francisco Bolivar Alvarez," rolled melodically off his lips before he caught up my hand, and lightly kissed my wrist. He smiled slightly and said, "Diego, to my friends."

This was Santiago Alvarez? I froze, momentarily stunned as Diego folded up the map and tossed it in his attaché case.

Don nodded admiringly. "Gee, I've got to learn how to do that kiss-the-wrist thing."

Diego pulled out a chair for me as I said, "Adie Sturm." I watched his face for a reaction.

He studied me for a moment. "Adie? Is it a nickname?"

"Yes, short for Adelina."

"Lovely. And Sturm means storm, does it not?" His brandy eyes watched me curiously. "Are you?"

"What?"

"A temperamental woman?"

"Sometimes."

His eyes crinkled at the corners. "Intriguing."

Don coughed politely. "Diego, this lady is taken—"

"Women aren't possessions, Don. They can only be taken if they wish it."

"Whoa! That's deep."

"Would you like something to drink, Adelina?" Signaling the server, Diego's square gold pinky ring with a black insignia flashed in the light. "A margarita, perhaps?"

"Thank you, but—"

"Come now, Adelina," Diego said, as the server stood waiting, "it's an afternoon of celebration here at the square."

"All right, thank you, but no salt, please."

Don picked up his beer. "I met Adie a couple of days ago,"

"I suppose it's common for people to meet up again in a small place like Cozumel." I glanced at Diego. Odd that he didn't recognize my name—especially if he sent the hit men.

"So, true," Don admitted distractedly, his attention riveted on a table at the rear of the restaurant. "Wow! Speak of coincidence. Those ladies—I met them at the disco last night. "You two wouldn't mind if I went over, would you?"

Not waiting for a reply, Don made his way over, greeting the freckled redhead and bouncy brunette with kisses. Whatever he said got them laughing. My guess was—he wouldn't be back.

"So kind of Don to leave us alone, wasn't it?" Diego set his beer down. "Jolly type."

"Yes, he seems nice if a bit—"

"Spacy."

I grinned. "But likeable."

"Let's not talk about him, Adelina. Are you here for long?"

"About a week."

"Hopefully we can become better acquainted during your visit."

I smiled slightly not sure what to say.

The waiter brought over my margarita in a large goblet. I stirred it and took a sip. "What do you do here, Diego?" My aim was to draw him out, find out if he had murder on his mind—specifically me.

"I have a firm called Royal Investments. Is your margarita to your liking?"

I nodded. "Excellent, thanks."

Diego leaned back in his chair and regarded me. "Are you interested in Cozumel investments?"

"Maybe, someday. I love the island."

"I have come to love it, too."

"You're not from here then?"

"No. My family is from Madrid originally. They settled in Mexico City twenty years ago. My parents still live there."

"What brought you here?"

116

"Sun, sea and a slow pace." Diego smiled. "How have you been passing your time?"

"Snorkeling, shopping—"

"Not sightseeing?"

"I am planning on seeing San Gervasio soon—with a friend." I took my sunglasses off and wiped a smudge off with my napkin.

"A female friend?"

"Um-mm."

Diego's eyes searched mine, but didn't follow up his question. "Has Don invested with you at Royal?"

"That is rather confidential. Are you always this inquisitive?"

"Sorry, I didn't mean to pry."

"Pardon me. I was unnecessarily rude. What about you? What do you do, Adelina?"

"I'm a travel guide and consultant. I take people on tours."

"Are you with a tour group right now?"

"No, this is a vacation, but I'm always researching, finding out things that would interest my clients."

I glanced over at Don, hugging both women close. The redhead shrieked exuberantly, "We're going with you, Don! We can share the wealth!" She kissed him hotly on the lips, where upon the brunette laughed boisterously.

Diego frowned, regarding Don and his companions before he turned his attention back to me. "Would your clients be interested in investment opportunities?"

"Some might."

On the podium, the band started up. Some of the crowd dispersed to sit, while others got up to dance. Diego moved his chair closer to mine to continue our conversation. Discretely, I peeked at Don and his lady friends from behind my goblet. One of them was sitting on his lap and the other was chugging back beer. Every once in a while we'd hear a hoot or a snort from their table. Indignant looks from the other patrons flew in their direction.

Above us the sky darkened. An awning covered our table, so I wasn't too concerned when the rain started. A cool breeze picked up and blew a strand of hair into my face. I was about to brush it away when I felt Diego's hand on my cheek, pushing my hair back.

"Your hair is very attractive." His fingertips rested on my arm, as his eyes met mine.

"Are you always this forward?"

Diego smiled and withdrew his fingers. "My turn to apologize. Sorry, Adelina. You haven't told me where you're from."

"I'm Canadian. I live close to Toronto. Do you know where that is?"

"Yes, I've been to Toronto and Montreal. Canada's picturesque, but somewhat cold in winter."

I lifted my glass and sipped the cool liquid. "I'd agree to that."

"With your sort of job, you must have traveled extensively." He leaned over to speak in my ear, his hand touching my shoulder lightly as the band picked up the tempo.

"Yes, the Caribbean and Europe." I had to get close to answer. I placed my hand at the back of his chair.

Seeing my difficulty, Diego drew his chair right up to mine and swung his legs away. "Have you been to Spain?"

I nodded. "I spent a month there."

Lowering his dark lashes, his eyes dropped to the edge of my lacy top. Diego's nearness made me shiver. I felt a strange undercurrent with him beside me. My hormones kicked in. This was nuts. For all I knew he was plotting right now to have me killed. Surveying the restaurant for his bodyguards, I sighted a slight fellow with a scarred face and a moustache sitting on his own, on the other side of the patio, inside Loritas.

I scanned the table next to Don. Was I seeing double? My margarita must be powerful. Two massive males sat silently staring in our direction—men that rivaled the biker from last night, and won hands down when it came to ugliness and bulk. They looked amazingly similar.

A gust of cool breeze disturbed the serviettes.

"You're cold." Diego glanced at the goosebumps on my arms. "I would put my arm around you, but I know that would be too forward for you."

"Yes, it would." I crossed my arms over my chest and rubbed my arms. "It will get warmer."

Diego glanced down at my legs. "That's something I wish all ladies would do."

"What do you mean?"

"Wear shorts. They like tight clothing here but you never see them in shorts. Mind you, some of them I wouldn't want to, but in your case, your legs are perfect. They should be shown off for a man to admire."

"Thank you, I guess."

Diego lightly stroked my forearm, sending a tingle down my body. "You're not accustomed to compliments, are you? Canadian men don't know how to appreciate a lovely woman. You deserve to be showered with adoration."

Skepticism must have been evident on my face because he smiled and shrugged. "Adelina, it's a cultural thing. I'm Spanish and we've been taught to place our women on pedestals. But, I wouldn't say this to any woman. I prefer intelligent blondes, like you."

"Intelligent?" I smiled. "How can you tell?"

"Your eyes sparkle."

A low vibration droned, followed by a high-pitched ring. What was that? Then it dawned on me. My new cell. I zipped open my purse and dug around for the phone. "Excuse me a moment, Diego? I've been expecting this call."

Diego nodded, as I said, "Hello."

"Adie, I'll be back in half an hour. Meet me at the bar?"

"Sure, see you." I ended the call and picked up my purse and packages.

"You look like you're getting ready to leave." Pulling his wallet out, he took a business card and gave it to me. "I'm having a luncheon for a few friends on my boat tomorrow. Could you come?"

"When?"

"Around noon."

"Well, I'm not sure what my plans are."

"My phone number is on the card. Call me and I'll send my driver around to bring you to the marina."

"What should I wear?"

"It's casual, but we're not leaving the harbor, so nothing too practical."

I smiled. "You mean leave my sneakers at my hotel along with my T-shirt and shorts?"

"You are astute, Adelina."

"Who's coming for lunch, Diego?"

"Don, my sister, maybe my former assistant. Don't worry." He seemed amused. "You won't be alone with me, if that's your concern."

I gathered up my umbrella and stood up. "Thank you for the drink."

Diego got to his feet and inclined his head politely, "I hope you will come tomorrow. I've enjoyed your company." Swivelling around to an old lady selling roses, he beckoned for her to approach. "Wait, a moment, Adelina." He tossed her a fiver, selected a red rose, and gave it to me with a flourish.

I handled the rose carefully, aware of the thorns on the stem, and placed it gently in my bag on top of my purchases. "It's lovely—so sweet of you, Diego. Maybe I will come." I caught the attention of Sandy and Joe and mouthed a good-bye. They waved back and I turned away to join the pedestrians on the cobblestone walkway. Glancing back at Diego, I saw him watching me as I merged into the crowd.

On the main harbor front street, Raphael Melgar, I bypassed silver shops, gift shops and t-shirt shops. Just west of the square, the road was blocked with construction machinery. The work crew must have left when the rain started.

The street was still full of muddy puddles where they had removed the pavement. Now, a half hour later, the sun lay low on the horizon, peeking out from behind fluffy clouds. I figured it would be faster to walk through the area to get to my hotel, albeit dirtier.

It was quiet. No traffic. A park was off to my left and a large hotel being renovated was situated across the street. Feeling bewildered by my encounter with Diego Bolivar Alvarez, my surroundings became a haze, and I, a sleepwalker. Diego was a paradox to me—charming, handsome and yet so amoral.

As I walked towards my hotel, avoiding mud puddles, I became aware of how alone I was. The sky was dark even though it was only late afternoon. Footsteps, barely audible, prompted me to glance involuntarily over my shoulder. I nearly froze in mid-stride but forced myself to continue when I saw the lanky man with the pencil thin moustache following—one of those men from Loritas. Had Diego sent him?

Further ahead, but too far away to be of any help, I saw a

couple holding hands, too aware of each other to notice me. From the corner of my eye, I watched the man. I picked up the pace but he was right there, maintaining the same distance between us.

Through the rubble of broken cement pieces and wood planks, I edged over to the other side of the street where an old fellow stood under an awning. I shot a glance over my shoulder. The tail was not far behind. I had to lose him. A pickup truck loaded with wooden planks was parked in the middle of the road. I sped around it. The uneven gravel was slippery. As I swiveled to look around, my heel twisted. A sharp pain shot through my banged up ankle. I paused a moment to breathe through the throbbing.

The old man smoking a cigarette studied me, inhaling deeply. I peered around the side of the rusty truck scanning the street. A mosquito landed on my forehead. Impatiently, my hand brushed it away. If I stepped out, he'd come after me, on the other hand, he might try to corner me behind the truck.

Just past the truck, my attention centered on two young men in their early twenties, leaning against a wall engrossed in conversation.

"Hola!" I yelled out desperately.

The more handsome of the two men, black hair curling over his ears, tilted his head and commented to his buddy. "Nice legs!" Then he called out, "Hey blondie, what's happening?"

I had to work it. I stepped out, telling myself to forget my pain, slid my hips into motion, and sauntered up to them. The first guy tilted his head and flashed a smile, his eyes running down the contours of my body. His body-builder friend, straight hair tied back in a ponytail stared in a macho Latin way.

"You alone, *mamasita*?" the first guy asked.

I checked across the street and spotted my stalker. "*Si.*"

"Speak Spanish?"

"A little."

He picked up my hand in his and rubbed my palm suggestively. "My name is Angel. We go for happy hour, but later I take you dancing, *si*?"

I had to remind myself that Latin women expect come-ons a few times a day, or so I'd read. It probably didn't help having these short shorts on either. I glanced at the guys—jeans, Nikes, designer t-shirts and gold bracelets. Vacationing Mexicans from Mexico

City, I'd bet.

I withdrew my hand. "Nice to meet you. I'm Adie." I smiled coyly. "How about we go to my hotel? It's happy hour there. I'm buying."

Angel laughed and said, "It is a change for a chica to buy the drinks," he shrugged his shoulders, "but why not?" His eyes shot across the street and yelled out, "*Cabron,* she's with me." The thin guy slunk back under the hotel awning.

From down the road, we heard a fierce roar. Startled, we swiveled around to see a mighty hippo of a man charging up the road as fast as his powerful legs could carry him, through rubble and around construction equipment, in the direction of the tail. The goon from across the street decided this was not his day. He raced into the alleyway between a shop and the Hotel Triste, disappearing out of sight.

Huffing loudly, Joe changed direction and ran up to us. He wiped his forehead with his hand and asked, "You okay?" just as Sandy rushed up after him.

"Where'd the guy go?" Her gaze flit down the street.

"Took off down there." I pointed to the laneway between the buildings on the opposite side of the street. "Thanks for coming after me, Joe, but I'm fine."

"No problem," Joe said gruffly. "I thought you might need rescuing, but," he went on, glancing at Angel glowering, "looks like you already got yourself some body guards." He frowned, eying the alley.

Sandy patted his arm. "It's too late." She grinned at me. "Joe's mad. Missed his afternoon bag workout and now this. Bad break, Joe."

* * *

It was happy hour and the bar was hopping. It was two for one and everyone and his cousin was there to party. Joe picked up a piece of shrimp. "Spoils for the victors, eh?" He tilted his back and tossed it down.

The bartender stood waiting for our drink order.

"I'm buying, Joe." I took a seat. "What would you like?"

"Thanks, Adie. Corona sounds good."

I lifted a brow at Sandy.

"Corona. You must have been scared."

I nodded. "It's been unreal these last few days. But how did you know to follow me?"

Joe chug-a-lugged his beer and burped loudly. "Just being totally aware, Adie. I saw him watching you. When you got up to leave he was in a mucho big hurry." He munched on a crab cake. gazing over to the opposite side of the round bar where my escorts sat having drinks on me. "But, hey, you outsmarted him."

I laid my package on the bar top and ordered a margarita, no salt. "Lucky for me, Angel and his friend were heading this way." I turned to Sandy. "Why don't you have the other margarita?"

The bartender shook up a green blend in record time and set two goblets in front of us.

"Sure, beats beer. You get sick of that stuff—" She stared in the direction of the entrance. "Wow!" She nudged me. "Look at that hottie!"

Wolf stood at the doorway, checking the room.

Sandy whispered breathlessly, "He's looking at you, Adie."

Blond hair ruffled up in a seriously sexy way, Wolf approached us. His eyes searched my face for an indication of my mood.

I indicated my companions. "Sandy—Joe, my friend, Wolf."

Reaching out, he shook hands first with Sandy and then did a guy hand-shake with Joe.

Handing Wolf the second beer sitting on the counter, Joe said, "Adie sure had us going today."

"Yeah?"

"One mean dude followed her."

Wolf paused in mid sip, set the beer back down and turned to me taking up my hands. "You okay?"

"Joe scared him off."

"Adie didn't need us." Joe grinned. "Got herself a Mexican escort service."

Wolf lifted an eyebrow inquiringly.

Sandy flicked her finger to the far end of the bar where Angel and his friend sat drinking beer. "She found those two goin' to a bar and joined them," she said, snapping her fingers, "just like that."

Angel lifted his beer and smiled.

I returned his smile.

Wolf's lips formed a straight line. "Adie has numerous talents." He brought the beer to his lips and drank deeply. "Am I correct in assuming you two are martial artists?

"Sandy's boyfriend, Steve, and I own the dojo." Joe said.

"Who do you think sent this guy?"

Joe shrugged. "This dude was sittin' at Lorita's watchin' her. Got up when she left and tailed her."

"You were with Sandy and Joe?"

"Earlier. Before I left, I was with Don and Diego."

"Diego?"

"Alvarez."

"Why were you with him?"

"Curiosity."

"Yeah? Well curiosity killed the cat and I don't want that happening to you."

"Well I was probably safer with him than you were with Daniella."

Sandy smirked when she heard this exchange. She nudged Joe. "Time to go, Joe. Steve will be wondering where we are." She faced us. "Nice meeting you, Wolf. Be careful, Adie."

I nodded.

Guzzling the last bit of beer, Joe set down the bottle and shook hands with Wolf. "Take care of her, man."

12

While Wolf was in the shower scrubbing off Daniella germs, I was getting ready for battle, making sure I was hotter than the competition. He was waiting on the couch reading one of the printouts and sipping a beer but knew enough to stop and look up.

His gaze trailed down the length of my clingy indigo dress to my strappy high-heeled sandals. "When you're angry your eyes get turquoise. Very sexy."

"When you lie your nose grows longer."

Wolf grinned. "Hey, you're not dealing with a wooden puppet here, Adie."

"No? You bounce around like one."

"All that will be explained."

"Well?"

"Patience—relax, Adie." Wolf took my hand and led me to the the elevator. On the way we bypassed a young couple. They held each other tightly, secure in their love. No shattered dreams—yet.

We walked out the side entrance to the parking lot. It was a balmy evening, only a slight breeze lifting my hair from its perfect hair-sprayed shape as Wolf eased the car onto the road. Of course my hair would only look like this for an hour max before it hung limp as overdone spaghetti.

Wolf observed me from the corner of his eye. "Feeling any better?"

"About you? We'll see, after I hear your story."

Wolf kept his eyes on the road. "It's more important to talk about what happened to you, Adie."

Off Avenue Benito Juarez, he found a parking spot. Coming around to the passenger side of the Jeep, he opened the door to help me out. Jeeps are high off the ground and stepping out with heels is extremely difficult. It also takes some manoeuvring to get out without having the dress ride up to my waist. I only somewhat succeeded with that, as Wolf swiftly lifted me out and set me down.

Wolf's eyes trailed down my legs as I steadied myself. His arm was hard and powerful. My heart beat faster. Stopping just short of the entrance to the restaurant, I sighed.

"We're almost there, Adie. Hold on. We'll get you fed in no time."

I arched an eyebrow. "What do you think I am, your pet?"

"Only if I get to stroke you." He gazed at me intensely. "I could really make you purr." His lips lowered to mine in a kiss that made me forget my anger.

Suddenly withdrawing his mouth, Wolf took a step backwards. "There, that's better." He peered into my eyes. "Back to Caribbean blue."

Before I could complain, he placed his hand at the small of my back, guiding me to the Maître d's stand of the Mission Restaurant.

"*Buenas noches,* Señor. Two?"

"Yes. Somewhere private, *por favor.*"

A roof covered the tables, but instead of windows, it was open framed with beams. We were led to a small table by a tiny bridge crossing a miniature brook.

When the server came I ordered lemonade. I wanted a clear mind and an explanation. "Tell me what happened after you took Daniella to the bar?"

"Not much. She had a margarita and got sloshed."

"You mean more drunk than she already was?" I leaned back in my chair. "And then?"

"Took her home."

"And that was it?"

"Yeah. Came back. Read a Royal Investment document." When I arched a brow he added, "You were already sleeping."

"And?"

"I covered you up. Looked like you were having a nightmare. You yelled out something."

"She didn't ask you to stay?"

Wolf grinned.

"Okay. Spill!"

"Maybe you don't want to hear this."

"She took her clothes off, didn't she?"

Wolf nodded.

"Everything?"

"Her dress."

"Let me guess—she didn't have anything on when she took it off."

"Just her shoes."

"It must have been incredibly hard to leave after that."

Wolf smirked at my pun. "Well, I told her we needed to get an early start, so seeing the dollar signs, she put on a robe and said adios."

"She probably slobbered all over you first, didn't she?"

Wolf gazed at the ceiling.

"It's a good thing you had a shower." I frowned. "So, what happened today?"

"She was all business." Wolf patted my hand. "Don't worry, Adie. I didn't let her have me. I'm saving myself for you."

At that point the waiter arrived with our food. When we were alone, I asked, "How was the east side?"

"Beautiful. We saw some abandoned cottages somewhere between Chien Rio and Bonita Beach."

"And?"

"The place would be a pain to renovate and run."

"How so?"

"No electricity and too far away to bring in a construction crew—too costly."

"How was it for snorkeling?"

"Waves are too high, but we could try around here before you leave."

That was another thing that was bugging me. Marg had reminded me that my hot roommate might be staying, and I'd be leaving him in the clutches of that barracuda, Daniella. I knew I shouldn't become attached— after all, he hadn't told me he cared. With his failed marriage, he might not want anything but a vacation fling. In my inner turmoil, I started to pick off a dry flake of skin on my lip.

I was jolted out of mutilating my lipstick as Wolf picked my hand off. "Don't ruin those sexy lips. Not that I blame you. You must be stressed—you've had a helluva day." He stroked my hand gently. "Something you should know. Alvarez has an account in the Caymans."

"Bank statement?"

Wolf nodded. "Among other things. Transfers to that account from the US and Canada."

"We really should look those over some more."

"Yup. And I phoned Hernandez and told him what happened. He said he'd be dropping by tonight to talk to you."

I sighed. "For all the good that will do."

"You mean because Alvarez has clout here?"

"I'm not so sure he's the one behind all this."

"What makes you say that?"

"Well, when I introduced myself, he didn't even blink. Absolutely no reaction."

"What kind of reaction did you think he should have?"

I rolled my eyes. "Get serious. If he's sending killers after me, wouldn't he know my name?"

"Maybe not." He shrugged. "He knows Marg and wants her gone. He has thugs that handle everything."

"I guess." I dipped a piece of lobster into the heated butter. "Oo-hh, this is *so* good."

"I knew you'd feel better with some food." His lips twitched. "A woman that likes to eat likes to..."

"What?"

"Nothing."

I gazed at Wolf. "It makes me so mad."

"What?"

"That skinny stalker. What gives him the right to harass me that way? I would have loved to have kicked him good—right in the balls."

"That would ruin his sex life."

"That type doesn't deserve to reproduce."

"You see Alvarez interact with this guy?"

"No, the creep was at Lorita's, but Diego wasn't looking at him."

"Let me guess. He was strictly focusing on you."

I grinned. "Except when Don started making a spectacle of himself."

"Don?"

"He saw these women from the disco and took off to sit with them. They were drinking beer like it was soda pop."

"Don likes to party. Why'd this bother Alvarez?"

"I don't think it was the drinking as much as it was Don shooting off his mouth."

"About?"

"Money. Apparently he's getting loads."

"Don must have invested with Alvarez."

"I asked Diego that, but he refused to answer me and said..."

"It was none of your business."

"FYI, Wolfster, except for that issue, we got along stupendously."

"You and Diego," Wolf said dryly.

"Yes, honey. We do." I had almost finished picking away at my veggies when I realized something. "What's Don's last name?"

"Carrera, why?"

"What if his name is in Alvarez's records? Couldn't he be behind the attacks?"

"Adie, there must be dozens of investors with Royal. They can't all be involved. Let's not go the conspiracy theory route." Wolf signed the check and stood up. "Come on. We've got things to do."

* * * *

The moon sparkled on the whitecaps drifting onto the shadowy shore. Wolf slid his arm around my shoulders and pulled me close. The investigation was a mess but my instincts told me I was getting closer to finding the murderer.

"You're cold. Why don't we go in."

"And look at those printouts?"

"They might have some answers."

As he gathered up the papers, I pulled my feet up under the skirt of my dress and rested against the pillows on the couch.

Earlier, I had placed the rose in a beer bottle and set it on the coffee table. The red petals had opened, as if waiting to be kissed. A soft spicy scent lingered in the air. It was easy to see why a rose could be such a powerful symbol of love.

Wolf caught me gazing at the rose. "You didn't tell him where you were staying, did you?"

"No. I'm not stupid."

"But you can be tricked."

"Just because he gave me a rose doesn't mean anything."

"It meant something to him. It's like bait when you go fishing."

"So, with one rose, he thinks he can pull me in?"

Wolf nodded. "But he doesn't know you like I do."

He set the paperwork on the coffee table and sat down beside me.

"And you think I need more?"

"Yeah, jewelry."

I nodded.

"Massage."

"Um-hum."

"Seafood and exotic drinks."

"Um."

"And..." his hands pushed the narrow straps of my dress down, "this." When he kissed my shoulder, a shock of electricity tore through my body. My head fell back on the pillow. His mouth torched my throat.

I wanted this man. Reaching back, I stroked his silky shirt feeling the firm back muscles underneath. His skin was warm and smelled of the ocean and soap. I closed my eyes and gripped the firm curve of his butt. As I stretched my legs, I brushed against him. The pain was intense. I cried out.

"Adie! What's wrong?"

Bringing my foot up, I touched my ankle. It was blue and puffy.

"Why didn't you tell me your ankle was swollen?"

"I twisted it walking in the construction area today. I didn't think it was so bad."

"You need ice." Wolf strode over to the fridge and checked inside. "I'll be right back. Don't move." He grabbed the bucket and closed the door behind him.

The buzz of the phone startled me.

Should I answer? What if it was Daniella tightening her lasso?

"Hello," I said hesitantly.

"Oh, hi, Adie. Are you as tired as I am?"

"Marg, am I glad to hear from you."

"Why, what happened? Did Daniella sleep with him? You poor thing! Did you break up?"

"She asked him to, but he left."

"Or so he says."

"True, he could be lying."

"They all lie, Adie."

"You're just cynical, coming from that horrible relationship with Boris. Have you heard from him by the way?"

"I phoned but he was so offensive. I told him I'd be back in a few days and hung up."

"How are things with Manni? What does he think about you leaving?"

"He wants me to stay. He's worried about Boris's temper."

"You two are pretty tight, aren't you?"

"Yes, but we've got a problem."

"Oh?"

"His sister, Anita wants me to convert."

"To what?"

"Catholicism."

"And you don't want to."

There was a pause. "I don't know—what's going on, Adie? You don't sound yourself. It's not just Daniella—did something else happen?"

"It's quite a story. After you left I saw some karate pals, Sandy and Joe. You met Joe. Anyway, I was telling them about the biker when I noticed Don sitting at another table with this sexy guy."

"Sexy? Who was he?"

"Think."

"Oh-hh—not Alvarez?"

"Bingo!"

"He must have been furious with you."

"Furious? He didn't know who I was or anything about me."

"What!"

"Strange, isn't it?"

"So what did you think about Mr. Smooth?"

"He is that. Actually, I like him."

"You are *so* weird, Adie. First a cop, then a criminal."

"So you think I have no reasoning skills?"

Marg chuckled. "Limited, when it comes to men."

"Thanks, girlfriend."

"Wolf must have had something to say about Alvarez or didn't you tell him?"

"I told him about us meeting. I didn't say anything about lunch on his boat tomorrow."

I heard Marg gasp. "Lunch with Alvarez! Where's Wolf now?"

"Getting me some ice for my ankle."

"What happened? You were okay when we went shopping."

"It hurt from that fight with the biker, but I forced myself to shop. When I left the plaza, I decided to walk back to the hotel. You know the road in front of the Hotel Triste? This creep followed me and I guess I wasn't watching where I was going. I twisted my ankle in the construction rubble."

"Oh my! What did you do?"

"I saw these two guys. I was so scared, I picked them up. We started walking to the Maria and they told the creep to go away."

Marg chuckled. "You amaze me! But, Adie, you're not going through with this lunch are you? Alvarez set that thug on you. He'll probably want to drown you next."

"*Au contraire!* It didn't seem that way to me."

"Adie, you're playing with fire. Wolf won't let you do this."

"He doesn't own me. Besides, he'll be busy looking at properties tomorrow."

"With Daniella?"

"Um-hum."

"So while the cat's away, the mice will play?"

"Investigating is not playing. And, Marg, someone is after me."

"You should have got that dye job, not me."

"Sure, clown red, maybe. Imagine the increase in my social invitations looking like a circus reject."

I heard the door open as Wolf came in with the ice bucket. He set it down on the coffee table, went into the bathroom and came back with a couple of towels.

"Listen, that man is dangerous and Adie…"

"What?"

"With all these men you're dangling on strings, do you think you'll have time to do any sightseeing with me?"

"Sure, San Gervasio. Call me, okay?"

"Right, see you soon then."

As I hung up and twisted around to drop the phone back onto the receiver, I felt Wolf raise my ankle and place a pillow under it. He wrapped it with an ice-filled towel and tightened it. "How's that?" He sat back and surveyed his work.

"Great. Thanks."

"I'll have the late afternoon and evening for you, Adie."

"You're busy."

"You're okay with that?"

"Sure, really, I understand."

"You do?" Suspicion entered his voice.

"You're here on business, and so am I."

"Sightseeing?"

"Um-hum." Diego's boat would count for that.

"I'm waiting for this call," he said checking his watch. "It would best if you kept off your foot tomorrow."

"Um-hum."

His cool blue eyes stared intently at me. "But you're not going to do that, are you?"

"I'll sit a lot. How about that?"

"I want you in good shape," he said, glancing at my body. "Not that you're not, but let's say in smooth running condition."

"Now you think I'm your car?"

"A sleek red Porsche, just waiting to be revved up and raced at top speed."

"And you think you can control this Porsche?"

"Ye-ah. I could race my hot little Porsche to new heights she's never dreamed of."

A low vibrating drone sounded. Wolf dug in his pocket flipping open his cell and started talking while he made his way over to the bedroom. Apparently the conversation was private. He closed the door. One guess. It was Daniella and she was hitting on him.

I picked up a pen and some printouts placing them on a magazine in my lap. All this high finance stuff was not my *forté*. Reading through names, dates, and money transfers for a few minutes, I could see why Diego would rather read a magazine. I saw Don's name, but as Wolf had pointed out, it didn't necessarily mean anything.

A knock on the door startled me. Limping over, I opened it cautiously.

"Good evening, Señorita Sturm," Officer Hernandez glanced at my foot.

"*Buenas noches.*" I motioned for him to sit on the rattan chair. He sat down with his legs primly close together. From his shirt pocket, he took out a notebook and pen.

"Señor Du Lac phoned about this man following you. Where were you?"

"Across from the Hotel Triste."

"What time was this?"

"Well, let's see—shortly before happy hour."

"Around five?"

"Um-hum."

"Describe this person, please."

"Thin, medium height, dark hair wearing a gray T-shirt and dark pants."

"Anything else you can remember?"

"Oh—a moustache."

"But you were hurt, Señorita Sturm."

I shook my head. "It's from last night. It got worse today when I twisted my ankle on the rubble on the road."

Hernandez said, "So, this is twice now, Señorita, which leads me to believe you have an enemy. Do you know who this could be?"

"Wish I did."

Rising to his feet, Hernandez inclined his head. "We will be on the alert for this man. We don't like to have our tourists disturbed here in Cozumel."

"Did you find the biker?"

He opened the door to the hall. "We didn't. Someone sighted him on the ferry but, unfortunately, we were too late."

I closed the door after him and sat back down. Sticking the checked off sheets into the flap of the magazine, I left the others on the table in a pile. The towel was soggy and I was getting tired. I limped over to the bathroom and emptied bits of ice into the sink. I was miserable and tired. From the hook I took my sleepwear and changed.

At the bedroom door, I paused and knocked. A moment later,

Wolf let me in. Still on his cell, Wolf was uttering monosyllables, the other person doing most of the talking. I got into bed and pulled the sheet up. With my eyes closed I tried some of those deep breathing techniques to try to relax and sleep. Breathe in clean air, and breathe out Daniella air. The last thing I remembered was a hand stroking my cheek and a kiss on my forehead.

13

He was coming at me with a knife. I couldn't block him. I had given in to fear. He kicked my ankle hard, bringing me down. Intense pain to the bone. The knife flashed before it came down into my chest. Bright red blood seeped between my fingers. I woke up with a groan and sat up in bed.

There was no blood. I checked my ankle, but no, the reality wasn't as bad as the dream. My ankle looked fine if you call green swelling good, although I was probably better off than he was. His nose could be broken. The blood had been his, but it could have gone the other way. A shiver coursed down my body. I ran my fingers through my hair. It felt damp and greasy, the way it always does when I have nightmares. But it hadn't all been a dream and now it was up to me to find out who was out there gunning for me.

Take care of your health. That's a karate mantra. It should have been my main concern but my intention was to stick to my own personal motto— *take care of my curiosity.* And today, my curiosity would be satisfied.

Getting myself in gear, I showered quickly, put on some makeup and phoned room service. If I was smart, I would do what Wolf had suggested—ice my ankle and rest. But Santiago Francisco Bolivar Alvarez had all the answers and I couldn't miss this opportunity.

When a waiter arrived, I motioned for him to set the tray on the coffee table, next to the vase with Diego's red rose. I needed to face a far greater challenge than walking. I had to wear sexy shoes and look enticing for Diego.

During breakfast, I put my mind on my wardrobe choice for lunch on the yacht. The closest I'd come was sandwiches and beer on a twenty-foot sailboat.

This, I got the impression, it would not be. What to wear for lunch with a billionaire? The white halter-top dress would be perfect. It was tight with a scooped neck and back, but not sluttish. My theory was, the better I looked, the more I'd get out of him.

Now for the hard part, I had to talk to Diego. Phoning guys can be difficult. Not so much if he's a plain Joe or if it's a business thing, but a drop-dead sexy guy like Diego is another matter. It's not like I knew for sure he was a criminal either. I couldn't deny the rush I felt being with him. It wasn't exactly like the hormonal volcano I felt with Wolf, but still powerful. And those eyes— brandy eyes, misting into green. I could see why it bothered Daniella when he broke up with her. And that was an even better reason to accept his invitation.

I punched in his number and waited, listening for the ring.

"*Bueno*," a man's voice drawled.

"Hola, may I speak to Diego, please?"

"Adelina?"

"Yes. I'm phoning about lunch."

"I hope you decided to come."

"I'd like to."

"Where are you staying?"

I couldn't tell him that. "Would it be okay if your driver picked me up at the Internet Café at the Chedraui Plaza?"

"Certainly. Can you be ready by twelve?"

"Yes, no problem. How will I know your driver?"

"He's driving a white Mercedes. I will tell him to look for a beautiful blonde. He'll find you. Adios, Adelina."

I took a taxi to the Chedraui Plaza. I wasn't about to put any pressure on my ankle. Inside, I paid for a half hour and logged in. I had e-mails.

Hey, Honey. What's shaking? You must be going native by now with that all over tan. LOL. Has Beige admitted to offing Reich and Farber? The police are hot to take her in for questioning. Ask her if she's ever been to Farber's house. Fingerprints. Bernie.

Marg could have been in Uma's house and she could have had access to roofies.

I opened Kharkovclues@hotmail.com next.

Hey, Adie. Beige is not what she seems. She stands to inherit five hundred thousand from Reich's estate. Also, Uma wasn't raped. Ilya.

This was a shocker! An inheritance like that would give her even more reason to collect Reich's money from Diego. The sooner his estate had the money, the sooner she'd collect.

Had she lied to me about her involvement with Reich? They

must have been having an affair. That money would be her ticket to freedom from Boris. Could she have planned to murder Reich and maybe Uma? Was it possible? I needed information to find out. Slick could help me on this. Quickly, I clicked an e-mail.

Hey, Bernie. Describe Reich for me. Height, weight. Thanks, Adie

I scrolled down to an e-mail from Boris. What if I was wrong, and Marg's hunch was right? Could Boris be behind it all? He liked control and Marg had left him. And he hated me for being her friend. I clicked it open:

TELL THAT COW TO GET HER FAT ASS BACK HERE ON THE FIRST PLANE OUT OR SHE'LL BE F'N SORRY SHE WAS EVER BORN AND SO WILL YOU. BORIS

Now he was threatening me! The biggest mistake Marg ever made was meeting him on that date site. Checking my watch, I noticed it was almost twelve. I went over to the window. A large, white car was parked at the curb. A man with a cap sat in the driver's seat. This could be it, I thought, stepping outside. Seeing me, the chauffeur got out, came around and tipped his hat. "Señorita Sturm?"

"Yes."

"Señor Alvarez sent me. My name is Ernesto. Please…" he said, opening the door and giving me his hand to assist me into the Mercedes. The soft black leather seat felt cool to the touch. Now I was definitely nervous.

"Have you been out to the yacht before, Señorita?"

"No, what's it like?"

"Very grand, Señorita. You will like the boat."

Yes, I might like the yacht, but what about the rest of them?

We were driving along the coast road when I saw the sign for the El Presidente and then one for the Marina. We slowed down as we approached the harbor. Parking close to the wharf, Ernesto switched off the engine and turned to look at me. "I will bring you to the yacht, Señorita."

I waited for him to help me out. Holding onto his elbow, I leaned against him as I walked, telling him about my sprain. He took care to give me his support all the way to a glistening white yacht. Dumbfounded by the size of the boat, I let go of Ernesto and stared.

"Adelina!" Diego called out from midship. Dressed entirely in white, Diego stood on the other side of the gangway, his dark wavy hair ruffled by the breeze. Reaching out to take his hand, I teetered unsteadily almost losing my balance. I clutched Diego's arm tighter than I meant to and tumbled into his arms.

"What is it, Adelina?" He examined my face. "Are you not well?"

"I injured my ankle and it's becoming difficult to walk."

"Let me help you—we will have you sit down." Diego guided me to the stern where a grouping of comfortable built-in chairs were arranged around a table. A tray with fluted glasses was set up.

A lovely woman in a silk teal dress sashayed over to us. Light brown hair brushed her shoulders. "Ah, Diego, your new friend. Introduce us."

"This charming lady is Adelina Sturm."

She smiled with even white teeth, a show-stopping smile.

Diego placed his hand on her back. "Let me present my sister, Carmelita. She's been waiting impatiently for your arrival."

"A pleasure to meet you," I said carefully. "Impatiently?"

"My brother exaggerates." She took another look at my face. "Is there something wrong, Adelina?"

"I injured my ankle and it's still a little tender."

"Then you must sit and let Diego get you some champagne to relieve the pain."

"Of course. It's chilling in the bucket. I'll open the bottle and bring it up. It's time the party began. The most important people are here, right, Carmelita?"

Diego made his way below, leaving us to stare at each other. Carmelita cut the ice. "I like your dress."

"Thank you. Yours is beautiful."

Carmelita grinned. "Now that that's out of the way, we can talk, um?"

"Sure. What's our topic?"

"Diego, what else?"

I smiled.

"So-oo—what do you think of my older brother?"

"He's sweet and considerate."

Carmelita arched an eyebrow. "Are we talking about Diego? He's the original bad boy."

"Oh, I'd agree he can't be trusted, but what man can?"

Carmelita laughed. "Ha, you've got that right! My husband is pond scum."

Footsteps sounded on the stairs and Diego appeared carrying a large bottle of champagne wrapped in a towel. Behind him, a man in a white uniform carried a tray with a selection of cheeses and crackers.

"You two seem to be getting along. Carmelita isn't boring you with tedious tales of her errant husband, is she?"

I smiled and took a cracker and a piece of cheese.

"This one is discreet, Diego, and has a sense of humor. Keep her."

"See, I told you—I knew you would appreciate Adelina."

"Not in the same way you do." Carmelita smirked.

Ignoring her comment, Diego poured champagne. He toasted, "Salud," and we clicked glasses. "Carmelita, Adelina and I are just friends, right now."

"Take note, of the right now, Adelina. That could change by the hour."

"Diego is capricious?"

"What else can you expect from a Libra? What sign are you, Adelina?"

"Sagittarius."

"Ah-hh, the fire-sign. Watch out, Diego."

Diego sat down on my armrest and slid his arm around my shoulder. "I like a passionate woman. By the way, you are looking exceptionally lovely today, Adelina." He glanced at my cleavage.

Keeping his eyes on me, he spoke to Carmelita. "What happened to Fede anyway? Doesn't he like parties anymore?"

"Not with me he doesn't. He's probably *in flagrante delicto* with his latest whore."

Diego grinned. "Divorce that bastard. He doesn't deserve you."

"True, but it's too much trouble. I think a diversion will do just as well." Carmelita gazed at me. "Where are you from? You don't sound American."

"Canada, near Toronto."

"Oh, really? Diego just spent last week there, didn't you?"

"Um-hum." Diego's eyes shot to the shore. "Guess who's

arrived—with friends?"

Don was with the two women from the restaurant. They boarded the yacht laughing boisterously, looking three sheets to the wind. Don's Hawaiian shirt matched his red face and the women had on serious skank-wear.

Diego took it all in his stride. "Carmelita, could you please run down and put on some music while I greet my guests?" As he took my hand, his lips brushed my wrist. "Be right back."

Sipping my champagne, I watched the commotion. While Diego greeted Don with a handshake, I couldn't help but notice what a squeezable butt he had. Maybe this champagne was over-stimulating my estrogen level. I wasn't sure if that was a horny hormone, but whatever it was, it was doing a number on me. Okay, I told myself. Forget sex for a moment and focus on the scenery.

"And that isn't scenery?" Hormone whispered.

"Of course not." Logical Voice piped up. "Look at those boats." So I did. There were large and small powerboats and a few sailboats in the harbor, just sitting there because nobody wanted to go out with the unpredictable El Norte blowing in.

"Sure, so what?" Hormone said. "Boats are boring."

Don, smiling broadly, staggered towards me with his drunken entourage, the women giggling nervously when they saw me. "Hey, Adie! You sure get around." He leaned over and stage whispered, "Dang! I was wrong—you weren't taken, after all, were you, darlin'?"

Diego appeared, overhearing the remark. "She's not mine yet. I need time to win her." He winked.

"Hah, you sly dog!" Don nudged Diego in the ribs. "You might have a bigger battle than you think."

"I'm not a prize, you two."

"No, of course not, Adelina. We're merely jesting," Diego said seriously. Don nodded in agreement.

Strains of Spanish guitar music filled the air, as a man appeared with a tray of what looked like pâté and caviar. Don and his women friends dug into the caviar. I opted for the pâté. Diego refilled everyone's glasses and called out, "Salud!"

The women were eager to party. The bouncy brunette, detached herself from Don's embrace and approached me, whispering, "Say, honey, you know where the head is?"

"Go down those stairs. Diego's sister is there. She'll tell you." I wondered what Carmelita's take would be on Don's harem.

The plump brunette stood there a moment, glancing around. "This boat sure is big…" Her voice trailed off as she spotted Diego speaking to the chief. "Gawd, sexy or what?"

I nodded, admiring Diego's body. "Chocolate cake delicious."

"Layered with extra thick fudge icing." She licked her lips contemplatively. "Good enough to eat, all right. I'd have seconds with him, no prob." She winked. "Talk to you later, honey." She took one last look and headed down the stairs.

Alone, I started thinking about what Carmelita had said. Diego had been in Toronto. Reich and Uma had both been murdered last week. He could have done it, but that was hard to believe. He wouldn't want any bloodstains on his clothing—too fastidious. But I suppose with all his money he could have arranged it. And there was that cashier's check that he didn't want to give to Marg. Fingertips stroking my hair startled me. Sitting on my armrest, Diego gazed into my eyes. "You looked so deep in thought. I have been neglecting you, Adelina. But I have something—open wide."

A strawberry popped into my mouth. "Um-mm."

He waited until I swallowed before he pressed another one to my lips. "Open, *mi amor.*"

I obliged, pleased by the attention.

"Now drink the champagne."

I drank.

"See how the flavors mingle?"

"Fabulous!"

"I made sure the champagne was chilled to exactly forty-five degrees Fahrenheit to give us the best possible taste." Diego examined the color of the champagne.

"Ah-hh! It's excellent."

"Dom Pérignon '90. I knew you would appreciate it. Do you like the foie gras?

Did he mean the pâté? "Oh, yes."

"But you haven't tried the oysters. You don't like them?"

"I like steamed, but I'm afraid I'm not keen on raw oysters."

"A pity. You know what they say about oysters…"

"No." I brushed up against him and ran my fingers down his cheek. "What do they say?"

Diego stroked the palm of my hand, meeting my eyes. "Then again, a woman such as yourself may not have the need for aphrodisiacs."

"Um." I withdrew my hand. He was so right. A cold shower is what I needed.

"You told me you'd been to Spain. Did you like it?"

"A dramatic country and friendly people."

"I agree—fascinating. See any art?"

"Goya and Velazques."

"Interesting you chose them. Quite a contrast, those two artists." Diego gazed at me.

"Because one paints about violent reality and the other…"

"Captures the innocence of children." He gazed down at me. "Do you have children, Adelina?"

"No."

"With your unusual features, your children would be very attractive."

"Unusual?" Did he think my nose was too long?

Diego whipped off my sunglasses, studying me silently.

"Diego!" Annoyed, I reciprocated by tugging off his sunglasses and dropping them on the table. Dynamite eyes! I should have kept my hands to myself. Distancing was needed. I was rapidly losing it. Those tingles were starting up high and working their way down.

"Calm down, Adelina. I like the way your eyes slant and your lips are exceptionally pouty." He leaned closer to press his lips against mine, pulling the back of my head closer. His fingers moved in my hair and then slid down my neck. His kiss became more persistent, his tongue flicking over my lips.

Don interrupted the mood with his shout, "Hey, Daniella, Wolf! Welcome aboard!" His round head thrown back in glee, he roared, "As you can see our host is temporarily out of commission."

Daniella and Wolf? They were here?

Diego walked over. "Hola, Daniella. Nice of you to come. And you brought Wolf. Welcome." Wolf and Diego shook hands. "Didn't know you two were dating."

Daniella and Wolf stared in my direction. I guessed by the downward turn of Wolf's mouth that he was not pleased. Well, I wasn't either. The man did cheat on me—there was no doubt in my mind.

Diego handed Wolf and Daniella glasses filled with champagne. He caressed my arm tenderly with the tips of his fingers as he spoke. "Let me introduce you to my friend, Adelina. She is visiting from Canada." He glanced at me. "Daniella is my former assistant and Wolf is from Toronto. Is it possible you have met Wolf, Adelina? I know that sounds ridiculous. Toronto is not a small place but—" Diego refilled my champagne glass.

"Hey, Adie." Wolf waved. "We've not only met but have known each other for years."

"What a coincidence!" Diego absentmindedly stroked my arm.

Her lips curled, Daniella regarded Diego's close proximity to me and frowned.

"But surely, Adelina, you don't know Daniella?" Diego's eyes flicked from me to Daniella.

"We've met briefly." Not liking the expression on Wolf's face, I took some cheese from the tray and loaded it on a cracker.

Diego furrowed his brow. "This is extraordinary! You know them both?"

Carmelita glided over to join us. "Ah-hh! What have we here?" Her gaze skimmed Wolf from top to bottom. "Just what we needed—an attractive man."

"Hey," Don protested. "What am I, chopped liver?"

"Not at all, darling. You have charm."

All the females nodded. Teddy bear charm.

Diego interjected. "Carmelita?" He placed his hand on her elbow, guiding her forward. "Meet Wolf."

Carmelita studied Wolf with interest. "How long will you be here in Cozumel?"

"A couple of months maybe."

"How nice. I'm Diego's sister, by the way. Why don't I give you a boat tour? Daniella looks so weary." She gestured to a chair. "Seat yourself, amiga, and relax." As Daniella's eyes shot daggers, Carmelita took Wolf's hand and led him to the stairs.

With a bark of laughter, Don approached the table for more champagne. "Hey, Daniella, I hope you're not serious about Wolf. He's a busy man." He shook his head. "So-oo many choices."

Diego squeezed Don's shoulder. "She has the right to move

on."

Don's brunette bimbo eyed Diego like a steak on a barbeque. She moved in closer. "Hi-ya, handsome, I'm Bambi. Don didn't introduce us. So thrilled ta meetcha."

Diego picked up her hand and brushed his lips on her wrist. "Diego. Are you enjoying yourself, Bambi?"

"Oh, yes. Your boat's super!"

Daniella stalked off to the far side of the boat, and plopped herself down in a chair.

The redhead sidled up to Diego's side, taking his arm. "Hi, sexy. I'm Bunny. How's about a tour?"

"Unfortunately, I can't now." He twisted out of her grip. "I believe Adelina was about to tell me about Toronto."

"Oh-hh." Bunny's face fell in disappointment. "That's okay, I guess." She masked her disappointment with a sad smile, towing Don away.

"You got rid of her," I said quietly.

"Only temporarily. She'll be back." Refilling my glass, Diego probed. "What's going on, Adelina?"

"What do you mean?"

"It's obvious to everyone here, with the exception of the bimbos and my sister. Are you and Wolf involved?"

Panic button. What should I say?

"I can tell by your silence, you are." He stroked my hair gently. "No matter, Adelina. But I'd like a chance to get to know you. Would you consider going to Tulum with me? It would be travel research for you."

I sipped the champagne reflectively. I did need to do that, but would it be smart going with him?

Bounding up the stairs, two steps at a time, a large beefy man stopped and stared significantly at Diego. Acknowledging him with a tilt of his head, Diego rose to his feet. "Will you excuse me, Adelina? There seems to be a problem."

I nodded, glancing at the massive bodyguard, a man I'd hate to encounter in a dark alley alone. There was something familiar about that face. Then it came to me. He and his bookend companion had been sitting at Lorita's watching us. Was the skinny creep another one of Diego's bodyguards? It was all getting so confusing. And I was finding it extremely difficult to concentrate.

I certainly didn't understand the ins and outs of high finance but I did know something about the Caymans and tax free deposits. Meanwhile, Carmelita was foiling Daniella's takeover plans if she was anything like her brother.

The redhead's high-pitched voice carried over the other voices. "Stingray Island! Love it! You can really take us to town with all that loot. Right, Bambi?"

I strained to hear more, but Don started groping Bunny, and peals of laughter followed with Bambi getting into the act, tweaking Don's behind. The three of them pranced around, dancing a convoluted salsa which ended with the three of them heaped on the floor.

Half closing my eyes, I took in the sun, filtered from behind a cloud. A whiff of ocean mixed with soap. I nearly jumped out of my skin when soft kisses tickled the back of my neck. A bolt of electricity shot down my body. When the lips withdrew, I remembered to breathe again. I swiveled around. Wolf grinned wickedly, before he strode off towards Don and the bimbos.

"Aren't you the sly one." Carmelita appeared beside me, holding a glass of champagne. Her eyes raked Wolf's athletic frame stretched out in a plush deckchair and sighed, her eyes flicking to Daniella. "But it looks like I'd have to take a number with both of you in the running." We watched as Daniella sat on the armrest of Wolf's chair, her fingers trailing through his hair.

Don boomed out, "You guys are too much. You two switch partners every few hours?"

"Jealous, Don?" Wolf replied casually. "Don't be, with such lovely ladies of your own,"

Bambi and Bunny tittered, eyeing him with interest.

"Wolf should go with us," Bunny said.

Don placed a finger over her lips. "Secret, remember?"

"Oo-ops!" Bunny hiccupped. "Do you have a boat, Wolf? Don said he might get..." Bambi elbowed her swiftly, stopping her mid-sentence.

"Some of your investments pan out?" Wolf asked.

"If they get any better, I'll quit my job and live here."

I wriggled uncomfortably, my legs numb from sitting, thinking all the while that Don was trying to hide something. When

I stood up, Carmelita helped me over to the other guests.

Don grinned widely, putting his arms around both of us.

"I feel like I'm in a candy store."

"No sampling allowed, darling." Carmelita leaned away from Don, her forefinger teasing his chest.

"Not even a kiss?"

Carmelita anticipated his move, quickly turning her head, letting Don's kiss miss her rosebud lips and land on her cheek.

Unperturbed, Don offered cigarettes all around. Bambi reached out for one. Carmelita shook her head and said, "I like specially blended cigarettes."

"Sorry, left my weed at home."

Carmelita mused, "A joint might help me forget about that cheating husband of mine." She sipped her glass of champagne reflectively. "But, I guess," she said, swirling the last few drops of champagne, "this might be just as effective."

"Forget Fede, there are other fish in the sea." Don chortled. "Besides, you're asking for too much, darlin'. You want a committed man, look in a mental hospital."

Carmelita frowned. "Cheating husbands should be committed." She picked up the champagne bottle and poured herself some more, lifting her eyebrow enquiringly at the group. Bambi held up her glass for a refill and Carmelita obliged. She looked at Don. "I haven't done anything naughty for a while, darling. I have a proposition for you," she said, grabbing his arm, propelling him away. Bambi and Bunny giggled uncertainly, and trotted off behind Don and Carmelita.

Left alone with Wolf, his inscrutable eyes met mine. I felt betrayed. "Excuse me," I said tightly, heading down the narrow stairs somewhat unsteadily, more aware than ever of my aching ankle and my injured pride.

The galley was spacious with a bar, fridge and a small stove. I bypassed a table that seated eight and went into the salon. Creamy leather couches were artfully arranged around a giant glass coffee table, trimmed with gold trim.

I nearly jumped out of my skin when a door slammed in the corridor. Suddenly the massive hulk of Diego's bodyguard stood before me. "May I help you, Señorita?"

My voice croaked out, "Bathroom?"

"Over there, Señorita," he said, pointing at a white door.

"*Gracias*," I said, stumbling as I missed my footing.

In two steps, the big guy grabbed my arm, but before I could scream, he growled, "Let me help you, Señorita."

Once inside, I shut the door behind me. It felt safe. A nice locked room. I inhaled and took in the decor. Elaborate gold taps and soap holders graced a marble sink. Real gold. Even the knobs on the oak cabinets were gold. Diego had money—lots. Enough money to hire hit men.

Cautiously, I pushed the door open and peeked my head around the edge to an empty corridor. With no one around I should check the place for clues. If Diego killed Reich and Claws, Marg would be off the hook. Strangely, I felt a little guilty. Diego had invited me for lunch with all the best intentions, or maybe the worst. Either way, it wasn't a chore kissing the man and now I was about to snoop into his personal stuff.

I crept cautiously down the hallway. Footsteps sounded behind me. I started. Strong arms encircled my waist, soft lips brushed my neck—my body molding into silly-putty. A hint of citron drifted to my nostrils.

"Curious? Want a tour?" Diego whispered in my ear.

I tilted my head up to brandy eyes.

"Let me show you the boat." With his hand on my waist he brought me to the next cabin. He flung the door open. "Guest stateroom with an adjacent head." A double bed and two bunk beds were arranged on one side while a sofa and armchairs occupied the rest of the room.

"Nice. Do you take people with you?"

"Carmelita and Fede. But hopefully, she'll divorce the scum and marry someone more committed."

I giggled, thinking of Don's insane asylum with committed men in straight jackets. Diego shot me a puzzled look before he took my hand, leading me to the next cabin.

Gesturing down the corridor, he said, "Crew quarters. They have the day off." We walked further to an oak door. He swung it open. "What do you think?"

Nobody could say Diego had Spartan taste. Center to everything was a large round brass bed covered with blue silk. A heavy cherry desk stood in the corner with a computer and printer, while on the starboard side a wooden table laden with a decanter, glasses and fruit sat under a large porthole. Italian marble tiles gave the already spacious interior an airy feeling.

"It's beautiful!"

Arms wrapped around me, Diego pulled me in and lowered his lips to mine, awakening my nerve endings with a zap. "You didn't answer my question before," he said, his voice husky.

"Question?" My brain had lost its functioning power.

He steered me over to a chair and assisted me into it. "Tulum. Will you go with me?"

Hormone shouted, "Yes, yes! I'd go anywhere with you!"

"Shut up," Logical sniped, "Get a grip! You don't know this man. He's a killer and you're next!"

"You can research the ruin and we could go swimming." Diego kissed my cheek. Tingles rushed down my body.

"Wise up, Adie!" Logical warned. "He wants to drown you and make it look like an accident."

But Hormone wouldn't let that one go. "No way! Can't you see he's turned on and wants you? Besides, girl, don't those kisses feel good?"

"That's crazy. She's already got a man," Logical argued.

"Don't be naïve," Hormone snarked. "Wolf's out of the picture. You saw him. He's in lust with Daniella. She's got her hands all over him. He didn't resist the barracuda, did he?"

"I would be a gentleman. I promise," Diego said soothingly.

I frowned.

"It's Wolf, isn't it? Forget him, Adelina. He's too busy to go, what with his latest acquisition." Was that a double entendre? "And I can see your relationship with him has its shortcomings."

"You mean because of—" He must mean Daniella. Surely he didn't mean there was something wrong with Wolf's package?

"Yes, Daniella, too." He unscrewed the lid of the bottle on the tabletop. "To really experience Mexico, you need to try some vintage tequila. This one's Jose Cuervo Reserva de la Familia. The agave is carefully cultivated for years and aged in oak barrels." He poured a generous amount of the brilliant coppery liquid into each brandy snifter, and passed one over to me. "Napoleon said, 'Champagne is good in victory and defeat'. Tequila is, however, the Nectar of the Gods. Try it."

Cautiously, I took a sip.

"What do you taste?"

"Vanilla, coconut, nuts maybe, with something else…"

Diego smiled slightly. "Tell me..."

"Something spicy?"

He nodded.

I drank a bit more.

"The peppery accents makes it," he said. "You agree?"

"Um-mm." The tequila was most unusual. I was intrigued.

"What?" Diego asked, noting my expression.

"The finish is fantastic! It's—" I sipped again, considering it, but remaining perplexed.

Diego smiled secretively. "There's a chocolate finish, Adelina."

"Aa-ah!" I sighed ecstatically.

With his chair pulled up close, I could feel the heat from his leg against mine. The drinks had relaxed me and I slumped back into my chair. When his hand stroked mine, my hormones involuntarily exploded. My mouth felt dry. I ran my tongue over my lips and took another sip.

"You like it?"

It? How would I know? I hadn't seen that part of him.

But if *it* was as firm and hard as the rest of him and if *it* were presented properly, maybe wearing one of those feel-good condoms. I giggled.

Diego looked amused. "Tomorrow's busy for me, but," he stroked my hand, "we could go Sunday. Why don't we take the nine o'clock ferry and return on the last one back?"

He took a business card out. "What's your cell number?"

"66-9009. It's easy to remember isn't it, with all those *6*'s and *9*'s?"

Diego smirked. "*6*'s and *9*'s are my favorite numbers." Checking the contents of my glass, and seeing a third of the tequila left, Diego picked up both glasses and took them to the night table by the bed. He came back and pulled me up on my feet. "Come, Adelina."

"Where are we going?"

"It will be more comfortable on the bed."

That started me giggling again. Of course, *it* would like to be on the bed. I started thinking of *it* with an elaborate raincoat. While I was contemplating color choices for the raincoat, I felt myself being lifted and carried to the bed where Diego gently placed me and climbed up beside me.

Why was I feeling so giddy? Diego reached over to grab a pillow, his arm brushing my breast, as he propped me up higher. He brought my glass up to my mouth. My lips parted and I let the tequila glide down my throat.

Diego's eyes sparkled green. "So you will go with me to Tulum?" He took my glass and set it on the night table. Pressing his lips on mine, his tongue flicked over my mouth before he slowly explored the sensitive skin on the inside of my lip.

My body responded.

"Say yes," he whispered, his hand stroking my shoulder.

I threaded my fingers into his wavy hair, loving the feel of it, so thick and soft, forgetting every reason I was ever on the yacht. Diego kissed my throat. His tongue feathered down until he found the perfect spot to drive me wild—the hollow at the base of my neck. The tingles in my core became so pronounced with every lick, that my hips began to subtly wiggle, entreating him for more. With one arm resting on my hip, his other hand reached up to my breast. Through the thin material of my dress, I could feel his finger trace around my nipple. I closed my eyes an instant and leaned my head back against the pillow, caught up in the sensation.

Breathless and mindless, Hormone whispered, "Yes!"

"What, sweet Adelinita? Did you say yes?"

I glanced up at Diego, whose attention seemed to be riveted on my legs, my dress having ridden up, exposing my thighs. Diego slid his hand away from my breast, sat up and undid the buttons of his shirt giving me a view of his splendid muscular chest. I reached to touch him tentatively, stroking his smooth warm skin, running my fingernails down his flat abs. Diego paused in the process of taking his shirt off, and grabbed my hand, his eyes glowing with desire.

"Adelina, will you?"

I nodded slightly, having lost the power of speech. But then I noticed my stilettos digging into his silk cover. I should take them off. Jerking up into a sitting position, I pushed Diego away.

"What is it, Adelinita?" His glance trailed down to my high-heeled shoe as I attempted to unbuckle the ankle strap. Seeing me fumble away, he bent down to help me. I twisted to get a better look. Our heads collided. This hurt, but I also managed to unbalance him. As he tried to right himself, his hand dropped down on my injured ankle.

A sharp agonizing pain! I screamed. Footsteps pounded to the room—my shriek bringing an unexpected audience. Heads peered around the door frame. First an astonished Bambi and then, a disapproving Daniella, followed by an amused Carmelita.

Through the women, Wolf and the bodyguard made their way into the stateroom.

Daniella took up a place beside Wolf. Her gaze shot daggers. "Your technique must be terrifying the poor dear. I thought I had taught you better than that."

Diego glowered. He was about to explain when I touched his arm to stop him. "It's not his fault. I hurt my ankle last night and Diego was helping me with my shoe."

"Obviously, it needs icing," Wolf drawled.

Daniella's words hissed through her teeth. "It certainly does."

Bringing my legs over to the side of the bed, I attempted to stand up. With the combination of the alcohol, high-heeled shoes and a throbbing ankle, I swayed dangerously.

Wolf rushed forward. Diego hurriedly grabbed my hips from behind.

"I've got her." Wolf smiled in satisfaction.

Diego nodded but kept his hands firmly on my hips.

"I'll take her back to her hotel and see that her ankle is iced." Wolf looked pointedly at Diego.

Daniella gave me a look of disgust. "Yes—ice her."

Bambi giggled.

Daniella gripped Wolf's arm anxiously. "Will you come back?"

"No. Adie needs me." Wolf turned to Diego. "Could your driver take Daniella back?"

Diego nodded, smiling slightly. "I'm sure Daniella wouldn't mind staying. We haven't finished partying yet, have we?" he said to the women.

Bambi laughed heartily. "For sure, Diego. Nice bedroom by the way." She stared lustfully at him, taking in his ruffled hair and his bare chest.

Diego jerked his chin, directing his bodyguard to go. The rest of us followed, Diego in the rear. Wolf supported me up the stairs to the gangway. Stopping Wolf to give me a quick hug, Diego whispered, "See you soon, okay?"

"Thank you for inviting me, Diego." I waved to the luncheon guests. They called out their goodbyes. Not Daniella, of course. The scowl on her face grew when Diego kissed me tenderly on the cheek. Wolf didn't look too pleased either, but he grinned happily when he swung me up and carried me away to the Jeep. Opening the passenger side, he manoeuvred me in and unceremoniously dropped me into the seat.

14

Wolf glanced at me as he backed out onto the Marina entrance road. I couldn't read his expression but there was a hint of a smile on his lips.

"You turned the wrong way—we're not going back to the hotel?"

"You noticed?"

"Are you implying I'm too wasted to notice?"

Wolf looked amused.

"Where are we going?"

"You like surprises, Adie," Wolf said, his mouth turning up at the corners.

Where did he get these ideas from? I hate surprises. Slouching in my seat, I closed my eyes. It was getting hotter and stickier. I wished I were wearing a tank top and shorts instead of this clingy dress. This dress was the problem. The scooped neckline was way too low. Diego must have thought I wanted him.

Not that he wasn't being considered, but I don't rush things. I like time to get to know my sexual partners. I felt terrible. First one tear squeezed out and ran down my face, and then another. I sniffled, trying to stop, brushing off a tear. Why hadn't I worn waterproof mascara? If I weren't a mess yet, I soon would be. I dug in my purse. Where was a Kleenex when I needed one? Finally, a tissue.

"We're almost there, Adie. Are you awake?" Wolf glanced at me and pulled over to the side of the road. "Is it your ankle, Adie? Do you think it could be broken?" He touched my tear-streaked face. "We need to get you to a hospital for an x-ray."

"No."

"It's hurting you, isn't it?" He lifted my chin with his finger and examined my face.

"No."

"But you're crying."

"I can cry if I want to!"

"Talk to me, Adie."

I sighed. I felt so down. "It's just—"

"Wait, we're almost there. Can you hold on just a little

longer?" He squeezed my hand before the car rolled out onto the main road. I blew my nose and wiped the smeared mascara away from under my eyes. He turned right where a sign read San Francisco Beach. An attendant stood there waiting.

"Hola, Señor, Señorita," he said happily, opening the passenger door for me. Extending his hand, he helped me step down on the parking lot. Wolf shut his car door and came around to my side. "I will take care of the Jeep for you, Señor."

With me leaning on him, we made our way past two stands selling jewelry and leather.

"Hola!" A dark haired Mexican lady called out when we approached. "I have beautiful jewelry for the lady."

"Maybe later," Wolf said, steering me away. "Let's go down to the beach and sit there."

As we passed the restaurant, a waiter inquired, "Table, Señor?"

"We'll be sitting at the beach for now." Wolf waved in the direction of some unoccupied chaise lounge chairs lined up near the water. He helped me over to a chair, waited while I wriggled to a comfortable position and knelt down.

"Let's take that shoe off."

When the waiter came by, Wolf asked him to bring a towel with ice for my foot, a lemonade and a Dos Equis.

"I'm cut off, am I?"

"For now. You don't need alcohol to have a good time."

"Are we going to have a good time?"

Wolf sat down on my chair and stroked my leg. "For sure…"

"This is a lovely place." I said wistfully taking in the long stretch of sand along the curve of the bay. "I wish we could go for a walk."

"Injuries take time to heal."

"I know." I should have stayed in all day at the hotel and iced it.

"Señor?" The waiter had brought a towel and a bag of ice.

"*Gracias.*" Wolf took it from him and wrapped up my ankle.

"*De nada.* Anything else I can get for you?" The waiter smiled.

Wolf shook his head and sat on the end of my chair. The sun was sinking low in the sky as we watched the young man return to the bar. We were alone at last.

I frowned, thinking of how I had messed up. Was Diego after me out of a Daniella rebound or was it purely a slut exchange for him? Now I felt worse.

"Why were you crying before?"

I massaged the pressure points above my eyebrows with my fingertips. I had a headache, probably the mixture of champagne and tequila. "I was feeling depressed."

"Just the booze."

"No, I've got reasons."

"You're angry with me?"

"Sort of."

"Only sort of?" With the sun setting, he fixed his cool blues on me. "You're pissed off, aren't you?"

"Okay, yes, I am." I glared at him. "Why did you go with her?"

"I was hungry."

"For food?"

Amused, Wolf replied. "We were planning to have some mind-blowing sex in the master stateroom but it was already occupied."

"That's *not* why I was there."

"Why did you go to the yacht?"

"Clues, Wolf. I thought maybe, I'd find out something about the murders, and Marg wouldn't have to get arrested. I need to talk to you about her."

"Marg?"

"Yes, she stands to inherit five hundred thousand from Reich's estate."

"Yeah? Reich was loaded."

"Yup. One of the Reichs—you know Reich Shoes." I twirled a strand of my hair, glancing up at the cerulean blue sky. "Marg thinks she can get that check from Diego. But can she? Does Diego need to pay it out?"

"That depends on the contract Reich signed when he invested."

"So, possibly, Marg is wasting her time?"

"My guess would be that Reich was a stockholder. That would mean he would be getting dividends and she wouldn't be allowed to take out his investment."

I adjusted the ice on my ankle. "Do you think Diego could be laundering money through the Caymans?"

"Drugs?"

"Diego's rich."

"His family's rich."

"So you think it's possible that he's doing nothing wrong?" I took a sip of lemonade.

Wolf gazed out at the small white caps. "Anything is possible with Alvarez."

I grabbed his hand to get his attention "Listen, I found out he was in Toronto when the two murders occurred."

"So was I, Adie."

"You're saying that's not a coincidence? He lives here in Cozumel, not Toronto. And Diego is more likely a murderer than Marg."

"Has she told you if she was having an affair with Reich?"

"I think something was going on."

"What about Uma—how was she murdered?"

"She was drugged and dumped into the Grand. The cold water killed her."

"So why would Marg want to kill Uma?"

"She hated her?"

"You don't just kill people you hate, Adie."

I suppose he was right, otherwise Daniella would be a rotting corpse inhabited by hundreds of generations of maggots by now. "Unless, the stress unhinged her."

Wolf chuckled. "Psycho-psychiatric counselor?"

"Okay, not likely, but I know someone else that is psycho."

"Who?"

"Boris."

"Glad I don't know him."

"He could have killed Reich and Uma."

"I can see Boris killing Reich out of jealousy, but why Uma? What could he have had against her?"

"It could be for some reason we don't know about. The other thing that bothers me is the money."

"Uma's?"

"Yes."

"She have family money?" Wolf asked.

"She had a settlement from Reich and she had wealthy boyfriends."

"Any other sources?"

"Ilya might know."

"Ilya?"

"The detective I met."

"And he will tell you this, how?"

"E-mail."

Wolf regarded me intently.

"I wanted to help Marg so we stayed in touch."

"That's how you know Uma was drugged?"

I nodded.

"Means," Wolf said.

"Huh?"

"Marg works in a hospital and she has access to drugs. She has *means*."

"That's why Ilya thinks Marg is a suspect."

"Wait, was she in Kitchener?"

"I thought she was in Cozumel but I don't know for sure. She was here before I arrived." I frowned. "I don't want to suspect my best friend."

"Tell me about Reich's murder."

"He was thrown over the fence, in with the pit bulls."

"The dogs killed Reich?"

"No, Ilya said it was a blow to the back of the head."

"I'll ask Bernie to find out more about Reich for me."

"Who's Bernie?" Wolf asked.

"This reporter I met."

"For a woman who's concerned about my commitment to her, you've sure got plenty of paramours of your own."

"Those guys are just acquaintances."

"What about Alvarez. He's an acquaintance?"

"I'm trying to figure things out to help Marg. I think he's involved."

"Sure, Adie." Sarcasm laced his words.

"You're mad about Diego?"

"What did you expect to find out in the master stateroom?"

"Well if he'd left, I could have looked through his papers."

"Why would he leave when you're lying in his bed?"

"On his bed, and he wasn't naked," I said pointedly.

Wolf grinned. "Only a matter of time…"

" He wouldn't have done anything with the door open."

Wolf smiled. "You underestimate your allure." He leaned in closer and kissed me, leaving me breathless. His hand stroked my waist, his fingertips gliding to my breast. I was aroused, too much so. He could tell.

"We should go back to the hotel," he said, his voice seductively low.

"What about dinner?"

"You're hungry?"

I nodded seriously.

He sighed. "I guess we could eat here."

I glanced at the yellow streaks of light on the ocean reflecting from the last rays of the setting sun. "This is a beautiful beach, Wolf." I stroked his cheek. "I'm glad you brought me here. I like seeing the sunset with you."

* * *

Dinner was basic Mexican. I was feeling more in control. The food had mellowed me out. Here I was with Wolf just taking in the stars, listening to the steady rhythm of the waves hitting the shore. The warm breeze blew in off the ocean shifting Wolf's sun-bleached hair onto his forehead.

"Ready to go?" Wolf asked.

"You seem awfully anxious."

"They don't have dessert here."

"And there's some at the hotel?"

Wolf smiled.

"I haven't forgiven you yet."

"Key word, yet?"

I grimaced at the thought of him with Daniella. She was *so* transparent. Why couldn't she find herself another playmate?

"What do I need to do to be forgiven?"

I couldn't tell him—he should know. I'd only succeed in seeming insecure and jealous. I shrugged in reply.

His clear blue eyes sparkled. "You're making me fight for

you?" He stroked my hand. "I like a challenge."

Back to the macho stuff. What was it with men? You'd think I was the Stanley Cup the way these guys were acting.

Back home, the entire male population watches hockey— that's ice hockey. It's all about body checking, slugging the opposing team members, and sitting in the penalty box. At least that's my impression. As far as I'm concerned, the only team sport that bored me more was football.

"You're drifting away, Adie."

"Hm-mm?"

A waiter came at Wolf's signal and brought the bill. I tried to suppress a yawn, getting Wolf's attention. "Don't fall asleep on me, Adie."

I yawned and rolled my stiff shoulders forward and then back.

"You could do with a massage," he said. The waiter handed Wolf the receipt and he stood up expectantly. "Let's go, Adie."

I was in a difficult situation. This would have been a good time to have my own hotel room. My emotions started wrestling in my brain.

"Let's face it," Logical said. "You don't really know Wolf at all. He's a two-timer— a big time player."

"Don't be a fool!" Hormone Voice argued. "He's yours if you want him and if you don't take him ASAP, Daniella will."

I stood up carefully. My ankle wasn't as sore. The ice must have helped. Wolf gave me his arm to lean on as we walked slowly out to the car.

The parking lot attendant smiled at us as we neared the Jeep. "Your Jeep is safe, Señor."

Wolf shook his hand with a couple of dollars enclosed in his palm. The man's grin widened. "Gracias, Señor." He waved as we drove off onto the side road leading to the main highway. I wished I had something to smile about. I was in a real fix.

15

Slumped back on the couch in the living room, I fixed my eyes on Wolf opening the patio doors and letting in the warm evening breeze. It was Santana tonight. They liked to alternate their musicians down at the bar. Soft Spanish rock I could live with. Happily, they avoided rap—music that would definitely do me in.

It had been a mistake to mix drinks, especially when I'm not used to drinking tequila or champagne. Wisdom should come with age. Obviously, I wasn't old enough.

"Wolf?"

"Yeah?" he said, coming back to the couch.

"In the bathroom in my green makeup bag, could you please get me some Aspirin?"

Wolf searched my face. "Headache?"

I nodded.

The phone rang as he entered the bathroom and left me alone to deal with that instrument of medieval torture.

I had to answer it or let it continue to jab every neuron in my brain. "Hello?"

"Oh, hi, Adie…" Marg said in an ultra calm voice.

Was she still on drugs?

"Did you have a nice lunch today?"

Oh, please! "Marg, I can't talk right now."

"Wolf is listening in, is he?"

"Meet me at the Java at ten?"

"We're still going to San Gervasio?"

"Yes, breakfast first."

"Shouldn't we go earlier then?"

"No, definitely not!" I would need to get caught up on my sleep to survive.

"What's wrong, Adie?"

"Too much." Then I remembered my shoe quest. "Oh, and I need to take a look in the Chedraui Plaza. Let's talk tomorrow, okay?"

Marg hesitated. "All right, Adie, take care."

I heard the phone click and glanced up to see Wolf holding a glass of water in one hand and two tablets in the other. Tilting my head back I swallowed the pills.

"A massage would help."

"What kind of massage?" I asked suspiciously.

"Head, shoulders…" he said, "but if you prefer the full body with extras, I could accommodate."

"I'll take the head and shoulders massage for now."

Wolf sat down on the couch. "Come here then."

I twisted around and leaned my back against his chest.

With his fingertips he massaged my temples and forehead, pressing down on the pressure points above my eyebrows.

They were playing some old Santana, *Black Magic Woman*. I get lost in this song. Carlos knows what he's doing. What could be more perfect than Wolf and this sexy music? Unfortunately, the last part of the track was louder and more demanding—something my headache-ridden brain couldn't handle. I strode over and slid the window shut. "What are you doing tomorrow, Wolf?"

"Finalizing my deal."

"How come everyone knows about this property except me?"

"You will, soon. I want to show it to you."

"When?"

"Soon. Adie, what are you up to tomorrow?"

"Curious wording."

"For my very curious woman."

"Am I your woman?"

"When you want to be."

"Lunch, shopping, and then I'm sightseeing with Marg."

Wolf frowned. "Take your cell phone and turn it on. I'll call. Now, let's get ready for bed." Seeing my stricken look, he smiled. "Don't worry, Adie, we can just talk or if you want, read." He walked over to the bathroom. "I'm taking a shower, okay?"

I nodded. Please don't come out wearing your usual post shower attire. I heard the water turn on and started visualizing—that wet hard body, soapy and succulent, waiting for my touch. Or maybe, I was completely out there with this. Did he even want to see me tomorrow?

What was that vibrating noise? Ah, of course, my cell. I opened my purse and took it out. "Hello?"

"*Hola, mi amor*. Are you feeling better?"

"Yes, thanks, Diego."

Wolf came out the bathroom door looking splendid in his white towel. He must have heard me say Diego's name, because he frowned before entering the bedroom.

"I hope you enjoyed the luncheon."

"Yes, I did very much. It was kind of you to invite me."

"I'm the one who is honored you could attend. How's your ankle?"

"It's better, thanks." Did he mean that first inquiry into my health was about my intoxicated state? "I'm sorry, Diego. The alcohol just crept up on me. You must have thought I was out of my mind."

"Not at all. You're sweet and funny."

Me? Funny maybe, but sweet?

"I look forward to seeing you on Wednesday. Bring your bikini, okay?"

"Is there a place to swim at Tulum?"

"There's a beautiful beach."

"Is the snorkeling good?"

"I wish I could say yes, but the beach is sandy and there's only a small section of coral off to the one side."

"Oh," I said disappointed.

"Think of it as research, Adelina. Besides, we'll have fun. Bring your camera. I'll make sure we have all the necessities."

Now that would be interesting, to see what Diego thinks is a necessity. "What time would you like to meet at the ferry dock?"

"I'll pick you up at nine-thirty."

"I'll phone you and let you know where."

"You are a woman of mystery, *mi amor*. Are you afraid if I know where you are staying I might be tempted to visit you?"

"Carmelita said you were a bad boy."

"True—I'm very bad."

I laughed. "When are we returning?"

"We'll take the ten o'clock ferry. Unfortunately, I have agreed to a meeting with an investor at Playa del Carmen before we leave."

"Oh…"

"Sorry, Adelina. He was very insistent. But don't worry, this meeting should be brief."

My eyes fell on the red rose Diego had given me—its petals fully opened. "Your rose is so beautiful, Diego."

"You are refreshing. There's an innocence about you, Adelina. So unlike my jaded friends."

"And you, Diego, are you jaded too?"

"Disillusioned."

"Well hopefully our time together will be a positive experience."

"I want this to be a beginning for us."

"I'm not here that long and you know I'm involved with Wolf."

"You would be happier with a man who truly appreciates you."

I laughed. "And you do?"

"I'll have to show you, won't I?"

"Just remember what you told me."

"What was that?"

"You said you'd be a gentleman."

"Um-mm, yes, of course."

Was he smirking right now? I needed an iPhone, with the built-in monitor to see his face. "*Buenas noches*, Diego."

"Good night, sweet Adelina."

I ended the call and hobbled into the bathroom. Taking my clothes off, I adjusted the water temperature and carefully stepped in. Shampooing my hair, I started thinking of those hazel eyes and then I remembered the rest of him and wondered what I was getting myself into. He wasn't easily forgettable but neither was Wolf. Why was it for months, I couldn't get a worthwhile date and now I had two steamy choices?

The hot shower felt good. Daniella had really pulled a fast one when she'd brought Wolf with her. She probably thought Wolf would break up with me once he saw Diego. And it was strange. These guys were so cool about the situation.

And what was this about Wolf being in Toronto during the time of the murders? Could Wolf have met Diego before he got to Cozumel, and if so, was he involved in the murders? And then there was Marg. What if she murdered Reich and Uma? Flights left weekends to Cozumel but there were frequent flights to Cancun only a short distance away. She could have lied about being here so much earlier. Bernie would know if it was physically possible. After wrapping a towel around me, I stepped into the bedroom. Wolf lay in the bed, a sheet covering his lower body.

"Are you feeling any better?"

"Why?" I said suspiciously.

"I could be persuaded to give you that full body massage."

I tucked my towel in tighter. "I just came in to get some clothes."

"You don't generally wear clothes to bed, do you, Adie?"

"Sometimes I do." I opened the dresser drawer and tugged out a red pair of boxers and a matching top.

Wolf sat up in the bed, the sheet dropping to his waist exposing his muscular lean body. "When's that, Adie?"

I turned to him. "When I'm feeling sick."

"If you come here, I'll make you feel better."

"What happened to talk or read?"

"We're talking."

I shook my head and sighed. "I'll be back." I took my sleepwear to the bathroom and changed. I frowned thinking of my dilemma. I didn't want to tell Wolf about my upcoming trip to Tulum. He wouldn't understand. But I had to know the truth. In my heart, I felt Diego liked me way too much to be behind all these attacks. Wolf was wrong.

Something had to be done about this dud ankle of mine. I had to drive tomorrow. Studying the bruise, I thought more icing might be the solution. I'd have to get the ice since Wolf was lying there with only a thin sheet covering him. Maybe he didn't have a robe either. I didn't dare ask him to get up. It would be tempting fate— that buff bod, revealed in its natural state. I didn't want my first time with him to be ruined by the throbbing in my temples—I liked my throbbing to be lower.

With the ice bucket in my hand, I peeked into the corridor. Seeing no one, I chanced going to the ice machine in my nightclothes. The hall was quiet. I wondered how late it was now. I glanced around to make sure I was alone. Good, I didn't like surprises, most of them being unpleasant. Although I had to admit that breathtaking sunset and the spectacular beach were a wonderful surprise. Wolf sure knew how to touch my heart.

I pressed the ice machine button and loaded up. On the way back to the door, some guys on a tequila high came down the hall, clowning around. As I stuck the card in, they whistled. I slipped into the room. I didn't look back, hastily shutting the door behind me.

My nerves were shot—men either attacked me or wanted sex. Sure, there was nothing wrong with sex but, it would be nice to have a guy that cared.

When I entered the bedroom with ice and a towel, I noticed Wolf was sitting up in bed reading a book. He looked up when I came in. "You okay, Adie?"

"Yes, I think so." I couldn't explain this. He probably wouldn't understand. It's different for a man. Everything is different for a man. It's basic—they think differently than women.

"You look pale. Something happened?"

I sat on the bed and plopped the ice bucket down with the ice bag inside. Wolf took the bag and filled it with ice. The sheet dropped down. I was disappointed to see he was wearing his boxers after all, or had he put them on after my lukewarm response? I shouldn't have been so short with him. Blame it on this stupid headache.

"I guess I'm just spooked. I was half expecting another guy with a knife when I went out into the hall."

"I could have gone." Wolf put an arm around me and stroked my cheek with his hand. "Adie, you can't trust Alvarez. He won't be happy when he finds out that you're Marg's friend."

"I don't have to tell him."

Wolf frowned. "You're planning to see him again, aren't you?" He dropped his arm and examined my face.

"Um."

"I'm not going to tell you what to do, Adie. Just do me a favor and tell me when, and where. I already know why."

I didn't want to ask him what he thought the why was. It was better not to talk about that, especially when I wasn't too sure. I nodded. Grabbing a few pillows, I arranged them behind my back. Wolf placed one under my foot and then tied the towel with bag of ice around my ankle. I closed my eyes. Wolf edged up close to me and placed his hand around mine.

With the pills and alcohol in my system, I drifted into an easy slumber. Having him near me made me feel so safe.

16

An annoying list of figures. From the table, I picked up another printout and scanned it, almost discarding it before my eyes caught a name. It was familiar. But I was blocked. It would come to me—eventually. Fifteen million. That was a lot of money to invest.

A bang on the door startled me. I dropped the sheet on the table. Did we get our signals mixed? Marg must have thought we were meeting here instead of the Java. I hurried over to the door and slid it open.

"Adie, what are you doing here?" Dressed in a Hawaiian shirt and black baggy shorts, Don stared at me in surprise.

"I, uh, well…"

Don pushed the door open, smiling broadly. "So Wolf won, did he?" He stepped in, his eyes flicking around the room and said, "Where's the big man, anyways?"

"He's not here, and he didn't win."

Don looked mystified. "But, you're here in his hotel room and it's," he checked his watch, "nine o'clock in the morning. Now, I'm not a detective, but I'd say something is going on between you two."

I wasn't too good at lying, but I gave it a shot. "After breakfast my ankle started hurting and he suggested I stay and ice it. He had to go somewhere."

Don seemed disappointed. "Too bad. I was hoping to ask him his opinion about this forty-five footer I was thinking of buying. He said his parents had one about the same size."

"Yes." I remembered that. Wolf blasting down the French River, suddenly stepping back and telling me to take over. Virtually blind without my glasses, I took us on a suicide run— massive boulders everywhere. Miracle of all miracles, we made it and Wolf never found out. Five years later I had corrective surgery. He would never know how close to death we'd been.

"You should sit down, Adie. You're looking pale."

I eased myself into the rattan chair and said. "He'll be back later today, Don."

"Yeah? But I'm busy, busy, busy…"

"Oh?"

"Got this meeting with a big honcho in Chien Rio this afternoon and then I'm out of here for a few days."

"Where're you going?"

Don's face flushed. Changing the subject, he asked, "How's Diego?"

"You saw him last."

"Yeah, but," he winked, "you've got the inside story. Bambi told me you two were pretty cozy."

I looked away. "Too much tequila."

"The expensive stuff."

"I don't think he's got anything that isn't expensive, do you?"

Don chortled. "No, and he's looking to add to his collection."

"What do you mean?"

"Ah," he shrugged, "you know, no offense."

"I'm not a thing, Don."

"A guy like that likes a classy woman like you."

I sighed.

"And a rich dude like Diego probably gets everything he wants."

"Well, I'm not ready for a commitment."

"Commitment?" He chuckled. "I was thinking he'd more likely want to set you up somewhere, you know, a high-class condo with everything you'd want," he guffawed loudly, "including Diego, of course." He squeezed my hand. "But I might be wrong. What I do know is that he's got it bad for you."

"Why, did he say something?"

"It's not what he said, Adie. The looks he gave you weren't exactly platonic. And, he was plenty pissed after you left with Wolf."

"Oh." I glanced at my watch and stood up. "I hate to rush you out, Don. It has been nice seeing you again, but I've got to go."

Don walked over to the door, and swung it open. "Can you tell him to call me? Wolf, I mean. I'm sure you'll see him later," he said his eyes twinkling, "or is it Diego's turn?"

"Oh, shut up, Don." I said, pushing him out into the hall. That was stupid of me. I shouldn't have answered the door. I was brain dead from too many pills and alcohol. I glanced down at my ankle. The bruising was turning yellow.

To be on the safe side though, my chosen sandals would be low and maybe I should bring my Nikes for hiking around the ruins. I found a plastic bag and shoved in the running shoes, along with my camera and purse.

A while later I walked into the Internet Café. I hoped Bernie had the information I wanted. I smiled triumphantly when I saw the message.

Hey, Honey! Strange stuff this. Reich was five-six and weighed one thirty. Little dude. Now you didn't ask but Uma was five six and weighed one ten. Both of them light weights. Do you think Beige did it? Is she strong enough? Bernie

This worried me. Marg is five foot five and I'd say under one hundred-thirty. But would she have the physical strength to push Reich over the fence? I pressed reply and typed.

Hey, Bernie. Thanks. No, I still can't believe Marg did it. Secondly, I think she was already here when Uma was murdered. I am wondering about Royal Investments and the owner Santiago Bolivar Alvarez. Adie

Before I started thinking my best friend was capable of murder, I needed to consider the obvious suspects. Checking my watch, I decided I'd better get going or I'd be late for breakfast with Marg.

It's only a half a block from the plaza to Rock'n Java, so I decided to leave my Jeep parked there. No use looking for parking in this town. There was some construction along the road and pedestrians were using the left side. As I passed by the seafood restaurant Wolf and I had gone to the other night, I started thinking about him. If he hadn't shown up at the yacht with Daniella or taken her back to her house the other day, I would have given in to my desires. I mean, he was probably worse than Diego, with his clever seduction techniques. I melted when I saw that slow sexy smile of his.

When I arrived at the Java, I spied Marg sitting at a table by the window. Her eyes were fixed on the military ship docked behind the café. I placed my purse on the table and grabbed the menu. "Hi, Marg."

"Hi, Adie. You're early."

"I'm usually late?"

She laughed. "For once we're both early. This must be a first."

"What are you having?" I glanced at the menu.

"Waffles. How about you?"

"Something that doesn't make me feel fat," I said glumly.

"You hardly have to worry about that."

"If I don't worry about it, my worst nightmare will happen."

"Ha! My worst nightmare isn't fat. It's Boris."

"Okay, I take that back—I have worse problems than gaining weight." I thought back to last night and the paranoia I had at the ice machine. "My worst nightmare is having another guy with a knife after me."

Marg's eyes widened in surprise. "What do you mean? It happened again?"

"Well, once is enough, and last night when I went into the hallway to get some ice from the ice machine, I was scared."

"You know, Adie, considering everything that's happened, how could you...?"

"What?"

"Go to Alvarez's boat for lunch knowing he's sent men to kill you?"

I studied her expression. She looked bewildered. It was hard to believe she could be devious enough to send thugs after me. Might be Boris after all.

A slim man with a craggy face approached the table. "*Buenas dias,* Señoritas. What can I get for you?"

Just having fruit would be boring. I'd be hungry in no time. Fried eggs and bacon were too greasy after all that alcohol. "French toast, *por favor.*"

"*Si,* Señorita." He turned to Marg.

"Scrambled eggs and waffles, please."

"*Gracias,*" he said, on his way back to the kitchen.

"I've been dying to hear about your lunch on the boat."

"It's a yacht and things started well. Diego's sister is really very nice."

"I got the feeling a lot more happened."

"Don came with two bimbos."

"To be expected, I guess. He's cute but really fickle, eh?"

"A California guy." I smiled. "You can't help but like him. He's cuddly and he reminds me of a teddy bear."

Marg giggled. "That's it. I couldn't put my finger on it, but, that's it." She leaned in closer. "Then what happened?"

"Diego had champagne and appetizers and we talked…" My voice trailed off thinking of the kiss we shared.

"You have a strange look on your face, Adie. Did he come on to you?"

I bit my lip.

"You let him kiss you, didn't you?"

I nodded. "I didn't think anything would happen because there were other people there."

Just then our waiter arrived with our orders. The French toast looked fabulous. My first forkful was above my expectations. The Rock'n Java takes care of a healthy girl's appetite.

"He's a smooth talker and you fell for his charm."

"Marg, you've got to admit the guy is sexy."

Marg frowned, as she cut up her waffle. "Most women would find him gorgeous, but not me. I don't trust him. I like nice guys, like Manni."

"Are you two kissing yet?"

Marg blushed. "It's gone a little farther than that," She added hastily, "but not too far."

"Well, I'm glad you found a guy that treats you right." I glanced at Marg's dreamy expression. She was seriously taken with the guy.

"He does. What a switch from Boris. I don't know what I ever saw in him."

"What are you gonna do when it's time to leave?"

"We're going to stay in touch even when I get back home. Maybe I'll come back here or he'll visit me." Marg's eyes took on a dreamy expression.

"Good." It was about time Marg had a romance.

"Now tell me what happened. You're not telling me everything."

"Daniella and Wolf arrived." I clenched my jaw thinking of Daniella, her fingers in his hair.

"Together?"

I nodded. "Yeah, they were as shocked as I was."

Marg chuckled. "I can see why. So she was trying to steal Wolf away."

"I'd say. She was all over him."

"She's a real man-eater. What did Wolf think about you with Alvarez?"

"He wasn't pleased, but he was cool. In fact, neither Diego nor Wolf was too upset."

"Really?" Marg stared at me with disbelief. "Why was that, Adie?"

I fidgeted uncomfortably. "It's some kind of macho thing. I think they've somehow challenged each other—either consciously or unconsciously."

Marg looked puzzled. "To do what?"

"Let me put it this way. I'm the prize and it's not marriage they're after."

"How callous! I can't believe they'd do that."

"Believe it."

"I can understand Alvarez having ulterior motives and being a manipulator because I think he's up to no good, but Wolf seems honest and he's protective of you."

"Well if that's true, why is he with Daniella?"

"You said he was looking for a place to buy and she's a realty agent, isn't she?"

"Yeah, I guess. So you think it's only business?"

"On his part." She paused. "But you haven't told me about Alvarez and I notice you are on a first name basis. What happened with him?"

"Well after he figured out that Wolf and I were seeing each other he asked if I would go to Tulum with him. He gave me a tour of the yacht and we ended up in the master stateroom tasting some very special old tequila."

"Oo-hh," she said, cluing in.

I nodded. "I had too much to drink and not enough food." I hesitated. Marg was a bit conservative when it came to sex. "He carried me over to the bed and started to kiss me."

"So," Marg's eyes widened, "he didn't, did he?" She stopped eating and sat upright.

"No," I worked on my French toast and had a sip of orange juice, "but he was making all the right moves and I was melting like fresh snow on a warm winter's day."

Marg mouth dropped slightly.

"Then he accidentally fell on my ankle when we were on the bed."

Marg's face scrunched. "Huh?"

"I twisted my ankle in the construction area. When Diego touched my bruise, I screamed and a bunch of people showed up at the door of the stateroom, including Wolf."

"Wasn't Wolf angry with Diego?"

"Hah, he just thought it was his chance to run away with the prize. Wolf told Diego my ankle needed icing. He picked me up and carried me away."

Marg sighed. "How romantic."

I sat back and reflected. "It was nice when he brought me to San Francisco Beach to watch the sunset."

"Ah-ha."

"Um-mm, but then I got a headache from all the stress."

Marg smiled. "Probably the drinks, Adie."

"We should get the bill. I need to look for those red shoes." I motioned the waiter who came over with the checks.

"What about San Gervasio?"

"We'll do that after, if that's okay with you?"

"You know my motto."

I cocked my head inquiringly.

"Shop 'til you drop!"

* * *

"So why the rush on the red shoes?" Marg asked.

We were on the escalator going up to the top floor of the Chedraui Plaza where the shoe stores were located.

"I need them for Christmas Eve."

"That's in two days."

"No kidding."

"Why red?"

"I have this low-cut red dress."

"You're going out on Christmas Eve?" Marg turned to me as we stepped off the escalator.

"I hope so. I'm going back on Christmas Day. How about

you?" I surveyed the store windows. We started walking towards one of the shoe stores on the other side.

"Manni wants me to stay over the holidays." Marg paused to check out a T-shirt sale. She picked up a brown one in medium and held it up to her.

"Will you?" I rummaged around and fingered a red tank top in a small.

"Yes, I've decided to stay until just after New Year's."

Marg's announcement grabbed my attention.

"Things getting serious with Manni?"

"Yes, and Boris has Libby for Christmas anyway." Marg smiled happily as we moved on.

I spotted a store with fashionable shoes, with some unusual styles by international designers. "I think this might be the place to find those shoes." My voice trailed off as my gaze fell on some red-satin, high-heeled sandals."

"You didn't say what you and Wolf are doing on Christmas Eve."

"That's because I don't know. The thing is, I want to be prepared." I picked up a high-heeled sandal with a black bow.

Marg smirked. "For what, Adie?"

I blushed.

"Tell, girlfriend."

"For all I know Wolf may have made plans with Daniella and I'm spending my last evening here alone." I stuck my foot in the sandal. It fit.

"He wouldn't do that, would he?"

"Wolf doesn't tell me anything. I don't have a clue about what he feels about me."

"Did you tell him about going to Tulum with Alvarez?"

The saleslady interrupted, asking if I needed help. "Could I see the other shoe, *por favor*?" She nodded and went off to the back of the store. I sat down on a leather chair and waited.

"Did you?"

"He guessed I was going to see Diego from my phone conversation. He said I should tell him where and when and that he knows why."

"He does?"

"Yeah, strange, eh? I don't even know exactly why." What

was Wolf thinking? Maybe he understood me better than I understood myself.

"Because, you're trying to help me?"

"That's true, but..."

Marg smirked. "You think he's hot."

"True again, but..."

"Because you think Wolf is cheating on you and you want to do the same?"

I frowned. She'd hit the nail on the head. There's just so much a woman can take from her own personal hottie without some retaliation.

The saleslady came over with the matching shoe and I put both of them on and stood up. I walked up and down the tile floor, checking my feet in the mirror.

"Wow, those are knock-out shoes!"

"Sexy," I said, surveying them. "Comfortable, too."

"You're lucky you can wear those type of shoes. My feet would be screaming by now."

"Can you picture these with a flame red dress?"

Marg nodded enthusiastically.

I mentally translated the price in pesos to US dollars and came up with about seventy dollars, which was about seventy-four Canadian. These shoes would be about two hundred in Toronto. But should I buy them? What if I wasn't going anywhere on Christmas Eve? Contemplatively, I paced the floor.

"Listen, Adie," Marg stood up and grabbed my hands. "I'll buy them for you. My Christmas present to you."

I stopped to stare at Marg.

"Yes, really! This makeover with the new hair style and color you arranged for me really made me feel great and I want you to have a perfect night."

I was touched. "Thanks, Marg. You're the best." I hugged her. How could I ever have believed she was involved in the murders?

The saleslady standing by patiently asked, "Should I wrap them, Señorita?"

Marg nodded.

I sat and waited for Marg to pay, thinking all the while about Wolf. I dreaded telling him about my plans with Diego, but I would have to tonight, no matter what.

From Avenue Juarez, we zoomed out of San Miguel and hit the highway. On both sides, the undergrowth was mostly shrubs and fields. A few blanket stalls were located on the right side of the road with the cheaper sort of multi-colored blankets.

Marg was telling me about living with Anita and her kids. "She has a shop that specializes in making tortillas and tacos. Something like the delis we have at home."

"What does her husband do?"

"Same thing." Marg glanced at a roadside stall with large multi-colored blankets selling for eight dollars. "They bring the kids to the shop when they're not in school."

"Do you think you could live here, in Cozumel?" I turned down the access road to San Gervasio.

Marg got a far-away look on her face. "If Manni and I became a couple..."

"You're not a couple?"

"According to Anita, I should get my marriage annulled and have lots of kids with Manni," she went on hastily, "after we get married, of course."

I smiled. "Then it's lucky we're going to San Gervasio today."

"Why?"

"You don't know anything about this place?" I smiled, amused at Marg's expression.

"I brought a guide book with me, but I haven't read it yet. So, being you're the travel consultant, Adie, fill me in."

"Well, San Gervasio was a site dedicated to the Mayan goddess Ixchel—goddess of fertility, midwifery, medicine and weaving. Mayan women from the mainland were expected to make a pilgrimage to her shrine at some point in their lives to help them get pregnant. It must have taken these women hours to paddle from the mainland."

"Poor things. Imagine wanting to be pregnant that badly."

"And they could die in the effort."

Approaching the access road we turned left and entered the jungle. Huge trees and bushes were everywhere. Only faint strands of sunlight filtered through the canopy of leaves. We drove slowly on the narrow stone road for about ten minutes.

My phone vibrated and then started its low-tone ringing.

I pulled up to the side of the road, knowing it would be

difficult to speak and drive.

"Bueno!"

"You're becoming more Mexican, hotter and spicier."

My heart missed a beat. "Wasn't I hot before?"

Wolf continued in his husky voice. "You've gone from being a spicy red salsa to an especially sizzling green salsa."

"Almost inedible salsa?"

"Believe me, you're edible, Adie," Wolf said softly. "Where are you?"

I flushed at his words, conjuring up all kinds of images. "Just entering, San Gervasio. Where are you?"

"Checking out my property."

"Oh?"

"I want to take you there tonight, after dinner."

"When's dinner?"

"Will you be back by five?"

"I think so." I got more excited as I pictured Wolf in a towel, fresh from the shower—slick and muscular.

"Six?"

I had to concentrate. "Hm-mm?"

"I'll see you at six, okay? Bye, sexy."

I clicked my phone shut and visualized his sensuous lips and his deep blue eyes with that wicked glint.

"Adie?"

Marg's voice knocked me out of my daydream.

"Adie? Is everything okay?"

"Um-mm."

"Is there something I should know? Was that Wolf?"

I wanted to hold on to my daydream. Wolf was temptation with a capital T.

"Adie?" Marg squeezed my arm to get my attention. Are you okay?"

"Yes," I said sharply, her nurturing irking me.

Marg sighed in exasperation as I turned the key, starting the engine. Driving in second gear, I eased down the road for a few minutes until I neared the ticket booth. After I paid and parked, I reached for my Nikes in the plastic shopping bag and put them on. With one last fond glance at the bag with the red sandals, I stepped down and walked with Marg to the road. I didn't bother locking the Jeep since the plastic windows were lying in the trunk anyway.

"Can you speak now or should I wait until you return to Earth?" Her lips were pursed and her hands were on her hips.

"What's wrong?"

"I thought you were ill." Marg's voice held an edge.

"I'm not. Sorry, I didn't mean to be rude, Marg. Wolf was just saying things that needed my full attention. Let me fill you in on this place. The site was established around one hundred BC and was still in operation when the Spaniards arrived in the sixteenth century."

"And I suppose the Spaniards ruined the Mayan civilization."

"Apparently, there was one shipwrecked Spaniard that helped the Mayans fight the Spanish." I remembered that because I was surprised by this information.

"Good for him."

I noticed the white road. "These roads are called Sacbe. All their sites were connected with these roads." At one ruin, we saw a sign labeling the building the Temple of Hands. "Do you think there are snakes here?" It looked like the type of place snakes might like.

Marg's eyes widened at the thought. "I hope not. I hate snakes."

I glanced at the lush foliage and the high trees shading the area. "The problem is most of these touristy places hush it up if they have snakes."

Marg shuddered.

The large first room had a small temple. "I suppose this could have been a house."

Marg read from her guide book. "During the period one thousand to twelve hundred AD, this temple was the overlord's personal shrine."

"Right." Entering the second room, I stopped and stared. "What are those?" I pointed at small red handprints.

Marg laughed. "It says here that this room might have been a daycare center."

"Seriously? That's weird." I swung up my camera and looked in the viewfinder. If I zoomed it in, I might be able to take a picture. Excellent. I clicked the button.

Marg seemed mesmerized by the little handprints. At this rate, she might want to start a family with Manni before she left the island.

"Let's go." Edging my way around the building ahead of Marg, I came upon the largest iguana I'd ever seen. It stared at me with big hooded eyes. About two feet long further up next to the overhanging tree, I noticed another one.

"Marg, come and look at this." I opened my camera lens and zoomed in for a photo.

Trekking carefully on a trail, she reached my side and glanced up. "What?" she said, puzzled.

I pointed at the pale green iguana, camouflaged on the stones.

"Oo-hh!" Marg gasped. "What's that thing?"

"An iguana. See its friend?" Their tails were long and striped black.

Marg tensed up. "Ew, Adie, they're big!"

"They're omnivores. They eat insects and leaves." I patted Marg's arm reassuringly. "Don't worry, they won't attack us. Let's go see those ruins. See that rounded arch just ahead?"

"That's the entrance to the road. The arch protects an altar to the goddess Ixchel," Marg read from a blurb in the guidebook.

"You leaving a sacrifice, Marg?"

"Don't have anything she wants anymore."

"Don't put yourself down." I took out my camera. "Go stand over there." Marg stood serenely under the arch and I snapped the photo.

"Listen to this, Adie." Marg glanced up from her book. "Apparently, a hidden priestess would answer questions, pretending to be the goddess."

"Too bad she isn't still here. She could clue me in on my relationship problems."

"Try communicating with Wolf," Marg advised me in her psychiatric counselor's voice.

"Every time we try, someone comes in the way."

"Alvarez."

"No. The problem is Daniella and her man-grabbing ways."

"He won't let himself be taken by that skank."

I wasn't convinced of that. Daniella was a force to be reckoned with. Men don't think with their brain—everyone knows that.

We wandered around the ruins, stopping at an unusual building with two rounded platforms. "What does the guidebook say about this one?"

"It's called the Murcielagos and was the most important building in the late classic period." Marg paused and skimmed through the information. "It was in use for centuries but was no longer the center of the village by one thousand AD."

"The historic value of these ruins is good, but I can't say they're too interesting."

"That wall with the handprints was charming." Marg's eyes took on a pensive expression.

"I think what I like," I remarked, surveying the jungle, "is the trees and wildlife." High above us, birds were squawking and flitting from tree to tree. The roots of some of trees reached down into the shallow water in between the ruins.

We tread carefully, anxious not to get our feet wet as we crossed the stone bridge.

"It is a pretty location, but I'm not too fond of lizards."

"I've seen enough of the ruins. How about you?" I wanted to have a closer look at the wildlife in the trees.

"If you don't mind, I'd like to get a few more photos from that angle." Marg pointed to a ruin on the other side of the pond.

"Sure. I'll see you at the Jeep in a while?"

Marg nodded absentmindedly.

I watched her amble over the stone bridge and disappear behind the trees. Taking my time, I watched some small animals screeching in the branches high overhead. It was a busy place. Bushes and trees were alive with bright flashes of color. I took pictures before I headed back up a roundabout path towards the small parking lot. The Jeep sat at the corner of the deserted dirt parking area.

I was feeling a bit depressed. I'd spent almost every night in Cozumel with Wolf. How would he react when he found out I was going to spend the day and the evening with Diego? Maybe I should be asking Marg if Anita had another room for me to hide in. I shrugged. But I had to do this. It was important to find out more. Buttered up, Diego would tell me everything I needed to know.

At the Jeep, I decided I might as well change back into my sandals. They'd be cooler with this oppressive humidity. No air conditioning in this vehicle. I remembered asking the guy at Hertz about air and all he did was point to the open window. If you wanted luxury you needed money.

I swiveled around, grabbed my plastic bag and pulled it off the seat. About to reach into the bag, I sensed a slight movement. Abruptly, I dropped the bag on the floor. At that moment, a narrow black head emerged.

The snake rose slowly up alongside the gearshift. I froze. Red-yellow-black. The pattern repeated, as more of the snake crawled out of the bag. Its head was small on the long body. I was sitting in the driver's seat too petrified to move. It slithered closer. I recalled something I'd read. Red and black, friend of Jack, red and yellow, kill a fellow. This snake was red-yellow-black—a deadly coral snake. The yellow-striped tail stuck up in the air and started waving slowly from side to side. With a concentrated effort I twisted away, threw myself onto the ground arms stretched in a side break fall, and rolled away from the car.

"Adie!" Marg yelled. "Are you hurt?"

I glanced over to where Marg stood fifteen feet away. I got up unsteadily and stepped away from my vehicle, eying the driver's seat. Marg rushed up. "What happened?"

I held my arm out to stop her, and whispered hoarsely, "There's a snake in the Jeep."

"Snake?" Marg paled. "Where?"

I pointed at the red-striped snake, hanging off the dark runner of the Jeep. Our eyes followed its descent onto the dirt parking lot. Creeping unhurriedly towards the undergrowth, the coral snake entered the tall grass and slithered away out of sight.

Heaving a sigh of relief, I faced Marg, my shoulders squared. My suspicions were escalating. Marg could have murdered Reich and his ex. It was also possible she had hired someone to attack me because I'd found out her secret. After all, she'd been conveniently gone when the snake had made its appearance.

"Where were you?"

"Me? I was taking photos…" Her voice trailed off at my expression.

"Tell me what you know about Reich's assets."

"His estate?"

"Yes, tell me. I want to know everything, Marg."

"Well, I don't know how much money he had exactly. He was very well off, I know that. He was one of the owners of Reich Shoes. But why is this so important right now?" Marg took out a Kleenex from her purse and started dabbing on the bloody scratches on my arm.

I brushed her hand away. "Tell me what you know, Marg."

Marg looked startled. "He did charity work and had a house in Beachwood. Drove a BMW—an expensive one."

I snapped, "How much did he say he was leaving you in his will?"

"He didn't tell me anything about that." Marg glared. "What are you implying, Adie?"

"You're saying you didn't know that you'd inherit five hundred thousand?"

Marg's mouth formed an *O*.

"When did you leave Kitchener, Marg?"

"The fourteenth."

"The day Tim Reich was murdered?"

"Yes."

So, she couldn't have murdered Uma, unless she was lying. Was Diego trying to kill Marg? Had he sent someone to plant a snake in the Jeep? "Did you phone Diego about collecting the cashier's check again?"

"I was planning to, but now that I'm staying here longer I didn't want to risk going there by myself after what happened the first time. I'm sure he's behind all these attacks on us. It would have been easy for him to send someone to follow us and place the snake in there. Don't you see, Adie," she said, her voice raised, "if you'd been driving when the snake popped out, we might both have been killed." She grabbed my shoulders, "You can't go to Tulum with Alvarez! He's dangerous!"

17

A red snake is similar to a large stop sign in the animal kingdom. It calls out danger! I had been close to getting a serious dose of venom—too close. My hands on the steering wheel trembled as I eased the Jeep out onto the highway.

Perspiration coated my brow. Beside me, Marg sat rigidly silent, her mouth tight. The scenery was a blur as my mind kept recreating the coral snake incident. When and how did it get in the bag? There hadn't appeared to be any other visitors at the time, but the ruins were large enough for people to have come and gone unseen, leaving a coral snake behind.

Marg spoke up quietly as we neared San Miguel. "You have to believe me, Adie. I had nothing to do with this. I wouldn't do anything to hurt you." She put her hand on my arm. "Listen to me. If I were involved, why would I leave my hotel and go and live with Anita? Tim paid for everything. It's a beautiful hotel and I've never been anywhere more luxurious."

She had a point, but I couldn't rid myself of all my doubts.

"Do you believe me?"

I nodded, not trusting myself to speak.

I turned onto Calle 4. An iron gate fronted a pink house with large hibiscus trees. Before Marg got out, she said, "I know you'll do whatever you think you should, but please be careful. If you go to Tulum, tell Wolf and give me your cell number. If I find out anything, I'll call."

"Okay." I dug in my purse for a scrap of paper. "Thanks for the shoes, Marg. They're beautiful." I wrote the number and gave it to her.

Taking the paper, Marg asked, "Will I see you before you leave?"

"I'm not sure. If I have time, I'll call you. Otherwise, I guess we'll see each other back home." I got out of my Jeep and over to where she stood on the sidewalk. I was feeling all emotional and out of control. A tear rolled down my cheek. "I'm sorry I doubted you."

Marg gave me a hug. "You had a close call with that snake. I understand how you could be confused by all this. You're a brave person and a good friend, Adie."

* * *

Wolf wasn't back. The place was mine. Plenty of time for a shower and time to relax before dinner. A hot shower would get rid of the kinks in my neck. Vacations were supposed to be a time to let go of stress. This one was obviously a dud. No, I was wrong. Cozumel was a breathtaking place with the most fantastic snorkeling and beautiful beaches, not to mention the two hottest guys I'd seen in a long time. I felt drained. A facial would help.

With my clothes in a heap on the bathroom floor, I grabbed a towel to wrap around. After I rinsed my face I applied a thin coat of bluish mud and decided to sit outside on the patio while it dried. I sank back into the chaise lounge and closed my eyes. With happy hour at the bar, it was busy down by the pool—Ricky Martin full blast.

The patio door slide open. Why did I do this to myself? I heard his voice before I saw his face.

"Where's that spicy naked babe I live with? Is she…" Wolf stopped mid-sentence. He grinned, studying my appearance. "The *Day of the Dead* isn't until November, Adie."

Silently, I stood, brushing by him on my way to the bathroom. After showering off, I shook my head at my stupidity. Daniella would never let herself look like that. She probably slept with her makeup on and hair sprayed in that perfect big-hair look. I might as well have handed the room key to the barracuda.

With my hair styled and a touch of makeup, I left wearing a towel. Wolf was stretched out on the couch, holding a bottle of beer in one hand and a printout in the other. His white shirt rolled up at the sleeves revealed tanned arms and the unbuttoned shirt allowed a glimpse of his muscular chest.

His eyes shot up. "That's my sexy woman." He patted the couch. "Join me. I've got your drink for you." He gestured to the strawberry daiquiri sitting on the glass table.

Cautiously, careful not to loosen my towel, I sat down at the edge of the couch near his long legs.

"What's going on with you?" He handed me the daiquiri and leaned back, watching me.

"That was a facial, Wolf."

He grinned widely. "I am not entirely ignorant in the ways of women."

"Well, I had the need to treat myself after what happened today."

"Not another crazy with a knife?" His face showed concern.

"This one wasn't a person." I took a sip of my daiquiri.

Wolf stared at me expectantly.

"A coral snake."

"Where?"

"In my Jeep, in the back seat in a plastic shopping bag."

"Strange things you buy, Adie."

I jabbed him in the leg. He held up his hands in surrender.

"Sorry, couldn't resist."

His face became serious. "What happened?"

"We were seeing the ruins. I ended up going back alone while Marg took some more photos. I had my sandals in there so I thought I would take off my Nikes and change back into my sandals. When I picked up the bag, the snake's head popped out."

"Shit!"

"No kidding," I said dryly. "I dropped the bag and threw myself on the ground so I wouldn't get bitten."

Wolf glanced at my arms, noticing the scrapes and scratches. "What happened to the snake?"

"It crawled into the jungle."

Wolf frowned. "Coral snakes are native to Mexico but not Cozumel."

"That's what I thought. If anyone would know, it would be you, Hawkeye."

Wolf took my hand. "Are you sure about it being a coral snake?"

I pictured the snake in my mind. "Red-yellow-black stripes."

Wolf was silent a moment and then said, "Not a friend of Jack."

I frowned. "There's something bothering me about this."

"Besides the fact that you could have died?"

I nodded. "You know how we discussed Marg inheriting

money?"

"Five hundred thousand according to your cop buddy."

"Yes. Do you think she could?"

"Set you up?" Staring into the golden hue of his beer, Wolf considered.

I nodded.

"Do you know when she left for Cozumel?"

"December fourteenth. Same day Reich was murdered, or so she said."

Wolf put his feet up on the table. "You don't believe her?"

I sipped my daiquiri appreciating the thick mixture of strawberry and rum. "I have to check this out. I'm going to e-mail Ilya."

Wolf frowned.

I took another sip of my daiquiri finishing most of it. "Thanks for the drink."

Wolf smiled. "Anything for you."

"Don't make promises you can't keep."

His eyes trailed up my legs to the towel. "Get dressed. I can't promise not to do anything right now."

* * *

I clicked on Ilya's e-mail address and typed.

Hey Ilya. You've got to help me with this. When did Marg arrive in Cozumel? Did she leave on December 14th? What was Uma's time of death? Thanks, Adie.

I pressed *send* and walked over to Wolf who was leaning against the door. "Done." I took his hand and reached to push the door open. He held it for me and we stepped outside into the night air.

The tourist crowd was out in droves as we strolled into the busy center square. Eager to sell their canvases, airbrush artists called out for us to look at their art, while children played around the shops. Standing in front of the booths, men kept shouting for us to see their wares as we went by. I shook my head and Wolf told them *manana,* tomorrow. *Manana* gave hope. It was better than never.

* * *

La Choza, a restaurant known for its native cuisine, was a few streets from the square and although it was reasonably full when we got there, they quickly cleared a table for us overlooking the street.

Open air, under a thatched roof, it was charming—murals on the walls and a Mexican trio serenading guests. When Wolf pulled his chair closer to mine, I could feel the warmth of his body. Time was running out. I would miss this man.

A waiter took our drink order, a daiquiri for me and a beer for Wolf. Our drinks had become predictable, unlike our relationship. "I'm going home on Christmas Day." I examined his face for a reaction.

Wolf leaned back in his chair, studying me. "When?"

"Afternoon, around two."

The waiter appeared with some salsa and chips.

Wolf took my hand in his. "I'll miss you. You've been a fascinating roommate."

"Roommate?"

Stroking his chin with his forefinger, Wolf said, "A situation easily remedied."

"Do we have plans for Christmas Eve?" I clenched my jaw in preparation for a letdown.

"We sure do." Wolf dipped a chip in some green sauce and gazed at me steadily.

"And they are..."

Wolf moved in closer, his lips almost touching mine and whispered, "A surprise."

An undeniable craving awakened. Then he kissed me—charging me with emotions I didn't know I had.

"Ah-hm." A polite cough from our waiter. Wolf's lips let up abruptly, his fingers slid down to my arm. The waiter placed our drinks on the table. "Are you ready to order, Señor?"

"Is it all right if I order for you this time, Adie?"

"Okay." I'm a picky eater, but by now Wolf should know what I liked.

"*Pollo de mole pablano. Dos, por favor.*" The server nodded and made his way to the kitchen. I knew the *pollo* was chicken.

The other, I didn't have a clue.

Making their rounds, the house musicians came over to our table and waited to see if we wanted them to play. Wolf nodded and they started to sing *La Paloma*—the dove. It was a romantic ballad that seemed just right for this evening with the soft lighting at our table, the warm breeze and the smoking hot man beside me.

We sat back in our chairs watching the guitarists strum their instruments, singing softly. I wasn't so sure what the Spanish lyrics meant but the melody flowed and Wolf's hand touching mine was strong and warm. Before the trio moved on they accepted his tip.

"That was sweet of you, Wolf."

"You needed that after a shopping bag filled with coral snake." He ran his finger down my cheek. "You're lookin' good tonight, princess."

"Thanks." That was the extent of my conversational ability. My active libido was jumbling my brain waves. I was thankful for the distraction of the waiter arriving with our order. The waiter explained that the restaurant cooked the chicken in the traditional way, slowly, to allow the flavors to blend. Put off a bit by the black sauce, I was none the less intrigued to try something different. I dug my fork into the chicken and tasted it.

"What do you think?"

"Delicious. This may seem weird, but I'd swear, there's chocolate in it."

Wolf smiled.

"There is? That's unbelievable." I stroked his hand. "I think you know what I like."

"I do."

I guess the ball was in my court, but I wasn't going to play. "What's happening with your property?"

"Lots." Wolf concentrated on his meal. I waited for him to continue. "Got a construction crew together and hired a handyman."

"Tell me about the property." Wolf's tan made his startling blue eyes more mysterious.

"It's a total of seven cottages right here in San Miguel."

"At the beach?"

"No, but only a few blocks away from the waterfront."

"You said you'd show them to me tonight."

"Did I?" he said absentmindedly, as he cut his chicken.

He had really shut me out this time. "You don't have to if it's too much trouble, Wolf."

He patted my hand. "No problem." He was done eating and here I was, only starting, having focused on my drink instead of my food. Big mistake. I felt the punch of it already. Picking up my fork I dug into the chicken coated with thick black sauce when I felt my hair being swept off my shoulder. His lips nuzzled the curve of my neck and trailed to my shoulder. I pushed him away. "Stop, I need to eat."

He looked amused. "Ah-hh, if only I was a piece of chicken."

"You think I don't pay attention to you?" I asked seriously.

"Do you?"

That was ridiculous! I thought of him constantly. I glared swallowing a mouthful of succulent chicken.

"Don't speak, Adie. I want you to get your energy back." His lips turned upward at the corners.

"Why?" I glanced at him.

"Your eyes are sexy, so turquoise. Does that mean you're angry?" he said, studying me. "Your eyes always get that color when you're pissed off about something."

I sighed. This man could drive me crazy in more ways than one. I changed the subject. "Did you see anything in the printouts?"

"Large transfers to the Caymans from various places."

"There was something I saw earlier today." It was bothering me.

"What?" Wolf asked.

"A name. It seemed familiar. I recognized it. It's in the back of my mind." I rubbed my forehead. "I just can't think of it now."

"Show me the printout when we get back." He glanced at my nearly empty plate. "Done?"

I nodded. "It was really good, Wolf."

The waiter cleared our table and asked if we would like anything else. Wolf shook his head and asked for the check. A minute later, the waiter had everything totaled and Wolf signed the receipt. I was wondering why he was in such a hurry especially when he glanced at his watch. As we left the restaurant, his cell phone vibrated. "Excuse me, Adie. Hello?" Someone on the other end did all the talking. Shoving his cell in his pocket, he turned to me. "Let's go for a walk. It's a nice night."

It was a warm evening and the streets were still occupied with vendors and buyers. The cruise ship people were long gone, but the town was alive with food smells and bright colors from the blankets, beach clothes and the glitter of the silver shops. We were heading away from the square but relatively close to the waterfront.

Passing a corner house, he stopped at a black wrought iron gate. Wolf inserted a key into the lock and opened the iron door. Curiously, I followed. Lights in the bougainvillea trees cast shadows on the paved walkway as we made our way slowly around the first cottage. The heady fragrance from the flowering trees pleasantly assaulted my senses. Wolf took my hand and led me along past another white stucco cottage.

"Why were these cottages for sale?"

His hair had a halo effect from the backlighting, but his face was in darkness. "They were built originally for the management staff of a hotel on the coast. Things went wrong and the hotel went bankrupt. These cottages have been empty for a year now, unsold. I thought I'd fix them up and rent them out."

We trekked on, around another cottage. There were gaps in the garden along the path. Wolf stopped and indicated the empty portion of the grounds. "Juan is getting some plants tomorrow to fill in these spots."

Just past the garden, I noticed some movement in the trees. Something brown with a striped tail and a long snout jumped down over the wall into a tree. "What's that?"

"A pizote."

"Huh?"

"They look a bit like raccoons." Wolf smiled at my furrowed brow. "Don't worry about them."

"You'll protect me if they have big teeth?"

"It's not them you should worry about."

My eyes shot to Wolf, but a shadow hid his expression. He took my hand and led me further along beyond a clump of trees. The light seemed brighter as we entered a clearing.

"This is beautiful!" There was a kidney-shaped pool with a cement deck on which a few lounge chairs were situated. Candles reflected flickering lights on the water. Further over, I saw a small table with plates, a box, and a coffee urn. "What's all this?"

"You told me how you loved chocolate. I ordered a chocolate cake from the bakery."

Bewildered, I brought my hands to my face. "You ordered cake especially for me?"

"This wasn't entirely unselfish on my part. I had an urge for chocolate tonight and it's hard to find chocolate cake here."

"But how did you manage to do all this?"

"This was part of Juan's first assignment."

"And he thought of the candles?"

"No," Wolf said, stroking my cheek, "but I told him to light them for us."

"How did he—oh, he phoned."

Wolf pulled out a seat for me. Wolf uncovered the small cake and cut two generous portions and served them on our plates. The remaining piece he placed in the cake box.

It was decadent—the smooth chocolate filling melting in my mouth. "This cake is like a dream come true. You don't know how much I've been dying to have chocolate."

"I've had a craving for chocolate myself."

"It must have something to do with Christmas. You know, everyone has chocolates." I forked up a large chunk of cake and brought it to my lips.

"It doesn't need to be Christmas to have urgings." Wolf's eyes glinted silver in the faint light.

"The pool looks so inviting." Steam rose from the surface of the water. "Is it heated?"

"It's been running all day."

"But you don't have any guests here, do you?"

"No. We're alone," he said softly.

I glanced around, suddenly nervous.

I saw the flash of Wolf's white teeth as he smiled. "It's for you."

"What do you mean?"

Wolf pulled me up from my chair. "You like new experiences, Adie." He gestured to the pool. "It's hot and it's waiting for you and me."

"You mean we should go swimming?"

"Now you're getting the idea."

"We don't have towels."

"We do." Wolf gestured to a basket I hadn't noticed next to the lounge chairs.

I ran a finger over my lips. "No bathing suits."

"We don't need any," Wolf whispered, taking my hand.

"But…"

"I promise I won't do anything, except…"

"Except what?"

"Kiss you."

I was puzzled. The Wolf I knew wouldn't just kiss me. What did this mean? I wasn't exciting him anymore? Could he be in love with Daniella? "That's it?" I asked tensely.

"I wouldn't want to disappoint you, Adie. I could do more."

"That's not what I meant to say. I'm not sure if this is right…" I wanted this man, true, but did I trust him? Had he ever said how he felt about me?

"It's right. Besides, it'll feel good."

My skin was damp with perspiration from the humidity of the night. It would feel great to be in the water in this private place with a sizzling man like Wolf. But, no, I wasn't ready for more. Not with all these doubts. I needed to know what I meant to him. I didn't need a repeat of my last relationship.

"Okay, pinky swear," I said, holding my finger up. "I'm serious, Wolf. Nothing but kisses."

Wolf grinned and pulled his pinky around mine. "You drive a hard bargain."

"You need to turn around, close your eyes and keep them closed."

Wolf turned away. "Is it okay if I start taking off my clothes?" He undid his belt buckle and then started on his shirt buttons.

"Sure, but don't turn around until I say so."

He slid his shirt off, slowly and deliberately, while I unzipped my dress. I stopped everything and watched. My breath caught, gazing at his muscular back and narrow waist.

He wasn't just taking his clothes off. It was a scintillating strip tease! Aa-hh! I stared as he dropped his jeans. No girls' night out had prepared me for this!

I closed my eyes, gathering my strength. Looking away, I

stepped out of my dress, folded it neatly and placed it on the lounge chair. Unfastening my bra, I dropped it on top, and quickly pulled off my low-rise panties. "Don't move!" I said, hurrying to the pool ladder. In my rush to get in, I nearly tripped and fell. Righting myself, I hurled myself into the warm water. Pure heaven!

I knew I shouldn't look at Wolf, but I did. He had turned around, but he kept his promise. His eyes were still closed. The candlelight backlit his figure, broad shoulders and chest, long legs. As for his package, I wasn't disappointed. "You can come in now," I called out before I swam off.

Water caressed my skin. I felt liberated without a bathing suit. At the far end, I started back with a sidestroke. Something brushed my foot. Could there be frogs in here? Or worse yet—snakes? Water splashed into my eyes and Wolf shot up to the surface in front of me. Treading water, he pulled me close. As my treading skills are limited, I put my hands on his arms to stay afloat. He went into a rescue position, partially on his back and pulled me along with him to the shallow end. When my back touched the rim of the pool, I warned him. "Remember what I said." Afraid he could see too much, I sank lower in the water.

"No touching?"

I nodded.

He grinned before he shook me loose. I dropped in, my head submerged. I shrieked coming back for air. Sputtering, I grabbed his shoulders and pulled up, "It's okay if it's arms."

Wolf grinned. "New rule?"

"Works for me."

From somewhere on the deck a cell phone started vibrating.

"Ignore that," Wolf said.

It had to be Diego about our date to Tulum. I turned towards the buzzing signal. Wolf's lips nuzzled my neck. I shivered as he teased my shoulder.

"I should get that." So aware of the hard body against me, I was hardly conscious of the words I spoke.

"They'll call again—if it's important."

The buzzing stopped. My breasts slid against his slippery strong chest. My nipples hardened. Wolf's hand on my lower back pushed me up higher. He bent his head and his lips captured a bud.

A sweet sensation jolted me. When he let go, I sank down a bit, my thigh brushing against his erection. He pushed against me and I closed in on him. His mouth met my parted lips, our tongues flirted, exciting each other. His firm slippery body slid back and forth against me until the pulsing in my core became almost unbearable. We kissed urgently. But there was something wrong with this. "Wait, you said…"

Wolf withdrew his lips, but kept his body pressed tight against me. "What?"

"Only kisses," I whispered.

"These are kisses." His mysterious eyes held my gaze.

I didn't want to think anymore. Why was I thinking anyway?

"You didn't say there was a restriction as to where."

Wolf brought his lips to my mouth again, moving them sensuously as his tongue explored my lower lip. I ached for him. The push of his tongue on mine lit a fire inside. I came up for air before I brought my tongue to his ear. I teased it and felt his body shiver in arousal.

Now, I needed him more than ever—so magnificent. Narrow hips and a tight firm ass. My fingertips ran up and down his thigh while my wrist brushed his rod. I stroked until I heard him groan with pleasure.

Transported by his magnetism, his very essence, I reached out for him and pulled his head closer, impelling his lips to press tightly on mine. My tongue met his. Hot molten lava rushed down my body. He stroked my breast, his fingers teasing until I quivered with expectation. I was swept into a dreamy pleasure ride—a hot wet ride that could only get wilder. I forgot everything I feared about love. I knew there should be no rules for us. He wasn't meant for rules and neither was I.

The phone buzzed again and again. The persistent interruption jolted my mind into a confused state. Jealousy reared its ugly head. Was he giving all this to Daniella? If I was falling for him, I needed the truth.

Wolf kissed my shoulder. Insistently, the phone kept up its annoying racket. I had to know, and yet, it would be so easy to lose myself in this. Why was I torturing myself? If I let him, I could escape, fly into it, soar high. We could—the buzzing was driving me insane. I jerked away, angry with myself and him.

Wolf murmured, his voice husky, "You don't have to take that call, Adie."

I stared at him, wondering what to do. Marg needed my help. I shook my head. It wasn't easy to speak, but if it was Diego.... "I have to," I said, without conviction, but I voiced it, and he took me at my word. He glanced at me, his expression unreadable before he released me and dived down under the water affording me a glimpse of flawlessly rounded buns.

I swam a few strokes and grabbed the railing, stepping up the ladder. Pulling a towel from the basket by the lounge chairs, I speedily wrapped it around me and rushed to my purse which I had left on the deck next to the table. No sign of Wolf. He was swimming underwater.

The phone was still ringing as I pressed the button.

"Hello," I said breathlessly.

"I hope I'm not interrupting anything."

"No," I whispered.

"There's a change in our plans for tomorrow."

"Oh?"

"My father is in town and wants to," Diego sighed, "discuss business with me. He'd like to meet with me for breakfast. Is it okay with you if we go a little later?"

At least he didn't want to cancel. "Yes, when?"

"We could take the twelve o'clock ferry."

I watched as Wolf swam up to the ladder.

"Just a minute, Diego. Hold on." I grabbed a towel and threw it to Wolf as he started up out of the water. He caught it and grinned. I was glad he wasn't angry with me for taking the call. I didn't want things to be difficult with us, but I didn't want to make another mistake and rush this relationship.

And seeing the look in Wolf's eyes, I was right about throwing him a towel. Who knows what he would have done if I hadn't. He wouldn't think twice about strutting around in the nude tempting me. I walked back to the lounge chair and sat down.

"Sorry about that, Diego," I spoke softly, aware of Wolf hearing every word.

"You're not alone, are you?"

"No." I glanced at Wolf coming up to me, a towel slung low on his waist.

Diego laughed, "Well then, you'll have to tell me tomorrow how much you want to see me."

"And you would know this because?"

"I saw it in your eyes, Adelina. By the way, how is your ankle?"

"It's fine, now."

"Good, we need to climb down to the beach. But don't worry, I'll help you."

"It's that difficult?"

"For the old and infirm, but you're hardly that."

"Should I bring a towel?" The lounge chair creaked as Wolf sat down beside me.

"No, Adelina. All will be provided. Towels, a blanket, food and drinks. Do you like lobster?"

"Yes, I love lobster, as long as I don't have to see the whole thing. I'm okay with the tail, though."

"*Bien.* Have a late breakfast and we'll have a picnic on the beach in the late afternoon. Oh, and we'll need to take the eight o'clock ferry back, since my parents are here."

"Weren't you planning on meeting someone?" Wolf wrapped his arm around me, nuzzling my neck.

"Yes, thanks for reminding me. I'll need to phone him. Would you like to meet my parents? They're staying at Carmelita's."

I hesitated as I felt Wolf's tongue explore my ear, finding it harder to concentrate on the conversation. Diego seemed so far away. High voltage charges raced down my body. I tried to block out Wolf as I took in Diego's statement. Meet his parents? Was he serious? He hardly knew me, but maybe things were different here in Mexico."

"You're not ready for that? Don't worry. We'll do it some other time."

I needed to think, but Wolf's kisses were so sweet.

"Stop," I whispered to Wolf.

"Are you with Wolf?" Diego asked.

"Um-hum." It was difficult to speak. Wolf pushed my wet hair away to gain access to my neck. His kisses trailed down to my shoulder.

Diego chuckled. "In that case, I'm glad I interrupted.

"What are you doing Christmas Eve? Would you like to spend

the evening together?"

"Ah-hh," I said, sighing with pleasure.

"Does that mean yes?"

I shrugged Wolf off, to process Diego's question. "I'm sorry, Diego. I already have plans."

"Don't tell me—Wolf. He beat me to it. What about Christmas Day? Would you have dinner with me?"

Wolf's hand slid under my towel.

"Oo-hh."

"You can? Good. When do you return to Toronto?"

I tried to speak coherently. "Christmas Day."

"Oh? A late flight?"

I could feel my towel being lowered. "No!" I hissed at Wolf.

"Adelinita, we must have lunch then." Diego spoke indulgently as if to a spoiled but somewhat backward child, who was totally confused, which I was. How could I think with this devil touching me? I almost dropped the phone. I stood up, tucking my towel back in and collected my thoughts.

"I'll phone you about eleven-thirty tomorrow."

"Ciao, mi amor."

"Bye, Diego." I clicked to end the call and glared at Wolf. "Wolf. You knew that was important. Why did you do that?"

Wolf grinned wickedly.

I shook my head in disgust. "You just wanted to distract me because I was talking to Diego."

"It worked."

I frowned. "I need to fill you in on my plans, Wolf, but first, I'm getting dressed and you," I said, pointing a finger at him, "are going to look away while I do."

"Does that mean you'll look away when I get dressed?"

I blushed, thinking how crazy I sounded after our pool experience. "Yes, and you won't turn around 'til I'm ready, right?"

"Don't trust me, Adie?"

"You are so bad!"

"And you are so sexy," he said softly.

I was determined to get control of this situation, so I kept telling myself—the mind is stronger than the body. Taking up my clothes, I strode over to a large flowering bush and stood behind it, out of his view.

Through the bush I could see Wolf drying himself off before he abruptly dropped his towel, giving me an eyeful. I pulled on my panties, my eyes averted, not wanting to think about how hot he was. With my bra over my breasts I attempted to hook it up, but my hands kept slipping.

"Need help?"

How did he know what I was doing? Could he see through the bush? My eyes shot back to an overhead light in a tree. It shone down on the pathway behind me, and on the bushes on either side.

"Turn around," I ordered, as I shook my dress over my head and pulled it down the length of my body.

He paused as he pulled up his jeans and glanced in my direction.

"No need to now, is there?"

Promptly, I slipped on my sandals and stalked out. He was fastening the buttons on his shirt, looking amused as I marched up to him. "You could see everything, couldn't you?"

He smiled. "Just as much as you." Wolf tucked his shirt in his jeans and zipped them up. He gazed into my eyes. "I liked our swim, princess. Did you?"

"Yes," I muttered, before his lips pressed on mine, intensely, searching for answers I didn't have, and couldn't give him.

When I picked up my purse and looked at Wolf expectantly, he scooped up the cake box and steered me down the shadowy path to the gate. We made our way into the main street, hand in hand, past brightly lit stores. I noticed a guy giving me the once-over. "I must look awful with this scraggly wet hair. They're all staring at me, Wolf."

An older woman in a long dress with a man frowned when she came up to us. As she trudged by, she vigorously tugged her hesitant male escort along with her, who kept on ogling me. Wolf grinned slowly, glancing at my chest. "It's not your hair they're interested in."

"What do you mean?"

"Let's put it this way—if you were in a wet T-shirt contest, you'd win first prize."

Oo-hh, no! I knew my skin had been damp when I dressed but I hadn't thought my bra was so sheer. With the cool evening air, a thin white cotton dress, I might as well have been topless.

"Wolf!" I said anxiously.

"Come on, Adie. We'll cross the street," he said, "it's darker on the other side away from the shops. You'll dry faster with the sea breeze."

"Oh-hh," I said miserably.

"Don't be embarrassed, Adie." He smiled fondly at me. "You look like a mermaid."

I pulled my dress away from my chest, hoping it would dry faster. "How can I go to the Internet Café now?"

"You'll be dry by then. It's quite a way from here."

The waves were rushing in loudly against the sea wall, but the night was clear. Wolf stopped and put his arm around my waist. "See the north star? There's the Big Dipper." His eyes moved upwards.

"Where?"

"Look at the horizon."

The sky was full of stars tonight but I could make out the constellation low in the sky. Wolf's arm felt warm around me. I leaned my head on his shoulder. "The Mayans thought the Big Dipper was the Jaguar God, chased away by Venus, the Serpent God." Seeing the stars made me think of Mayan temples and the astronomy they studied centuries ago and my thoughts flew to my upcoming excursion to Tulum. I paused, wishing I didn't have to tell him. "Wolf, I'm seeing Diego tomorrow."

"Where?" Wolf's cool blue eyes met mine.

"We're going to Tulum."

"When?"

"The ferry dock at twelve."

"You're sure about this?" Wolf squeezed my hand. "We don't know who's been sending these bastards after you."

"Don't worry about me, Wolf. I can take care of myself." I said, with confidence I wasn't sure I had.

"Yeah, karate woman," he said dryly. Then he tried reasoning with me. "You can't handle this by yourself, Adie."

I wasn't sure I could either but I didn't want him to think so. I took karate because I'd been attacked a few years ago. Karate had given me confidence and control again. "Let's not argue about this. Diego won't hurt me."

Wolf fell silent beside me as we strolled away from the shops.

The road was under construction for a block or so. Bulldozers and trucks cluttered the street in between huge gaps in the cement.

"This was where I saw that guy."

Wolf put his arm around my shoulders. "You'll be home in three days. Why not leave it alone and with any luck you'll arrive in Toronto in one piece."

"Diego has this business meeting. I could listen in and see what I could find out. And I know I can get something out of him about Reich and Uma."

"Why is that, Mata Hari?" Wolf glanced at me. "Because he's so in to you?"

"Hah, little do you know, Wolf Du Lac. He asked me to meet his parents."

Wolf stopped in his tracks. "Seriously?"

I nodded. "Do you know anything about them?"

"Might be something we need to find out. The internet might have some info on his father. Do you know his first name?"

"No, but I have Bernie digging around for me. I'll check my messages."

"Are you meeting his parents?"

"No-oo. I don't think I'm ready for a commitment."

"Why does that not surprise me?"

"As if you are."

"Me? You think I've got a problem with commitment? I've spent every evening with you since you got here and you take off with another man just as we're getting close."

"Sex is not commitment, Wolf."

"You don't actually believe Alvarez wants a commitment with you, do you?"

"He seemed sincere about me meeting his family."

"He just wants you to think he's ready for marriage. It's bait, Adie."

"You mean like the rose?"

"Yeah, the rose, the champagne, the tequila and the yacht."

"And all guys think women want to get married."

"Sure, women have biological time clocks." Wolf smiled engagingly at me as we stepped back on the sidewalk.

"Sounds like a bomb ready to explode."

He chuckled and pulled me close.

I glanced up at him. Animal magnetism—that's what he had and more. He was confident, cool and in control of any situation.

Just ahead I could see the Chedraui Plaza and the Internet Café on the other side of the street.

I reflected on his statement. "Marg's bomb is going off. If she and Manni get married there'll be little ones soon."

"So, Marg isn't just having a fling?"

"You should have seen her today at San Gervasio looking at the children's handprints on the wall."

"Marg doesn't seem the type to be ordering contract killers."

"I know. She was really sweet today and bought me these beautiful red high heels. I've been looking everywhere for some red sandals and when I found them she gave them to me for Christmas."

"Can't wait to see you in them."

"How about Christmas Eve?"

"We could find a place to put them to use." He glanced at me. "When does your date with Alvarez?"

"We're taking the eight o'clock ferry back. He wants to meet his parents at Carmelita's. I told him I didn't think I'd go."

Wolf's black Jeep was parked in front of the Internet Café. The lights were on inside.

"He won't give up. You might end up meeting the Bolivar family," Wolf said, as he held the door open. While Wolf paid I sat down and logged in. There were three new messages in my mail.

Hey, Adie. This is what I found out about Santiago Alvarez. He's rich, but you probably know this. Got his initial investment start with daddy's moolah but made enough on his own to expand operations to Toronto and Montreal. Francisco Bolivar, the dad, runs a billion dollar import-export firm from Mexico City and has a hand in Royal Investments. Do you think Alvarez had a contract out on the Reichs? Could be he got greedy, offs them, and takes their money? We've got to talk. When do you come home? Bernie

Then there was one from Ilya.

Hi honey. Checked out Marg's story. She left Kitchener on December 14 and spent the night at the Airport Hilton in Toronto. Took a late flight into Cancun with a connection to Cozumel on December 15 giving her time to go back and murder Uma. Her fingerprints are all over the house. She had drug access. Uma's time of death is between nine o'clock December 15 and three in the morning, December 16. Beige has changed her return time to January third. Be careful. She's dangerous. Ilya.

No, I wouldn't believe that. Marg gave me the shoes I always wanted. That was special. Only a good friend would do such a thing.

My eyes shot to the next e-mail. Oh-no! I wanted to just delete the message, but I couldn't ignore it. The jerk could be the murderer. I took a deep breath and clicked.

ADIE, WHERE IS THAT BITCH? SHE'S IGNORING THE COURT ORDER AND YOU'RE AIDING AND ABETTING. SHE CAN JUST STOP WHORING AND GET HER ASS BACK HERE. WHEN I GET DONE WITH HER, SHE WONT HAVE AN ASS TO PEDDLE. BORIS

I motioned for Wolf to sit down beside me. "Look at this. Is he a sicko, or what?"

Wolf read the e-mail. "The abusive husband type."

"Makes a woman want to reconsider marriage."

"You're considering marriage?"

I bit my lip. "I have to start thinking about it again. My birthday was two weeks ago."

He kissed me quickly. "Happy Birthday. That biological clock is ticking, isn't it?

I nudged his ribs. "Read the other e-mails."

Wolf scanned them and commented. "Two, possibly three suspects, I'd say.

"Okay, we can go now." I touched the cotton material on my breasts. It seemed drier but to be on the safe side, I said, "Hand me that cake box, Wolf. I should have thought of this earlier."

"Can't wait 'til we get back?"

"The box, please."

Puzzled, Wolf handed me the box and then smiled. "Oh, I see, a boob protector."

I rolled my eyes at him as I stood up and held the box in front of my chest with my arms wrapped around it.

"A big loss to mankind."

I ignored his comment and waited as he opened the door.

The breeze was cooler now and clouds had started covering the night sky. Were we in for some rain?

"Adie, I'll take it now," Wolf said, reaching for the box. "We're going in the Jeep. No need to hide your assets anymore."

He turned the key in the ignition and started the motor. "If you get back early tomorrow, we could still go out."

The Jeep pulled out into the nearly empty street and we made a right towards the Hotel Maria. I started yawning, tired from eating, drinking, walking and swimming. Wolf was capable of tiring out any woman.

Wolf glanced in my direction, "Tired? Let's go to bed."

Seeing my expression, he added, "I could do with a good night's sleep—so don't do anything to excite me, eh, Adie?"

"Maybe you should sleep in the bathtub. I could fill it with cold water for you."

In the parking lot, Wolf turned off the engine. "Heartless woman. I have needs, too." Wolf grinned slowly. "Not as explosive as time clock needs, but nonetheless powerful."

"You can't have your cake and eat it, too."

"Why not? That's our plan, isn't it?"

"I wasn't talking chocolate cake here," I said seriously.

"Oh?"

"You know what I mean." It was dark in the car and I couldn't see his eyes.

"Explain."

"One word, Daniella Consuela Whatever!"

"That's three words, Adie." Wolf took the key out and walked around to my side. I gave up. He wasn't about to tell me anything. That was clear enough. I opened my car door.

Taking the cake box with me, I slid my legs down to the ground. As I landed, Wolf was there to take my elbow. He swung the door shut and took my hand as we headed to the front door of our hotel.

I must have looked more decent now, with the box in front of me. I only attracted an occasional glance from other tourists. Wet hair was not unusual on this island known for its diving sites. Not that the dress was the type of clothing worn for scuba outings but they might have thought I changed on the boat.

When we got in the room I noticed the red light flashing on the room phone. I set the box down and picked up the receiver, calling the switchboard operator. I asked about our messages. She told me there were two. I picked up the pen by the pad and waited. One was from a Mr. Don Carrera for Mr. Du Lac, the number left was 48-4457 and there was a second message from Miss Beige with the phone number 38-2456. I hastily scribbled the numbers on the pad.

Outside, a light drizzle was just starting to come down. I looked at Wolf who was placing the cake in the fridge. "Don and Marg called." I called over my shoulder. "The first number is for Don. I'm getting changed, okay?"

"Sure." Wolf sat down on the couch and started to punch in some numbers. I went into the bedroom. While I tugged on a clingy pink top and low-cut boxers, I remembered I had to phone Marg.

18

"So what did Don want?"

Wolf surveyed my outfit. "Nice and tight in the right places, but it's not necessary to wear clothes for my benefit, Adie. I want you to feel perfectly comfortable."

I ignored that. "Don?"

"He didn't answer his cell."

"Oh, I forgot to tell you something."

"What?"

"He was here this morning looking for you."

"And?"

I blushed. "He seemed to think…"

"But, you told him, you were only my roommate."

"Well, not exactly. I said I had to ice my foot and I told him you went somewhere."

"So why did he come?"

"He just said he was thinking of buying this forty-five footer and wanted to know your opinion."

"Don must have come into a lot of money," Wolf said thoughtfully. "He was doing fine before, but a large power boat? I told him my family had one at the cottage."

Hm-mm, that cottage was where I had discovered my sexuality. Wolf would have been part of my discovery, but he moved on to another girl, according to my mom.

Back to the investigation. What did the two murders have to do with Don? If I had consumed less champagne, maybe I would have recalled the conversation on the yacht more clearly. I was about to tell Wolf what I'd overheard, when my cell buzzed.

Wolf grimaced. "Not him again."

I reached into my purse and pulled out my phone. "*Bueno.*"

"Hi, Adie." Marg's voice trembled.

"It's okay. I'm not angry with you."

"That's not why I phoned. Something happened. I was watching the news station from Cancun and they described an accident. Brace yourself, Adie. It's not good."

"What?"

"Don's in critical condition."

"Oh, no!"

Wolf glanced at me with concern. I put my hand on his leg and sat down. "Tell me what you heard."

"Apparently, Don was driving on the east coastal road and his car rolled over the embankment."

I whispered to Wolf, "Don's been hurt in an accident!" I spoke to Marg. "What caused it?"

"That's all they said. Do you think it has anything to do with what happened to us? Could someone be trying to get rid of all of us? This is really scary, Adie."

"I'm going to see what I can find out. I'll call you tomorrow when I get back from Tulum. If you hear anything else, could you let me know, Marg?"

"Yes, of course, Adie. I hope he's not going to die…"

"Me too. Good-bye, Marg. Thanks for calling." I clicked the phone shut and turned to Wolf. "Don's in critical condition. He went off the east coastal road."

He grabbed my hand. "Is he in the hospital here?"

"I don't know," I said uncertainly.

"One way to find out." Wolf picked up the hotel room phone and pushed in the operator button. "Police station, *por favor*. I would like to speak to the officer in charge of the accident involving Don Carrera." Wolf pressed the speaker-phone button.

There was a pause and his call was redirected.

"Hernandez," a gruff voice said abruptly.

"Hola, Officer Hernandez, Wolf Du Lac."

"Is there another problem regarding your friend, Señorita Sturm?" Hernandez inquired politely.

"No, not this time. I just heard about the accident involving Don Carrera. We're friends. Could you give me details?"

"We are looking into the matter. It seems Carrera's car was pushed off the road. Do you know who could have done this?"

Wolf frowned. "You're saying this was not an accident?"

"Correct. At first we assumed it was a matter of drunk driving. There was alcohol on his breath, but when we examined the vehicle, we found traces of paint and dents in the side, as if a car had made several attempts to force Carrera off the road."

"The car rolled off?"

"*Si*. If you know the east coastal road at all, you will know it is narrow and the embankment is rocky."

"Where is he now?"

"Cancun."

Wolf thanked Hernandez and phoned the hospital, asking about the status of Don Carrera.

"Alive. We will know better soon. He is drifting in and out of consciousness but we are hopeful. Call again."

"Would I be able to see him?"

"A short visit only."

"*Gracias, adios*." Wolf hung up the receiver and glanced away.

Touching his hand, I looked up at his face. He was visibly upset. "Are you going there tomorrow?" I went to the fridge and got out two bottles of water and handed one to Wolf.

"I think so. I'll check with my workers first and then take the ferry across."

"Call me on my cell phone when you get there, okay?"

Wolf patted my hand. "Sure."

I stroked his cheek. "Think positively, Wolf. We have to believe he'll be okay."

Wolf stood up and walked over to the patio doors, shoving them open. Some nouveau flamenco music drifted up from the bar area. Below us, people were talking and laughing.

Up here, gloom had set in. I followed Wolf onto the balcony. "Someone had it in for him."

Wolf's eyes searched the dark waters of the Caribbean, as if looking for answers. "My guess is Alvarez."

"Diego likes Don, though."

"It could be something else entirely—something illegal."

"Weed?"

"Maybe. He came into this money suddenly. Enough to buy a large power boat." Wolf sat down on one of the chairs on the patio.

"A large shipment could bring in a lot of money."

"I didn't tell you what I overheard on the yacht." I moved behind his chair and started to massage his back and neck muscles.

"What?"

"One of those women he was with, kept going on about

partying with the money and something about Stingray Island. Where's that?"

"The Caymans." Wolf swiveled. "He could have an account there. Is that what you heard?"

"I'm not sure. One of them kept shushing the other one up. This morning Don told me that he was going away for a while."

Wolf's forehead furrowed. "So both Alvarez and Don have accounts in the Caymans."

"Why would someone want to kill him?"

"He knows too much." We watched the flickering lights of cruise ship out in the harbor.

"It could have nothing to do with Diego," I said, resuming my massage, kneading his neck muscles, in a circular motion.

"Except for the fact that they've gotten very chummy."

"I could phone Diego and ask him if he's heard anything about Don's accident. He might give himself away."

"The trouble with that is you can't see his expression when he tells you."

I scratched my head thoughtfully. "It's a good thing then that I'm going to Tulum with him tomorrow."

Wolf shot me a look. "Going any place with him is not a good thing. Santiago Bolivar Alvarez is bad news."

* * *

Alone, doing my morning stretches, I thought about Don. Wolf had good instincts about people, but maybe his judgment was clouded by his own personal feelings—his animosity to Diego. One thing I knew for sure was that someone was after me and I had to find out who.

Sitting down on the couch, I started skimming the printouts, searching each sheet for the missing link. My eyes riveted on a name. The murderer? But I had to eliminate the other possibilities. It was the only way to be sure.

I placed the printouts back on the table and stood up to go. There was a restaurant across from the ferry dock I wanted to try for breakfast.

The sun peeked through the clouds as I set out on the boardwalk. Tourists and locals alike were strolling along the waterfront, enjoying the slightly cooler air the El Norte had brought in. Hopefully, the weather would stay clear. I still wanted to do some snorkeling with Wolf before I left for home. That is, if he forgave me for this date with Diego.

Wolf and Diego—those two were like honey pots for a fly. That wasn't the problem. Trust was. When Jay jilted me, something had died inside. But I was over that now—at least I thought I was. I was a woman who had broken a few hearts myself. I needed a man who cared. It wasn't about sex either. The man I chose had to satisfy me in more ways than one. But this time love would have to find me.

When I reached the ferry dock, I waited until traffic cleared and crossed the road. The outside of Las Palmeras was open to the street. A young Mexican woman stood at the doorway holding menus. I was about to ask for a table when someone called out.

"Adie! Over here!" A brunette in a low-cut top waved to me from one of the tables.

I wrinkled my brow, trying to place her. Pretty and plump. Then it dawned on me. It was Bambi, one of Don's bimbos. I told the server holding the menus I'd be joining a friend.

"Hey, Bambi."

"Hey." She glanced at me. "Cute top. I like the lace edges. You wanna join me for brunch?"

"Sure, thanks." I took the seat across from her. "Are you here by yourself?"

She nodded, her face serious—worry lines around her mouth. "Did you hear about what happened to Don?"

I nodded, and was about to say something when our server came over with salsa, chips and menus. I knew what I wanted so I didn't bother to look. "*Huevos rancheros* and coffee, *por favor*."

Bambi waved the offered menu aside. "Toast and coffee."

When the waiter left for the kitchen, I sat back and stared at her. "Were you with Don?"

"No, I had Montezuma's Revenge. Bunny was worried about me, so she stayed behind. Don had to meet an important investor. He was told to keep the meeting hushed up."

"Where was this meeting?"

"Don told me it would be down the road from Chien Rio. That restaurant on the east coast."

When the waiter set down my coffee I added milk and a sweetener. "How did Don seem about the meeting?"

Bambi stirred her coffee reflectively. "Nervous."

"Did he know the investor?"

"No, and I wondered why he'd want to meet with Don."

"Don's been helping with PR, but Diego runs the company." Bambi eyed me furtively over her coffee mug.

I nodded encouragingly.

"Diego paid Don a huge amount."

I leaned in. "Do you know why?"

"He didn't want me to say."

I grabbed Bambi's hand. "I can help. If someone tried to kill Don, and you know whatever he knows, you will be next."

The color drained from her face. She pulled away, staring at me worriedly. "I'm just a secretary from Buffalo. Bunny and me came here for a good time. We liked Don and we didn't think he was in any trouble."

Our waiter brought over the toast and eggs. "Is there anything else?"

Too bad he couldn't provide me with answers. I shook my head and waited for him to leave. "What did he do to get the money?"

Bambi glanced away.

"Tell me." I touched her hand. "This person means business. He won't hesitate to make sure you and Bunny are out of the way."

"All right, you win." She sighed. "Don found out there were complications to the north island condo project. Millions were pouring in from Canada. Diego was putting the money into an account in the Caymans. He could have stopped taking new investors when things weren't working out, but he decided to let everyone think things were going off as planned. Diego gave Don the money to keep his mouth shut about the snags."

I cut up my eggs. "And did he?"

"The day you met Diego at Loritas, Don told us everything. You and Diego were both gone by then. It was late and Don was getting a bit wasted. So were we. When the drinks kept flowing we started singing, you know that song, *Money* by Pink Floyd. We didn't know all the words, but we got into it and did the cash register noises until the waiter told us to keep it down."

"Did Diego ever tell Don to shut up about it?"

Bambi nodded.

"Do you think Don asked for more money?"

"No, he was happy with the payoff and don't forget he has his own investments."

"Blackmailers end up dead."

Bambi dropped her spoon. "You think Diego ran him off the road?"

"He wouldn't do it personally, but if he thought Don had become too greedy he'd have his people to do it for him."

I sipped my orange juice reflectively.

Bambi fidgeted in her chair. "Jeez, Buffalo is not as complicated as Cozumel."

I had another thought. "The meeting Don had could have been with the guy that ran him off the road. He's lucky he's not dead. Have you found out anything about Don's condition?"

"Bunny phoned from Cancun this morning." Bambi buttered her toast absentmindedly. "She went over there late last night. She couldn't afford a hotel so she'll be back today sometime. Don was awake for a few minutes." Bambi's leg spasmed up and down. "He spoke to Bunny this morning and then fell asleep."

"Wolf went over to see him."

Her eyes went spacy. "He's a hot looking guy. Is he yours?"

"He's a free man." Not that I wanted him to be necessarily, but he wasn't too concerned about a relationship with me.

She perked up. "You mean he's not your boyfriend?"

"Well, he is for now." I met her eyes. "I'm going home on Christmas Day. He may forget all about me." My voice had an edge. "You want him?"

"I didn't mean anything by that. Just wondered." Bambi pulled back nervously. "You were with Diego when I first saw you and then Wolf took you back to your hotel. I wasn't sure who you were with. Don was laughing about you switching men."

"Oh," I said, my temper flaring, "so your threesome is more normal?"

Bambi said defensively, "Don couldn't decide who he liked more and we both liked him, so we thought we'd share."

"Well, I'm not sharing." I said defiantly, grimacing at the thought of Daniella.

"You mean you want both of them!" Bambi said, astonished. I shrugged. "Maybe."

Bambi laughed, boisterously, pushing my arm. "You go, girl!"

"I don't know what Diego is really like. He could be a despicable human being capable of murder..." I mused.

"Or, he could just be—" Bambi grinned, "a very bad boy."

"I'm spending the day with him."

"You're brave. What if he suspects you know something? Aren't you afraid?"

"My friend Marg is going to be arrested if I don't find out more about these murders in my home town."

Bambi glanced up over her coffee cup. "Murders?"

"Yes, they're all tied into Royal Investments."

"So that's why you're going out with Diego?" she asked incredulously.

"That and he kind of intrigues me." I pictured Diego's amber eyes that changed to a misty green.

"His ass intrigues me." Bambi smirked.

"He's sexy all right." I thought of his lips and how he kissed.

Bambi shook her head in disbelief. "Wow, two hotties! You've got a lot going for you, Adie."

I frowned, contemplating the last few months of my life. "When I get home, I'll probably be down to zero."

Bambi grinned. "Where's home?"

"Kitchener, near Toronto. Have you heard of it?"

"Have I ever! I *love* Oktoberfest! Buffalo is only three hours away. How about you? Have you been to Buffalo?"

"Shopped and skied there."

"Cool!" Bambi shrieked. "We're practically sisters."

I smiled. Bambi was something else. Pulling up my beach bag, I got out my cell.

"Oops, I forgot to call Diego."

When the waiter brought over our bills, I drew out my credit card just as my cell buzzed. I pressed the phone icon. "*Bueno.*"

"Hi, Adie. You still going with him?"

"As far as I know. I haven't spoken to him yet. How's Don?"

"He told me there were two guys in the car. One was a bodybuilder type. Neither of them looked Mexican."

This was beginning to come together. I was more certain than ever that my hunch was right.

"Don't get Alvarez angry, Adie. I want you alive, breathing and sighing."

"Sighing?" I asked, still thinking about my theory. "Why should I be sighing?" What was he talking about?

"I'll have to refresh your memory when I get back. But I'd really like to hear you moaning."

Then I clued in. I closed my eyes for a second, capturing the feeling I'd had with him kissing and touching me—I had been so turned on in that swimming pool. "Wolf…"

"Yeah, Adie?" Wolf's voice was husky.

It was like a match sparking into flame. I whispered, "I'll see you tonight."

"Bye, princess," Wolf said softly.

I pressed end. Bambi stared at me. She licked her lips. "That must have been Wolf." She grinned broadly. "Sounds like phone sex."

I sighed. "He's good at it."

"He's a keeper, Adie."

The smile on my face hadn't disappeared by the time I signed my bill. As I placed the receipt into my wallet, my phone vibrated.

I clicked it open and said, "Hello?"

"*Hola, mi amor*," Diego said smoothly.

"Diego, I'm so sorry I didn't phone you."

"You are coming?"

"Yes, but you won't need to pick me up. I'm at Las Palmeras."

"Excellent, I'll walk out to meet you then."

"Okay. See you soon." I wondered what a person like Diego would wear to the beach.

"Adios, Adelina," Diego said softly.

I ended the call only to see Bambi eying me sadly, a tear gathering at the corner of her eye.

"What's the matter?"

"You're *so* lucky. You get to spend the day with Diego and the night with Wolf. I get to spend the day with myself and the night with Bunny." She wiped her eyes.

I patted her hand. "Don will recover and you three will be happy once more."

Bambi sniffed. "I hope so or I'll be on that plane back to

snowy Buffalo.

* * *

He looked like a model for Calvin Klein jeans—an elegant profile, medium-length, wavy black hair and a tight ass encased in blue designer jeans. A white T-shirt revealed strong arms and a body that worked out. Diego was gazing out at the distant cruise ships in the harbor and didn't notice my approach. When I came close, I caught a whiff of citron.

"You haven't been waiting long, I hope? I lost track of time."

"Don't worry about it, *mi amor*." He took my hand and kissed my wrist. "You look lovely, as always. I will be envied by every man that sees you with me." He glanced at his Rolex. "We should hurry though. The ferry leaves in five minutes." He put his arm around my waist and guided me to the entrance of the ferry. Handing over the tickets, Diego looked around and signaled someone. "I'd like to introduce you to my right-hand man. Churo, this is my friend, Adelina Sturm."

The huge scary bookend from the yacht stepped forward and bowed slightly.

"*Hola*. We met on the yacht the other day."

The bookend said nothing, looking puzzled.

"It was Churo's brother, Luis, you met, *mi amor*. They're twins."

No wonder, I thought I was seeing double that day at Loritas. There were two of them at a table near the wall.

"Churo will be coming with us today, but don't be concerned, we'll have our privacy."

As we strolled over the gangplank into the ferry's main level, I started to worry. I was supposed to be the spider catching the fly, but was I devious enough to spin the web?

The ferry had plenty of passengers on the main level, most of them settled in the chairs. Diego thought we should sit at the window and motioned for Churo to leave us.

"You look anxious, Adelina. Do you get seasick?"

"Sometimes." My stomach was churning with stress.

"We could go up on the deck." Diego regarded me intently. "Is there something else wrong?"

"Don't you feel out of place here?"

He laughed. "You've got the impression I'm only comfortable on a yacht?"

"You have a wealthy background. I don't."

Diego stroked my hair gently. "There's no need for you to be wealthy as well, Adelina. I have enough for both of us."

"Your friends must have all gone to prestigious universities." There was advantage to wealth.

"Most of them went to university," he shrugged, "but some came out no wiser."

"Where did you go?"

"London School of Economics."

I stared at him. "See, that's what I mean."

Diego glanced sadly at a couple of teens jostling each other near our seats. "But I didn't graduate."

"Why?"

"Too much partying." Diego frowned. "I was young and stupid. I made all the wrong choices."

"Yet you went to law school, didn't you?"

"Eventually." Diego leaned closer. "What about you, Adelina? You're an intelligent woman. Didn't you have the chance to go to university?"

"Couldn't afford it. I ended up taking travel courses. Later, I picked up some psychology and art courses."

"Then with psychology you should be able to understand me. I, on the other hand, will need some guidance as to what pleases you." He brushed my hair aside at the nape of my neck, touching my skin lightly. He leaned in nearer, his eyelids lowered, his full lips closing in on mine. His kiss set off quivers that started high and ended low. Startled, I drew back. "Why don't we go up on deck?"

He looked amused, as he ran two fingers through my hair. "Of course, *mi amor*, but you can't escape your feelings."

I didn't reply. Grabbing my beach bag, I stood. Diego let me go ahead up the nearby stairs. Behind me, he placed a warm hand on my lower back.

Families and business people milled around the deck, watching the shoreline gradually getting hazier and unclear as the ferry moved away. It was sunny up on the deck and a light breeze blew my hair in my eyes.

Diego pointed ahead. "Look, you can see the shore already."

I turned towards Playa del Carmen in the distance. Small waves hit the side of the boat, rocking it gently. I held onto the railing, leaning over to look down at the water. It sparkled a brilliant blue with the sunlight on the crests of the waves. I felt Diego's arm go around my shoulders pulling me closer. "Why did you decide to come with me today?"

"I wanted to see Tulum."

"That's it?" His eyes challenged me.

"There are things I have been wondering about—questions I have."

"Oh, are you trying to delve into my psyche?" Diego smiled. "I have many questions for you, too. But you can start with one, and then it will be my turn."

"And you will answer me honestly?"

He grinned. "If you answer me."

"What do you mean? You won't tell me anything unless I answer your question?"

Diego smirked. "I think this game will be fun, don't you?"

I wasn't too sure about that. I'd have to approach this cautiously. I didn't want to bring his guard up. I had too much to lose.

The wind blew a strand of hair in Diego's eyes. He brushed it away impatiently. "What's your question, Adelina?"

What was a non-threatening question to start with? Had Daniella been seriously involved with Diego? Was that why she was so upset when he paid attention to me on the yacht?

"How long were you dating Daniella?"

He regarded me intently. "My question for you is—how long have you been seeing Wolf?"

"About a week," I said, thinking how close we had become in such a short time.

"Daniella and I started seeing each other shortly after she came to work for me. About a year ago."

"Serious?"

Diego held his hand up in a stop gesture. "That's another question. Remember you must answer mine first." Diego's eyes twinkled.

"Which is?"

"Were you ever married or engaged?"

"That's two questions. Which one do you want answered?"

Diego smiled. "I like the way you play. You don't let your opponent get away with anything."

"Are we opponents, Diego?"

"Just for this game, Adelina, and then, let's get friendly," he said, stroking my hand. "Were you ever married, *mi amor*?"

"Fortunately, no." I withdrew my hand.

Diego grinned. "You think it would be a negative experience?"

"It's your turn to answer, not to ask."

"Back to Daniella?" Diego shrugged. "She was serious. I was not."

"I get the feeling you rarely are." Diego was the sort to play around. I was beginning to feel like a mouse captured in a cat's claws.

Diego took my hand and led me to the chairs on the deck. "I am about some things. Isn't it my turn?"

I nodded.

"Were you ever engaged?"

"Briefly, but maybe it was all in my head." I sat down in the deck chair.

Diego laughed as he took the seat next to me and said, "Love usually is."

I tried to pin him down. "Have you ever been in love, Diego?"

He made a wide gesture to his surroundings. "I'm in love with life."

"So, that's a definite no."

"Listen to you." Diego slipped his fingers around a strand of my hair and played with it. "You're such a cynic. I'll need to instill some romance into your life."

"You don't have much time for that, Diego. I'm leaving Christmas Day."

Diego gazed at me with lowered lids, his eyes misty green. "For you, Adelina, time frames don't exist. The world is a small place, accessible, no matter where you live. I can fulfill your fantasies."

I smiled. "First, you need to find out what they are."

"You are a tease…" He lost his train of thought as he eased his lips on mine. His fingers touched my hair as I got another taste of him. His kiss was sweet, but I couldn't let myself get into his net. Abruptly, I pulled away. This date had a purpose. I couldn't lose sight of why I was here.

"You keep withdrawing from me, Adelinita. I can't believe you really want to," he said softly.

"Believe—" I pushed him away.

He smiled, undaunted by my gesture. With the sudden commotion of the people on deck moving towards the stairs, he caught up my hand and pulled me up on my feet with him and said, "We're coming into Playa del Carmen."

"How are we getting to Tulum?"

"Churo's driving us. The car's parked a few blocks from the square, so we'll walk there. Is that okay, Adelina or would you rather take a taxi?"

"Sure, my ankle's much better. I could do with some exercise."

Diego's eyes scanned my body appreciatively. "You're one of the fittest women I've ever encountered. You'll have to tell me all about your exercise routine." He waited for me to join him and I grabbed my beach bag, stepping in front of him, behind the group descending the stairs.

The crowd streamed out onto the gangway. We joined the general exodus on the wharf leading past Señor Frogs to the town of Playa del Carmen. Diego took my hand as we wandered together by the shops selling blankets, gifts and jewelry. Everywhere there were vendors eager to make sales.

"Have you bought any souvenirs yet, *mi amor*?"

I stopped to look at some silver necklaces. "No, I don't need anything but I'll get something for my mom."

"Oh, what does she like?" Diego asked, fingering a knife with a mother of pearl handle.

"Jewelry or maybe a shell." I glanced over at some conch shells on display.

"A shell?" he asked skeptically.

"Not everyone wants diamonds."

Diego gave me a fleeting look. "You don't like diamonds?"

"I have a diamond ring but I prefer colored stones."

"What about silver?"

"I love it, especially silver with turquoise." I showed him the pinky ring I had on with an ornate silver setting. "I bought this in Acapulco a few years ago. It's not expensive, but turquoise is lucky for me. It's my birthstone."

"Turquoise is meant to protect the wearer."

"It's very important for me then." I thought of how someone wouldn't mind seeing me dead. Could it really be Diego?

Diego looked puzzled. "Why?"

I hesitated, having said too much.

Misunderstanding, he said, "You think you need protection from me?"

"No, as long as you behave yourself."

Diego gazed into my eyes. "It's hard for a man not to respond to you."

"I can only imagine."

"You are a cruel woman," Diego said lightly. He stopped at the corner of the main street and waited for the traffic to clear before we crossed.

"There he is." Diego's eyes shot ahead. "In the Mercedes."

I could see Churo in the driver's seat reading a newspaper, as yet unaware of our presence. Approaching the sedan's door, Diego opened it for me to get in.

"*Hola,*" I said to Churo.

Churo grunted something incomprehensible in reply. In the driver's mirror, I could see his mouth twist in a semblance of a smile. I got the distinct impression Churo found communication painful and smiling more so. Leaning forward, Diego gave him instructions rapidly in Spanish, or at least that's what I imagined he told him. For all I know, he could have told him to stop by the beach and drown me, as I was no longer of any use to him. I caught the word Tulum which led me to believe one of us, at least, was going there.

Diego brought his gaze to me. "I was just telling Churo, we want to drive quickly. We don't want to waste this beautiful day sitting in a car, do we?"

"You're right. Sometimes the clouds move in too fast and it ruins the day. But of course we're not going snorkeling, so I guess it's not as important."

"No, but it would be enjoyable to spend the time sunning on the beach with you."

I glanced at Diego who was trying to see around Churo's large head. Further up the street we veered swiftly left onto the highway to Tulum.

"How far is it?" I shifted back against the leather seat.

"About sixty kilometers." Diego peered at the road over Churo's massive shoulder.

Pebbles started flying with the abrupt contact from the tires.

"How long does it take to drive there?"

"At the speed we're going, I'd say we can make it there in a half hour." Diego glanced at me and took my hand. "Don't be concerned, Adelinita. Churo drives well and the road isn't busy."

I wasn't about to tell Churo, Diego's personal mastiff, to slow down. Guys like showing off, zipping along in a finely tuned vehicle but to be honest, I liked speed, too. I sighed, thinking about my little red Miata that had died on me. "You don't like to drive, Diego?"

"I have a Ferrari Spider that I take out." He smiled slightly.

I laughed. "You make it sound like a woman."

"It's temperamental like a woman. I have to handle it just the right way." He added, "I would have driven it today, but Churo is helping me with something and my car takes only two people."

Diego's fingers stroked my hand. "It's my turn to ask a question."

"All right, go ahead."

"How deeply are you involved with Wolf?"

I shrugged. "I haven't figured that out yet."

He nodded understandingly. "Do you want to know why I like you?"

I nodded.

"You are unpredictable."

"True. Are there other reasons?"

"You'll need to forfeit another question if you want to hear more."

"I'll save that then. Are you honest in business?"

"That's a paradox. Honesty and business."

"That isn't possible? Business with integrity?"

"Only in an ideal world. Business isn't about ideals. Money

221

isn't made with virtue." Diego gestured to the passing landscape. "Many of these entrance ways we have passed are to various hotel complexes. If they weren't built, you wouldn't be able to do your job as a travel consultant, would you? And yet, every hotel built destroys the environment, doesn't it?"

I nodded. "Unfortunately, that's true. People want to see the world. With new technology, it is faster and easier to travel everywhere. What's wonderful about Cozumel is that it's mostly unspoiled by development. I guess I'm guilty of loving Cozumel the way it is. I wouldn't want it to change."

"As long as it's only Cozumel you love."

"I'm not ready for love." The love subject annoyed me.

"Don't get angry, Adelinita." He patted my hand. "It's my turn to ask a question. Do you still want to play?"

I breathed deeply, letting go of the ghosts in my past.

"You're right, Diego. It is not worth getting upset about. Ask your question."

He took up my hand. "Would you come back to Cozumel?"

"Definitely." I regarded my handsome companion. "Now it's my turn."

He watched me expectantly.

Gathering my thoughts, I glanced out the window to avoid seeing those hazel eyes with the greenish cast. He was like that coral snake, hypnotic—difficult to ignore, even more difficult to escape.

Suddenly, with a jolt, I was thrown towards the window on the right as Churo swung the car to the side of the road. My eyes widened when I saw an old man on a bicycle wobbling across the road, seemingly oblivious to the oncoming traffic.

Diego spoke sharply to Churo in Spanish. "My apologizes for Churo's negligence."

"No need to apologize. I'm sure Churo did his best with the situation."

"You're right. People in Mexico are so unaware of laws and regulations, intentionally so," he said cryptically.

I gave that some thought as I watched the palm trees alongside of the road zooming by. Was Diego intentionally ignoring laws, defrauding people? How was he connected to the murders? I had to get him talking about business. That was the key.

Diego's hazel eyes gazed at me curiously. "You seem deep in thought."

"I was thinking of your investment company. What kind of projects do you have?"

"Mostly condos. I just opened one here on the Mayan Riviera, close to Tulum."

"Are we stopping there?"

He shook his head. "I don't think you're ready for that one."

"Why?"

Diego grinned wickedly. "You like nude beaches?"

I tossed my hair back. "I was on one in Jamaica." Not that I was into it. I kept the bikini on strolling down that beach. When a nude guy on a lounger hit on me, I tore my eyes away and said a quick goodbye. "Your condo has a nude beach?"

"More like the whole thing is."

"What! Really?" That was bizarre. Who would have thought there were nudist resorts here?

"I should give you a brochure in case you ever get a client who likes the nudist life."

Bernie. He was the type to go crazy on a vacation. "Sure. I'd heard about nude beaches here, but I didn't think there were nude resorts."

"Mexico is liberal when it comes to nudity."

"What's it like?"

"A nude resort? I don't know personally. I'm not interested in the experience. It's for tourists."

"So it's just to make money?"

"That's what it's all about," Diego said emphatically. His eyes drifted to a wide entrance way. "This is it."

We entered a parking lot with a shopping center at one side. Several tourist buses lined up stood empty, along with some Jeeps and taxis parked in the other spaces. What caught my eye was a high stone wall fortifying the ruins. It reminded me of the medieval castles I had seen in Wales.

"At one time there were wooden and palm houses around this wall," Diego said. "The city itself was built around six hundred AD."

"Did the Mayans always build walls around their cities?"

"No, they were rare, although the name Tulum means wall.

But it wasn't called Tulum until after—" Diego broke off, instructing Churo in Spanish. From the trunk, Churo started taking out baskets. While he was so occupied, Diego and I started walking, stopping to pay for tickets before we entered the portal in the wall.

Ancient stone structures. The one straight on was shaped like an Egyptian pyramid with many small steps leading to a platform at the top. Groups of tourists were everywhere, some with guides speaking French or German.

"The first Europeans must have been blown away when they saw all this. It looks so medieval," I said, staring at the pyramids. "I read somewhere that the Maya inhabitants fought off the Spaniards."

"Perhaps, but my ancestors came upon Tulum when it was already in its decline."

"So the Spaniards didn't destroy this city?"

"The city was abandoned." Diego gazed at me significantly. "Spaniards aren't always the bad guys, Adelina."

19

"Oh, I'm so sorry. I didn't mean to put down your heritage."

Diego squeezed my hand reassuringly. "Why don't I take a picture of you?"

"Alright." I took my camera from my purse and handed it to Diego.

He aimed carefully and snapped the picture. Then stopping a passing tourist in a loud shirt and baggy shorts, he asked him if he wouldn't mind taking a photo.

The burly guy nodded and told us to stand closer together, joking as he gestured, "Put your arm around her, buddy. The litt'l gal looks lonely." Diego drew his arm around me as the man aimed the camera. Chunky shouted, "Hey you guys, say Christmas." The scowl I had should have cracked the lens. Diego, sensing my discomfort, whispered, "Please put up with him, Adelina." He yelled out, "Do you mind taking one more?"

"No problem, buddy. Hey, cutie, look happy!" When he returned the camera to Diego he winked and trudged off.

"You really don't like Christmas?"

"That's why I'm deliberately missing it."

"Christmas Eve would have been fun with you." Diego steadied me as my ankle turned on the uneven ground. "Too bad you made plans with Du Lac. Is he going back to Canada soon?" We approached a large ruin where a crowd gathered in front.

"Not that I know of. He bought some cottages that he's renovating. He's staying to get them fixed up." My stomach tightened into a knot. I dreaded the thought of Wolf staying here.

"If he had invested in my company, he would have left for Canada already, maybe even before you arrived. You would never have seen him. We'd have a fresh slate—no ghosts from the past."

I was silent thinking what ifs.

"Let me ask you something, Adelina. When you get home, where does that leave you?"

"Single."

"You see? Du Lac is like a pebble in a lake. Skims the surface for a few seconds and then sinks—never to be seen again." Diego flashed a white smile. "You'll like the Temple of the Frescoes." He took my hand and led me to a building to the right of the courtyard.

A guard stood outside the building telling visitors it was closed to the public for restorations, but when he saw us, he nodded respectfully and said, "*Buenas tardes*, Señor Alvarez." He motioned for us to enter the gallery. Maya murals covered the walls along with masks and the symbols of nature's fertility—corn, rain and fish.

"Look up there, Diego." I pointed. "What's that?"

"That's Chaac. He's one of the Maya Gods, god of rain and fertility." He motioned to another mask. "That one is Itzamna, the creator."

"You make a good guide."

"That's positive."

"I didn't say I didn't like you, Diego."

"Sometimes I wonder."

"That's because you're used to women dropping into your arms whenever you snap your fingers."

"I can't imagine you'd have any difficulty getting dates."

"There are dates, and there are dates."

"True." He grinned. "But remember, some men are better than others." Falling in step beside him, we came upon a tiny structure with an arch on both sides. Crouching, Diego led the way.

The arch was so low, I had to bend down to make it through the tunnel. "These people were shorter than I am, Diego. Imagine that!"

"Vertically challenged for sure."

"Not everyone is blessed with tall genes."

His eyes traveled down my legs. "You're blessed, Adelina. Jeans would only hide those lovely long legs."

Not knowing what to say, I asked about the pyramid ahead. "We can't climb it, can we?"

"No, not any more. But don't worry, we shall see the view from the cliff. The ruin over there," Diego pointed to the structure, "is the Temple of the Descending God. The figure is upside down."

"Why upside down?"

"He's the Bee God," he smiled, "looking for a sexy flower to pollinate."

"Right. He's a busy god. Reminds me of someone I know."

"Du Lac?" Diego took my hand and we strolled north.

"From what I've heard, you're no slouch in the romance department either."

"But I can stop looking when I find that perfect flower. See that building with the round base? It's the Temple of the God of the Wind. Gets very breezy on the edge of the cliff. The wind is strong enough to blow a slender girl like you right to the bottom."

I glanced at the sharp rocks on the hill to the beach far below. "I'll stay away from there then."

"I'm afraid that is a dilemma. Tulum is unique—the only ruin built overlooking the ocean, Adelina. We can't go down to the beach for lunch without standing on the edge so why not take in the view."

My fear of heights was pushed onto the back-burner as we approached the cliff. "It's beautiful," I said, taking in the turquoise waters and the tiny sandy cove. "How do we get to the beach?"

"That'll be the challenge. It's thirty-nine feet down." Diego took my camera and pointed. "Sit there. I'll take your picture."

Perched on the rocky precipice, I tried to get comfortable. Below, the beach looked idyllic. "If this beach were more secluded…" I was distracted by a hiker passing by. There was no visible path only dirt and rocks. With a walking stick he started the sharp descent to the beach below.

Diego joined me, sharing the sharp edged boulder. "Yes?"

"Oh, yes, this place is a lot like the beach I saw in Cozumel."

"Playa San Francisco?"

"On the north end—fantastic snorkeling. My friend was just blown away. When Marg saw that giant parrot fish, she couldn't believe it." I stopped. Diego had the oddest look.

"Marg is your friend?"

That was a mistake. I shouldn't have mentioned her, I thought, noting the irritated expression on Diego's face.

"Marg Beige?"

My eyes darted to the rocks below. Shifting uncomfortably, I felt insecure sitting here.

Diego touched my arm. "Why didn't you tell me you knew

her? She said she checked out my construction site with a friend," he said sharply. "That was you?"

"Um-hm."

Diego's eyes narrowed. "Why were you there?"

I didn't know what to tell him. "I was researching for my job."

"That's not the whole story, is it? That woman phoned again this morning."

I tried to explain. "She was paid to get Reich's check, Diego."

Diego's full lips twisted. "Is she obtuse? I told her to forget it. There's no point in her staying and waiting. His estate will get a check." Diego clenched his jaw. "Then she told me she went on a trip with her friend to investigate my scam."

Why did Marg tell him all this? She knew I would be seeing Diego. Didn't she know this would upset him? I wanted him to trust me, talk to me, and now everything was ruined.

Diego took my hands in his. "She said her friend knew about Reich."

"That's true. I know what happened." The cliff was high, a long way from the bottom. The rocks were huge and jagged, the incline practically vertical.

His voice took on a hard edge. "Why did you hide this from me?"

"I wanted to tell you, but I didn't have a chance." The people down on the beach seemed miniscule, so far away. A wave of dizziness hit.

"She thinks I'm a crook, making shady deals, conning people into investing in the north island project. Do you think I'm up to something? Is that why you came today—to dig into my business?"

I glanced up at him, nervously. My stomach did a somersault. "Marg thinks you're behind all the attacks."

"What do you mean?" Diego gripped my hands tighter.

This was the wrong approach. Now he seemed really angry. My mouth felt dry. It was hot on the cliff even with the wind blowing on my face. I stared at the distant beach.

My hair swept into my eyes. My heart pounded. A thin film of perspiration coated my brow and neck. I felt like I was running a race with no finish line. My eyes closed for a split second to fight off the dizziness. What if he pushed me? Was there anything that would break my fall? I shivered. My eyes shot to the vegetation growing between the rocks, small shrubs barely surviving the heat. Don't give in to fear. Stay calm. Take control. "A mugger attacked Marg outside your office."

Twisting my wrists, I pulled my hands out of his grasp and got up. Diego copied my lead and stood, forcing me to look up into his eyes. Outweighing me by at least sixty pounds, all he needed to do was to push me—my head would hit one of those sharp rocks and I would die. It could be easily explained for someone like Diego. Who would question an accident? After all, he was Santiago Francisco Bolivar Alvarez—a man of importance in Mexico.

Diego gripped my shoulders. "You think I had something to do with that?"

My left hand located and held his right hand on my shoulder, while my other hand formed a spear. My voice rose accusingly. "There were more attacks—a man shooting at us and a guy waiting for me in my hotel room with a knife."

As he absorbed this, I caught him by surprise, jabbing him in the base of his throat. The pain caused him to loosen his hold. With both my hands I pushed his arms up and out, stepped back, and kicked him hard in the chest. Diego grunted and doubled over, the breath knocked out of him. Hurriedly, picking up my beach bag, I thrust past him and forced my trembling legs to run.

As I sprinted past a ruin and a group of Chinese tourists, I heard him call out, "Adelina, wait!"

Sandals with two-inch heels aren't the best for racing on uneven ground and my progress was slower than I'd hoped. If I made it to the other side of the ruins I would be safe. There were tour groups and a person at the ticket booth. He wouldn't dare try anything. I turned to see him about ten meters behind, gaining distance rapidly.

My escape came to a stop as I ran into someone solid—a flat stomach, like a stone wall covered in cotton. I felt my arms restrained by powerful hands. My eyes flicked up. *It was Churo!*

20

"Help me, Churo!"

The big man spoke, his voice low and guttural. "Señorita, what is wrong?"

Diego caught up to us. Swinging me around to face him, he spoke haltingly. "Adelina, why did you do that? You can't believe I would hurt you?"

I edged into Churo for protection, backing away from Diego. "You were so angry. I thought you were about to throw me off the cliff."

"I am not one of those bastards out to kill you, Adelina. I'm disappointed you would think so badly of me. Why didn't you tell me about all this? You don't trust me?"

"Marg was sure you were behind the attacks. She warned me you were dangerous and that we were both a threat to you. You knew both victims. The fact is, someone has been sending thugs to kill us and you seemed the most likely person."

"When were these attacks?"

"Monday a guy attacked Marg. Tuesday, on the north end of the island, they were gunning for both of us."

Diego stared at me intently. "Adelina, don't you see? It couldn't be me."

"Why?"

"We met at Loritas on Thursday. Don't you remember? I'd never seen you before."

I thought back. I had wondered why Diego didn't recognize my name when we had met but Wolf and Marg had convinced me that Diego was masterminding everything.

"I see now—that's how you injured your ankle." He touched my arm gently. "And the scratches?"

I nodded. "I had to jump out of my Jeep."

Diego waited.

"There was a coral snake in my shopping bag."

"Damn it, Adelina! I can't believe you would think I would have wanted you dead." He grasped my hands. "I'm a lover, not a fighter, unlike you. What are all those moves anyway?"

"Karate." I stared at him, searching his face for some sign of sincerity. "If what you're saying is true, you'll need to explain everything to me. Will you do that?"

Somberly, Diego nodded. "I'll tell you what I know about Reich." He turned to Churo. "Is everything ready on the beach?"

"*Si,* Señor Alvarez." Churo looked at me.

"Our lunch is set up for us, Adelina." Diego's eyes searched my face. "Do you trust me now?"

I glanced at Churo. He nodded slightly at my unspoken question. "All right, Diego, but no more secrets, eh? If you aren't trying to kill me, someone else is, and I need to find out who."

"May I hold your hand?" His lips turned up at the corners as he asked, "You won't hurt me, will you?"

* * *

My beach bag slung over his shoulder, Churo effortlessly scaled the rocks ahead of me. I slid a few times, but Diego's hand steadied my climb down. Finally, we were standing on a powdery white beach.

A scattering of people relaxed in the sun. It was a beautiful cove, but apparently we were headed somewhere else. Churo led the way along the shore. Soon enough we came upon an isolated stretch of pristine beach. Sparkling with sunlight, the Caribbean's waters lapped gently on the sand. Churo veered over to a group of boulders. It was a natural wall. A gap about three feet wide opened onto an oval area of beach about the size of a large room. I was surprised to see a tiny hibachi, a patterned-red blanket and coolers.

By the rocky wall, a mustached man with longish brown hair stood strumming a Latin ballad. Singing along softly, he looked out at the ocean.

Diego seated himself on the blanket and motioned for me to join him. He reached over and pulled off the cooler lid, took out a bottle of red wine and a corkscrew. "I think we could all do with some of this, hm-mm?"

"You did all this for me?" I was astounded. My instincts were right. Wolf and Marg didn't trust Diego but, it couldn't have been him. "How sweet. I didn't expect all this."

Diego smiled brilliantly. "Neither did I."

I sat down beside him and took a glass from him. Diego poured wine into our glasses. "Check the color, Adelinita. It's from California."

Swirling the wine in my glass, I commented, "It looks almost purple."

"Taste it, *mi amor*."

"I'm surprised you would call me that after what I just did."

"You are a fiery woman, Adelinita." He fingered a strand of my hair. "I like that about you, but I can't say my body is pleased with all the abuse. I'll probably have to sit around the dinner table tonight with my parents, an ice pack tucked under my shirt. Luckily, you didn't kick me further down. I don't know if I could have forgotten that as easily." He sipped his wine. "But why don't we let it go, Adelinita? You forgive me for frightening you?"

He seemed genuinely repentant. I nodded.

"It's from the Napa Valley," Diego said enthusiastically. "A Jacob Franklin Petite Sirah."

I tasted the wine and found it softly flavored of fruit and something else. "Smooth."

"What do you notice about it?"

"Fruity, maybe plums?"

"Um-hum. You've got an excellent palate." He turned to me, his eyes twinkling. "What I like is the chocolate flavor."

"How perfect." The man couldn't be that bad if he liked chocolate.

The musician brushed the strings of his guitar and we sat silently for a moment listening to him.

"He's good, Diego."

"I heard him at a bar a while ago—in Cancun."

"And you just hired him for today?"

Diego nodded. "We needed the ambiance."

"I think," I said, glancing at the sea, "you'd have it right here without doing anything. Remember, I don't get to see the ocean as often as you do. My hometown is covered with snow, with any luck."

"And if you're not lucky?"

I took up a handful of fine sand and let it run through my fingers. "Brown grass or slush."

Diego furrowed his brow. "Why live there?"

"It's where my work is."

"But you're a tour guide. You could live anywhere, couldn't you?" Diego swished the wine around in his glass. "I could give you a job here."

I laughed. "I'd have to take a Spanish course first."

"I could arrange for you to have a crash course in Spanish," he said smoothly.

"What in two days?"

His index finger pushed a strand of a hair away from my eyes. "You'll need to come back here, then."

"I will. You don't have to coax me." The waters of the Caribbean were so blue, so alluring.

While Diego refilled my glass, Churo came over to one of the coolers and took out a package and a small pot. With a barbeque tong he placed some lobster tails on the grill as well as a miniature pot. Leave it to Diego to think of something like this. "What's in the pot, Churo?"

"Salsa to baste the lobster, Señorita. The lobster tails have already been marinated and now they need a sauce."

"I'm impressed. You're a chef as well as a bodyguard?"

Diego grinned. "Churo has many talents."

Oo-hh! That didn't really reassure me. What if one of his jobs was putting coral snakes in cars or taking pot shots from boats? And if Diego had a crew of security men, who's to say one of them wasn't Apeman, the biker dude, or that creep following me? I wasn't sure what to think anymore. "Diego, you said you'd tell me about Reich."

"I did. Why don't we have some salad at the same time?"

He reached into the cooler, taking out bowls and salad forks. Diego spoke between mouthfuls. "I met Reich in Toronto through another investor. He had money to spend and wanted to get into something more lucrative. I told him the profits would be big if everything went well. Investing is always a risk. Personally, I thought the man was a little off, but what did I care? I'll take anyone's money. It's their choice, isn't it?"

"What did he invest in?"

"Company stocks. At the time I was dealing with two developments. I told you about the nudist resort already. The other project is a condo development on the northern part of the island."

"Why didn't you give Marg the check?"

"Well, first of all, you need to understand Reich didn't know what he was talking about. He wrote me a letter asking that all of his investment money be returned. I e-mailed him that it wasn't possible. He received dividends quarterly—the next one at the end of December. If he wanted, he could get another stockholder to buy him out, but he would have to arrange that himself. Then your dippy friend came along and asked for the money. I told her to forget about it. It wasn't doable. It would be sent to his estate."

"So why didn't you tell Marg?"

"I did. She wouldn't believe me. She thought I was trying to cheat Reich because I wouldn't give her the two million he'd invested. I explained it all to her, but she looked at me like I was growing horns—the devil incarnate. I spent half an hour clarifying Reich's situation, and then I told her to go. When my secretary showed her out, she was still babbling on." Diego emphasized his point with his fork. "She's obviously intellectually challenged. Secondly, I can't understand a woman with your sophistication being bothered with such a dowdy dolt."

I could imagine that Marg would have had a problem believing all this, especially if Reich had convinced her that everything had been arranged. She wasn't business oriented, being a psychiatric counselor, and all. Marg found business just as confusing as I did, maybe more so and she didn't trust Diego at all. "I know she doesn't understand business, but Diego, she is intelligent." Then I thought about the goon who'd gone after Marg.

"Do you have a big hairy ape-like bodyguard, Diego?"

"No, Adelinita, unless you think Churo is gorilla-like." He tilted his head, regarding Churo in amusement. "I admit he's big, but not that hairy. But seriously, Adelina, I have three men working for me, Churo, Luis and Eduardo. You've met Churo and Luis. Eduardo has been in Puerto Vallarta on vacation for the last week. He's thin and tall, not hairy, though."

If he was telling me the truth, what did this mean? None of those descriptions matched the thugs. According to Bernie, Diego had a Toronto office. He had a lot of investors, one of them being

Claws. "What about Uma?"

Diego twisted his lips. "Met her with Reich and some other investors. Attractive, if you like the pencil-thin chic type."

"Someone didn't like her. She's dead."

Diego scanned the water. "I was wondering about that myself. But none of my other investors have been murdered or at least I don't think so."

While we had been busy eating and talking, Churo had finished barbequing the lobster tails. He served them up for us. My first mouthful was amazing.

"Awesome, Churo. I wish I could take you home with me."

Churo flushed with pleasure. "*Gracias,* Señorita Sturm."

"Perhaps I should have cooked for you," Diego whispered in my ear. His breath set off a shiver of delight.

As I ate, I noticed our guitarist had decided to call it quits. Picking up his guitar, said something to Churo and waved good-bye. Hastily, Churo threw the utensils and pots in the cooler and called out to the young man. The guitarist stopped and waited for Churo to join him. The two of them made their way in the direction of the beach we had left behind. We were alone, but this time I wasn't frightened. I wasn't entirely convinced of Diego's innocence, but I couldn't see why he would murder his investors. I handed my plates to Diego, who placed them into a bag in the cooler, along with his own.

"Have you got your bathing suit on?" Diego pulled his T-shirt off over his head.

I nodded, removing my tank top. With my shorts off I sat back on the blanket watching Diego unzip his jeans. His body was perfect—wide shoulders, good pecs, tight abs and muscular legs. With every sip the potent wine increased my appreciation.

Diego sat down next to me, inspecting me in my purple string bikini. "A very attractive bikini. You look lovely, however, with so much skin exposed, I think you need some sunscreen. I wouldn't want to be responsible for a burn." He dug out a bottle from the side pocket of the first cooler and dropped a small dab on his palms and rubbed them together. "So your workout is karate?" He lightly applied the lotion on my back in a circular motion. "I like your muscle tone. Maybe I should take it up."

"You must do some sort of workout." I closed my eyes and let the rays of the afternoon sun warm my skin.

"Tennis and the gym, mostly. You know, I'm not used to an athletic woman. Spanish women usually don't work out."

"Oh, why not?"

"Tradition, I guess." He laughed. "They prefer shopping and eating."

I glanced at Diego. "Carmelita doesn't look like the eating type."

"She's more cosmopolitan." He shrugged. "Stress keeps her thin."

"You mean her two-timing husband causes her grief?"

"She isn't an angel either."

"Runs in the family?"

He smiled enigmatically and refilled our wine glasses.

"This is my last one, or I'll be asleep soon. This wine is strong, isn't it?"

"*Si, mi amor,* but soft in the mouth." Diego picked up the sunscreen again and stroked my shoulders gently, his hands coated with lotion, working his way down my arms. I closed my eyes again, enjoying the sensation.

His contact was soothing, relaxing my tensed up shoulders. I wasn't done with questioning Diego but my body was loosening up and telling me to let it go. My back leaned into Diego, feeling the slight pressure of his lips on my neck. His tongue caressed my ear lobe and circled in and around. His breath on my skin sent quivers down my body. He whispered, "You're a fascinating woman and so very desirable."

I didn't know what to say, so I said, "Thank you."

"No need to thank me," Diego said softly, running his hands down to my waist. He kissed my shoulder and then gazed at me from heavy-lidded eyes. "I thank you. Your presence makes this simple beach paradise for me." He held my glass up to my lips. "Finish the wine, *mi amor*. It's too good to waste." I had a last sip and he placed my empty glass in the cooler. Picking up the suntan lotion, he rubbed it in his hands before he spread it on my back, working his hands under the strings of my bikini, loosening the ties. It felt good—the sun, the warm balmy breeze on my skin, and the soothing waves lapping against the shore.

Pushing my shoulder towards him, he turned me about to face

him. "Your eyes are beautiful—so blue and slanty. You're like an exotic flower opening up to the sun."

I stared at him, touched by the poetry of his words.

"Your lips are pouty and full, perfectly formed to excite a man." Diego's eyes flickered green before he brought his generous mouth down on mine. I knew I shouldn't have been drawn into his kiss, but Diego was hard to resist. His hair brushed my cheek as he eased his lips off and took hold of the strings of my bikini tied around my neck, loosening them. His lips pressed against my neck sent tingles down my body. I could feel his hand on the outside of my thigh gently stroking. "Your skin is like satin—silky smooth, so enticing."

Tentatively, I reached out, exploring his firm back, running my fingers down his sides and resting them at his waist. My lips brushed his shoulder, tasting sea salt and a hint of sweat. It wasn't unpleasant. This way he was less perfect and more real. Mentally, I compared him to the other man that drove me crazy.

Wolf was magnetic—my attraction to him so strong it was like fireworks when he touched me. I melted in his arms. His eyes reeled me in with his lustful looks. He was the sea god. But Diego had his own power, easing past my protective shield, making me feel special. There was no other woman diverting his attention, he had eyes only for me and he was devastatingly handsome.

Diego had lifted himself up on his elbows, his gaze focused on my breasts. He lowered himself slowly, his mouth kissing a mound where it wasn't concealed by the thin layer of fabric. A spark ignited at the tip of my breast and started a flame that grew with every kiss. His fingers searched under my top and found what he wanted, a nipple that became erect at his touch. I felt a tug on my bikini strings and an unexpected breeze blew on my exposed chest as Diego seized my bikini top. The wine had slowed me down, but I reacted quickly, clutching my hands to my chest only somewhat managing to cover my breasts. "Diego! What are you doing with my top?"

"This is a topless beach, Adelina. I thought you might like the feel of the sun on your breasts."

"If I had wanted to be topless, I would have decided that on my own, wouldn't I?"

Diego grinned mischievously, his eyes on my chest. "Ah-hh,

but your breasts are so beautiful. Surely you wouldn't want to deprive me of the pleasure of looking?" His hand smoothed a strand of my hair and he added softly, "I've never met a woman quite like you, Adelinita."

"That is so nervy. I should smack you."

Diego smirked. "You like abusing me, don't you?"

"You? It's me that's being abused!"

Diego stroked my cheek gently. "I would never hurt you, sweet Adelina, my exotic flower. I can't help myself. When I'm with you, I feel like nothing else exists. You are an enchantress that has put a spell on me. I want to take your clothes off so that I can feast my eyes on the loveliest woman in Mexico."

"You said you'd be a gentleman. You promised."

"All is fair in love and war, Adelinita. My intentions were good at the time," he said apologetically. "Don't be angry."

Diego held up my top. "I'll help you put it back on."

I was about to say I'd do it myself, but that would have been worse. "Tie it around my neck, Diego."

While he was busy with that, I reached out to grab the top to pull it over my breasts. Unfortunately, I lost a string and one breast popped out. Diego was quick to capture and cup it lovingly before he pushed it back into my top. He then tied my strings at the back and sat down beside me with a grin.

"Is that better, Adelinita?"

Before I could answer, my phone started to vibrate.

"Excuse me." I dug around in my bag and pulled out my cell. "*Bueno*."

"He hasn't got you naked, has he?"

I blushed guiltily. "No, he has not! What kind of a question is that?"

"Are you all right?"

"Yes."

"Are you sure?"

"Um-mm, where are you?"

"Close by. Are you still coming back on the eight o'clock ferry?"

"Yes. I'll see you tonight, okay?"

"For sure, Adie."

Shutting the phone, I eyed Diego who had settled down on the blanket stretched out like a cat. "You are bad."

"I know. Lie down, *mi amor*."

"And why should I?"

Diego stretched his arms out. "Because it's so pleasant and we can soak up these rays."

"And give you another opportunity to rip off my clothes?" I asked sharply.

"Ripping sounds fun, but I wouldn't dare. You'd probably poke my eyes out next."

"That's an idea."

Diego patted the blanket. "Lie down, *mi amor*. Do you want me to tell you anything else?"

I sure did, but would he? I lay down on the blanket and touched his arm. "Where do you keep your money?"

Diego yawned. "In a bank."

I touched his cheek, reminding him. "You said you'd tell me everything." Our eyes met and I pleaded, "You must tell me, Diego. Someone is trying to kill me."

"Maybe you should be thinking why? Do you know something you shouldn't know?"

Should I confide in him? No, there was too much doubt left in me. I wanted to believe him, but I couldn't just yet.

Diego's arm encircled me. "Adelinita, you could come and live with me until you leave. I have security guards. I can protect you more than Wolf. When you get back to Canada, surely the attacks will desist."

"I'm not so sure. It all has to do with these two murders in Kitchener."

"Kitchener? That's a city about one hundred kilometers from Toronto, isn't it?"

"Um-hmm. That's where I live." The sun was so hot on my skin it was difficult to imagine being home in the middle of winter. It was worse yet, to think of being back with someone out there trying to kill me.

Diego stroked my hair. "You look so sad. I wish I could bring a smile back to those lovely lips."

"I'm glad you opened up to me. I don't know who to trust anymore."

"What about your friend, Marg? Can you really trust her? I

would think she might have an agenda."

"Why?"

"She can't let up on the idea of taking back the two million. What does she gain from this?"

"Reich was her patient. They got to be close. He trusted her. She was paid ten thousand to get the check." I frowned. "There's something else. I just found out she inherits money from Reich's estate."

"So she'd want him dead, wouldn't she? What I wonder is why he didn't come here himself?"

"Apparently, Reich suffered from paranoia and had a fear of flying."

"Crazy, eh?" His glance fell on my bruised ankle. "Now, tell me about these attacks on you."

He listened as I told him. His brow furrowed as I related the part about the biker with the knife.

"This man was American?"

"He didn't speak much except to swear at me. But, yes, I think so."

"You said he had a knife and you had just finished showering. Did he…violate you?"

I found it difficult to speak.

Diego brought his hand on top of mine. "I'll send my men out to find him. He needs to be taught a lesson. It won't take away the pain, Adelinita, but at least the bastard will think twice about assaulting women."

"He didn't rape me, Diego. Not that he didn't want to. Wolf came just in time."

"I'm glad for that, *mi amor*. But still, we don't need him raping any other women, do we? A bastard like that deserves worse than death."

Hearing him talk like that confused me further. "But you're a lawyer, don't you believe in just recourse?"

"I am a man first, a lawyer second," he said softly, "And I like you, Adelinita, very much. Are the police still looking?"

"I don't think so. I should have checked, but then something else happened just after I met you at Loritas. A man followed me from the restaurant. I reported this as well."

"This is outrageous! I'll speak to the police commander. He's my cousin. I know Cozumel doesn't have much of a police force, but surely they can find this thug."

"Officer Hernandez said the biker was sighted on the ferry, but I didn't hear anything else."

"So this bastard is walking around sightseeing as we speak?"

"I suppose he could be."

Diego scratched his head. "You mentioned a snake before. Where did this happen?"

"San Gervasio when I was with Marg."

"Marg again? Wouldn't you say this is too much of a coincidence?"

"I admit I was suspicious, but I can't imagine her doing this." I massaged my forehead thinking it over. It was all beginning to make sense. "It's getting late and it's hot. Why don't we go for a swim?"

* * *

The sun was low in the sky when we came out of the warm water. The salt bit my skin, but it felt good swimming the clear waters of Tulum, an effortless paddle with the salt giving me the extra buoyancy. When we came in, I was tired but more at ease. After all, Diego hadn't tried to drown me and he had told me the truth. There was something still to be discussed and I had to broach this topic as soon as possible.

Diego grabbed some towels from a bag and handed me one.

"Could I help you dry off?"

"I think I can manage that." I used the towel on my legs and arms. "I'm sure the sun will do the rest." Giving the towel back I lay down on the blanket. I felt sleepy, but I needed to stay awake. "Diego, what do you know about Don's accident?"

Diego dropped the towel and sat down beside me. "I heard it was bad. My cousin called. He said it wasn't an accident."

Diego lay down on the blanket, leaned on his elbow and looked up at me.

"Didn't you have reason to believe something would happen to Don?"

"Why would you say that?"

"Weren't you paying him off?"

"This is Mexico, Adelinita." Diego yawned.

"And you're telling me this because?"

"Things work like that around here," he said, matter-of-factly.

"Blackmail is customary?"

"Payoffs are a good way to keep friends close."

"But what if he wanted more money?"

"What exactly do you know about this?"

"Don had knowledge that could hurt you financially. Am I right, Diego?"

"You never cease to amaze me. What else do you know?"

"Did he threaten you?"

"Don?" Diego shrugged. "You know Don. He's harmless."

"Then why pay him at all?"

"So he stays enthusiastic. I had nothing to do with Don's mishap. It's possible he was running with the wrong crowd and someone wanted him gone." He patted the blanket, indicating I should join him.

I lay down beside him. "It wasn't you, was it?"

"No, a reminder would be sufficient if he started pulling the plug on my venture."

"And this venture is legitimate?"

"It's not a sure thing, but it has possibilities." Diego moved in closer.

"And if he got greedy?"

"I would mention one word—Eduardo."

"And did you have to?"

"No, Don was happy with his payment. He's not a fool." Diego put his finger on my lips. "Surely, I've told you enough. I'm not your enemy or Don's. I'm your friend, Adelinita."

His hand stroked my hair. "I could be more," he said, as his hand gently pushed me towards him until our lips made contact. The tip of his tongue entered my mouth. When his firm body pressed against me, I felt tingles race down my body. His eyes sparkled green. "You feel it, too—but it's you and Wolf, isn't it?"

I nodded.

Diego gave me a sidelong glance. "I believe we could have something special, but I'm a patient man. I can wait." Closing his eyes, he curled up towards me, placing his hand on top of mine. "Rest with me, sweet Adelinita."

The late afternoon sun was still strong and I wondered if I should reapply some sunscreen, but I was too lazy to reach into my bag. Maybe Diego could do my back. "Diego?" I glanced over. His eyes were closed. He lay still. Diego had dozed off.

I watched him sleep, envious of his dark lashes and wondered why these men I liked were so blessed, unlike me, needing a daily application of mascara before I could confront the world. A mixed up world with a murderer threatening me. But lying here next to Diego, I began to forget and relax.

The wine, the swim and the hypnotic rhythm of the waves overcame me, and I, too, drifted into a light sleep.

***

There was something delightful in the air. I breathed it in. My eyes opened a slit.

"I have a surprise for you, *mi amor*."

Fully awake, I sat up. Overhead the cerulean blue sky had citron poured into the rosy hues. The beach was practically deserted now, but the breeze was still warm and comfortable.

"That smell, Diego, can only be one thing."

"Yes." He grinned, pleasure brightening his face.

"Chocolate?"

"Mayan hot chocolate."

Curiously, I gazed at Diego and then at Churo, who was busy at the hibachi stirring the contents of two different pots.

"Tell me about it."

"It's an ancient Mayan recipe. Ground cacao, cinnamon, chili, maize and sugar."

"The Mayans had a thing for chocolate?"

"They had chocolate with all their meals and gave gifts of chocolate to their gods."

Diego handed me a tiny cup and saucer and placed one in front of him. "Is it ready?"

"*Sí*." Churo came over with a pot and poured the mixture carefully into our cups. Diego handed him a mug and he poured another one for himself.

I became conscious of my clothing, or rather, the lack of it. My bikini had dried in the sun and I felt the need to cover up, sitting here with two men eyeing me. Reaching into my beach bag, I pulled out my shorts and stepped into them.

"Getting dressed so soon, Adelinita? It's not necessary, it *is* a beach." Diego said. Churo smiled. I think he found Diego amusing.

"I assume we're almost ready to leave?" I tugged my top over my head.

"I suppose we'll have to." Diego sighed. "I'm not looking forward to this meeting. But he's a major investor and he wants more details about this condo venture. Apparently, he's rushed for time and wants to meet me on the ferry."

"This is the development that isn't going well?"

"With money in the right pockets…" Diego shrugged. "Unfortunately, he fails to understand that things take time in Mexico. I'll try to explain the situation to him. I'm sure it will be quickly resolved." He took a sip of hot chocolate and then spoke to Churo. "When we get to the ferry, Churo, perhaps you could go directly to the deck and I'll bring Adelina down. I heard it might rain later today."

Churo nodded.

I tried the hot chocolate and wasn't disappointed, but then chocolate rarely disappoints me. "It's very good, Churo."

"*Gracias,* Señorita."

"This was a great idea, Diego. You are such a creative thinker."

"I often have excellent ideas; unfortunately, they are not always feasible."

"You mean the condo deal?"

He smiled wistfully. "It could make millions…"

"You could explain it to him."

"He's in a hurry to live abroad." Diego frowned. "And something else bothers me…"

"What?"

He shook his head. "Nothing—I'm not sure what it is exactly."

He glanced at me intently. "You'll be seeing Wolf tonight, I suppose?"

I nodded, finishing the chocolate. "Do you think he's involved with Daniella?"

Diego flashed even white teeth. "Daniella wants him."

"Even I know that, Diego."

"She'll do anything to have him."

"She tends to be too obvious."

"It works for her. When she wears those tight outfits, a man notices."

"It's when she takes them off, I get concerned."

Diego chuckled. "Her needs are strong."

"What is she like?"

"Ambitious. Her goal is to marry a rich man."

"You weren't rich enough for her?"

"My family wasn't enthused about Daniella and at the time I wasn't ready for a commitment." He shrugged. "In hindsight, I'm glad I broke up with her."

"Why?"

"Emotionally, she's a fish."

"Hey, I like fish. Daniella, on the other hand, I'm not keen on."

"My mother thought she was rather indecent."

"And what would she think about me?"

"She'd like you. You're not motivated by money like Daniella. Mind you, there would be some opposition because you're not Spanish, but then again, my mother's not entirely either, and my father didn't mind marrying her."

"Oh?"

"My mother's from France."

"How did she meet your father?"

"She was on holiday in Mallorca and so was he."

"That's romantic."

"That's what she wants for me—love, marriage and children."

"So does my mom. She doesn't think she has enough grandchildren, and Diego, I hate to say it, but I'm getting closer to the big three-oh."

"You, Adelina? How could you lead me on like this? I thought you were barely twenty."

"But, Diego…"

I saw a faint hint of a smile.

"That was totally insensitive." I jabbed him. "I feel so old."

Diego kissed my cheek. "My apologies. If you're old, I'm ancient at thirty-one."

"It's different for men. They want younger women for their partners and the emphasis is always on the woman's appearance."

"You'd look lovely at sixty."

"If I live that long."

"I would make sure that you are safe. My house in San Miguel has a security system, not to mention Luis and Churo. I don't want you to be alone. If for any reason Wolf is not with you, phone me and I'll give you the guest bedroom or if you prefer, my room is also available." His eyes twinkled mischievously. "Of course, I'll be in my room with you to insure that you are safe."

"That's a joke. I think I know what your intentions are."

Diego brushed a strand of hair away from my eye. "I'm a normal heterosexual male. You can't tell me Wolf's intentions are any nobler than mine?"

"At least he usually asks."

"He knows how fierce you are and doesn't want his teeth knocked out."

I said, "He has nice teeth."

"And I don't look good to you?"

I stroked his cheek affectionately. "You're very handsome and you know it."

"*Gracias.*" Diego took my hand and kissed my wrist. "I hate to end this afternoon, Adelinita, but we'll need to go if we're to be on time for the eight o'clock ferry."

By the time we returned to Playa del Carmen, heavy dark clouds blanketed the sky. Diego regarded them with concern as we boarded the ferry. "There is a storm coming in, Adelinita. I hope they don't delay the ferry."

"They would do that?"

"Sometimes they don't cross at all."

"At least hurricane season is over."

Diego frowned. "True. Last month was bad."

"Some hotels on the waterfront were damaged, weren't they?"

"Too many hurricanes this year. It's certainly not good for business or pleasure. Life isn't perfect here in Cozumel, *mi amor.*"

"Life isn't perfect anywhere, Diego."

"Ah-hh, I forgot your cynical side." He squeezed my hand lightly. "I'd like to make you happy, Adelinita."

We sat down in some seats near the windows. A few droplets

of water appeared on the glass.

"I guess that all depends."

"On?"

"Every woman wants a special man that respects, loves and protects her."

"I could be that man for you." Diego touched my hair gently.

"You could?" I asked skeptically.

"I admit I don't love you, but that takes time, and I would make sure you are protected and avenged. Now that last criteria, respect, you should have no doubt about that one."

"You don't act like you respect me."

He grinned. "My respect has grown in direct correlation to the pain inflicted on me."

"Women let you get away with too much."

"Perhaps." Glancing at his watch, Diego got up. "I hate to leave, Adelina, but I need to go. My meeting shouldn't be more than twenty minutes. I'll be back soon. Will you be all right?"

"Of course, don't worry about me."

Diego strode over to the stairs and smiled at me before he turned to go up the steps, holding the railing.

21

Diego seemed sincere but he told me his ventures were marginally legal, and he had neglected to mention his bank account in the Caymans. This meeting with his chief investor could be a breakthrough. Clutching my beach bag, I carefully made my way up the stairs.

The wind had picked up and it started to rain. I hid behind a pillar near some seats. Near the bow of the boat, I could see Diego talking to a tall gaunt man. Eduardo the hit man? The wind drowned out their conversation making it impossible to hear their words. Raindrops came down harder and my clothes started to get wet. I placed my bag behind the post and strained to hear the conversation. They were a few feet apart, Diego shrugging his shoulders as the other man emphasized something emphatically with his hands.

The appearance of a bulky man behind Diego was the return of my nightmare. It was the biker who had attacked me in my hotel room! He was creeping up closer to Diego, carrying a wicked-looking knife. Where was Churo?

I wouldn't let him kill Diego. I shouted, but my voice was lost in the wind. I raced up, screaming, "Diego, behind you!" It was then that I slipped on the wet deck.

Diego turned into the biker blocking him with his forearm.

The biker swiped. Diego kept on going, his fist connecting with the goon's shoulder.

The thug suddenly froze, a look of disbelief in his eyes before he jerked, his legs giving out from under him, and he crumbled, falling backwards onto the deck. I watched a dark red stain spread on his chest. How? Still crouched on the deck, I swiveled around to the wiry gray-haired man, holding a long barreled gun—a silencer.

The man frowned, not altogether pleased with what he had just done. He looked familiar. I'd seen him before, a while ago. My hunch had been right all along. It was him. My insight had come too late.

The man smiled but it was an ugly smile. His voice was raspy in the wind. "Ah-hh, Adie Sturm. Storm is a good name for someone like you, a shit-disturber and major bitch. This time you haven't ruined anything, though it would have been easier if I hadn't shot Kowalski. He could have finished off Alvarez, but this way I've got two birds with one stone."

"Dr. Hamilton Morgenson." I stood to face him. "CEO of Central Hospital and Uma's boyfriend."

"Smart, but not that smart. You hid Beige, but you were too cocky to keep yourself hidden, weren't you? No disguises for the vain Miss Sturm. It wasn't difficult for my boys to find you, the way you strut your stuff. Too bad my little pet didn't finish you off. You don't like snakes, eh, Sturm?" He glanced down at the unconscious biker. He added dryly, "Kowalski was salivating to get a bit of your action. When I finally sent him, he was royally pissed he didn't get to *do* you."

"Shut up, Morgenson! You have no right to speak to her like that." Diego glared at him angrily. "She's not one of your whores. Treat her with respect!"

We turned to Diego, clutching his arm, his fingers red with blood.

"Big powerful man, aren't you, Alvarez?" Morgenson sneered. "You're nothing without your guard dog." Morgenson motioned with his chin to the far corner of the deck. "He won't be guarding anyone anymore."

"Churo's dead—you killed him?" I started for the spot where Churo lay but Morgenson waved his gun for me to stay.

"Don't cry for him, Sturm. You and your spic friend, here, will be joining him in hell soon." Morgenson laughed derisively.

"Why are you doing this?" I shot a look at Diego. He was as wet as I was but that wasn't what worried me. A steady flow of blood from his wound dripped down on the deck.

"Alvarez didn't tell you about his little nest egg in the Caymans, did he?" Morgenson hissed, "We both put in millions," he turned to Diego, "but you loused it up. Why didn't you off Carrera—a liability, babbling in public. Doherty heard it all. He should have killed him that night, but he was too busy following this bitch.

"Don was harmless, Morgenson," Diego said calmly.

"Hah! Carrera was nothing but a blackmailer. Fortunately, I

had the foresight to arrange a much needed accident." Morgenson frowned. "It wouldn't have been long before other investors heard there were problems with the condo development, would there, Alvarez?"

"Problems can be solved." Diego stared steadily. "Politicians come around eventually, Morgenson. Now put down that gun."

Morgenson snarled. "Don't patronize me, boy! You think I haven't thought this through? We both signed for that tax free account and if you're dead, it's all mine." He pointed his gun at me. "And this interfering bitch gets to join you." He flicked his eyes in my direction. "Where is that stupid friend of yours anyway?"

"Marg is safe away from you," I said defiantly.

"I should have fired the conniving cow." His lips peeled back, eyes wild with rage. "She snooped into my affairs and coaxed everything out of Reich! And then the stupid idiot left her files for you to steal, didn't she, Sturm?"

I needed to gain time—keep him talking. "Why did you kill them, Morgenson?"

"Reich was a loose cannon and well, Uma, was Uma—boring and greedy. She made the ultimate error when she shot off her mouth to Reich." He gripped the gun tightly, pointing it at my chest. "It was time for a change, anyway. Yes, a younger woman, without Uma's delusions of grandeur."

I glanced sidelong at Diego. His face was pale—his arm was coated with blood, the wound long and deep. I pulled off my top.

"What the fuck are you doing?" Morgenson leered at my breasts in the bikini top. "If you think stripping will distract me, you're out of your fucking mind." He steadied himself, his back against the railing as the waves rolled the ferry.

Ignoring him, I folded my top several times and reached over and placed it on Diego's forearm. "Press on the wound, Diego."

"Isn't that something?" He snickered, wiping the rain from his eyes. "Tough little Ms Sturm helping out the rich spic boy? Well, forget it. Your number's up! Game over."

I needed to divert him to make my move. Morgenson stood close to us a couple feet away. He couldn't miss at this range. I had to remember what to do, and to do it fast, or we'd both end up dead.

Diego's eyes narrowed. "Put down the gun, Morgenson. You're delusional if you think you can leave this country alive after you kill us. You don't know who you're dealing with. Put it down now and I'll let you live."

Morgenson shot Diego a look of disgust. "You're in no position to bargain, are you, Alvarez?" He shifted his gun to point at Diego's head. "Too bad it's raining. I would have liked to see the sweat of fear on your face."

I shifted my position around to Morgenson's gun arm. With my left hand I made a windmill motion that knocked his arm up high and around. With the edge of my hand, I struck near the elbow. Morgenson winced. The gun dropped to the deck, firing as it hit.

The boat lurched. The gun slid under one of the seats behind a pillar. Morgenson sprang down on the deck, on hands and knees searching for the gun. I leapt in, pushing him aside with my knee. The force of his fist threw me into a deck chair.

A familiar voice interrupted the hunt. "Looking for this, Morgenson?" Soaked to the skin, his wet blond hair slicked back, Wolf appeared from behind a pillar, pointing the gun at Morgenson.

"Du Lac? What do you have to do with this?" Morgenson's eyes shifted from Wolf to me and back again. "I see—you and Sturm, eh?" He lunged forward. Grabbing my hair, he forced me to the railing. "It's your fault, you interfering bitch! You got him involved." With his arm around my chest, I was Morgenson's human shield. "Drop the gun, or Sturm goes overboard!" he bellowed through the rush of the wind.

Wolf's steely blue eyes glittered dangerously. Hesitantly, he dropped the gun.

"Now, kick it here."

Wolf shoved the gun closer to Morgenson. At the same time, I poked my hip out and with my fist pounded him in the groin. Morgenson doubled up in pain, loosening his grip. I elbowed his chest and shook him off. Wolf pounced, going for the gun. Morgenson anticipated his move, kicking him in the temple. Wolf swayed, dazed from the blow.

The ferry lurched. Something struck my leg—hard. I flinched. From behind the post, a heavy bucket rolled over and banged into my shin-bone.

Morgenson snatched up the gun. Taking advantage of my pain, he gripped my bikini top, dragging me along. At the railing, Morgenson's guffawed loudly. "Surprise, Du Lac. She's shark bait anyway! How long do you think she'll stay afloat, boys? I'd estimate less than one minute. Think of that Alvarez. Don't you feel just a little guilty for involving her?" He pushed me towards the railing, still holding the gun. The dark waters pounded against the ferry, the waves rising in huge crests.

Alvarez edged closer to Morgenson, one arm behind his back, his wounded arm hanging limply. Morgenson gripped me tightly, waving his gun around.

"Neither of you have the balls to come for me." He laughed wildly. "Hah! Here I am an old man and I'm taking you both down." He swerved to Wolf. "I would have expected more out of you, Du Lac, an outdoors type. Too much sitting behind a desk, eh—making deals, overpricing your bids." He cackled gleefully. "Money can't save either one of you now."

He lifted me over the railing—my upper body suspended over the edge. Only Morgenson's hold kept me from the swirling waters of the Caribbean.

"Wolf!" I cried out in panic.

"Morgenson!" Diego called out over the rush of the waves. "Spic boy has something for you." As the boat rocked to one side, Morgenson paused a split second to twist towards Diego. I heard him gasp first and then grunt as if someone had struck him. He tottered, unbalanced, leaning over the railing, before he let me go.

"No!" I screamed, feeling myself slipping from his grasp. The dark waters churned below. I knew I didn't have a chance in hell of coming out of this alive.

A hand gripped my leg, wrenching me back. I made aching contact with the wooden deck. The ferry rocked. Wolf rolled on top of me. Squirming away, I shoved him off. As he stood, Wolf took me up with him. The black agitated ocean had taken a prisoner. Morgenson was gone.

A few feet away Diego leaned back against the railing, a bloody switchblade in his hand. There was a faint smile of satisfaction on his face.

***

"*Señor* Du Lac and *señorita* Sturm." Officer Hernandez glanced at my bikini top and bloodstained shorts. "*Señor* Alvarez told me how you saved him."

Cold and shaky—more miserable by the minute, the last thing I needed was the police. "I would like to get back to my hotel."

"Of course, soon. Señor, would you like to be brought to the hospital? You may have a concussion."

I glanced at the large purplish bruise on Wolf's temple. He stood unsteadily, his arm draped around my shoulders. "I'll be all right. Señorita Sturm will be with me."

Hernandez nodded. "Be aware of the symptoms—vomiting, dizziness, disorientation or memory loss. Wake him every two hours to see if he is experiencing problems, Señorita."

I nodded. "I will."

"Good." Hernandez checked his notes. "Do you know the name of the other man, Señorita?"

"Kowalski."

"He was shot by the man named Hamilton Morgenson?"

"Yes. He'd been hired to kill Señor Alvarez."

"He matched the description of the man that attacked you in your hotel room at the Hotel Don Juan. Was it him, Señorita Sturm?"

"Yes, and the other man that followed me, the man with the moustache, his name is Doherty. At least that's what Morgenson told us."

"Why did Morgenson shoot Kowalski?"

I pushed my wet hair away from my forehead. "It was accidental. He intended the bullet for Señor Alvarez."

"Did either of you see what happened to Morgenson?"

"No. He fell overboard. At least, I assume he did."

Wolf nodded.

"I see," Hernandez said, tightly. "Do you wish a ride to your hotel?"

"No, thank you. I'll drive Señor Du Lac's Jeep back. Could you help me?"

"Certainly." Officer Hernandez held on to Wolf's arm to

steady him as we trudged over to the black Jeep.

"I may have to contact you to complete my report. The coast guard will be on the watch for Morgenson." He turned to me. "One more thing. Morgenson wanted to shoot you, too, didn't he, Señorita? Were these attacks you experienced instigated by him?"

"I think so."

"Why did he want to kill you, Señorita Sturm?"

"He didn't want anyone to know what he was doing and I figured it out."

"Did it involve Señor Alvarez?"

"Indirectly." I touched Officer's Hernandez's arm. "Will Señor Alvarez be all right? He's lost a lot of blood."

"Don't worry, Señorita Sturm. There are experienced people at the hospital."

Wolf handed me the keys and I unlocked the vehicle. Officer Hernandez took my battered rescuer to the passenger side and helped him in. He shut the door and waved good-bye as I manoeuvred the Jeep out onto the road. I had to ask. "Did you see what happened to Morgenson?"

Slumped at an angle in the passenger seat, his eyes closed, he murmured, "He fell into the ocean."

"Diego killed him?"

"Maybe."

"What happened to the knife?"

Wolf shrugged his shoulders.

In the hotel parking lot, I looked at Wolf. His face was pale under the tan. "Do you think Diego told Officer Hernandez what really happened?"

"I don't think they want the whole story."

* * *

It was an experience walking through the ritzy lobby area of the Hotel Maria, with bloodstained shorts and a bikini top, supporting a man—everyone's eyes watching us. If they had the idea we were divers they must have thought we'd had a struggle with a shark. They would have been right. Morgenson was a predator all right. But now he was the victim.

We took the elevator to our floor. Inside the room, I helped

Wolf with his wet clothes and brought him an Aspirin before filling up the ice bucket and a plastic bag.

Wolf made himself comfortable on the bed. He took the bag from me and smiled that slow smile of his. "We're still going out tomorrow."

"I didn't know I had a date with Superman."

"With a little rest, I should be primed by tomorrow. Then I could show you what Superman can do for his little Wonder Woman."

I smiled. "I'm sure you can, but for now just sleep."

"Go take a shower, Adie. I can tell you're dying to get cleaned up."

I smiled. "Thanks to you, I'm not dying."

"You've got plenty of time to thank me."

I took out a pink top and boxers and glanced back at him before I went into the bathroom.

He looked wiped, but he was as sexy as ever. Then, my thoughts went to the struggle on the ferry. I sighed, thinking how lucky I was to be alive.

When I got out of the shower, the room was dimly lit by the bedside lamp. Wolf had fallen asleep, his arm under a pillow, his muscular shoulder exposed. I ran my hand down his shoulder, feeling the velvety texture of his skin. I hated to wake him. "Wolf?" I whispered. He stirred, but didn't wake up. I put my fingers under his chin gently, moving it slightly. "Wolf?"

"Princess?" he said softly. Warm arms wrapped around me as he pulled me close, his lips meeting mine. Then his head fell back on the pillow, his eyes heavy.

"Go back to sleep, tiger."

He didn't need to be told twice. He slid back. The sheets rustled as he shifted into a more comfortable position, his breathing unhurried as he fell into a slumber.

I set my alarm for two o'clock. He was groggier the second time but managed to mumble something affectionate. The third time, he muttered, "Adie, go back to sleep. I'm good. No worries." My final time, Wolf growled, "Go to sleep." He rolled over, his back to me.

22

I awoke to the sounds of soft breathing near my ear. Wolf had curled himself close to me as if he needed my protection. Not likely, but it was flattering to think of Wolf requiring my comforting presence for anything. I decided to let him sleep and went into the bathroom, showered and got myself ready—hair and makeup. In the bedroom, I couldn't remember if Wolf and I had planned anything except the use of my red-hot shoes sometime tonight.

I didn't see any reason to dress up, so I tugged out a pair of tan shorts and a blue scoop-necked tank top and slipped into a pair of crocheted wedge sandals. I was about to leave when I decided to write Wolf a note, in case he woke up while I was gone. On my way out I picked up my camera and purse off the dresser. In the elevator, my cell phone rang. I dug it out of my purse and answered.

"*Bueno?*"

"*Hola, mi amor.*"

"Diego, are you all right?"

"Yes, Adelinita. I'm so sorry. Will you forgive me?"

"There is nothing to forgive."

"We still have a date for breakfast tomorrow?"

"Yes, ten o'clock?"

"Where are you staying?"

"I'm at the Hotel Maria. Why don't we have breakfast here?"

"At the beach restaurant, *mi amor?*"

"Yes, but are you sure you're all right?"

"Nothing serious was damaged. Don't worry I won't faint away during breakfast. I wish I could see you today, but I know you have plans. I will have to while away the hours—relaxing, sleeping and dreaming of your beautiful lips."

I laughed. "Rest up today, then. Good bye, Diego."

"*Ciao*, Adelinita."

* * *

My curiosity had almost killed me. Most of it was clear now. Only a few loose ends. I had to share what I knew but there was something to be done first. This five star hotel had a gift shop with everything from fancy wrapping paper to lingerie. A good half hour later, with the necessary items, I headed to the camera shop. They told me they would have my photos ready with special instructions within the hour. The computer room was empty. I logged in and checked my mail.

There were e-mails, but before I read them I had to send one.

Hey guys, got the story on the murders. If you want to know what and why, meet me at the airport and take me home. I'm coming in on December 25, North Jet flight 204 out of Cozumel arriving 18:20. Adie.

I skimmed the work e-mails. Ingrid and her irritating messages could wait. The rest were from potential clients. I answered those.

Afterwards, I returned to the camera shop and selected a frame. Shopping completed, I limped into the lobby area. Last night hadn't been good for my ankle and I was beginning to feel it. As I plopped myself down on a comfortable rattan chair, propping my foot on the matching footstool, I took out my cell and pressed Marg's number.

When a lady picked up, I asked to speak to Marg. It seemed forever before they located Marg and she came on.

"Hello?"

"Hey, Marg."

"Adie! How did it go?"

"It was bad. We were almost killed on the ferry. The person behind it all was Morgenson, not Diego."

"Morgenson, the CEO? What do you mean, almost killed!" Marg gasped.

"He tried to kill us last night and he was behind all the attacks. Morgenson is dead. It's a long story."

"I can't believe this! Who's we? You and Wolf?"

"And Diego. But we're all okay, now." I scratched my chin. "Oh, Marg. Something I couldn't connect..."

"What?"

I absentmindedly fingered my package. "You met with Reich at your house, right?"

"Yes, he came to give me the travel package and a cashier's check."

I could hear a child crying in the background and then a high-pitched voice screaming something in Spanish. I concentrated on the loose end. "How do you think Reich turned up dead at your neighbors?"

"I don't know. I asked him to take a look at my fence. I gave him a hammer and nails. He said he'd lock up."

My mind raced. Noise, a party, and then there was the murder weapon on the table. It would have been dark by the time Morgenson came. He could have waited for Marg to leave and followed Reich to the fence. He must have struck him with the hammer and tossed him over the fence to the pit bulls. "Ah-hh!"

"What, Adie?"

"That's why Ilya thought you did it!"

"Huh?"

"There was a hammer lying on the table in the living room. I didn't see any blood so he must have cleaned it off and left only a trace so that he could frame you for the murder. Your fingerprints would have been on it."

"That makes sense, but what about Morgenson's?"

"He must have worn gloves, so you became the prime suspect. Motive, opportunity and means."

"What do you mean?"

"You were still in Toronto when Uma died and you would have gained from Reich's death according to his will. It was your hammer and you had access to drugs at the hospital."

"I didn't think of that. No wonder Kharkov was nasty on the phone. He wanted me to come back. Adie. He must have wanted to arrest me."

"Yup. Well now you can relax. I'll let Ilya know when I get home. Just know you're off the hook. I've got to go, Marg. Call me when you get home." I had too much to do today and no time to waste.

When I entered the suite, I heard the water running in the shower, and taking advantage of the opportunity, I went into the bedroom and got out my present for Wolf. I decided not to wrap it. Instead, using the silver paper I had purchased downstairs, I wrapped Diego's larger gift. I hid the other articles away. In the dresser I found my red string bikini and put it on with the matching paraeo before I made my way to the living room.

It was a clear sunny day, not a cloud in the sky. The El Norte was gone. I slid open the patio doors and stood still, looking out at the sparkling blue waters—so different from last night.

A fresh ocean scent assailed my nostrils. Strong arms held me tight as lips brushed my neck. "We need to get out of here to enjoy the day, Adie."

I agreed, but was sorely tempted to say, no, let's stay. "Where would you like to go?"

"Bonita Beach?"

"Sure. Give me a minute and I'll be ready." Wolf headed into the bedroom and emerged moments later in a bathing suit and a blue t-shirt. "I have some towels and the snorkeling gear is in the Jeep. We can eat there, eh, Adie? Can you hold out that long?"

I regarded him steadily. "I don't mind waiting."

His eyes met mine. "Some things are worth waiting for."

* * *

Bonita means beautiful and it was—a pristine beach with the surf relatively calm. This was a rare find with this side of the island known for its strong surf and temperamental undercurrents.

Wolf threw the towels on the beach and I spread them out next to each other. A waiter appeared out of thin air and asked us if we wanted drinks.

"How about quesadillas, Adie?"

"I'll have a piña colada, too."

The waiter turned to Wolf. "A drink for you, Señor?"

Wolf nodded. "Sol."

As the waiter headed to the bar, I said, "We have a lot to celebrate."

"It's Christmas Eve today, Adie. Is this the day you would celebrate with your family?"

"Yes. How about you?"

"Yeah. Mike is probably back in Kitchener."

"Rolf and Darla are at my parents' house tonight with the ever delightful Tasha."

"Not your favorite type of get-together?"

I touched his hand tentatively. "I'm glad I'm here with you instead. This is a perfect place for my last day."

"Tomorrow is your last day." He frowned. "Or are you saying that because this is the last one with me? Are you seeing Alvarez?"

"Yes, a farewell breakfast."

"He hasn't bled to death?"

"That's kind of mean. He was really hurt, Wolf."

"And I wasn't?"

"How are you feeling?" I studied his purplish bruise. "You were really out of it last night."

"It's hard work keeping up with you."

"It wasn't easy waking you up every two hours either. You got to be pretty grouchy."

"That's because you didn't wake me up for anything important, Adie."

The waiter came over with our food and drinks. We clicked glasses.

"How did you get that bump anyway, Wolf?"

"In the process of saving you from drowning at sea, Morgenson kicked my head before he fell overboard."

"You are my hero." I bit into a quesadilla, conscious of the heat rising to my cheeks.

"And you promised to show me eternal gratitude."

"Mm-mm." I glanced at him. "Tell me why you were there on the ferry."

Wolf stared at me. "You needed my help."

"And you knew this because?"

"I put two and two together. Don described the man in the car and I remembered to look at the printout you found before I left and saw Morgenson's name. His description matched with the man Don saw. I met Morgenson at the hospital a few weeks ago when I put in a bid to construct the addition."

"Did you see him with Uma?'

"Not sure. What did she look like?"

"Dark, thin and stylish."

"Not my type."

"And your type is?" I said, flirtatiously.

"Sexy," he leaned in kissing me slowly, shivers coursing down my body, "like you."

"Just sexy?" I thought of how Daniella might be considered sexy.

"Sizzling."

I tilted my head. "And you can tell this because?"

"Your eyes close when I kiss you and your hips move in the most seductive way."

"You're good at kissing."

"I have other skills yet untried."

I smiled. "I'm sure." I searched his face. "Where were you yesterday afternoon?"

"Close by."

"Where exactly?"

"Tulum."

"You mean you were stalking me on my date?" I sat up, staring at him.

"I got there in time to see you running away from Alvarez."

"Oh, that was because…"

"He made a suggestion that really turned you off."

"Diego is not perverted."

"How about dangerous?"

"He tends to be a bit Old Testament."

Wolf raised an eyebrow.

"An eye for an eye—avenging the enemy."

"He doesn't seem to mind killing people."

I sipped my piña colada, considering his remark. "I don't think you really understand. I told him about the biker and how he wanted to rape me. He thought the creep should be taken out."

Wolf frowned. "I guess I'd agree with Alvarez on that. I should have gone after the bastard. But by the time I saw him again Morgenson had already shot him."

"I hope Churo's okay."

"You liked the guy?"

"He was nice and can he *ever* barbeque lobster." I grinned.

Wolf stroked my cheek. "And I know how you like to eat."

"So what exactly did you see when I was at Tulum with Diego?"

"I saw him making moves on you."

"And how did you feel about that?"

"Playing psychiatrist, are we?"

"Just wondering."

"Finish your lunch and we'll try some snorkeling." Wolf zipped open the equipment bag.

Pensively chewing the last bit of quesadilla, I considered how Wolf was avoiding his feelings.

On a nearby table, I placed my plate and glass and came back to get my gear. "The snorkeling may not be as good here."

"I agree, but if we go to the reef, we might see something."

The warm salty water felt pleasantly cool after the heat of the sun on the beach. When we got to chest height we started swimming towards the reef. About twenty feet from the reef, I spotted something on the surface of the sandy bottom. I motioned Wolf to join me. In five feet deep water I could almost touch the mottled brown disc shape with a thin long tail—a stingray. Wolf made a circle with his finger and thumb. It was like finding a hidden treasure. With my hand in his we swam to the reef.

The cloud of sand in the water made the fish harder to spot. Sergeant majors curiously swam up to our faces, eyeing us inquisitively with their yellow eyes. The ridged coral was brownish gold in the hazy water. A red-banded parrot-fish shot out from behind mountainous green star coral where a brilliant turquoise fish fed. It was definitely an escape from reality, watching the world under the sea—a feeling of ultimate freedom.

Wolf edged around the mound of coral. I let him go on alone. I was more cautious. A current battles a swimmer and the swimmer doesn't always come out on top. I hoped Wolf wouldn't let his adventurous nature reel him into danger. He did what he wanted to do, not always what was good or safe. I guess I owed him big time for backing me up. I had been too proud to play the helpless woman and there was that other matter. He didn't seem too pleased about my breakfast plan with Diego, but I couldn't see why I should change my plans. It wasn't as if Wolf had declared his undying love for me, or even some hint of continuing our relationship at home. As far as I could see, he was just not pleased about me spending any time with another man. But what about him? Daniella was lurking around, biding her time until I left to make her play for him.

From behind the purple fan coral, a school of blue-striped

grunts shot out, surrounding me. Something caused that mass exodus. I looked beyond the reef. Long silvery bodies—barracudas. Three of them, near the surface. I'd had enough excitement in my life. I backed up and headed in towards shore. Wolf could have that experience without me. On the way I spotted a red filefish and lingered there a moment, watching it feed on some seaweed. Worried, I didn't want to abandon him. Not that I could really help him if the current did push him out to sea, but…Something brushed my arm. Startled, I saw Wolf. He had somehow circled around and was now swimming next to me.

Lack of sleep, and the after effects of last night, had taken a toll on my body. I felt a chill. Motioning that I was going back to shore, I wished I knew what he was thinking about us. Was there an *us* for him? Wolf signaled an *okay* and we headed back together.

The sun was strong and hot. I sat on my towel, staring at the ocean.

Wolf glanced at me. "Will you miss it?"

"I won't be happy to go back to the winter."

"Yeah, I know what you mean." His brilliant blue eyes gazed at me. "Do you want to see me again?"

"Not too possible is it, since you intend to stay here?"

"I thought maybe I'd fly home for New Year's Eve. Would you like to go out then, Adie or do you have someone stashed away?"

"No, I haven't worked on that angle yet." I smiled. "I could pencil you in."

"Do you want to go dancing?"

I lay down on my stomach and tilted my head to him. "Mm-mm. I'd like that."

Wolf lay down and pulled me closer. "We dance well together." His eyes lowered and he kissed me slowly. I wanted it to go on; his lips moved on mine with such passion, but he withdrew and stared at me intently. "Why don't we go for a walk?"

"Sure. I'll take my camera. I wouldn't mind a few shots of the bay." I zoomed in on Wolf staring out at the ocean and clicked.

He turned around, grabbed the camera from my hands and told me to go further into the waves. The surf splashed up from behind. I must have had a surprised look on my face as he snapped the picture. His eyes held a satisfied expression when he checked the picture.

"I'd like that one."

He handed me the camera and I swung it over my shoulder. I had a feeling we were going to do more than walk. Could it be he was actually going to talk to me? I mean really talk, the way women do with other women?

We came upon an outcropping of rocks and he extended his hand for me to hold onto as I scaled a few large ones. Then I let go and jumped down to the other side. It was an isolated place far from the beach crowd. I stood alone with nature and Wolf. The waves rushed in stronger—the water a brilliant sapphire, like Wolf's eyes.

"I haven't cared about anyone since my divorce. When you were nearly thrown overboard yesterday, I realized how strongly I felt about you."

"Was this a good thing?"

He frowned slightly. "Yes and no."

"So you'd rather have a fling?"

"Nothing wrong with those."

I pivoted and shot a dark look to the ocean.

He pulled me back around to him. "But I wouldn't mind getting to know a crazy woman like you a lot better." His lips turned up at the corners ever so slightly.

"Why don't we go back to the hotel and change? I need to try out my red shoes."

***

We took the east coast island road south to the point, and then navigated our way around to the west side of the island. The sun was setting as we parked at the hotel. I was desperate for a shower—anxious to feel human again.

At the suite, Wolf held the door open for me. "We don't have to go anywhere tonight, Adie. I mean," he said softly, "I could call room service. We could hang out. You wouldn't have to go to the trouble of dressing up."

I pulled off my wet top and shorts. "And the hair," I said, smiling, sticking my fingers in the salt-matted mess, "I could just leave it?"

He tilted his head, scanning my bikini-clad body. "My focus wouldn't be on your hair."

I reached up to his cheek and stroked it, meeting his eyes. "You'll like my dress."

"Sounds like an order."

"It is." I shut the bathroom door behind me and took a quick shower. On my way to the bedroom, a towel wrapped around me, I peeked into the living room. Wolf was sitting on the patio staring out at the ocean. He was in a strange mood but so was I. At first it had taken some getting used to—sharing space with a man. Now it was very familiar yet soon I'd be on my own again.

I put those gloomy thoughts away as I worked on my hair and makeup. After all, it was my last night.

In a revealing flame-red dress with a scalloped hemline and matching satin sandals, I posed at the patio doors. Intuitively, Wolf turned. His gaze flicked to my cleavage and slowly moved down. "Gorgeous." He walked over. "You're right. I do like your dress." His hands touched my face and trailed down my neck to my shoulders. "But it would be nothing without you in it."

I was suddenly shy. "Thanks," I said softly, my breath catching at the sight of him dressed in black, a stark contrast to his streaky, blond hair.

Wolf reached into his pocket and took out a velvet bag with a drawstring. "Before we go, I thought you might like your Christmas present."

Curiously, I pulled the strings open, and lifted out a silver chain with a delicate heart shaped pendant, a bright blue topaz asymmetrically mounted on one side. "It's beautiful. Will you help me put it on?"

Wolf picked up the necklace, encircled my neck and closed it carefully. "The stone matches the Caribbean blue of your eyes." He gazed at me intensely before he took my hand. "Let's go down to the beach restaurant."

The dancing and food was wonderful and though I enjoyed it, the unaccustomed shoes and dance maneuvers tired me. I was more than ready to get back to our hotel suite. When we came in, Wolf said, "I ordered sangria, Adie. They said they'd bring it right up."

"Perfect. I want to give you your present, but why don't we wait until the sangria comes."

"Sure," Wolf said, smiling mysteriously, before he disappeared into the bedroom, reappearing with a large gold box. "For you, but you have to share."

"Chocolates." I sighed, when I opened the lid. "Perfect." Choosing one, I savoured the flavour, not eager to swallow. "Chocolates are a health food."

Wolf nodded solemnly, in agreement. "They release endorphins. Always a good idea."

"The pleasure principle released." I selected another truffle. Wolf's lips parted as I deposited a chocolate in his mouth. Before I pulled my hand away he caught my fingers in his mouth and sucked the chocolate off my fingertips.

"You taste as good as the chocolate," he said softly.

"That is a compliment." I picked out another truffle and held it a second, waiting—his lips parted to receive the chocolate.

A knock on the door brought a waiter with our sangria and glasses on a tray. Wolf signed the bill. After the waiter left, he filled our glasses with the sparkly crimson mixture.

He lifted his glass. "To Christmas?"

I nodded. "A memorable Christmas." We clicked glasses—the ice cubes tinkled, breaking into tiny ice floes between the slices of lemon. Our eyes met.

Wolf found a soft round truffle and brought it to my lips. He teased me a moment, circling his index finger around my mouth, before he gently pushed the chocolate into my parted lips. I let it glide in, holding it in my mouth a moment, feeling the texture of the chocolate before I allowed myself to chew and swallow.

"And how is this Christmas for you?"

I smiled. "It has promise." When I finished the last bit of sangria, I whispered, "I'll get your presents."

Moments later I came out of the bedroom. He was caught off guard as I stepped out wearing a red lacy bra, matching thong, and high-heeled sandals. I pointed to my bra.

"Your presents are here. Reach in for the first one."

"That's tricky. Your bra is already quite filled."

"You can manage." I sat on his lap. "I hope you like it."

"From what I've seen, it's everything I ever wanted." He

pulled my bra strap down over my shoulder and reached into my bra.

His fingers smoothed over my breast as he pulled out the bracelet. Tearing his eyes away from me with some difficulty, he said, "Very nice," examining the heavy silver. "I don't usually wear jewelry, but you've chosen well."

"Let me put it on your wrist for you." I brought the bracelet around and closed the clasp.

"May I open the second one?"

I nodded, and he pulled out the fabric of my bra to reveal a tiny package. "Ribbed for added enjoyment." He smiled engagingly. "Are you sure this isn't your gift?"

"That one is to be shared."

"That's it?"

"Not quite. The last present is right here."

"Here?"

"Sitting on your lap."

"I'll have to open it then, won't I?" he said, his hands unsnapping my bra as he eased his lips to the top of my breasts. The tip of his tongue journeyed into the valley between my breasts. A rush of heat surged down my body as he pushed off the bra. My nipples hardened with the touch of his hands.

Effortlessly, he lifted me and placed me on the thickly woven cotton rug. Bodies entwined, our lips met. My mouth parted, allowing his tongue to caress mine. I pressed back. Our kiss was feverishly passionate. My lips tightened on his tongue before I slowly released him.

As I started to kick off my high-heeled sandals, his hand stopped me. "Keep them on," he said, his voice husky, his eyes following the curves of my body. Then he lowered himself over my stomach, holding onto my hips, his fingertips massaging me while his tongue flicked delightfully lower.

I exhaled in a rush. "Was that my appetizer?"

Pulling away, he unbuttoned his shirt. He shrugged his shirt off and let it drop to the floor. Mysterious eyes fixed on me as he said softly, "You deserve more than that, my spicy woman—so much more."

I watched as he slid off the rest of his clothes. I wasn't disappointed, either. No, definitely not. Hard, lean and totally male—everything I ever wanted.

He sat back, watching me, picking up my foot and massaging my arch. "You've made me wait a long time—years."

What a sweet sensation, I thought, stretching out my other foot for a similar treatment. "Patience is a virtue."

"And I will proceed virtuously into the garden," he said, his voice husky with desire.

"Garden?"

"Garden of Eden." Wolf lay down beside me, his arm pulling me close.

"Oh yes, your mother said I was taboo. I'm no longer forbidden?"

My question was left unanswered as his hand pushed my head close and our lips met. His tongue entered my parted mouth and flicked over the sensitive skin on the inside of my lips. Fire coursed down my body. My hands reached for his waist, trailing to his narrow hips, eager to touch him.

His tongue withdrew to explore the contours of my ear, his breath warm and moist. I exhaled slowly, enveloped in the stimuli. I wanted him to experience the sensations I felt. My lips wandered to the base of his neck. His velvety skin aroused me. I took in his scent of soap floating on an ocean breeze. I heard the intake of his breath as my mouth captured the skin at the base of his neck before I released him.

Soft lips caressed my shoulder while his hands wandered from my hips to the curve of my belly and upwards. My breast molded in his hand. His brought his head lower. His tongue feathered hotly on my enflamed body. Lips tugged and eased off. My breathing became heavier as his fingertips teased.

Pushing me towards him, he caressed the small of my back with his lips. I lifted up my hips, shivering in anticipation. He slid my thong off. On the rug, we explored each other. I tingled with his touch—my body pulsed for him. Sighs turned into moans. I tried to focus on him but his persistent attention distracted me. I was being lifted, higher and higher into a gigantic tidal wave, spiraling uncontrollably in the surf—a wave of joy. My fingers dug into his hair while his lips sent me into a heady, rapturous state. From somewhere far away, I heard throaty moans. Through the haze of my euphoria, I realized they were coming from me.

Propelled into another world that was heavenly bliss, I was consumed. Screams released from somewhere I hadn't been before.

"You taste so good, princess." His hands caressed my curves like a sculpture—gently and sensitively.

My fingertips explore his chest. Soft groans escaped his lips. I felt empowered. This magnetic man needed me as much as I wanted him. I brought myself towards him. With my breath on his ear, he shivered and sighed. As he gripped me firmly, his silken tongue caressed my skin. I lifted my head, watching his sapphire eyes heavy-lidded, drifting far away.

Behind me now, his chest against my back, his fingertips gently kneaded. I sighed and closed my eyes, leaning against him, so aware of him and the sensations he was provoking. I felt his burning lips on my shoulder. I wanted him, and he gave it all to me until we were both lost in the heat. I was captured in his dream. I felt transported into a world with no beginning or end, where nothing existed except him. Pain and pleasure. I trembled and cried out. Wolf's hair brushed against my cheek. I held on to him as we flew into bliss. He groaned like a man who had found nirvana.

The warmth of his arms surrounded me, as we passionately kissed. I closed my eyes, my breathing ragged.

"Your present is unforgettable, princess," Wolf whispered in my ear. He carried me to the bedroom. We lay down holding each other until sleep overtook us.

This time when I woke him in the night, it wasn't to see if his cognitive functions were up to par. He wasn't gruff either, his mouth softly responsive as our lips met his. We didn't speak—we didn't have to. He knew what I needed.

His lips searched, igniting my flame. A manic roller-coaster ride to the top and then a wild sensation going down. I let myself go, shuddering uncontrollably.

Then we did what we both wanted—so much. Our covers fell off as we rolled together. My smoldering passion torched and I pushed myself closer, my urges enveloping me, burning volcanic flames. Fire enflaming fire. We became one, his chest against my back, holding me close.

Scorching hot embers from his fingers to my core. Sweat covered our bodies. He moved faster. I floated into a cloud of ecstasy. Under his touch, I was caught up in the sheer joy, his body tight against me. I tensed, but I didn't want it to stop. I became part of him. Pushed past that precipice, I cried out. We collapsed. From deep in his throat, he groaned. Together we drifted away into a deep sleep.

* * *

The sun crept into our room through the wooden slats of the blinds. I sat up, watching Wolf sleep. He still had the bracelet on from last night.

Careful not to wake him, I showered quickly and dressed for my date with Diego. Before I left, my eyes swept over my lover. His bruise had turned green and his face was pale through his tan. With the sheet barely covering a hip, he slept, his features almost angelic, his blond hair tousled. I smiled knowingly. His sensuous lips and strong jaw gave him away. He'd be the last person anyone would call innocent.

I closed the door quietly behind me, leaving him to dream. I took the elevator down to the Hotel Maria's beach restaurant. Searching the tables, I spotted Diego sitting next to the balcony overlooking the sea, wearing a sling over his white cotton shirt. His face was drawn, but his dark-fringed brandy eyes were as attractive as ever.

When he saw me, he stood up. "You shouldn't overexert yourself, Diego." But he remained standing, greeting me with a kiss on the cheek before he sat back down.

"Adelinita, you are radiant this morning. You slept well last night?"

I nodded, whereupon he frowned, remarking dryly, "I shouldn't have asked. I am a glutton for punishment."

"And you had your share."

"True, but it's all over with."

I searched his face. "Diego, do you think you killed Morgenson?"

"I can't say for sure, with the boat rocking and you dangling over the railing. Hopefully, yes."

"His body—was it found?"

"No. His corpse will float in eventually."

"H-m-mm, first Reich, then Uma, and now, a corpse for Cozumel."

"He deserved to die, Adelina. He wanted us all dead."

"Where did you stab him?"

"You like those sort of details?" He grinned. "Of course you do. You're quite a combatant. I was impressed." He squeezed my hand. "You're a courageous woman."

"I would have been overboard if you hadn't stabbed him."

Diego smiled slyly. "Morgenson was misinformed as to my skills, especially with knives. Not all rich men rely on their bodyguards. In answer to your question, it was in the chest area." He pursed his lips. "Unfortunately, with my other arm cut, I wasn't able to hold onto you."

"Luckily, I have another hero."

Diego's mouth tightened at my words.

Interrupted by the waiter who took our order, our conversation stopped until he discretely disappeared from sight.

Diego reached for a floral-rose package with a silver bow and pushed it towards me. "Merry Christmas, *mi amor*."

"You shouldn't have."

"Open it, Adelina."

Carefully, I undid the bow and pulled off the wrapping paper that covered a narrow black box. I lifted out a leather case. Squeezing the buttons on the lid, I clicked it open. A silver necklace inlaid with turquoise stones lay on a velvet bed.

"It's beautiful, Diego." I handled the delicate necklace. "You remembered turquoise was my birthstone."

"It's your protection. Will you wear it for me? I'd help you, but unfortunately…"

"Of course." I picked up the necklace, wondering what to do with the other one from Wolf I had on my neck. Deciding they could look good together, I secured the clasp.

"You are the perfect woman to wear it. The artist would be pleased."

Our waiter arrived and set down our breakfast. "Señor Alvarez, Señorita Sturm." With a flourish, he placed the serviettes on our laps. Bowing to us both, he backed away, as if he were having an audience with the king and queen.

I caressed both necklaces with my fingers. They were lovely.

"Thank you, Diego. But it wasn't necessary." I glanced at his untouched plate. I picked up my fork and knife and started cutting up his omelet for him.

Diego stared at me intently. "You saved my life." He took my fork away and put it on the table, taking up my hand again, kissing my wrist. "There is another present." He smiled slightly. "I don't mind the attention, but I wish I could use both my hands right now."

"Oh?"

"It makes me feel powerless, and…"

"What?" I picked up my fork and started my omelet.

"Less of a man for you."

My eyes scanned his athletic body, and worked their way up to face, his classic features and his generous mouth. "You are a very attractive man, and don't forget sometimes women like their men to need them but I can tell it's difficult for you. No ripping my clothes off today, eh?"

His lips twisted reflectively. "I'm not giving up on that concept, *mi amor*." He picked up his fork and had a mouthful of omelet.

"I have something for you, too, Diego."

"There's no need for a present. What you did is my present. I owe you my life."

I stroked his fingers. "And I owe mine to you. So, therefore, we are even in the debt department."

"I will always be in debt to you. There was no need for you to get involved and by doing so you put your life at risk. Look deeper into the box."

I lifted the velvet lining of the leather case and peeked underneath. A small envelope with my name on it lay inside. Curious, I flipped it open with my fingernail. A card with a key taped on it fell out. I held it up.

Seeing my baffled expression, Diego explained. "I am giving you a piece of Cozumel. A condo in San Miguel for you to use whenever you need it. There is a number to call on the back. Just leave a message. Someone will come and make sure it's clean and ready."

"I can't accept this, Diego. It's too much."

Diego stroked my hair gently. "Call it a loan, then. I don't want anything from you except a call to say you're here. No obligation. I will respect your wishes."

I nodded. "Under those terms, I accept the key. But I may return it at some point. You wouldn't get offended?"

"There is no need to ever return it. Unless the sea takes it in a hurricane, you are the owner of the condo, not me."

I stood up and leaned close to kiss his cheek, but he turned his face to catch my lips, and my kiss became his kiss. I sat down, my face flushed. "Just when I think I've tamed the lion."

"That's your mistake then—calmed yes, tamed no."

"Diego, tell me what happened to Churo."

He frowned. "He's in the hospital in serious condition, right now." He brightened. "But the doctors are optimistic."

"Good. Now tell me why Morgenson wanted to kill you."

"He had millions at his disposal and wanted to hide it in the Caymans. That's where I came in. He thought if he invested in my company I could put the funds in the Caymans in a bank account in our names. And I did."

"Do you know where all his funds came from?"

"I can guess."

"And your guess is?"

Diego sat back, watching me in amusement. "You're an intelligent woman. Figure it out. Hospital administrator..."

"You think he embezzled it?"

"Probably did it for years."

"How was he going to get away with it? The Canadian government could extradite him from any country for those murders."

Diego stroked his chin reflectively. "South America wouldn't be so easy."

"Um-mm." I sipped my coffee, gazing at him—wavy dark hair, incredible changeable eyes and kissable lips.

"Adelinita, I wanted to ask you something." The top few buttons of his shirt were open, revealing the contours of his chest and a gold chain with an unusual medallion. He was devastatingly handsome and unclaimed. I broke out of my reverie to remember I, too, had a gift. From the chair beside me, I snatched up a gift wrapped package and handed it to him.

"This is not necessary."

"It's a memento."

"Now you have me curious, but do me a favor, *mi amor* and open it for me?"

I nodded and undid the paper, pulling out a framed photograph. I set it on the table.

"Ah-hh, just what I wanted," Diego said, staring at the picture of us at Tulum. "We had a good time on the beach." He chuckled. "Not so much on the cliff. That was a bit too eventful." He picked up the framed photo. His eyes met mine. "Is there more to this photo?"

My lips turned up at the corners. "What do you mean?"

Diego placed the picture down on the table but it tipped over face down. His glance fell on the cardboard, noticing a number penned in. "Your phone number?" His eyes met mine. "That's what I was about to ask for. I have your cell number, but perhaps you would miss my call. I would like to see you when I come to Toronto."

"Call me."

"There's promise in that."

"Not necessarily." I rested my chin on my fingertips. "I'm not sure what's better for me."

"You mean, who's better…"

"I should go, Diego," I said, standing up.

Diego rose to his feet. "Parting from you is sweet sorrow," he said softly. His arm dropped around my waist, bringing me in. "I could be the right man for you." He leaned in to kiss me, his lips urgent, hinting at his underlying passion.

I ran my fingers down his cheek, before I picked up the box and walked away. When I reached the lobby, I swivelled around. His eyes were still on me. He brought his hand up and waved. I waved back. I was beginning to think he really did care for me.

* * *

A few hours later, my plane made its approach into Lester B. Pearson International Airport. Toronto glowed with an expanse of yellow lights scattered across the city—the CN Tower, the Skydome and everything else that made it familiar.

I was home and he was still in Cozumel. Was I a fool to think we ever had anything together, or ever would have? My thoughts went back to Marg, as I waited in the lineup at Immigration. With the information Diego had given me and Hernandez as a contact, Morgenson had a motive for murder. Marg was off the hook.

I scanned the crowd. Then I saw them. Bernie and Ilya stood at the exit. When I got past the roped in area, Slick said, "Hey honey, nice tan." He smirked. "Betcha it's all over, no tan lines, eh?"

Ilya took my suitcase. "Adie Sturm, Nancy Drew of the twin cities. So what happened?"

I put my finger on his lips and smiled mysteriously. "Patience, soon. Where's the car?"

"We're in the parking garage." Slick steered me ahead. "Who did it?"

"Hold on." Digging in my purse, I grabbed my cell. Yes, my phone with the strange number, my gift from Wolf. He wouldn't be concerned about me now. I was gone and he was still there, in Cozumel with Daniella. Ilya looked at me inquisitively when I sighed.

The snow blew horizontally through the air outside out the windows. "Merry Christmas, Mom—I'm home. See you tomorrow?" I stuck my cell back into my purse. The good thing was I had missed the family get-together. The bad thing was I was back here in the land of ice and snow. Did I still hate Christmas? This one sure hadn't been boring or predictable. And in another week, it would be New Year's Eve—a new year holding the promise of exciting possibilities.

www.AnastasiaAmor.com
Anastasia.Amor@hotmail.com
https://www.facebook.com/Anastasia.Amor.author
http://anastasiaamor1.blogspot.ca

ABOUT THE AUTHOR

OKTOBERFEST WOMAN OF THE YEAR FINALIST, GLOBAL and EPIC AWARD NOMINEE, ANASTASIA AMOR is a university psychology and education graduate. Amor believes in balance.She is the proud mother of two, a pet-mom and a teacher. She also speaks German and is learning Spanish. Art and writing are her passions but she loves to dance and is a known chocoholic. Canadian culture and twenty years in Mexico, researching Mayan Mexico inspired the Adie Sturm Mystery Series. As a martial artist she puts realism into Adie Sturm's fight scenarios. Researching DEAD DELICIOUS she learned to scuba dive. Psychic experiences, Cuban journeys and karate training sparked the fantasy-paranormal HAVANA HEAT. Her Canadian heroines are intelligent and fearless as well as sensual. Amor also writes erotic romance.

PRAISE for ANASTASIA AMOR

DAYS OF THE DEAD: *ADIE STURM MYSTERY* "…murder, hot romance, intrigue, and suspense…Adie is a modern-day, sexy Agatha Christie…charming and quite captivating…put together well!"
—***4 Stars***! *ReviewYourBook*

"…You never can tell just what will crop up… a fun read, and will be very welcomed by fans of the series." ***4 Books***! —*Long And Short Reviews*

THE CURSE OF THE CARNAVAL: *ADIE STURM MYSTERY*
Epic Award Nominee
5 out of 5 stars "Just when you thought it couldn't get any hotter…"
—*Michelle Stinson Ross*

"Adie's back and it's hotter than ever, way hotter. And far more dangerous."
—*ChrisChat Reviews*

DEAD DELICIOUS: *ADIE STURM MYSTERY*
Global EBook Nominee
"***Dead Delicious made me a huge Adie Sturm fan***…. strong, sexy, and independent…Amor has incredible skill in how she unfolds the element of mystery while keeping the sensual atmosphere alive. Her sexy voice rings loud throughout, making us yearn for our slice of sun, sea, sand, and irresistible male company. *I absolutely loved this book!* …the colorful band of tour group members who will have you laughing one minute and tearing your hair out the next….fun, fast-paced, drop dead sexy, and keeps your pulse racing in more ways than one.
*Anastasia Amor is truly the queen of steamy mysteries." —**Highly recommended!***—*Natalie G. Owens, An Eternity of Roses.*

www.ingramcontent.com/pod-product-compliance
Lightning Source LLC
Chambersburg PA
CBHW051247260626
47162CB00002B/657